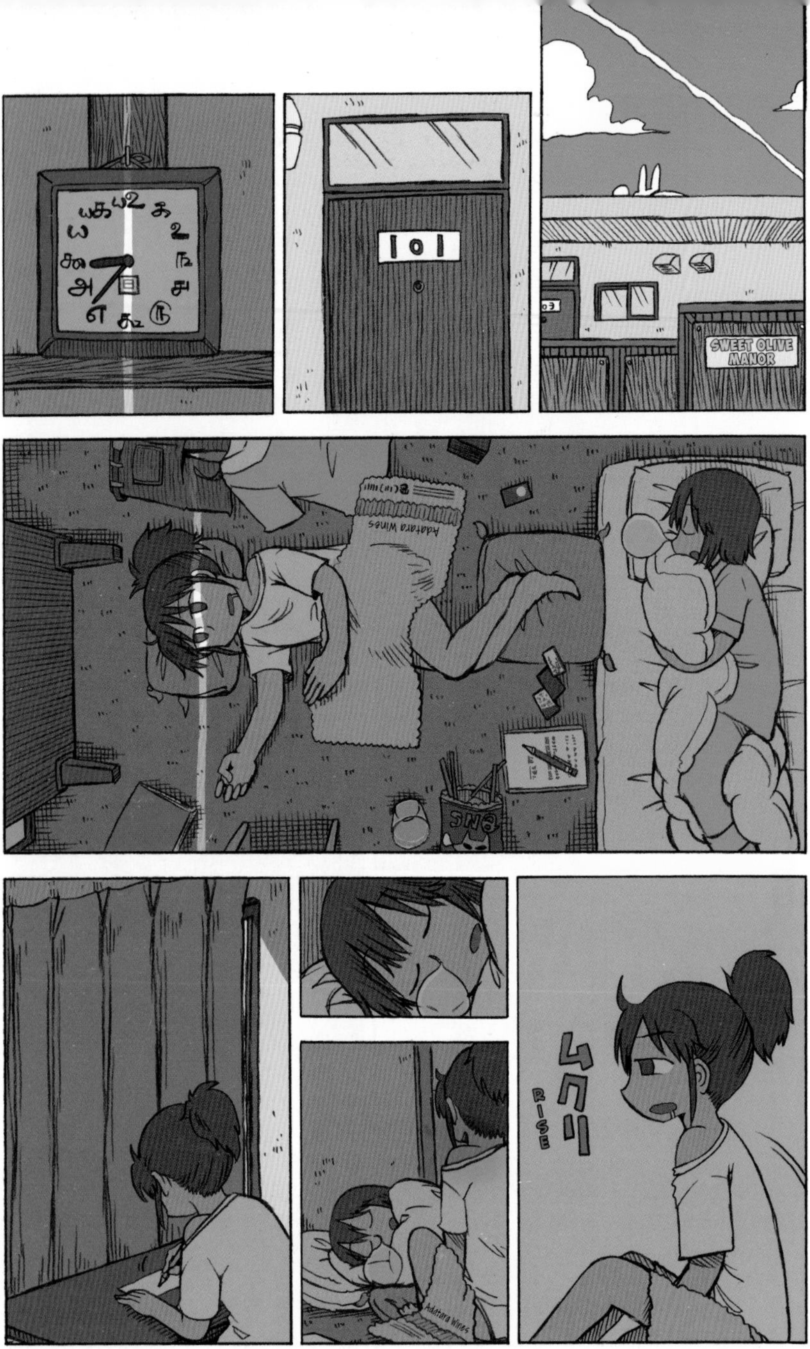
SWEET OLIVE MANOR
101
Adatara Wines
ムクリ
RISE
Adatara Wines

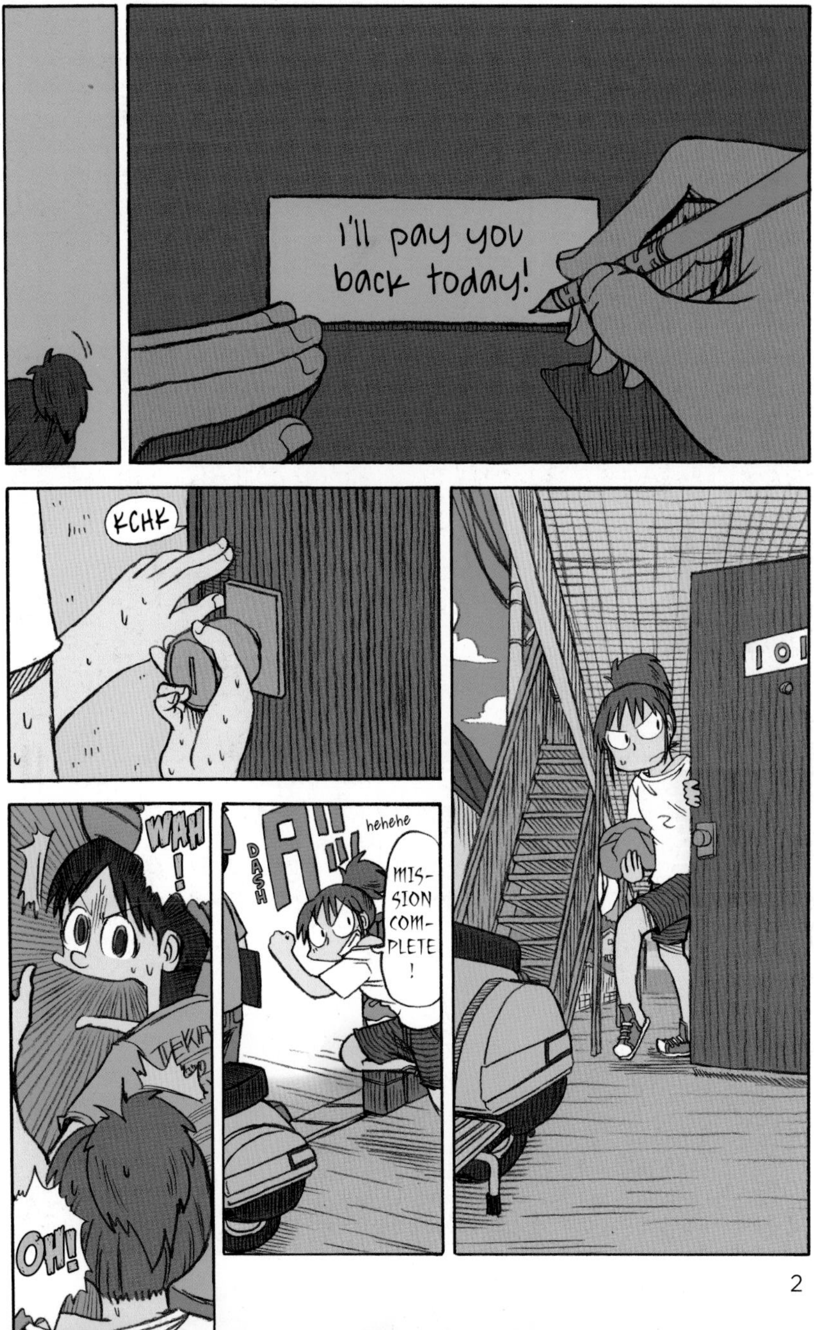
I'll pay you back today!
101
KCHK
hehehe
MISSION COMPLETE!
A!!
DASH
WAH!
OH!

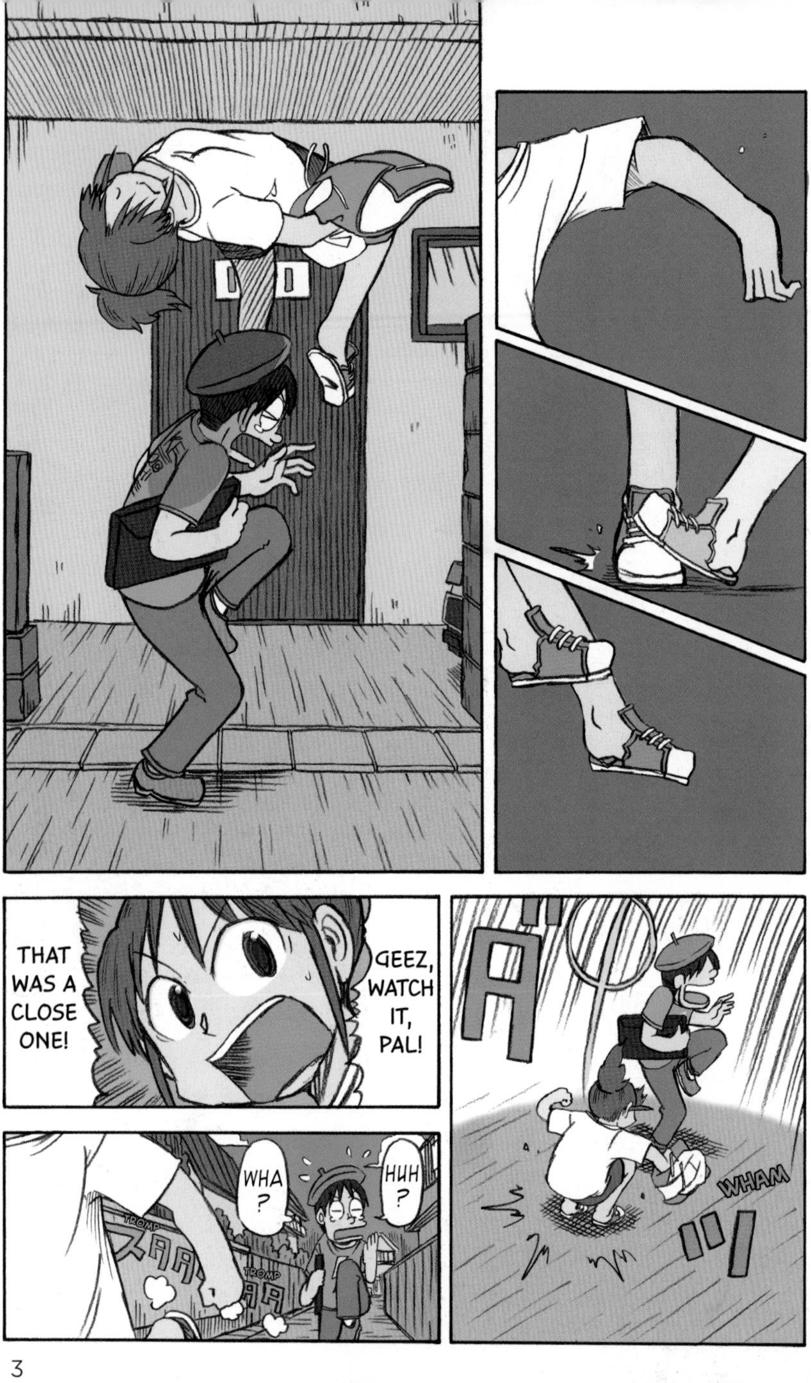
WHAM
GEEZ, WATCH IT, PAL!
THAT WAS A CLOSE ONE!
HUH ?
WHA ?
TROMP
TROMP

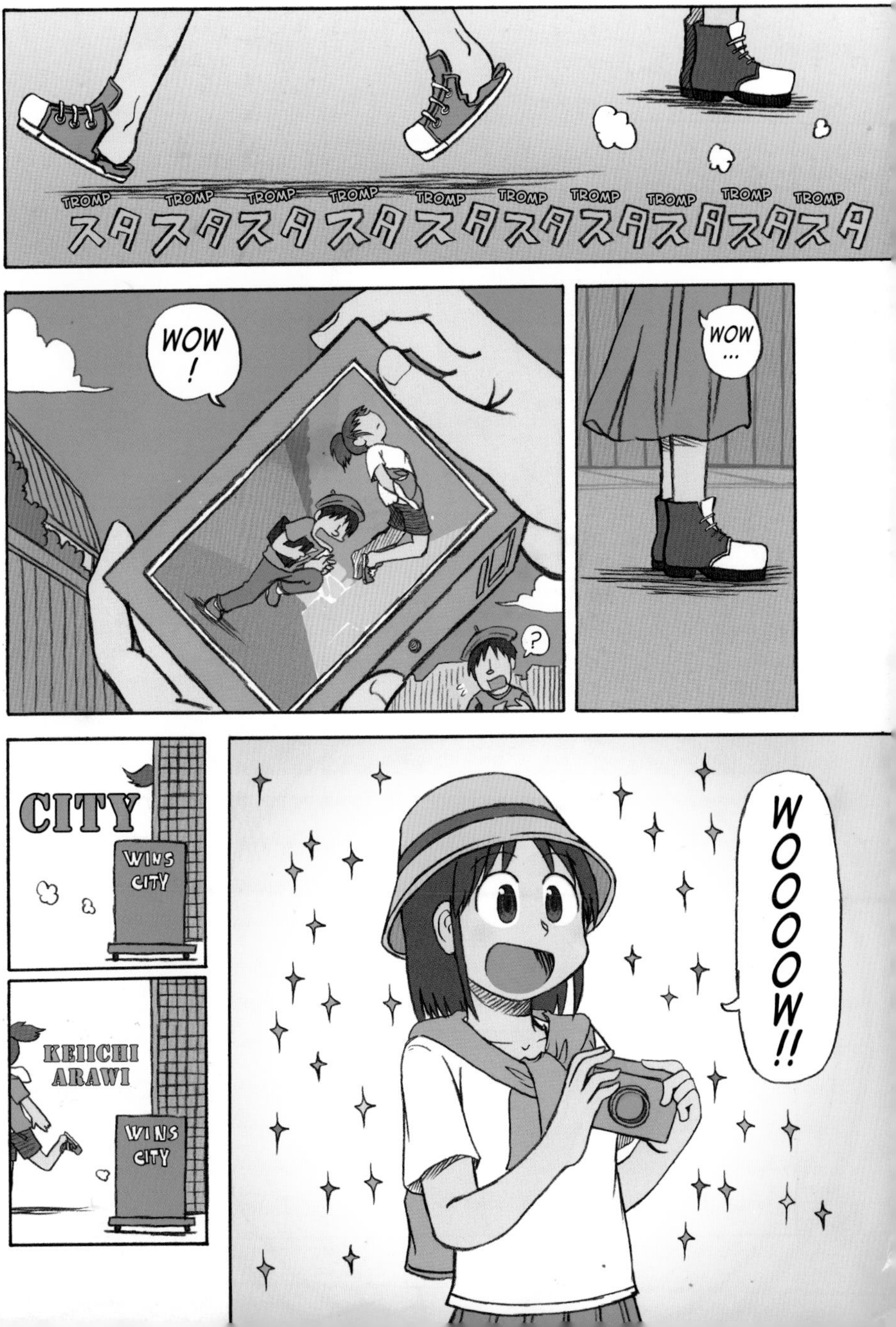
TROMP TROMP TROMP TROMP TROMP TROMP TROMP TROMP TROMP TROMP
スタスタスタスタスタスタスタスタスタスタ
WOW ...
WOW !
?
WOOOOOW!!
CITY
WINS CITY
KEIICHI ARAWI
WINS CITY

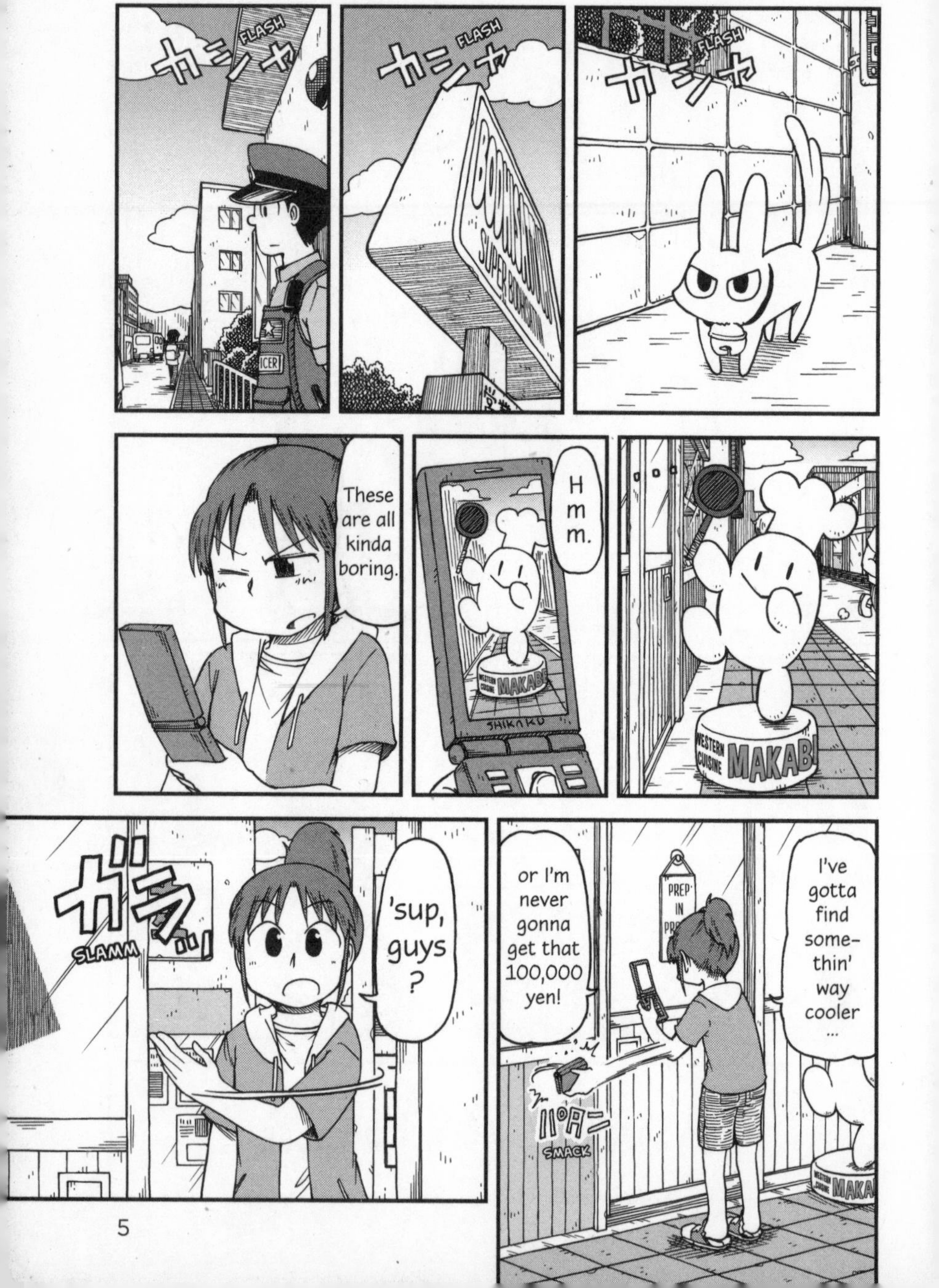
FLASH
FLASH
FLASH
Hmm.
These are all kinda boring.
I've gotta find somethin' way cooler ...
or I'm never gonna get that 100,000 yen!
SMACK
SLAMM
'sup, guys?

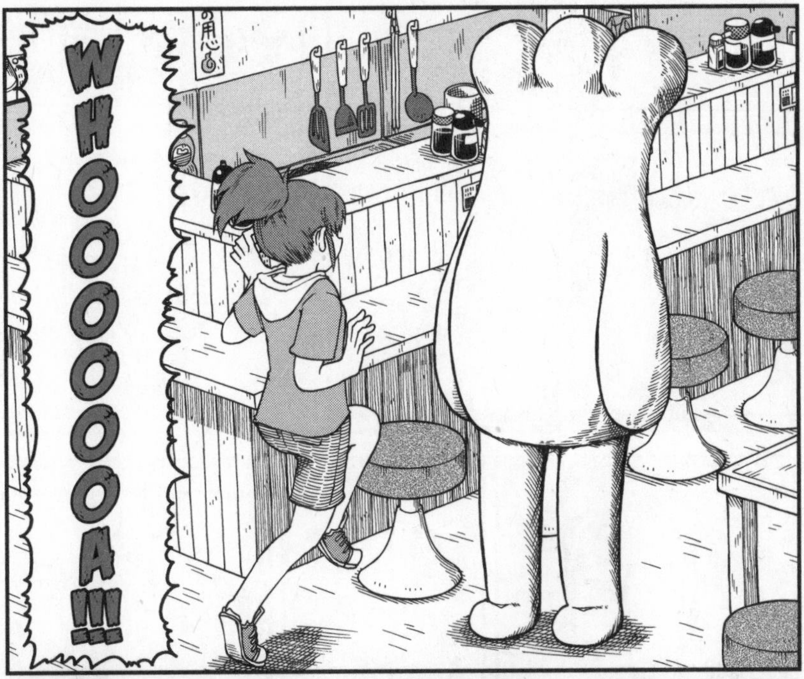
の用心
WHOOOOOOA!!!

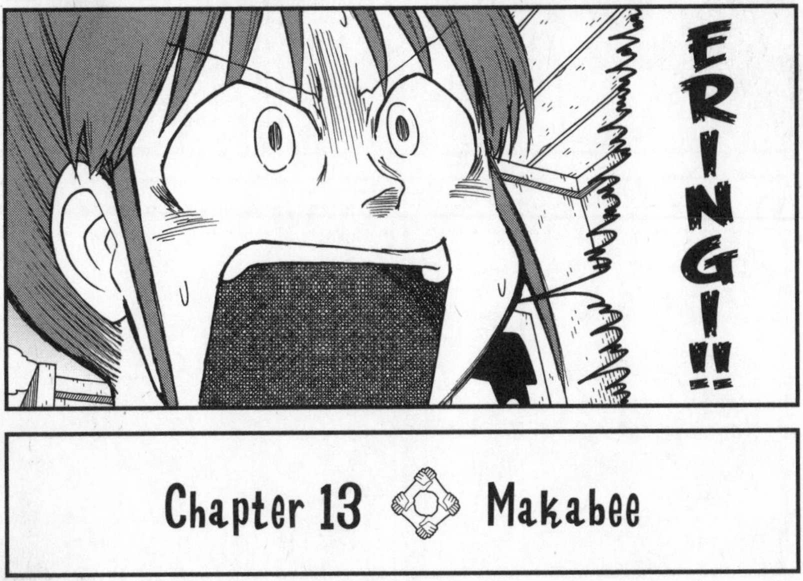
ERING!!

Chapter 13 Makabee

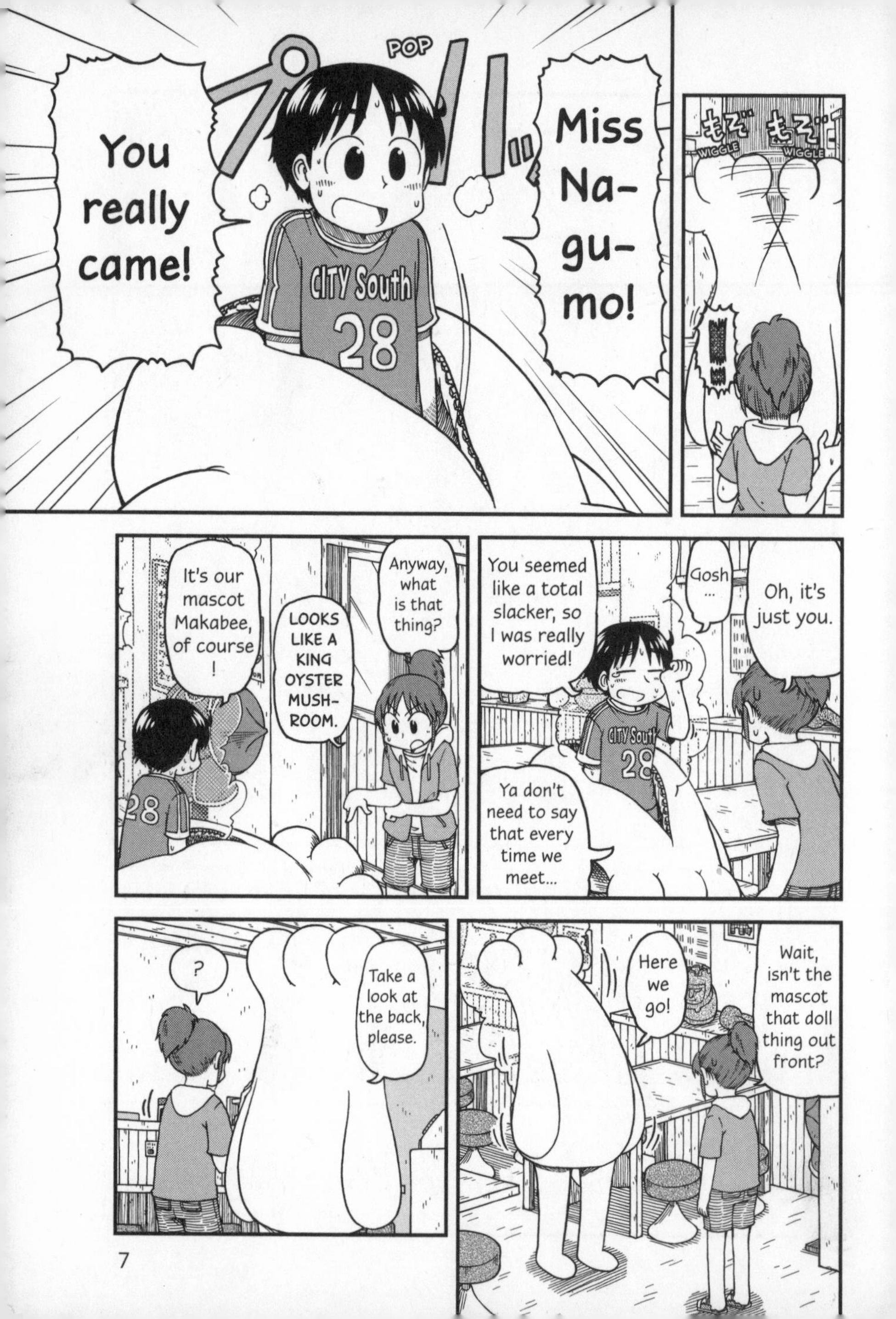
もぞ
WIGGLE
もぞ
WIGGLE
!!
POP
Miss Na-gu-mo!
You really came!
CITY South 28
Oh, it's just you.
Gosh...
You seemed like a total slacker, so I was really worried!
Ya don't need to say that every time we meet...
Anyway, what is that thing?
LOOKS LIKE A KING OYSTER MUSH-ROOM.
It's our mascot Makabee, of course!
Wait, isn't the mascot that doll thing out front?
Here we go!
Take a look at the back, please.
?

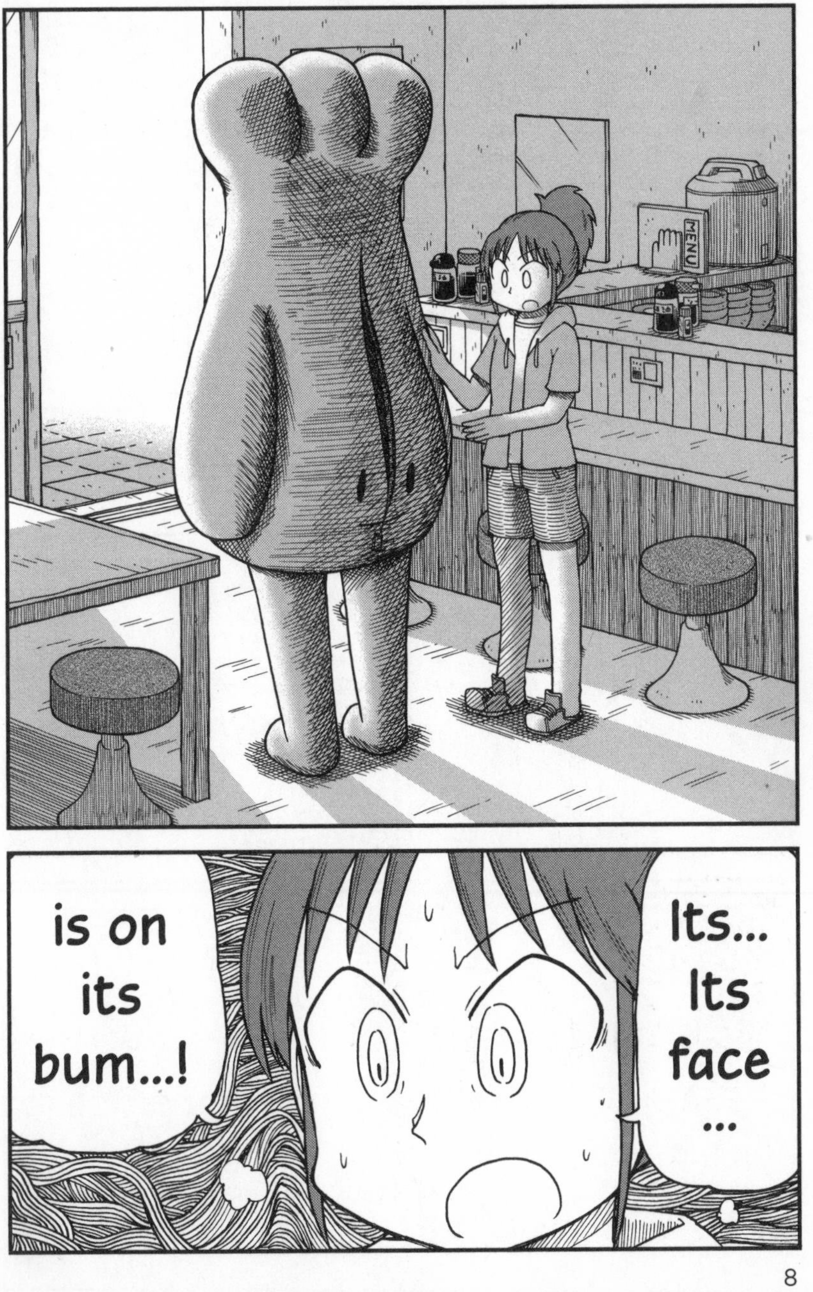
MENU
Its... Its face ...
is on its bum...!

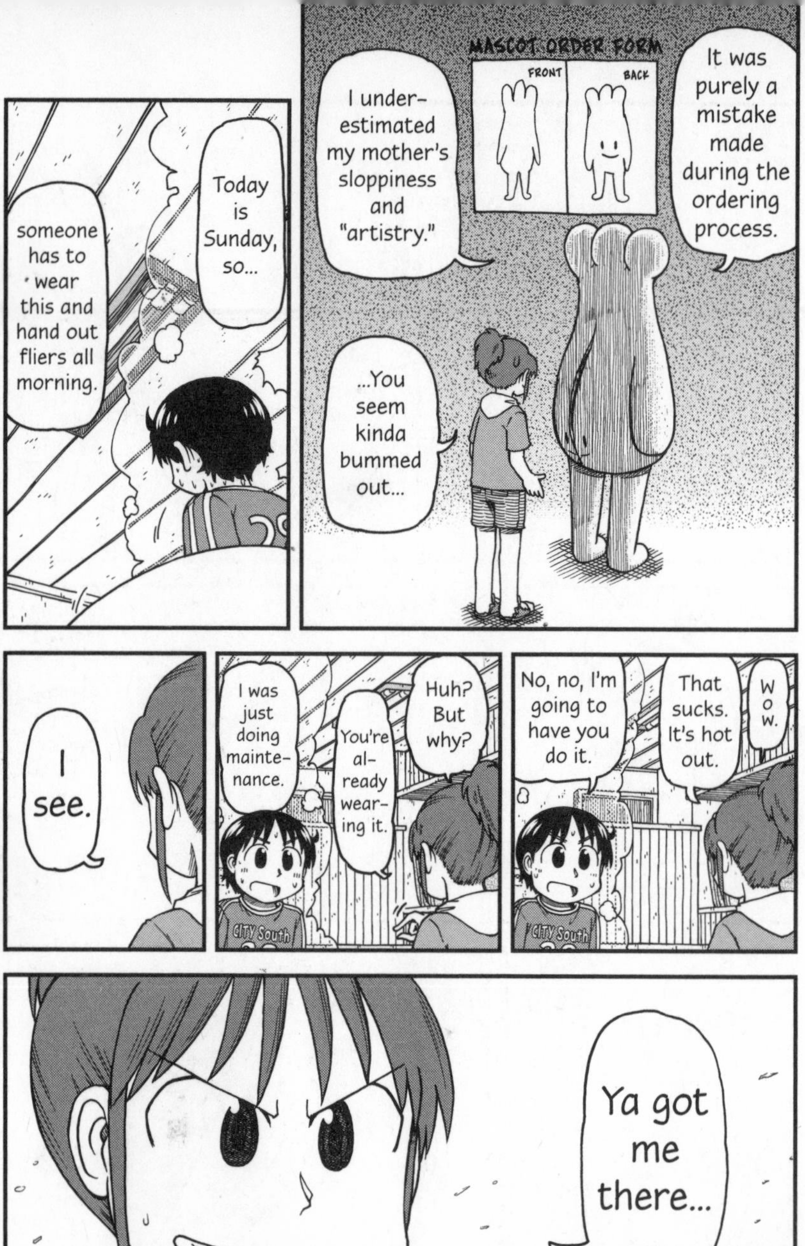

It was purely a mistake made during the ordering process.
MASCOT ORDER FORM
FRONT
BACK
I under-estimated my mother's sloppiness and "artistry."
...You seem kinda bummed out...
Today is Sunday, so...
someone has to wear this and hand out fliers all morning.
Wow.
That sucks. It's hot out.
No, no, I'm going to have you do it.
CITY South
Huh? But why?
You're al-ready wear-ing it.
I was just doing mainte-nance.
CITY South
I see.
Ya got me there...

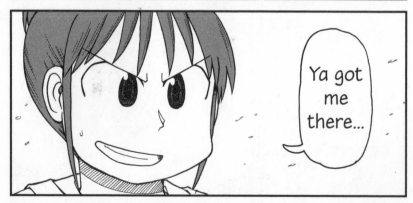

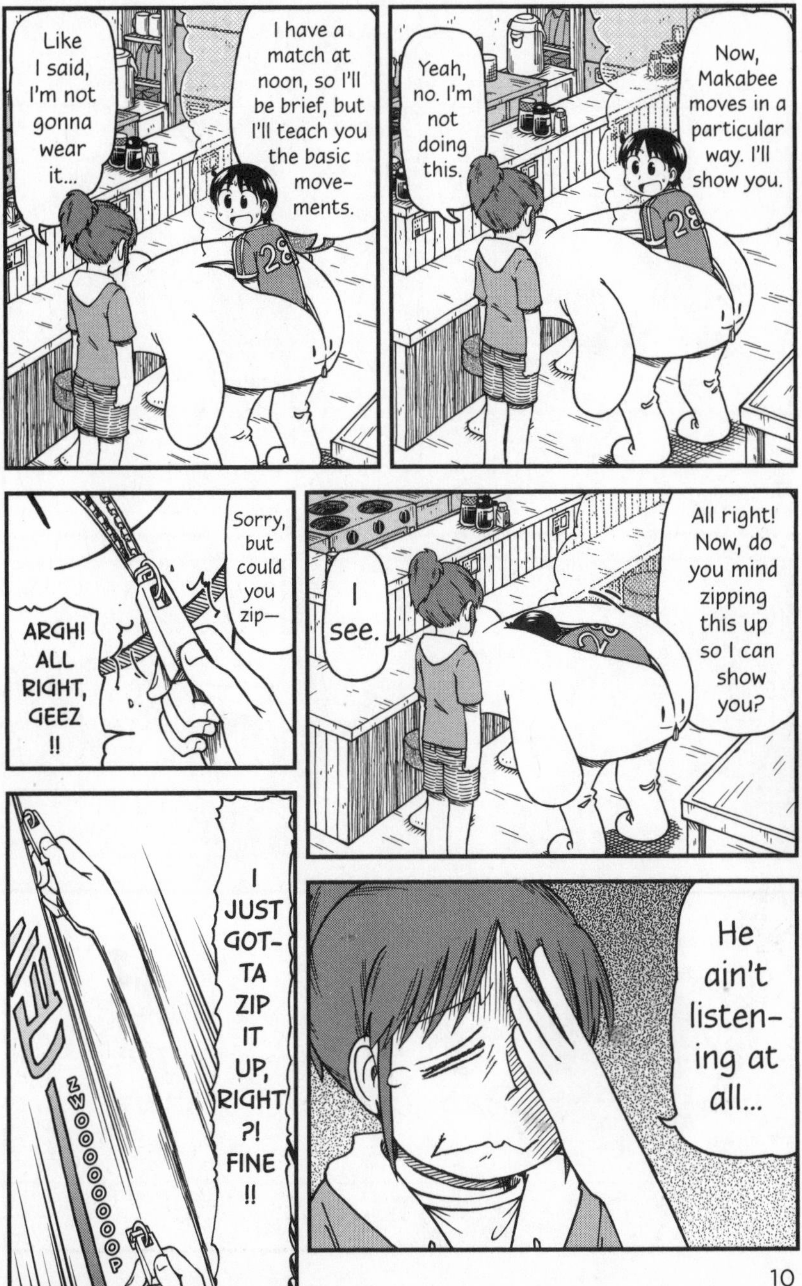
Now, Makabee moves in a particular way. I'll show you.
Yeah, no. I'm not doing this.
I have a match at noon, so I'll be brief, but I'll teach you the basic move-ments.
Like I said, I'm not gonna wear it...
All right! Now, do you mind zipping this up so I can show you?
I see.
Sorry, but could you zip—
ARGH! ALL RIGHT, GEEZ!!
He ain't listen-ing at all...
I JUST GOT-TA ZIP IT UP, RIGHT?! FINE!!
ZWOOOOOOOOOP

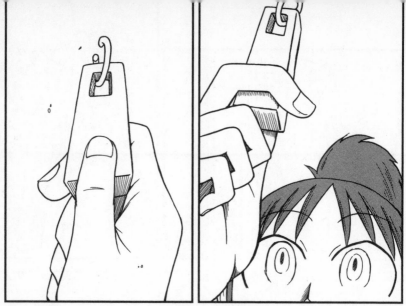

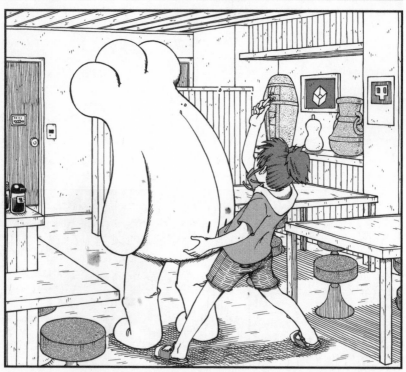

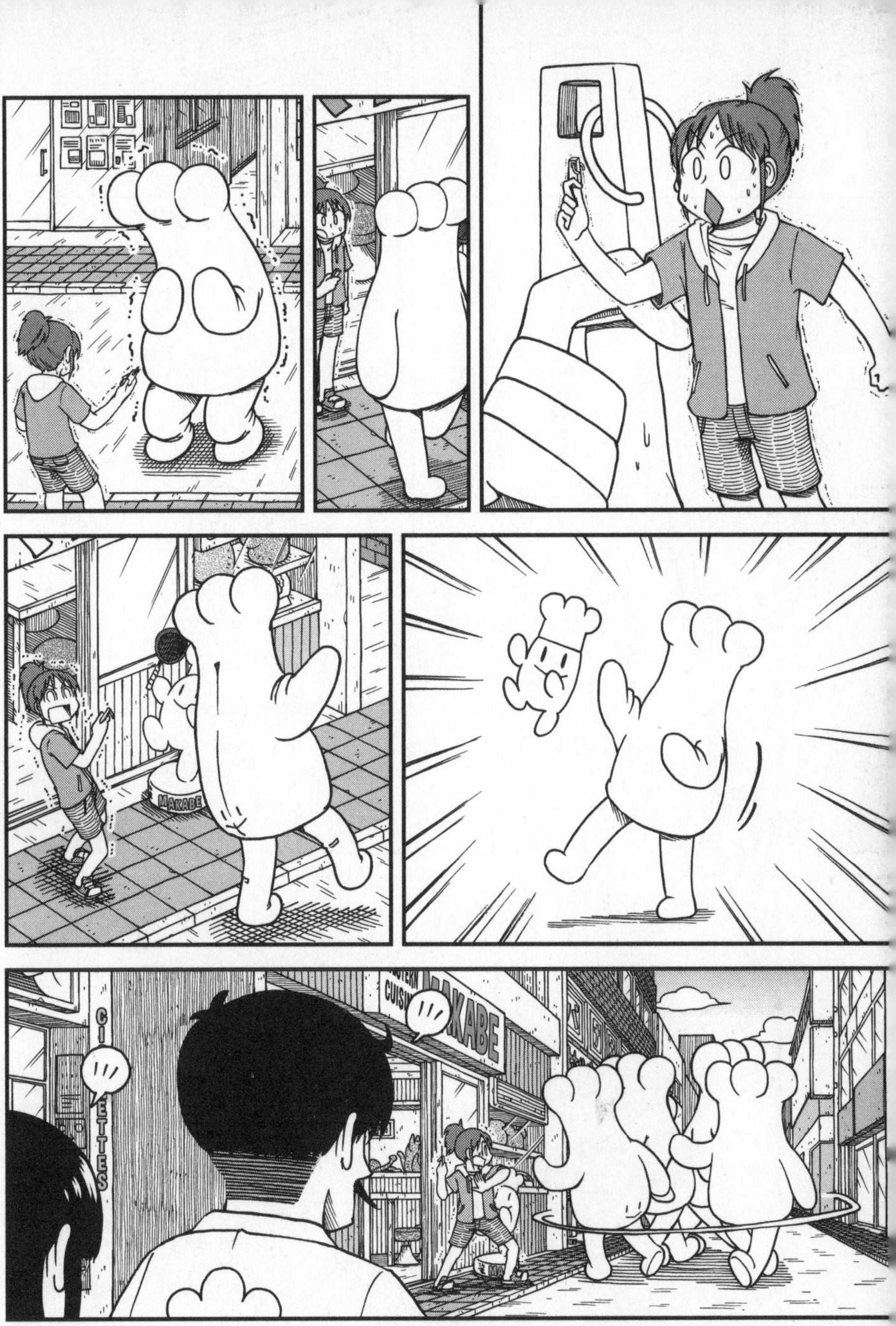
MAKABE

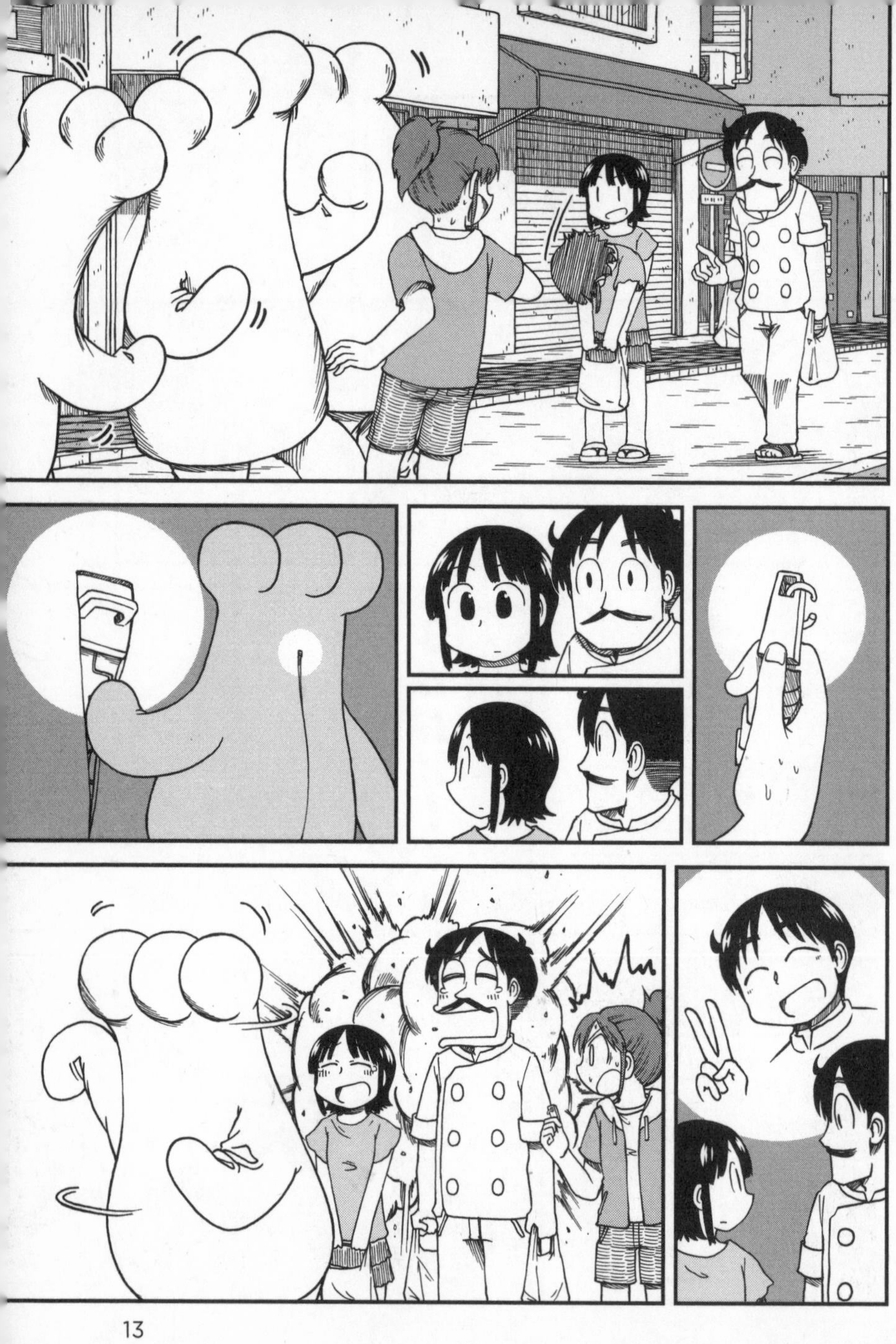

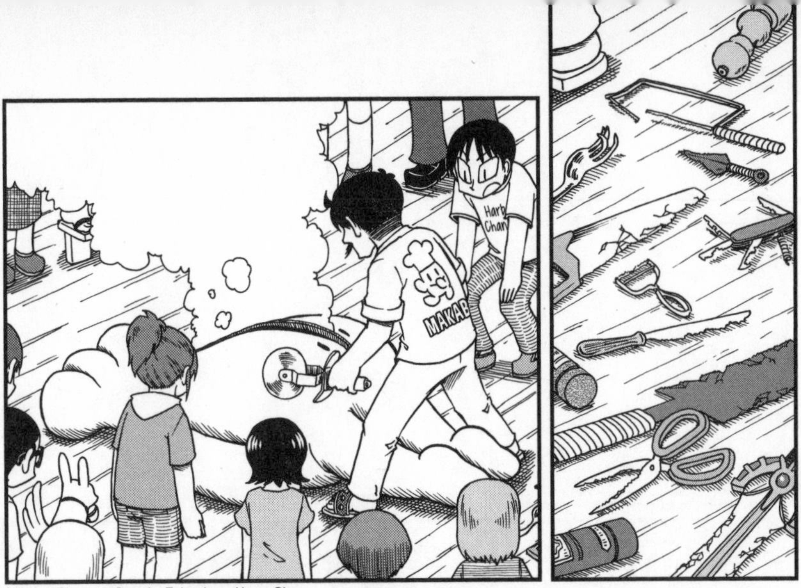

* Harbor Chanson: Song by Enka singer Haruo Oka

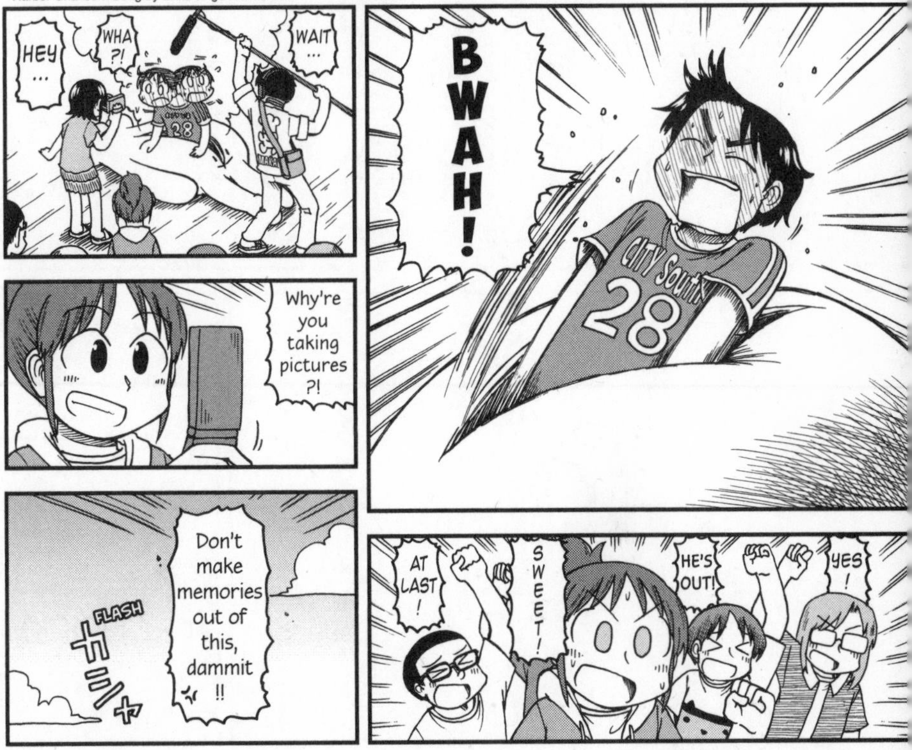
BWAH!
WAIT ...
WHA ?!
HEY ...
Why're you taking pictures ?!
YES !
HE'S OUT!
SWEET!
AT LAST !
Don't make memories out of this, dammit !!
FLASH

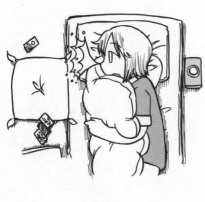

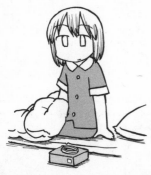

CITY

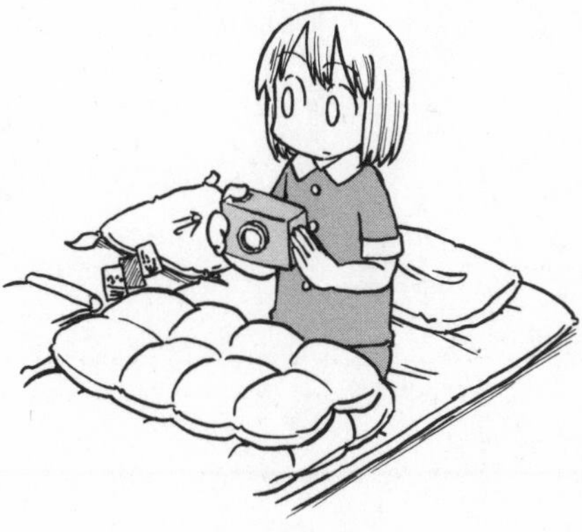

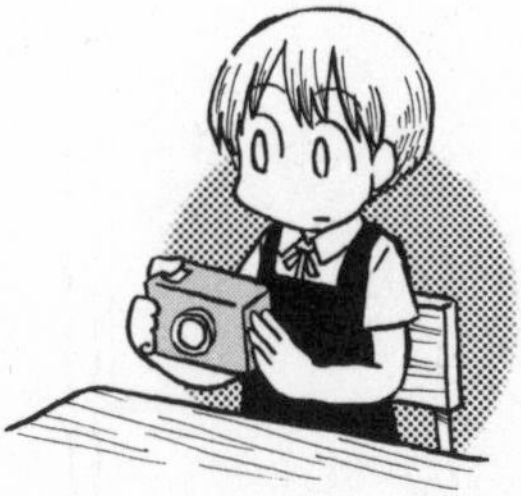

CITY

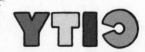

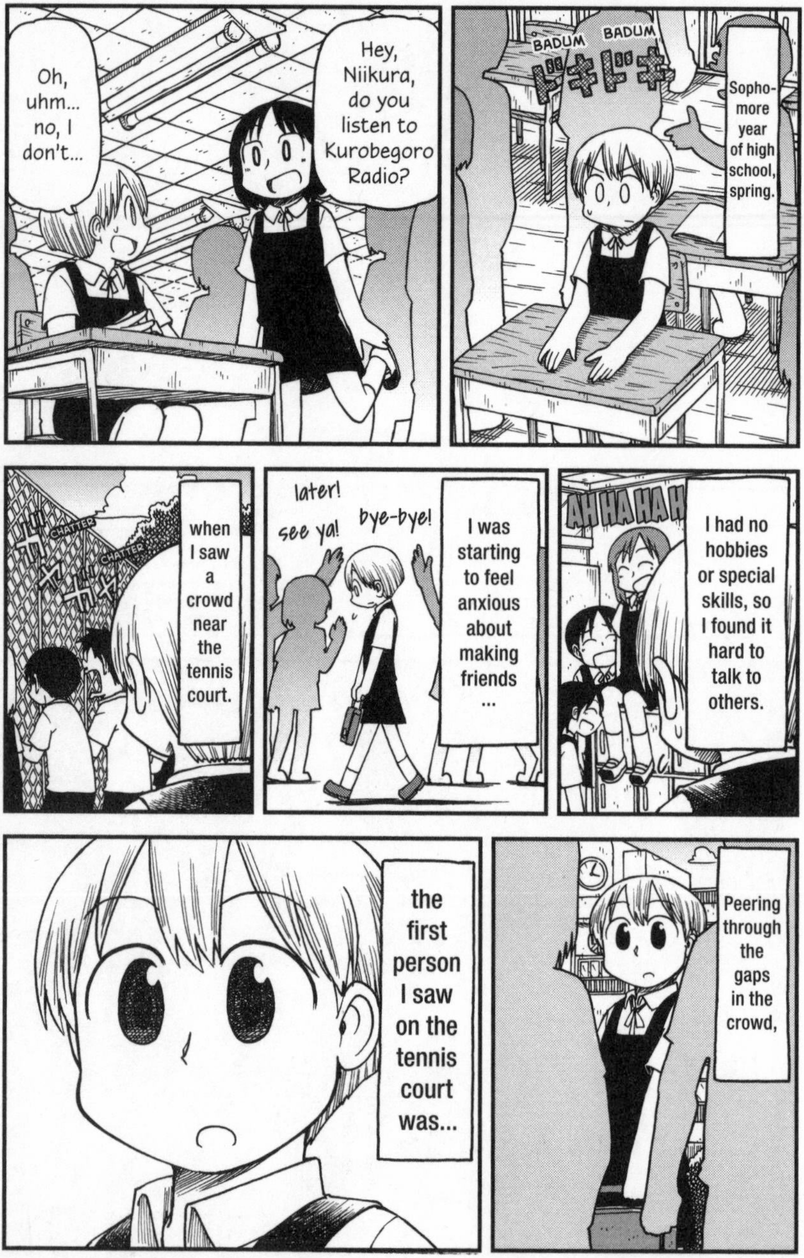
BADUM BADUM
ドキドキ
Sophomore year of high school, spring.
Hey, Niikura, do you listen to Kurobegoro Radio?
Oh, uhm... no, I don't...
AHAHAH
I had no hobbies or special skills, so I found it hard to talk to others.
I was starting to feel anxious about making friends ...
bye-bye!
later!
see ya!
when I saw a crowd near the tennis court.
CHATTER
CHATTER
Peering through the gaps in the crowd,
the first person I saw on the tennis court was...

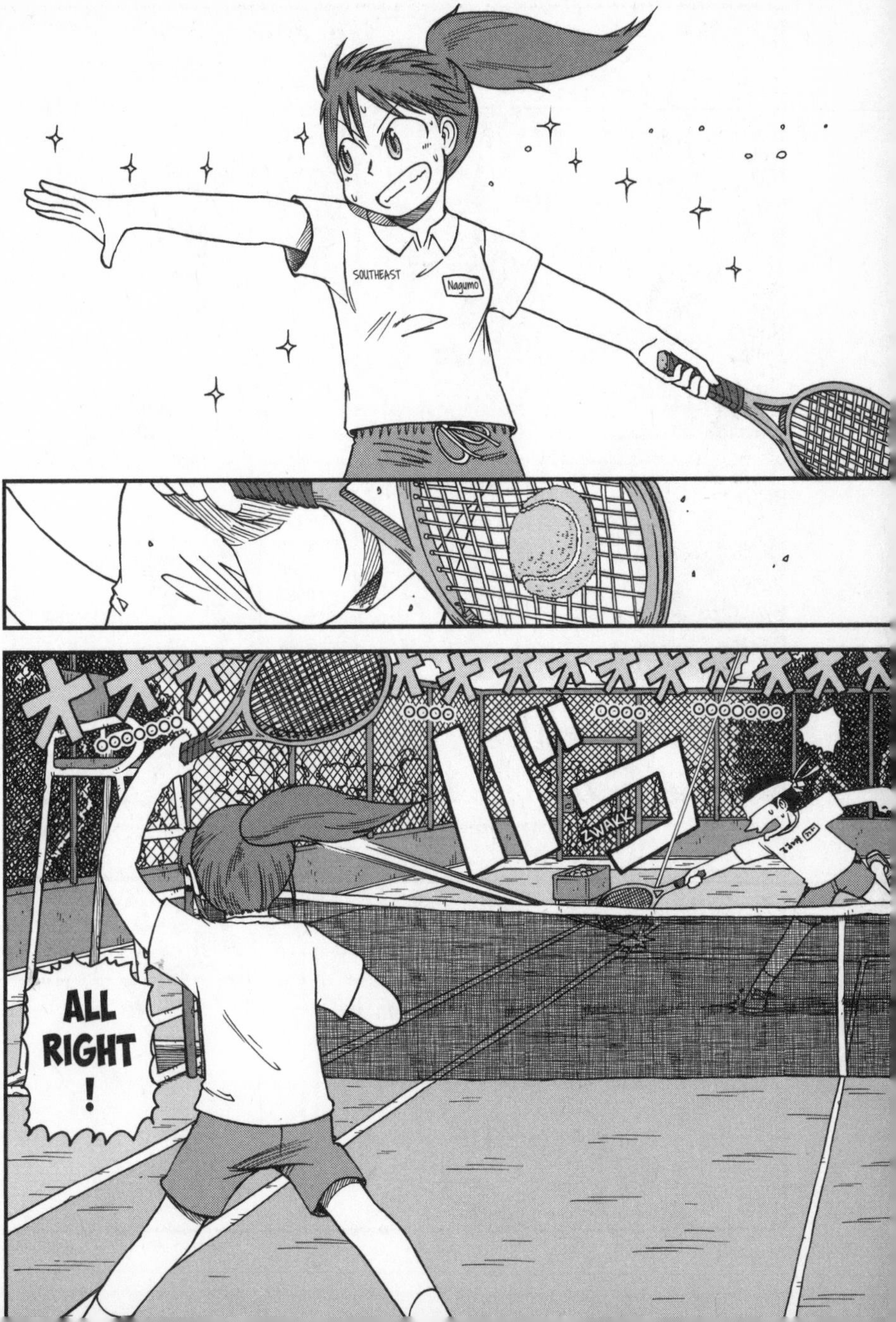
SOUTHEAST
Nagumo
オオオオオオオオオオオオオオ
バコ
ZWAKK
ALL RIGHT !

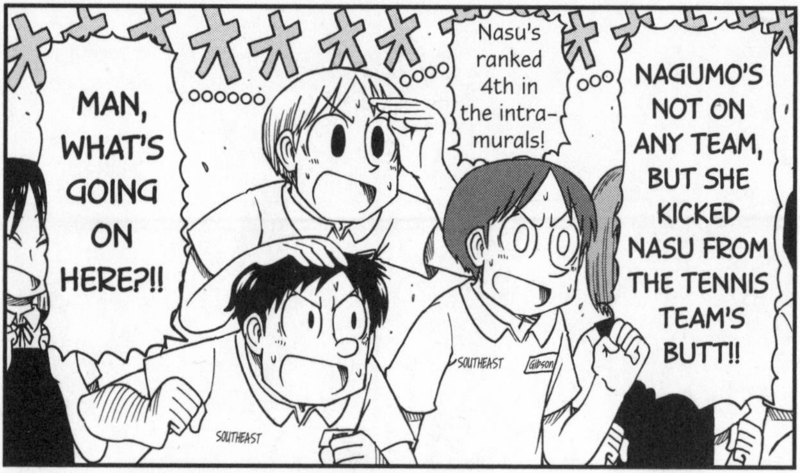
NAGUMO'S NOT ON ANY TEAM, BUT SHE KICKED NASU FROM THE TENNIS TEAM'S BUTT!!
ooo
Nasu's ranked 4th in the intra-murals!
oooo
oooooo
MAN, WHAT'S GOING ON HERE?!!
Gibson
SOUTHEAST
SOUTHEAST

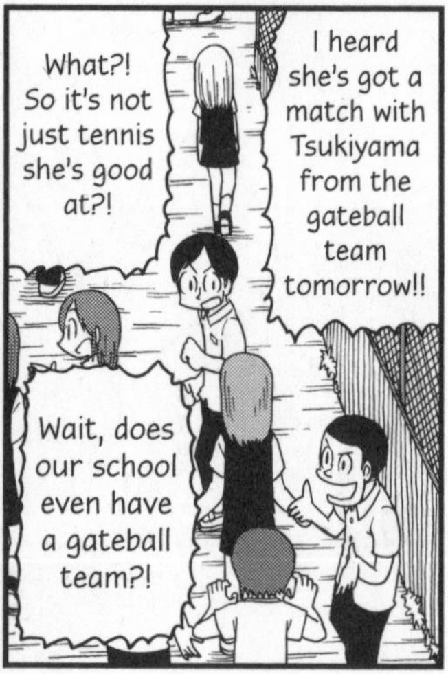
I heard she's got a match with Tsukiyama from the gateball team tomorrow!!
What?! So it's not just tennis she's good at?!
Wait, does our school even have a gateball team?!

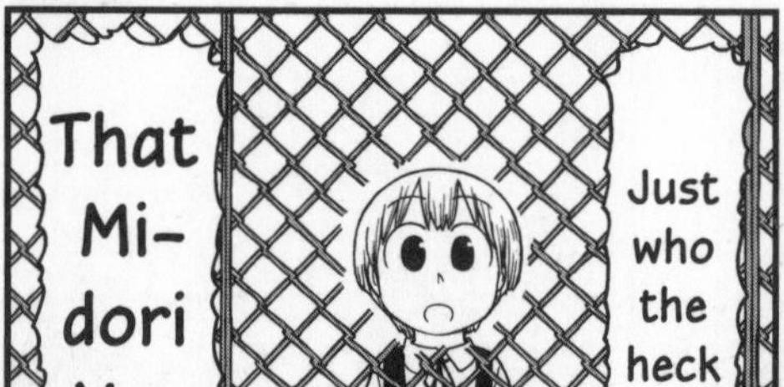
Just who the heck is that girl?
That Mi-dori Na-gu-mo!!

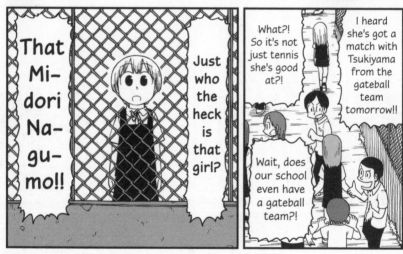

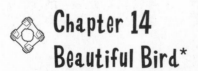

Chapter 14
Beautiful Bird*

*The kanji for "Midori" means "beautiful bird."

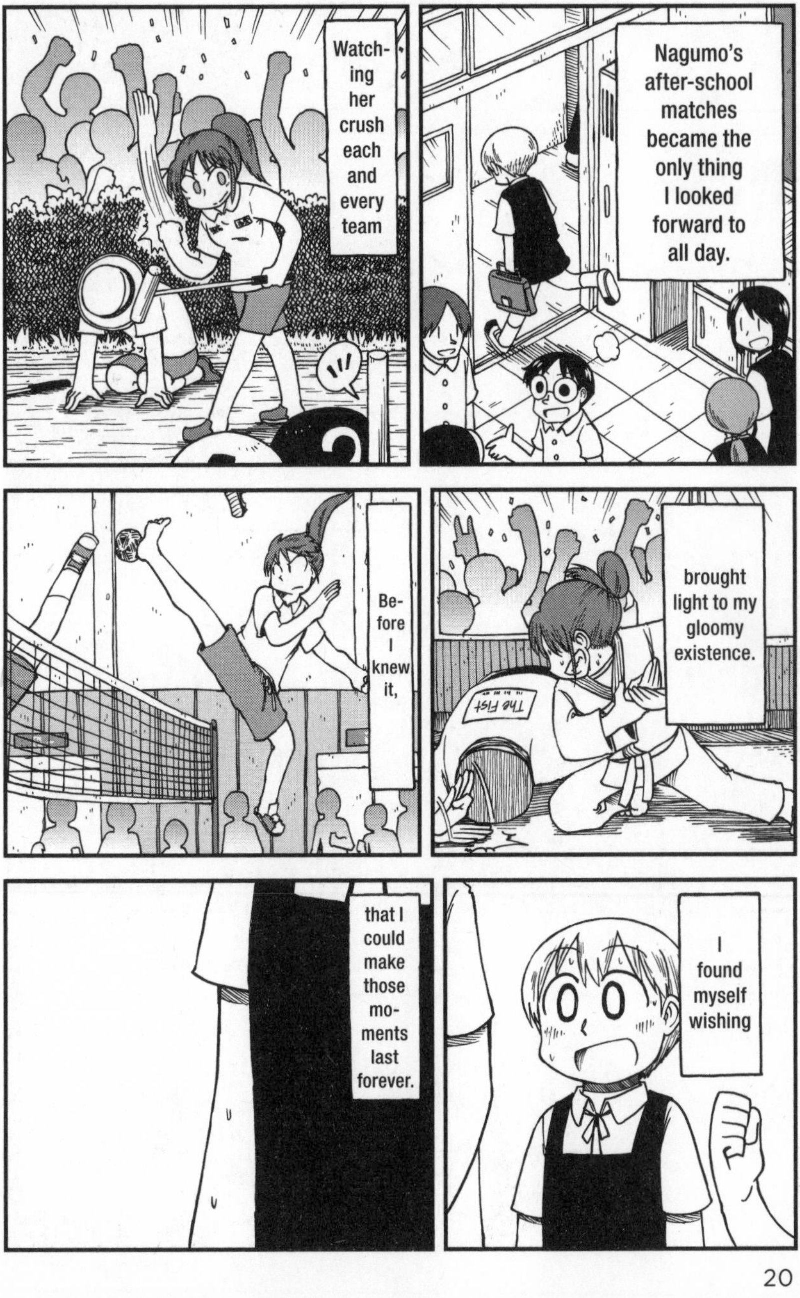
Nagumo's after-school matches became the only thing I looked forward to all day.
Watch-ing her crush each and every team
brought light to my gloomy existence.
The Fist
Be-fore I knew it,
I found myself wishing
that I could make those mo-ments last forever.

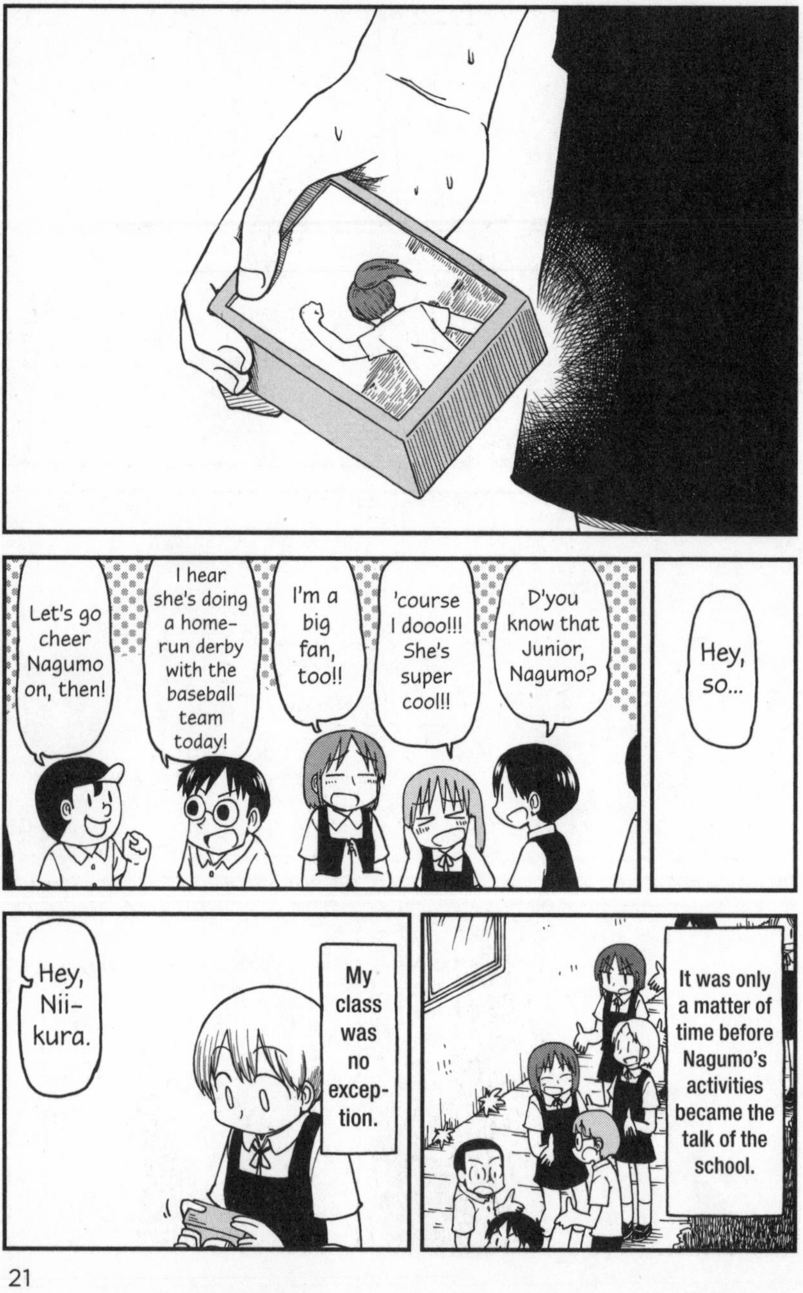
Hey, so...
D'you know that Junior, Nagumo?
'course I dooo!!! She's super cool!!
I'm a big fan, too!!
I hear she's doing a home-run derby with the baseball team today!
Let's go cheer Nagumo on, then!
It was only a matter of time before Nagumo's activities became the talk of the school.
My class was no exception.
Hey, Nii-kura.

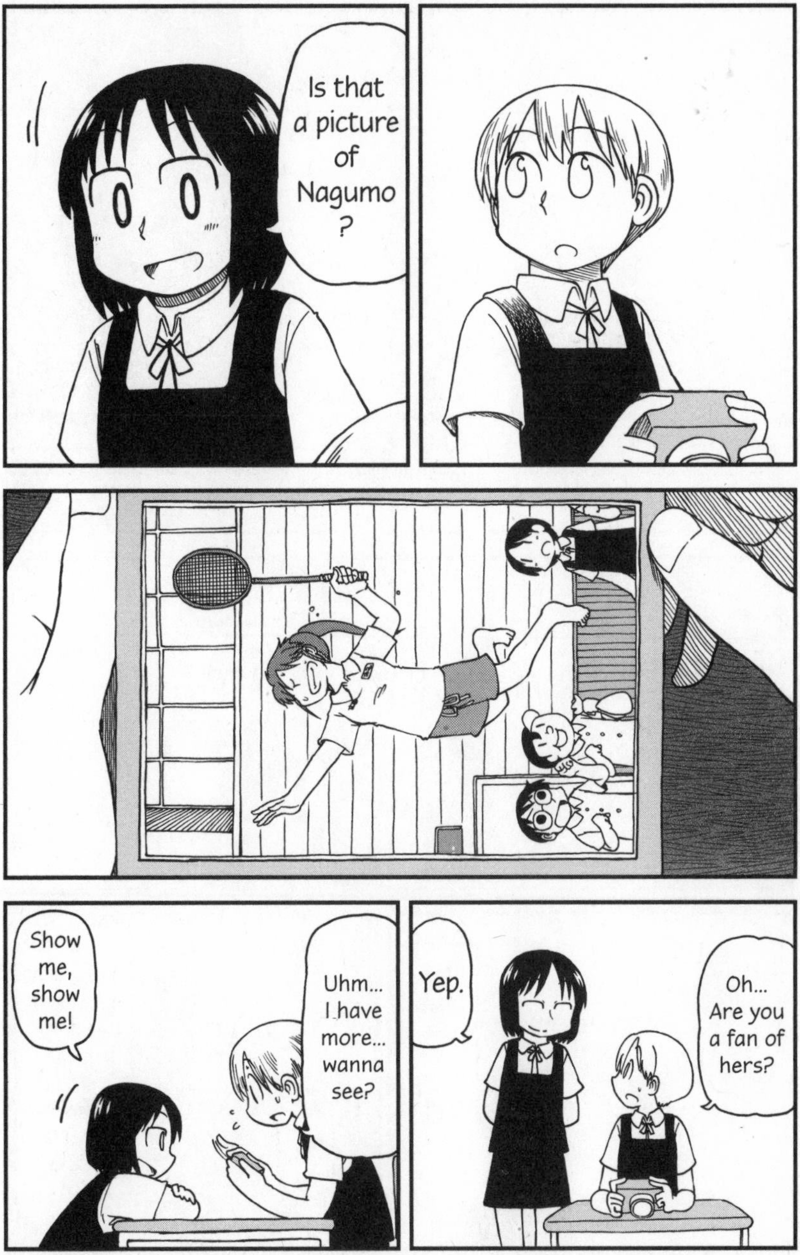
Is that a picture of Nagumo?
Oh... Are you a fan of hers?
Yep.
Uhm... I have more... wanna see?
Show me, show me!

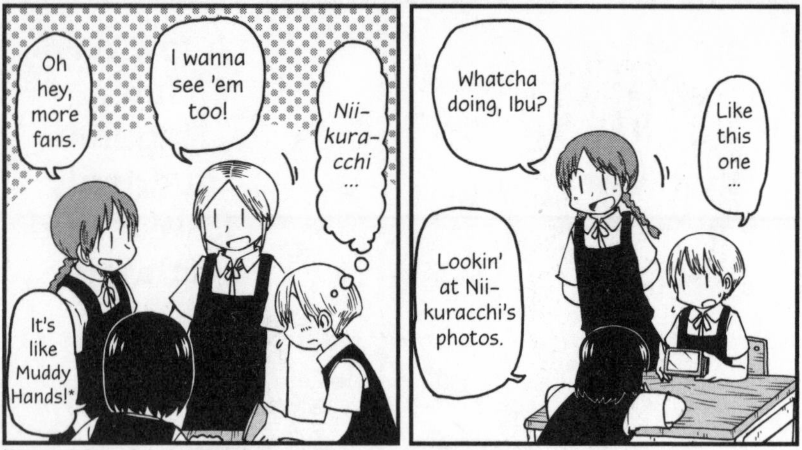
Whatcha doing, Ibu?
Lookin' at Nii-kuracchi's photos.
Like this one ...
Nii-kura-cchi ...
I wanna see 'em too!
Oh hey, more fans.
It's like Muddy Hands!*

*A monster in Dragon Quest that summons more of its kind.

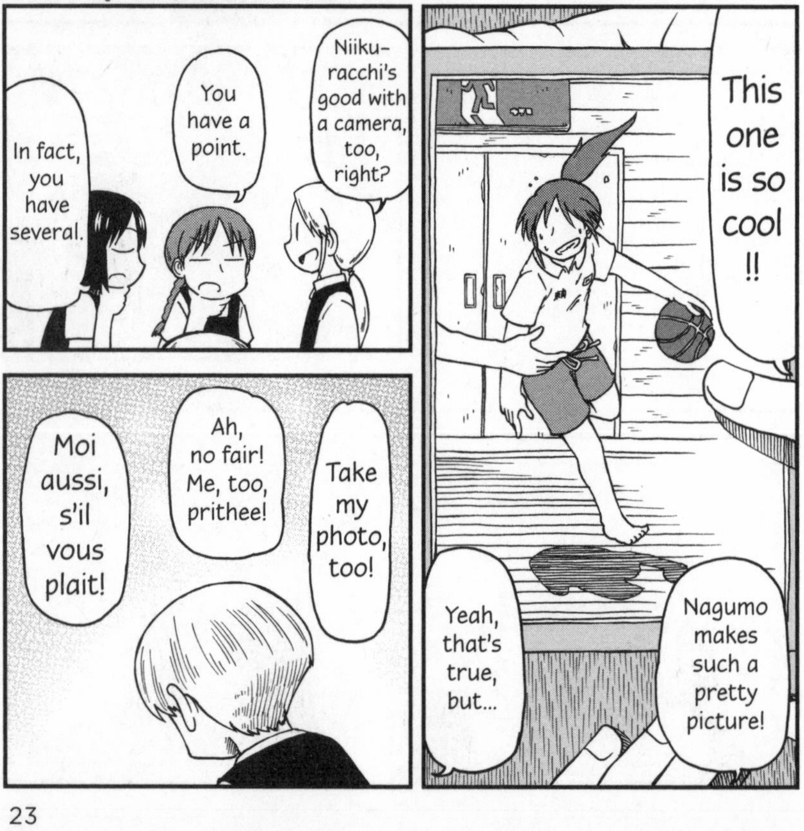
This one is so cool !!
Nagumo makes such a pretty picture!
Yeah, that's true, but...
Niiku-racchi's good with a camera, too, right?
You have a point.
In fact, you have several.
Take my photo, too!
Ah, no fair! Me, too, prithee!
Moi aussi, s'il vous plait!

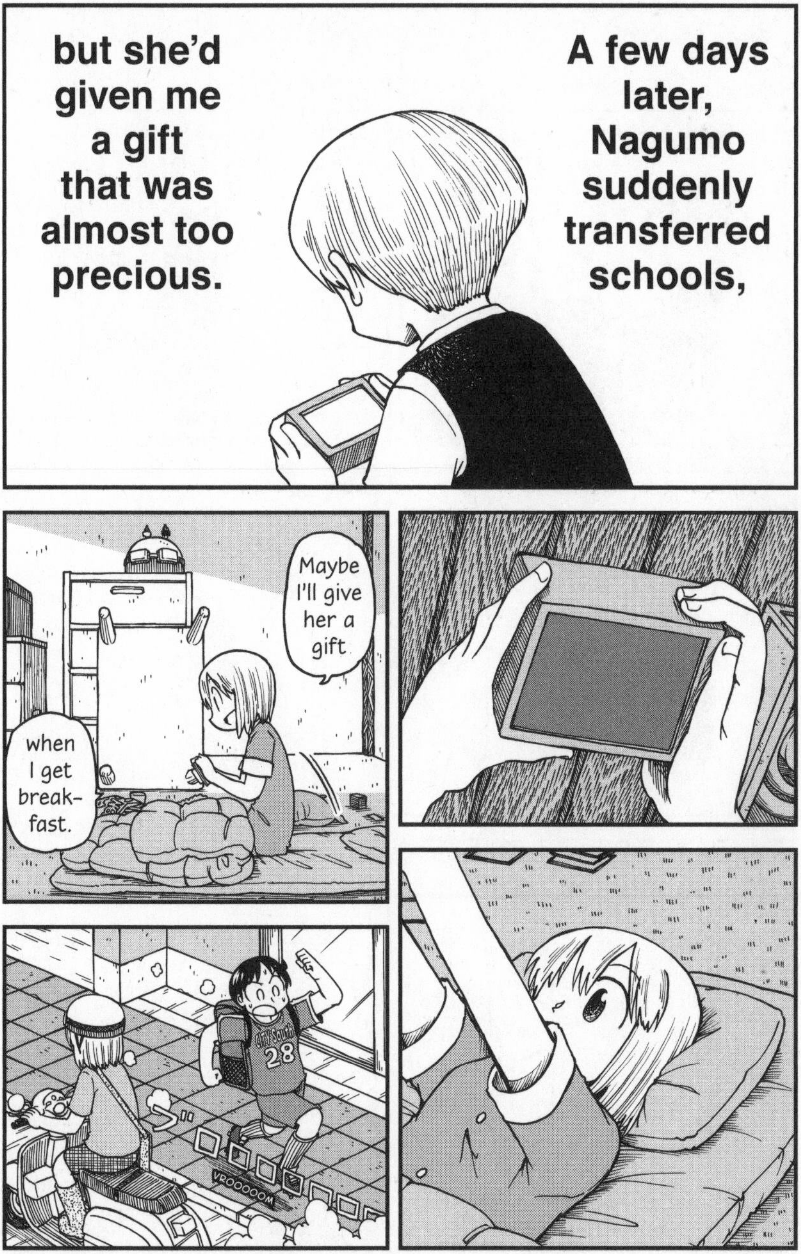
A few days later, Nagumo suddenly transferred schools,
but she'd given me a gift that was almost too precious.
Maybe I'll give her a gift
when I get breakfast.
VROOOOOOM

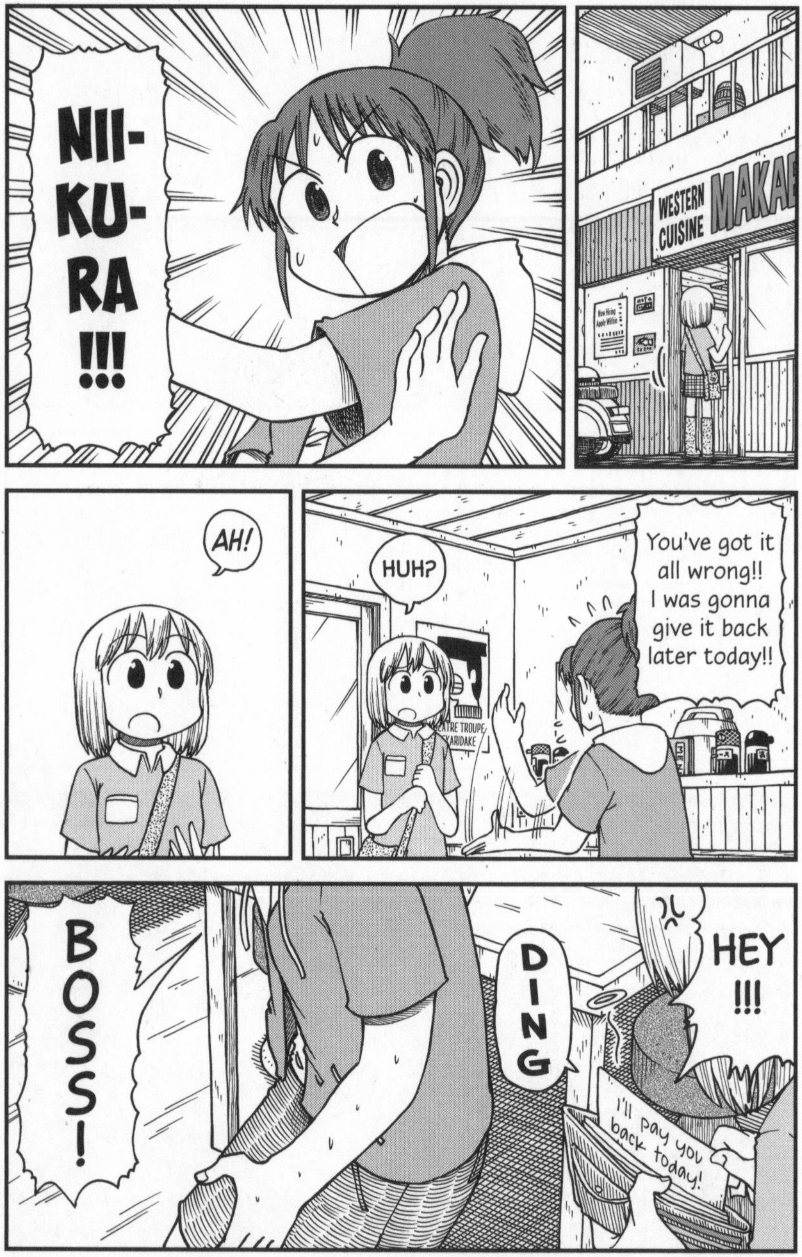
WESTERN CUISINE
Now Hiring Apply Within
NII-KU-RA!!!
HUH?
You've got it all wrong!! I was gonna give it back later today!!
AH!
HEY !!!
I'll pay you back today!
DING
BOSS!

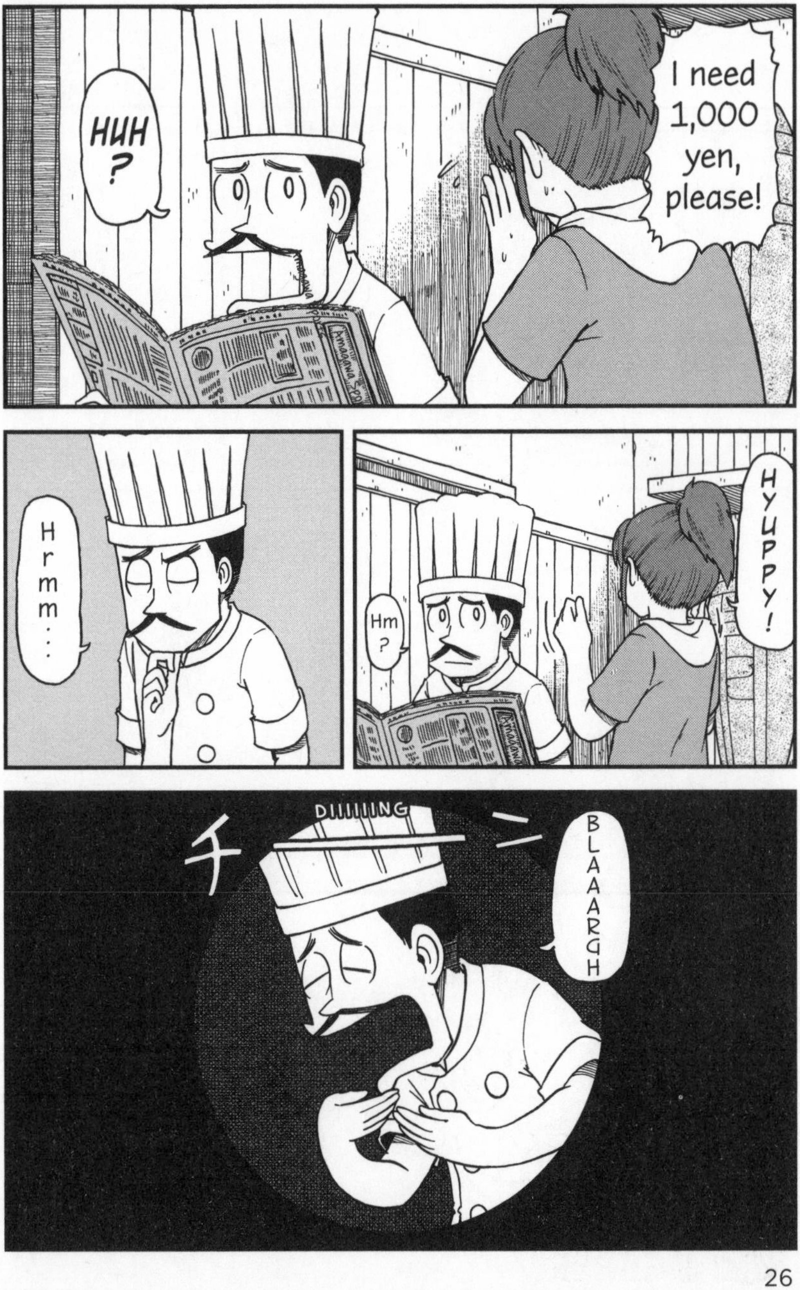
I need 1,000 yen, please!
HUH?
HYUPPY!
Hm?
Hrmm...
BLAAARGH
DIIIIIIING
チーン

UN
DEUX
TROIS

CITY

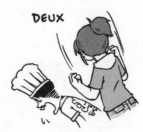

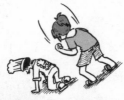

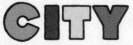

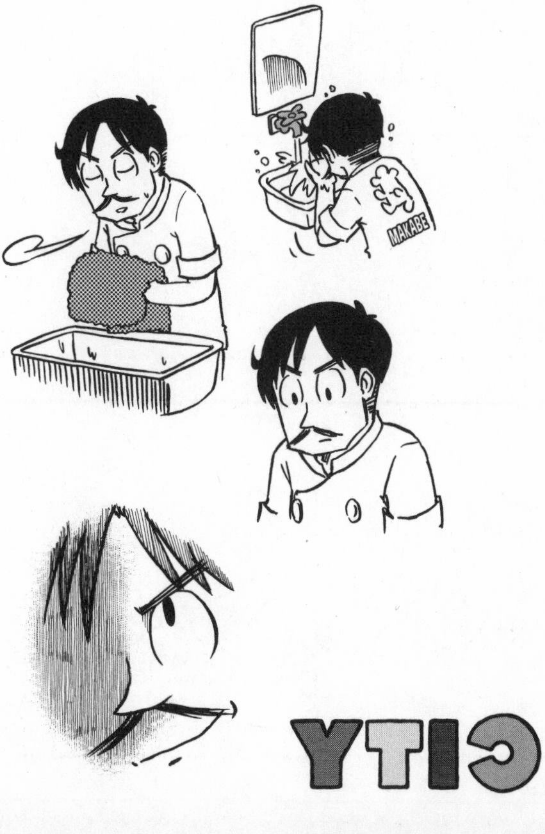
MAKABE

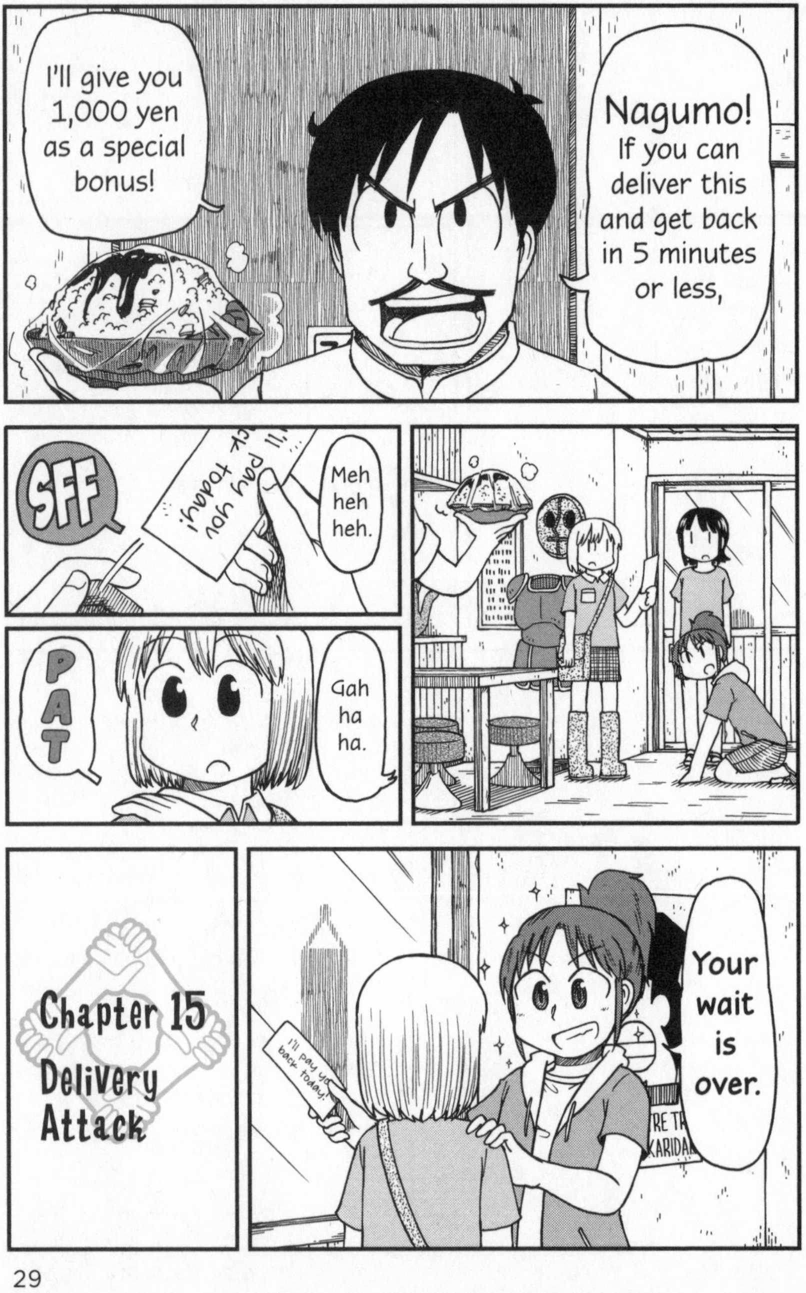
Nagumo! If you can deliver this and get back in 5 minutes or less,
I'll give you 1,000 yen as a special bonus!
Meh heh heh.
I'll pay you back today!
SFF
Gah ha ha.
PAT
Your wait is over.
I'll pay you back today!
Chapter 15
Delivery Attack

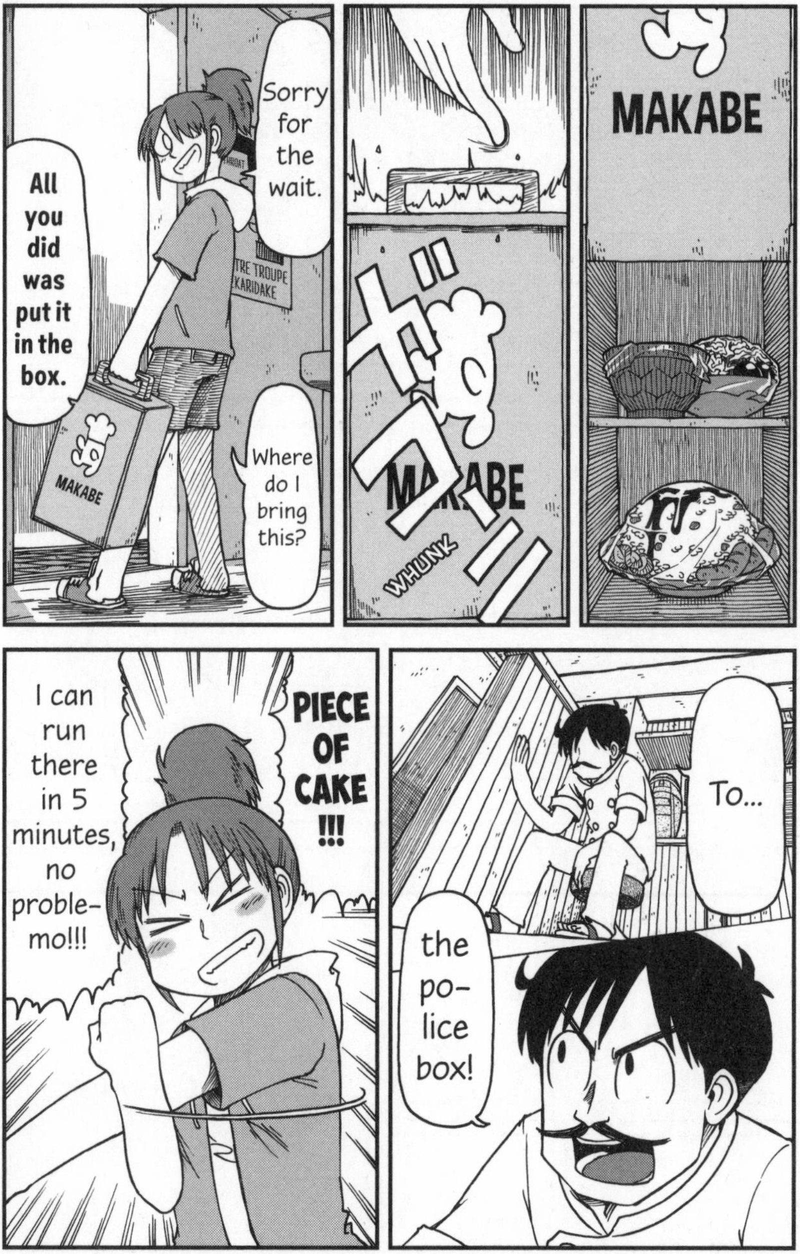
MAKABE
MAKABE
WHUNK
Sorry for the wait.
All you did was put it in the box.
MAKABE
Where do I bring this?
To...
the police box!
PIECE OF CAKE!!!
I can run there in 5 minutes, no proble-mo!!!

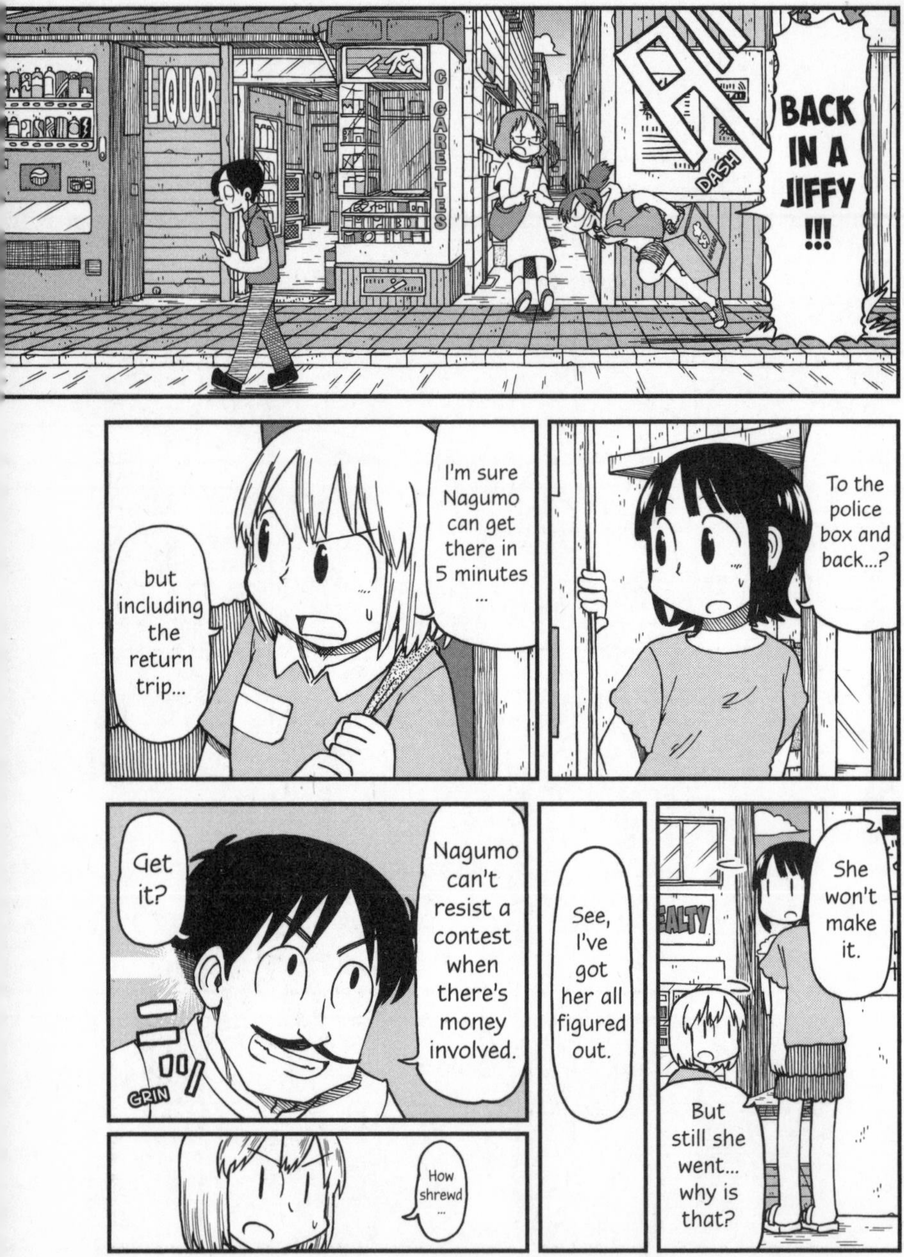

LIQUOR
CIGARETTES
DASH
BACK IN A JIFFY!!!
To the police box and back...?
I'm sure Nagumo can get there in 5 minutes...
but including the return trip...
She won't make it.
But still she went... why is that?
See, I've got her all figured out.
Nagumo can't resist a contest when there's money involved.
Get it?
GRIN
How shrewd...

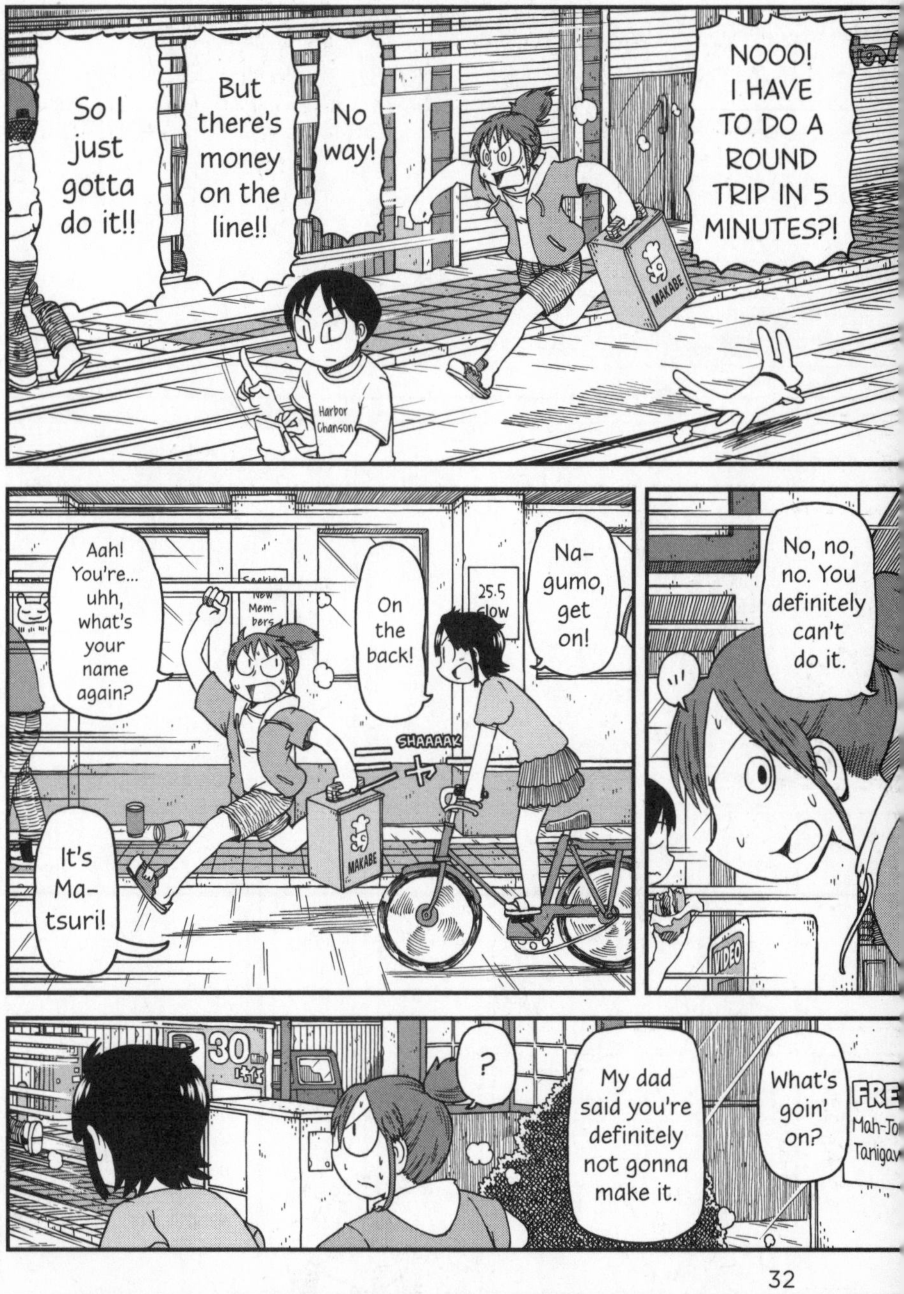
NOOO! I HAVE TO DO A ROUND TRIP IN 5 MINUTES?!
No way!
But there's money on the line!!
So I just gotta do it!!
MAKABE
Harbor Chanson
No, no, no. You definitely can't do it.
VIDEO
Na-gumo, get on!
On the back!
Aah! You're... uhh, what's your name again?
Seeking New Mem-bers
SHAAAAK
MAKABE
It's Ma-tsuri!
What's goin' on?
My dad said you're definitely not gonna make it.
?

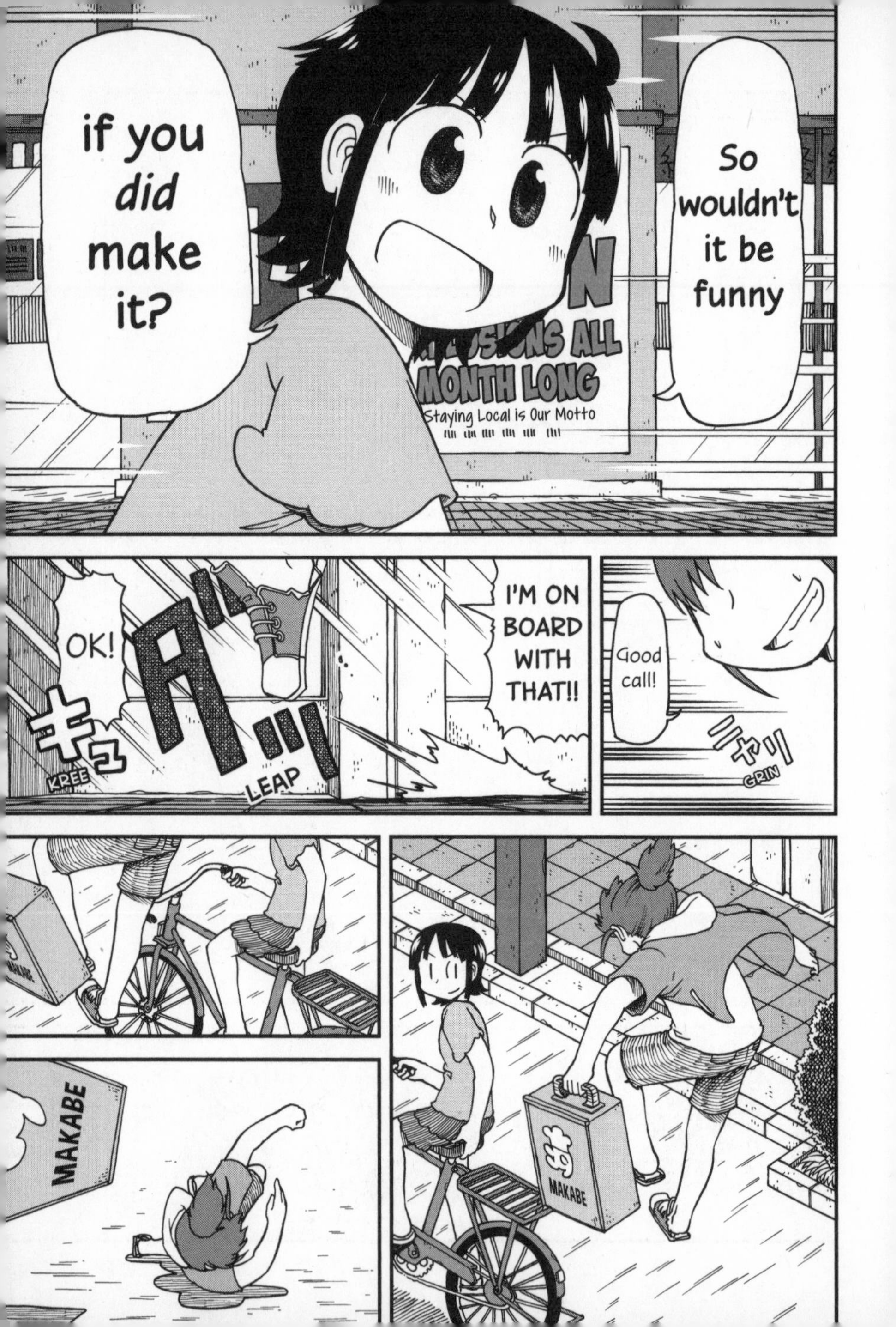
So wouldn't it be funny
if you did make it?
MONTH LONG
Staying Local is Our Motto
Good call!
ニヤリ
GRIN
I'M ON BOARD WITH THAT!!
ダッ
LEAP
OK!
キュ
KREE
MAKABE
MAKABE

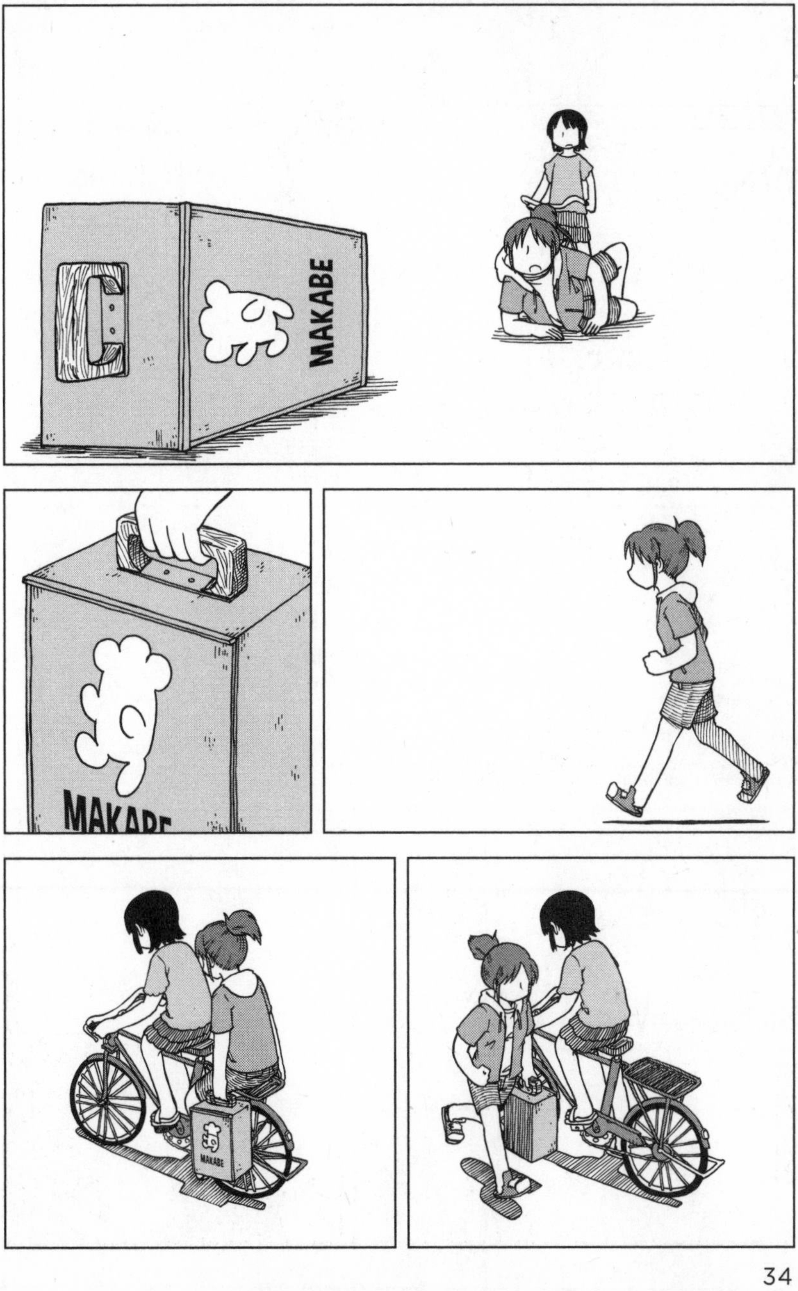
MAKABE
MAKABE

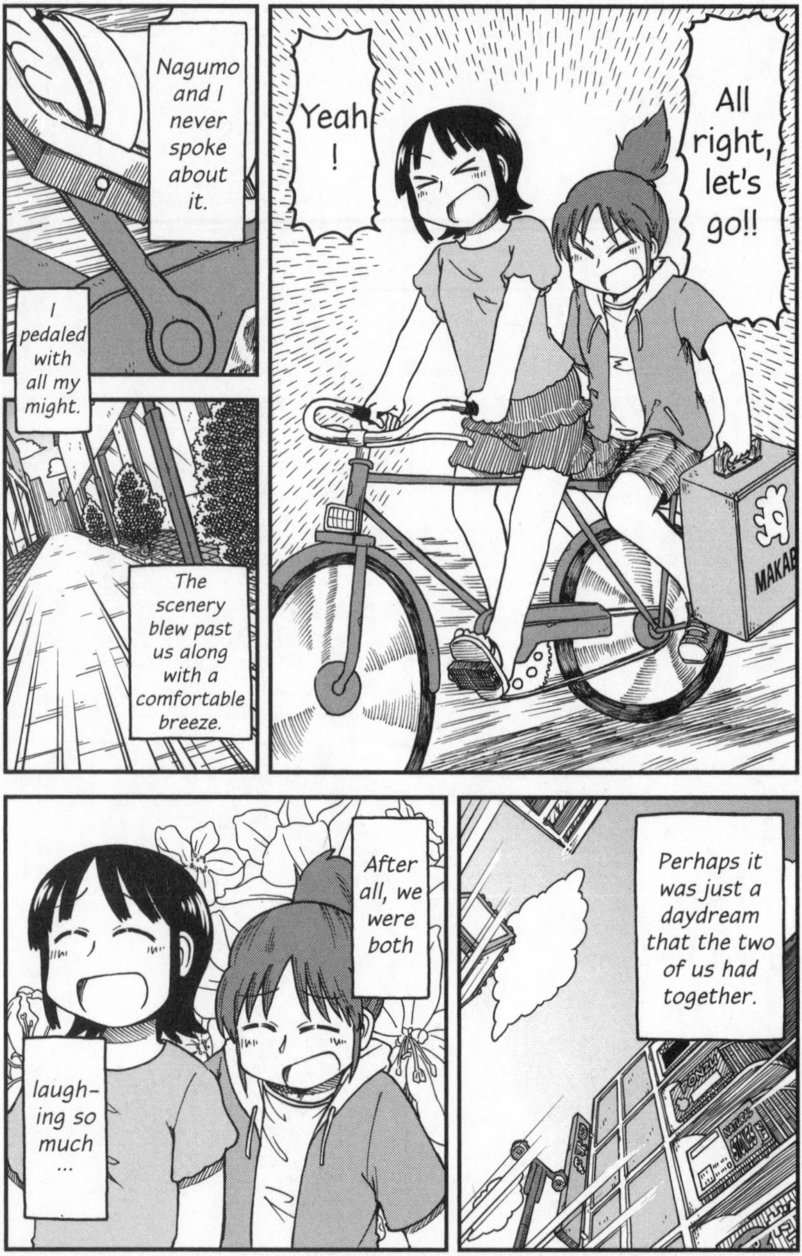
All right, let's go!!
Yeah!
MAKAB
Nagumo and I never spoke about it.
I pedaled with all my might.
The scenery blew past us along with a comfortable breeze.
Perhaps it was just a daydream that the two of us had together.
After all, we were both
laughing so much...

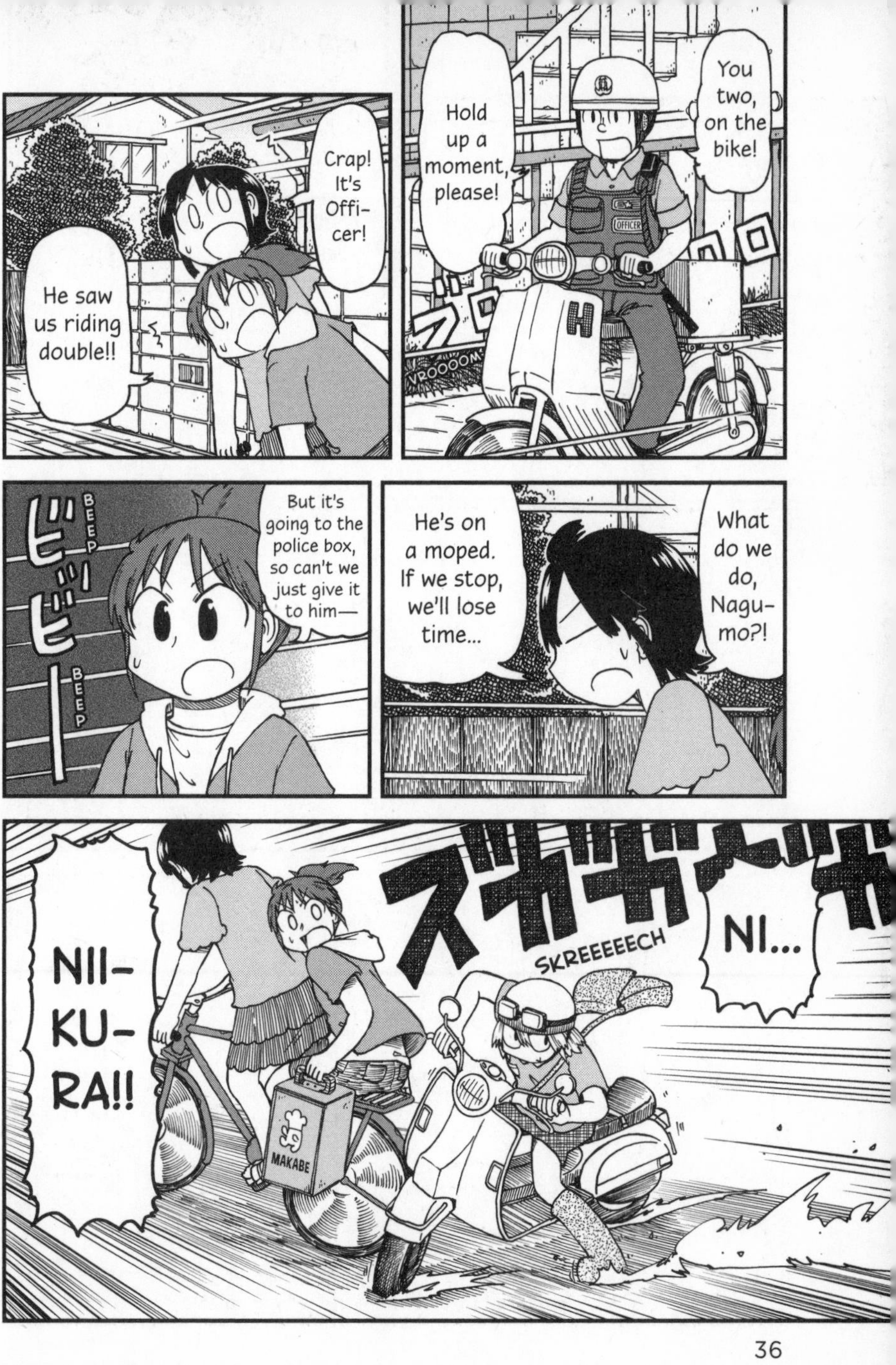
You two, on the bike!
Hold up a moment, please!
OFFICER
VROOOOM
Crap! It's Offi-cer!
He saw us riding double!!
What do we do, Nagumo?!
He's on a moped. If we stop, we'll lose time...
But it's going to the police box, so can't we just give it to him—
BEEP
BEEP
NI...
SKREEEEECH
NII-KU-RA!!
MAKABE

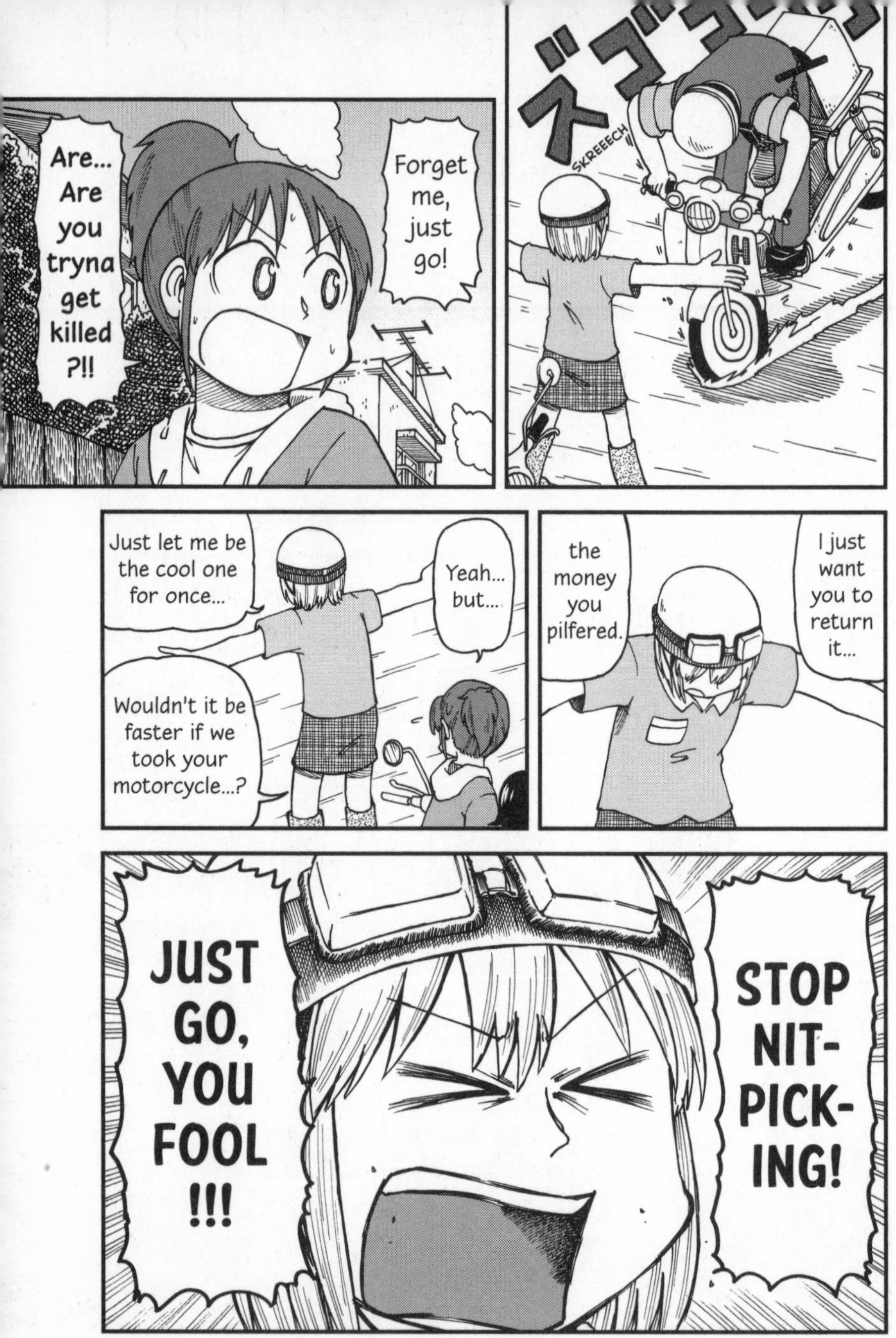
SKREEECH
Forget me, just go!
Are... Are you tryna get killed?!!
I just want you to return it...
the money you pilfered.
Yeah... but...
Just let me be the cool one for once...
Wouldn't it be faster if we took your motorcycle...?
STOP NIT-PICKING!
JUST GO, YOU FOOL!!!

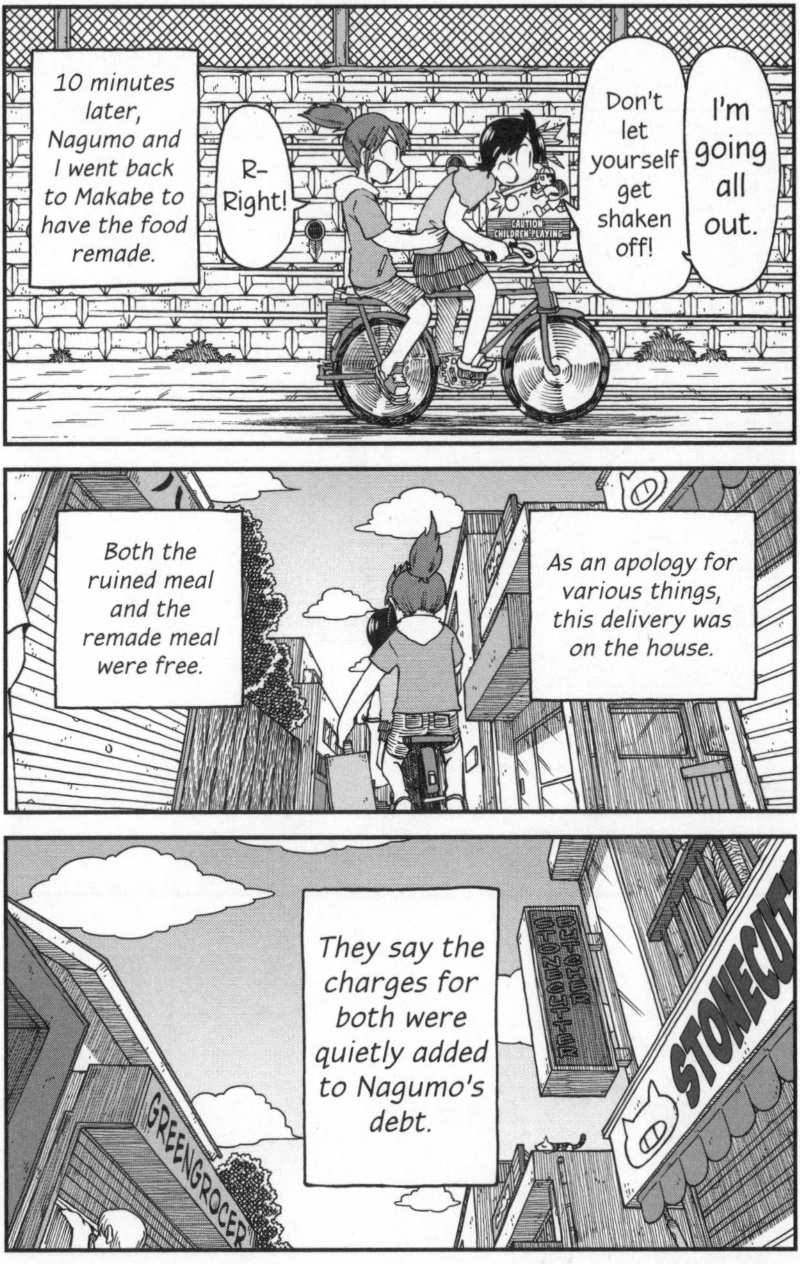
I'm going all out.
Don't let yourself get shaken off!
CAUTION: CHILDREN PLAYING
R-Right!
10 minutes later, Nagumo and I went back to Makabe to have the food remade.
As an apology for various things, this delivery was on the house.
Both the ruined meal and the remade meal were free.
STONECUT
They say the charges for both were quietly added to Nagumo's debt.
GREENGROCER

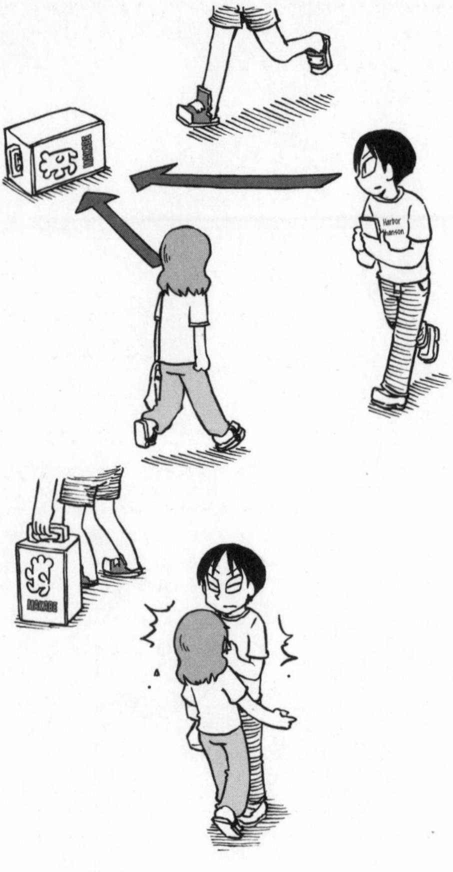
Harbor
MAKABE

CITY

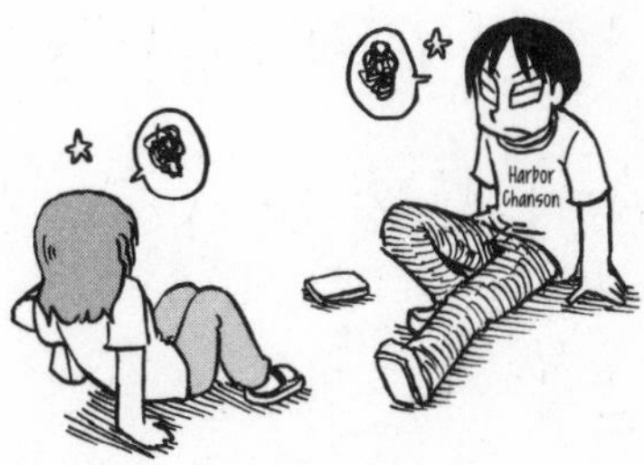
Harbor
Chanson

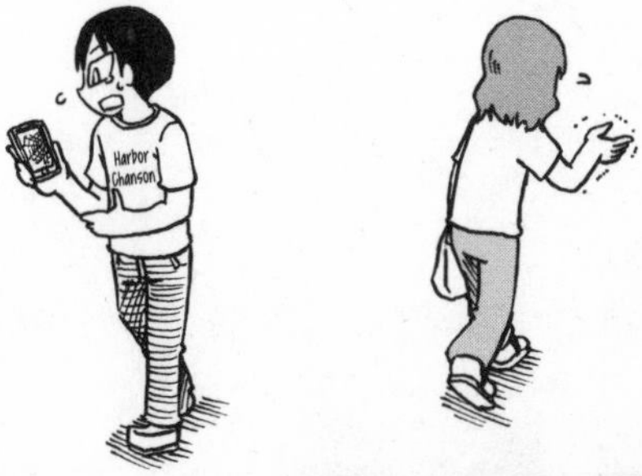
Harbor
Chanson

CITY

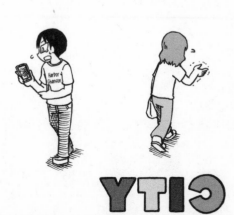

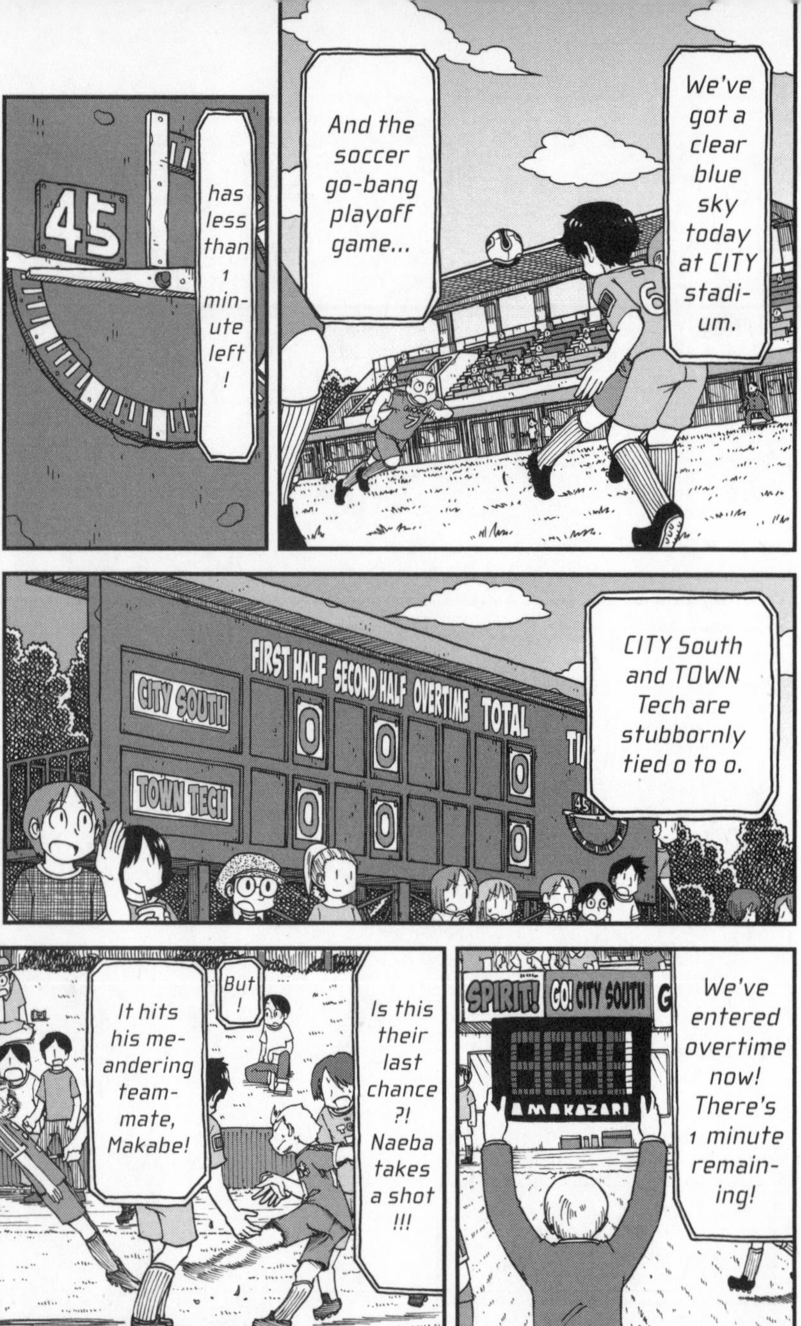
We've got a clear blue sky today at CITY stadium.
And the soccer go-bang playoff game...
45
has less than 1 minute left!
FIRST HALF SECOND HALF OVERTIME TOTAL
CITY SOUTH 0 0 0
TOWN TECH 0 0 0
CITY South and TOWN Tech are stubbornly tied 0 to 0.
SPIRIT! GO! CITY SOUTH
AMAKAZARI
We've entered overtime now! There's 1 minute remaining!
Is this their last chance?! Naeba takes a shot!!!
But!
It hits his meandering teammate, Makabe!

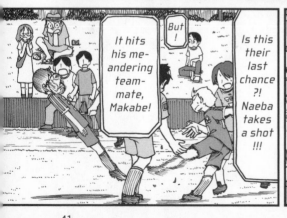

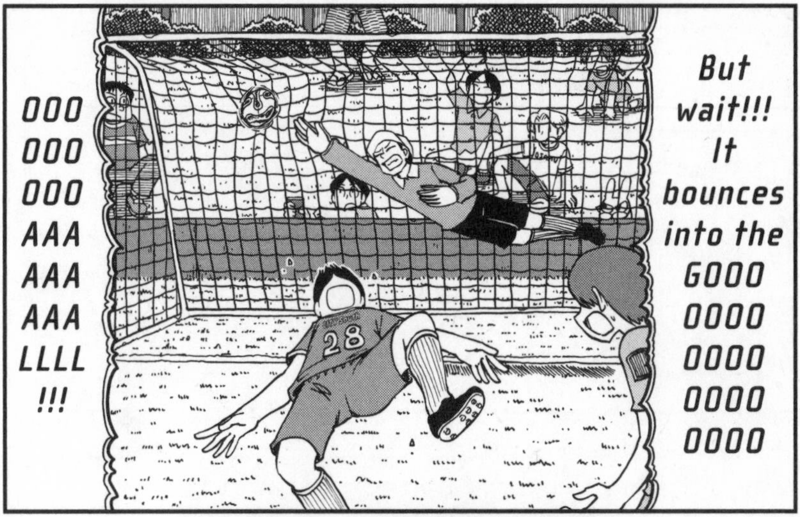
But wait!!! It bounces into the GOOOOOOOOOOOOOOOOOOO
OOOOOOOOOAAAAAAAAALLLL!!!

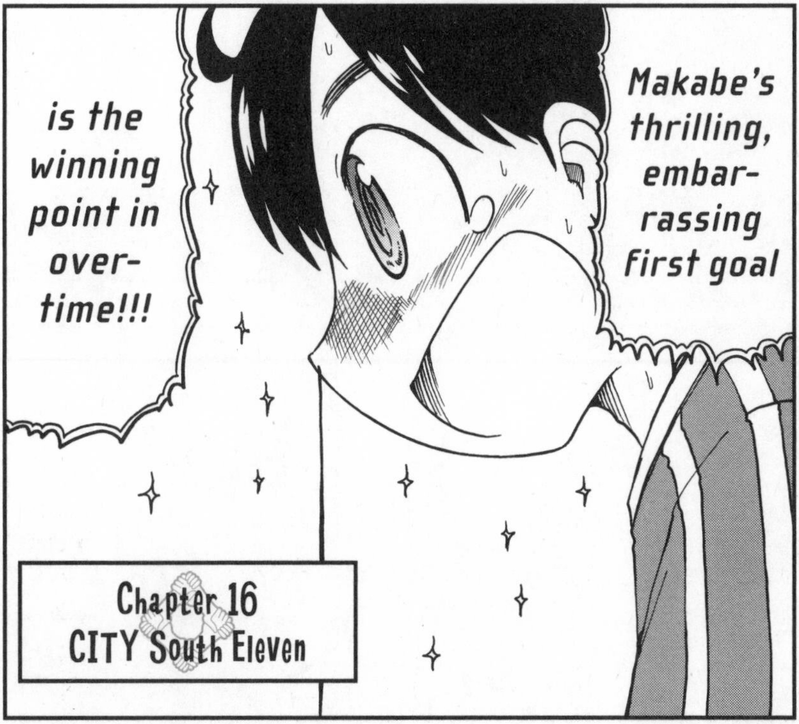
Makabe's thrilling, embarrassing first goal
is the winning point in overtime!!!
Chapter 16
CITY South Eleven

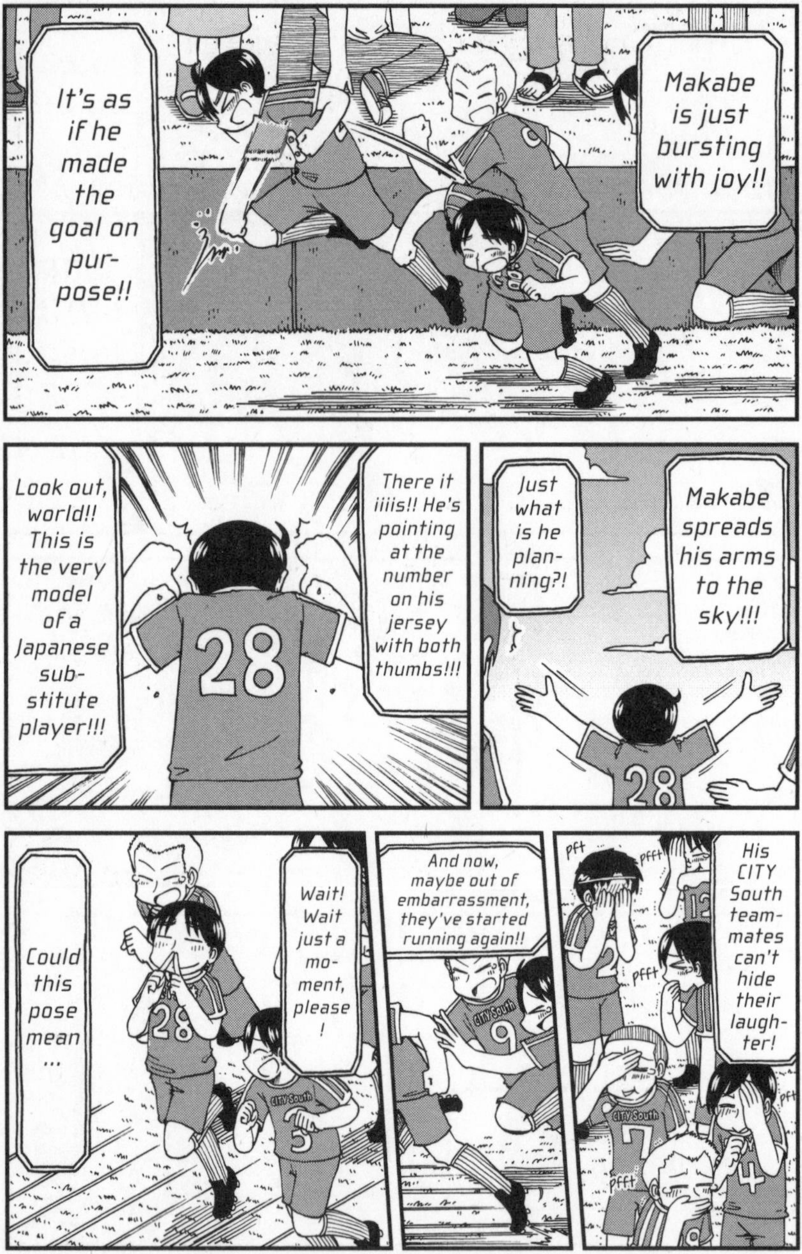
Makabe is just bursting with joy!!
It's as if he made the goal on purpose!!
Makabe spreads his arms to the sky!!!
Just what is he planning?!
28
There it iiiis!! He's pointing at the number on his jersey with both thumbs!!!
Look out, world!! This is the very model of a Japanese substitute player!!!
28
His CITY South teammates can't hide their laughter!
pfft
pfft
pfft
pfft
pft
CITY South
And now, maybe out of embarrassment, they've started running again!!
CITY South
Wait! Wait just a moment, please!
Could this pose mean...
28
CITY South

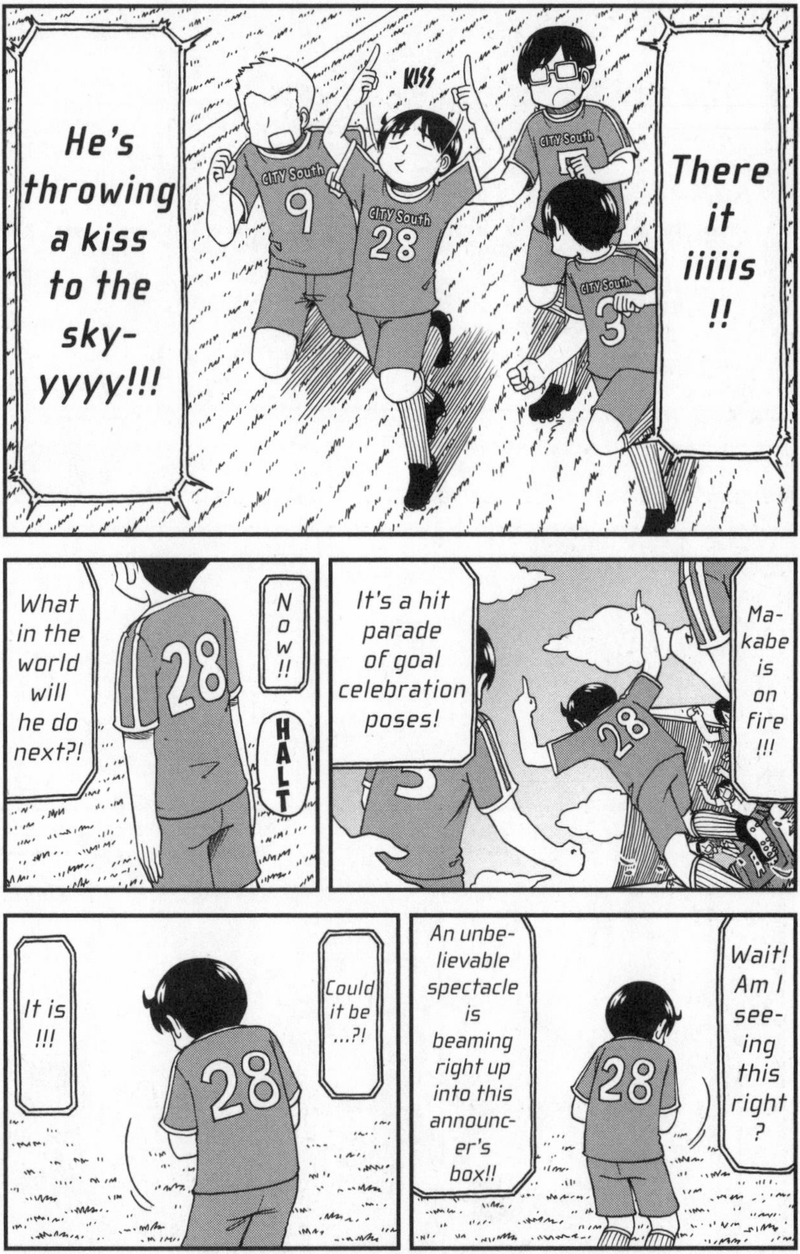
There it iiiiis!!
KISS
He's throwing a kiss to the sky-yyyy!!!
CITY South 9
CITY South 28
CITY South 3
Makabe is on fire!!!
It's a hit parade of goal celebration poses!
Now!!
HALT
What in the world will he do next?!
Wait! Am I seeing this right?
An unbelievable spectacle is beaming right up into this announcer's box!!
Could it be ...?!
It is!!!

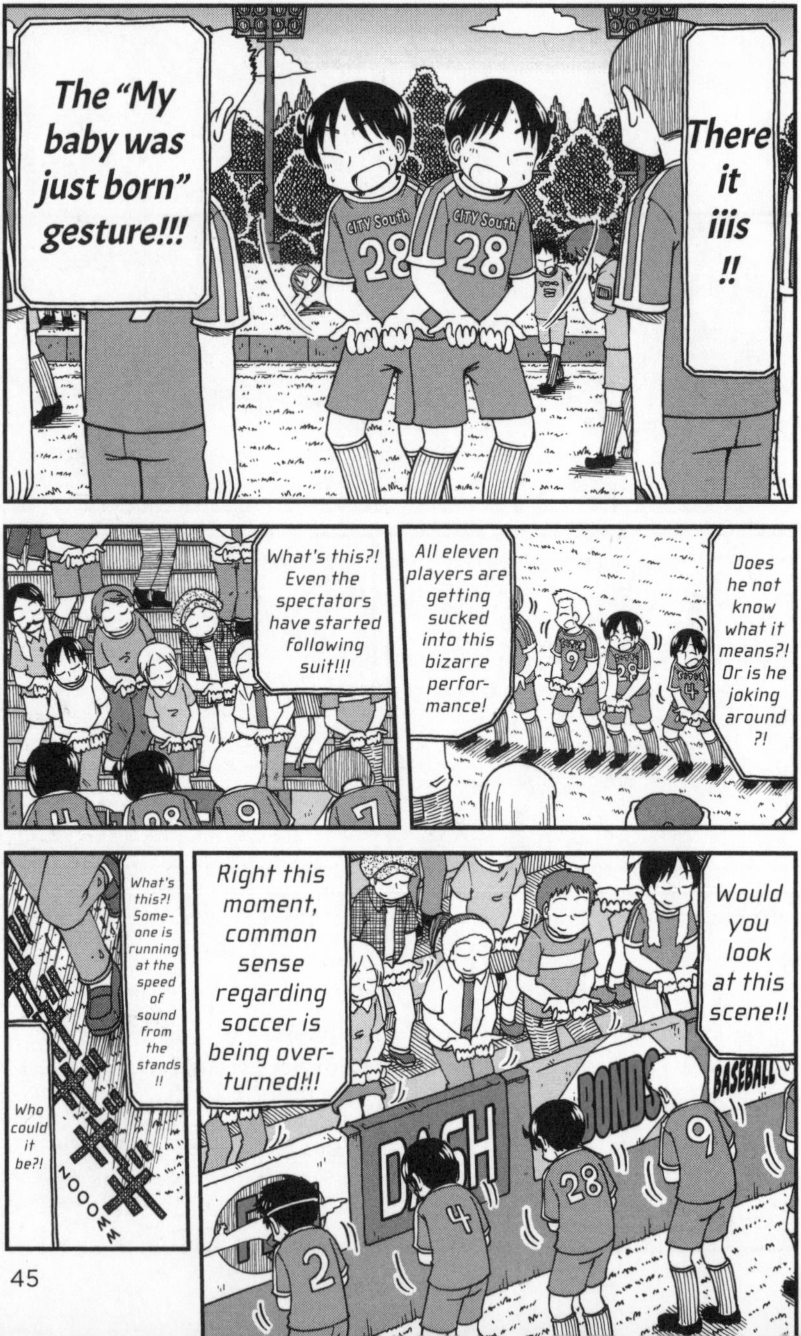
There it iiis !!
The "My baby was just born" gesture!!!
CITY South
CITY South
Does he not know what it means?! Or is he joking around?!
All eleven players are getting sucked into this bizarre perfor-mance!
What's this?! Even the spectators have started following suit!!!
Would you look at this scene!!
BASEBALL
BONDS
DASH
Right this moment, common sense regarding soccer is being over-turned!!!
What's this?! Some-one is running at the speed of sound from the stands !!
Who could it be?!
WOOOON

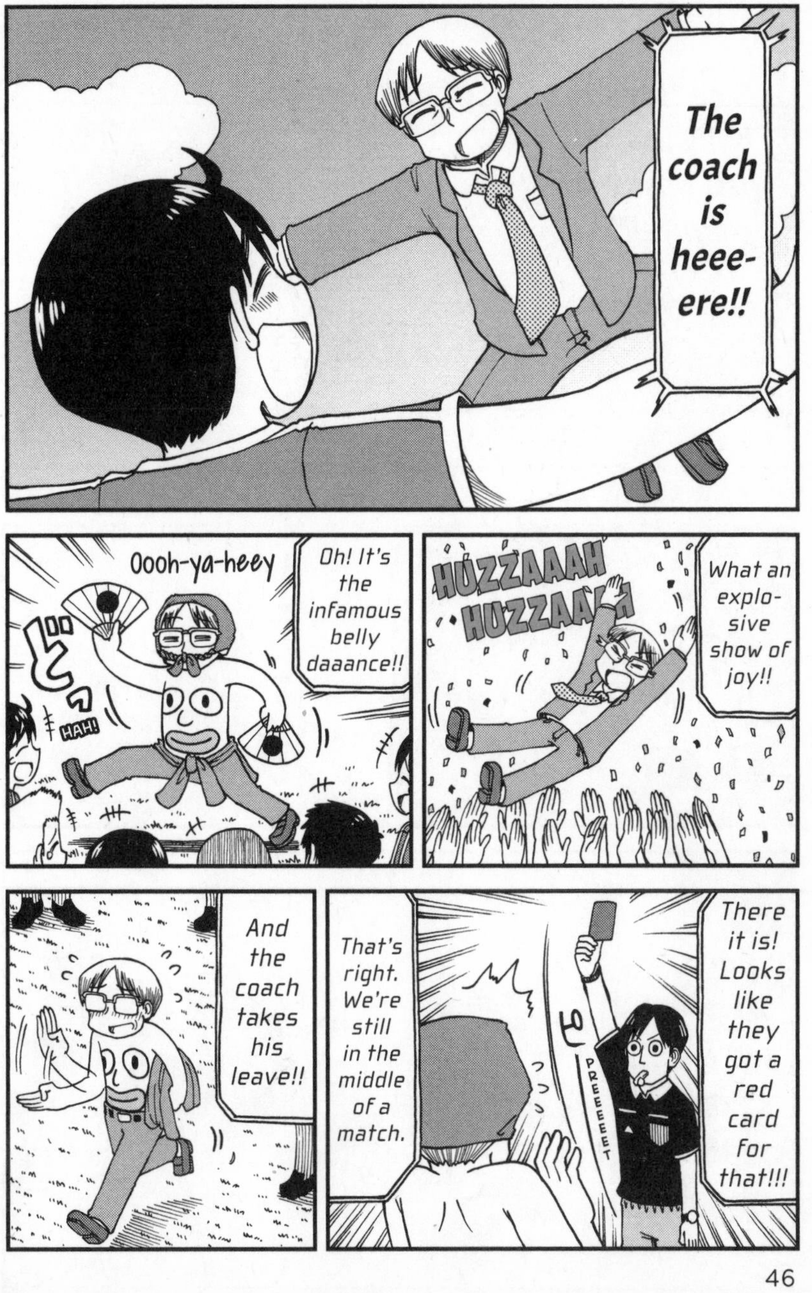
The coach is heeee-ere!!
HUZZAAAH HUZZAAAH
What an explo-sive show of joy!!
Oooh-ya-heey
Oh! It's the infamous belly daaance!!
HAH!
There it is! Looks like they got a red card for that!!!
PREEEEET
That's right. We're still in the middle of a match.
And the coach takes his leave!!

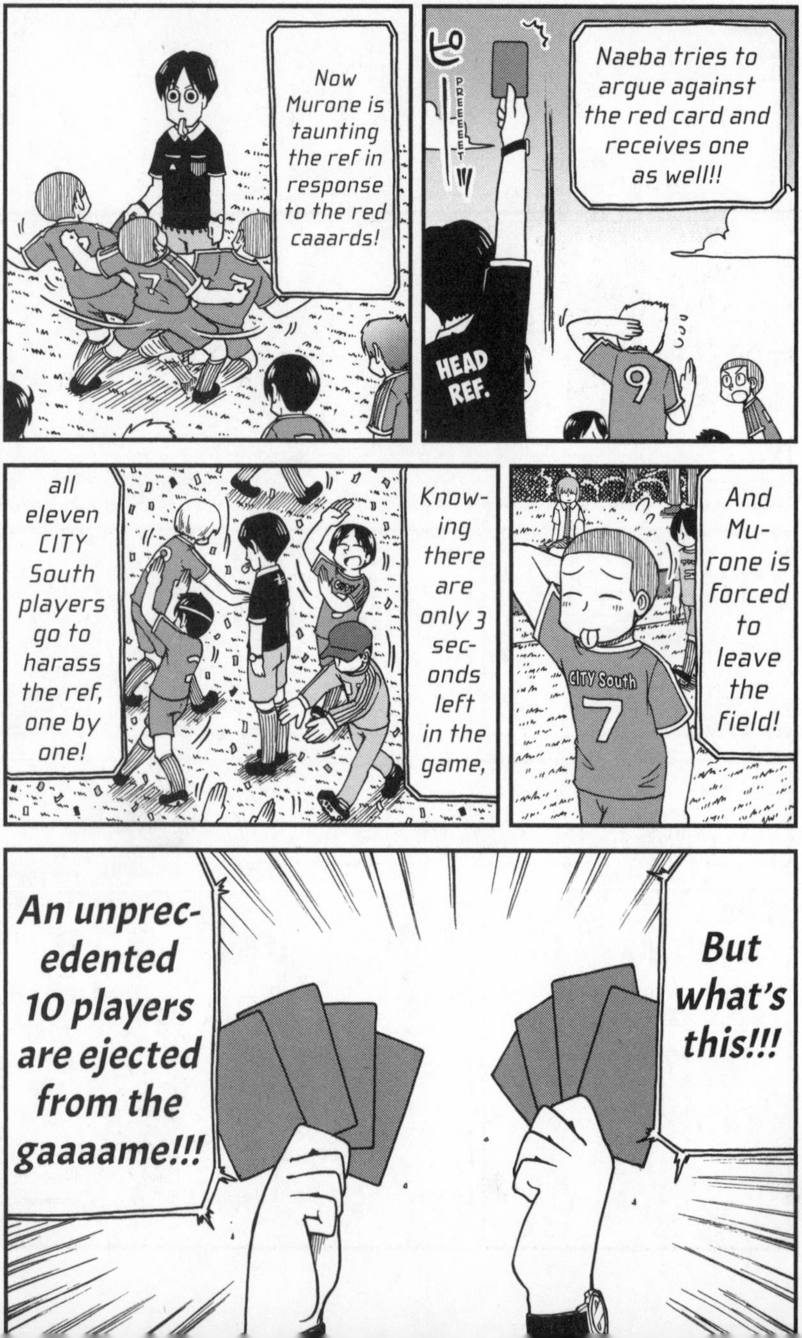
ピ
PREEEEET
Naeba tries to argue against the red card and receives one as well!!
HEAD REF.
Now Murone is taunting the ref in response to the red caaards!
And Murone is forced to leave the field!
CITY South
Knowing there are only 3 seconds left in the game,
all eleven CITY South players go to harass the ref, one by one!
But what's this!!!
An unprecedented 10 players are ejected from the gaaaame!!!

The last man standing is Makabe!
So!
What will he do?! Will he be dealt a red card?!!
CITY
28
He's thinking, he's thinking!!
ポクポクポクポク
TAP TAP TAP TAP
CITY South
28
If no one's left on the pitch, will the other team be able to score a point in the last few seconds?
But wait ...!
チーン
DIIING
......
THERE IT IIIIIIIS!!
HEAD REF.
28
HE'S EJECTED FROM THE GAME IN ONE GOOOO!!

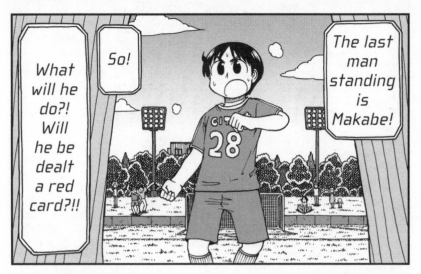

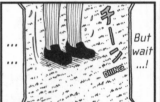

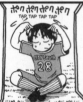

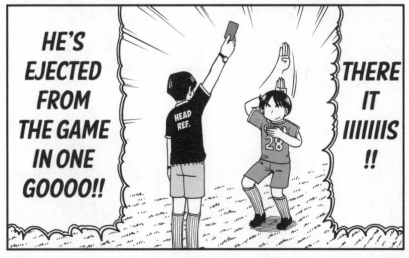

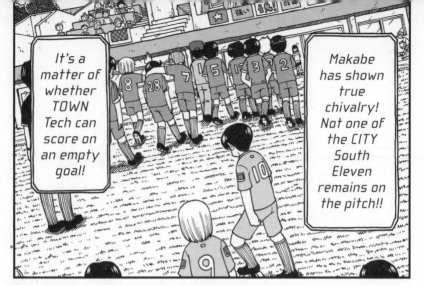

Makabe has shown true chivalry! Not one of the CITY South Eleven remains on the pitch!!
It's a matter of whether TOWN Tech can score on an empty goal!
This is it!!
The starting whistle is...
Now ...
Wait just a min-ute !!!
Is this ...
COULD IT BE...?!
TWEEEEE

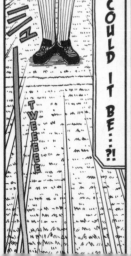

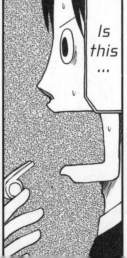

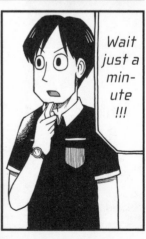

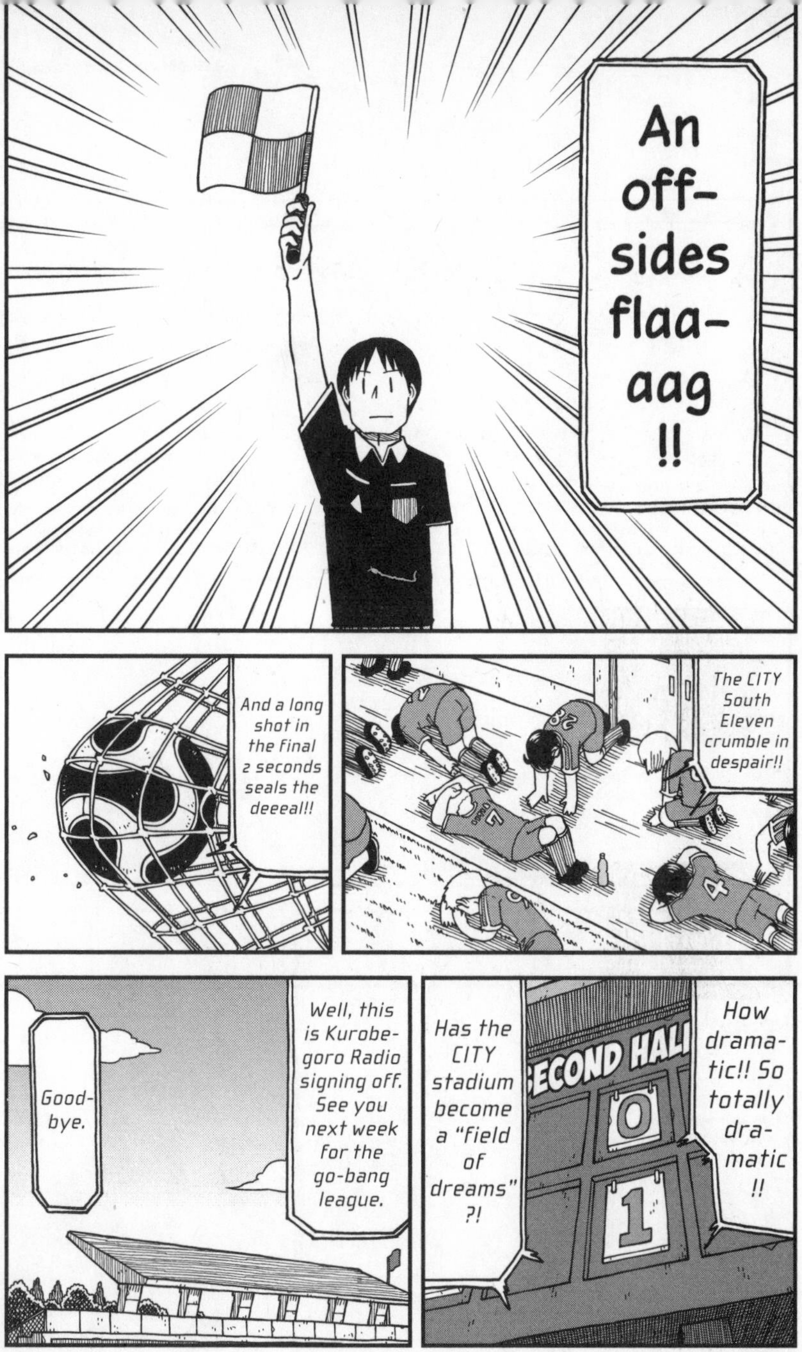
An off-sides flaa-aag!!
The CITY South Eleven crumble in despair!!
And a long shot in the final 2 seconds seals the deeeal!!
How drama-tic!! So totally dra-matic!!
Has the CITY stadium become a "field of dreams"?!
Well, this is Kurobe-goro Radio signing off. See you next week for the go-bang league.
Good-bye.

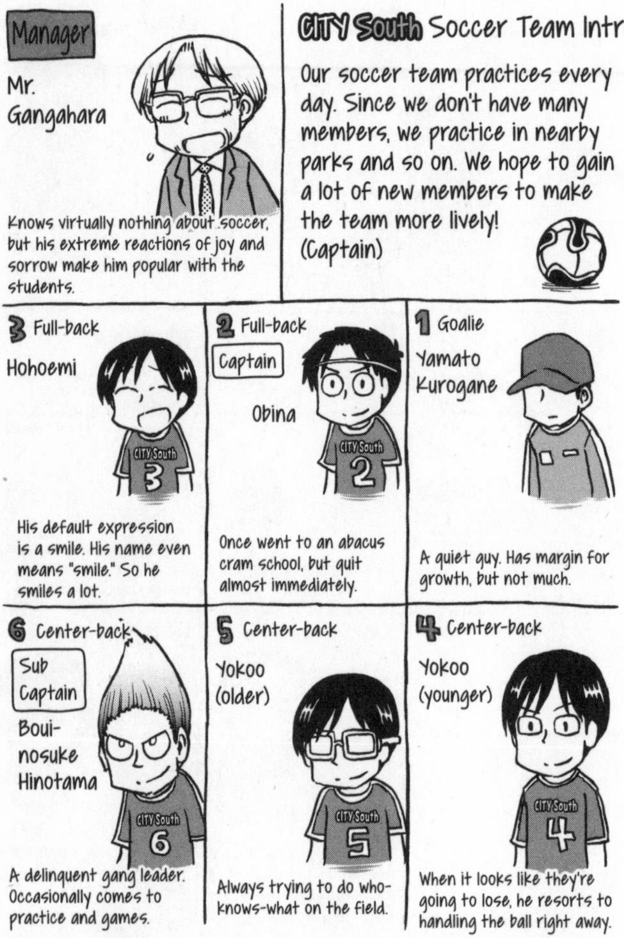

CITY South Soccer Team Intro
Our soccer team practices every day. Since we don't have many members, we practice in nearby parks and so on. We hope to gain a lot of new members to make the team more lively! (Captain)
Manager
Mr. Gangahara
Knows virtually nothing about soccer, but his extreme reactions of joy and sorrow make him popular with the students.
1 Goalie
Yamato Kurogane
A quiet guy. Has margin for growth, but not much.
2 Full-back
Captain
Obina
CITY South 2
Once went to an abacus cram school, but quit almost immediately.
3 Full-back
Hohoemi
CITY South 3
His default expression is a smile. His name even means "smile." So he smiles a lot.
4 Center-back
Yokoo (younger)
CITY South 4
When it looks like they're going to lose, he resorts to handling the ball right away.
5 Center-back
Yokoo (older)
CITY South 5
Always trying to do who-knows-what on the field.
6 Center-back
Sub Captain
Boui-nosuke Hinotama
CITY South 6
A delinquent gang leader. Occasionally comes to practice and games.

CITY

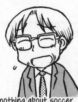

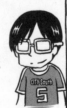

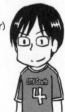

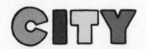

7 Midfielder

Murone

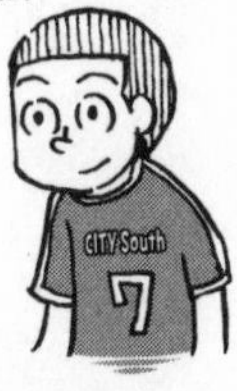

Quick on his feet, but absurdly weak when it comes to money and girls.

8 Gamer

Shirogane

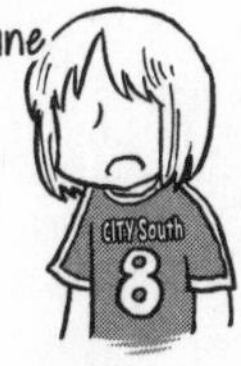

Was on a 300-game winning streak until his joystick died.

9 Forward

Naeba

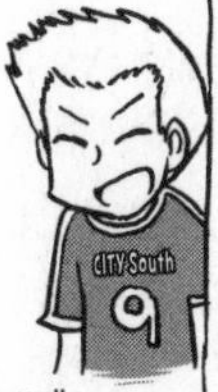

Does really, really reckless shots really, really often.

10 Midfielder

Genjirou Masago

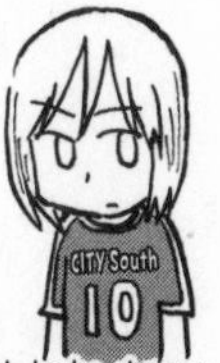

Skilled enough to be chosen for the CITY Invitational, but gets injured a lot.

11 Forward

Kasuga

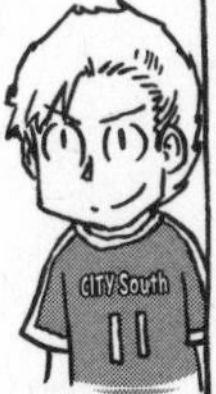

Blood type: Rh-null.

12 Spy

Iwao Gongen-yama

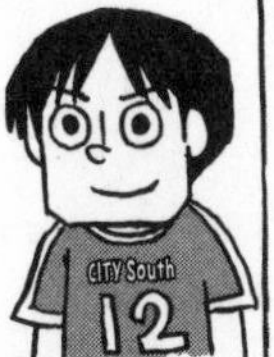

A spy sent in from another school. Joined the team as camouflage.

18 Forward

sub

Kurobe

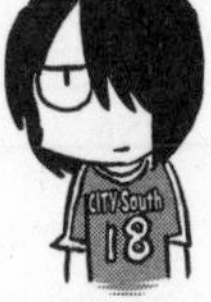

An inattentive, self-centered Juliet. Puts on a little smile with bonanzagram in hand.*

28 Midfielder

sub

Tate-waku Makabe

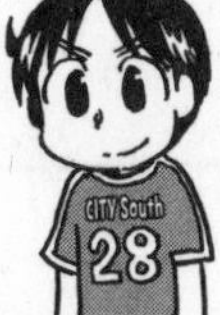

Was never able to come to Saturday practice because he had to work at his family's restaurant, but that recently changed.

*References to songs from the 1986 BOOWY album "Just A Hero."

CITY

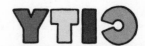

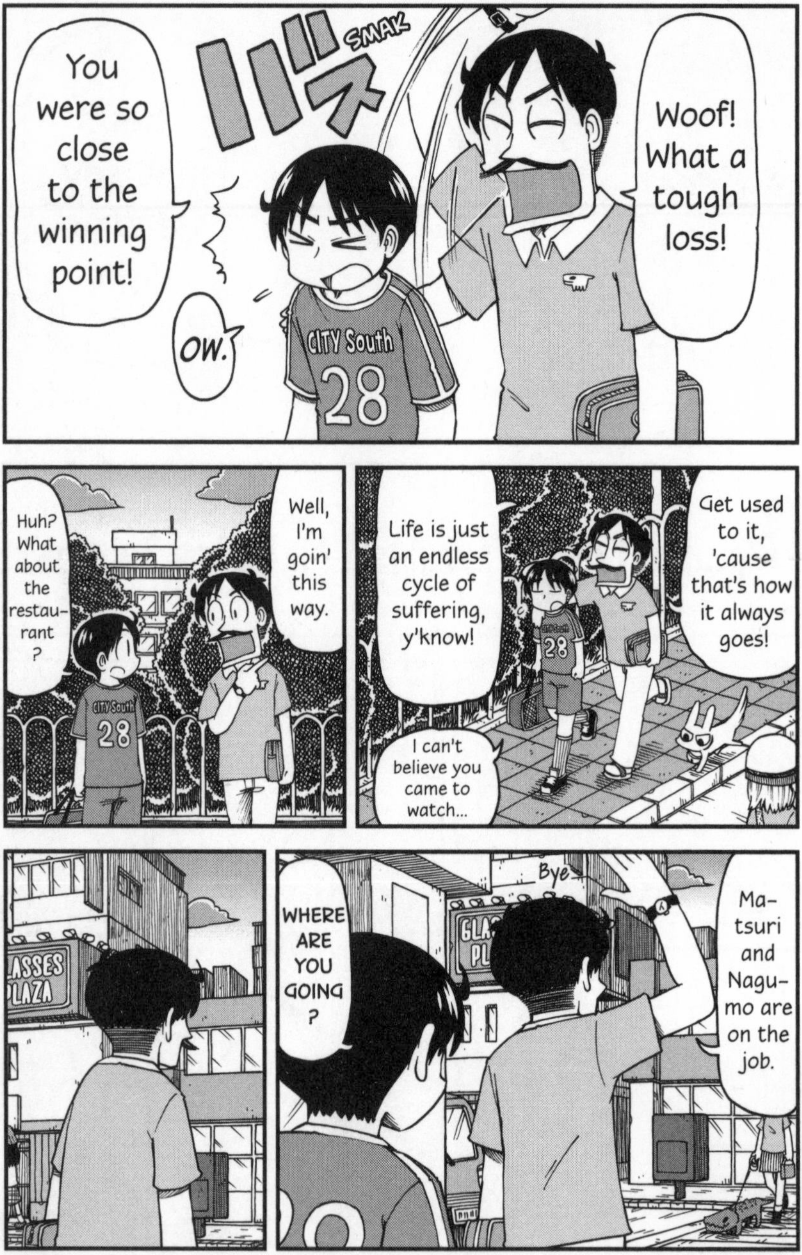
Woof! What a tough loss!
SMAK
You were so close to the winning point!
OW.
CITY South 28
Get used to it, 'cause that's how it always goes!
Life is just an endless cycle of suffering, y'know!
I can't believe you came to watch...
Well, I'm goin' this way.
Huh? What about the restaurant?
Matsuri and Nagumo are on the job.
Bye
WHERE ARE YOU GOING?

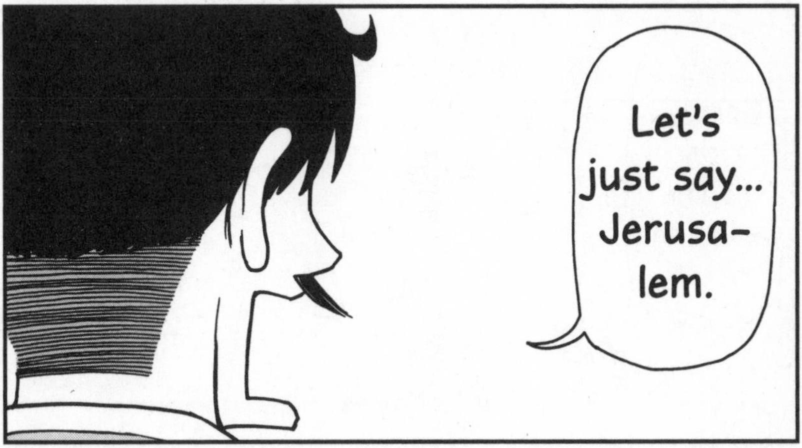
Let's just say... Jerusa-lem.

Chapter 17 Tsurubishi Makabe's Twilight

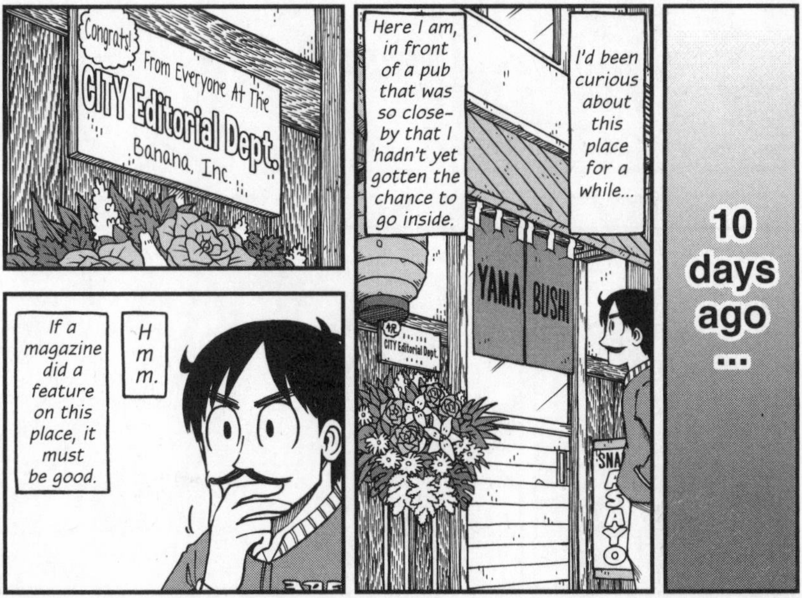
10 days ago ...
I'd been curious about this place for a while...
Here I am, in front of a pub that was so close-by that I hadn't yet gotten the chance to go inside.
YAMA BUSHI
CITY Editorial Dept.
SNA ASAYO
Congrats!
From Everyone At The CITY Editorial Dept.
Banana, Inc.
Hmm.
If a magazine did a feature on this place, it must be good.

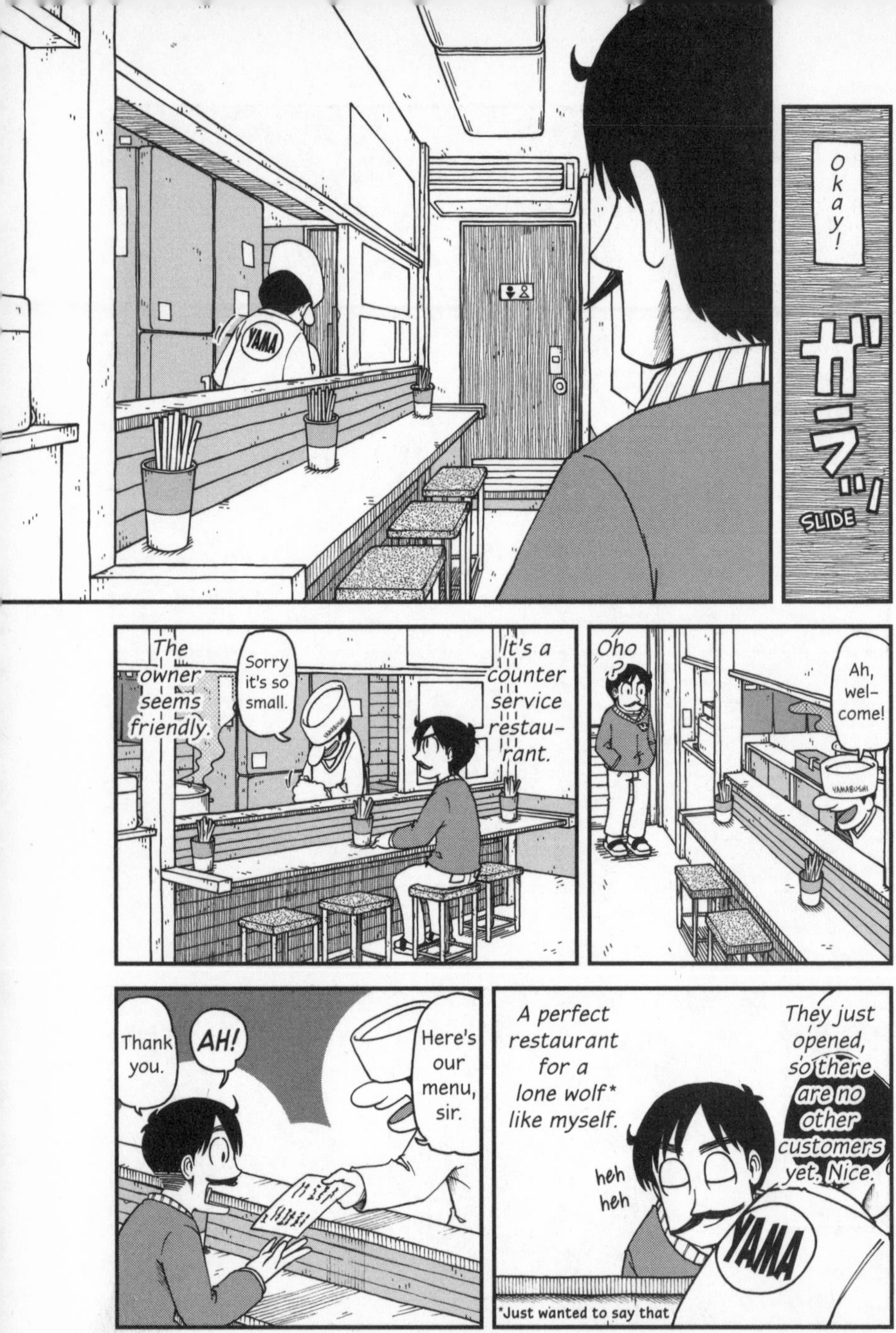
Okay!
ガラッ
SLIDE
Ah, wel-come!
Oho?
It's a counter service restau-rant.
Sorry it's so small.
The owner seems friendly.
They just opened, so there are no other customers yet. Nice.
A perfect restaurant for a lone wolf* like myself.
heh heh
*Just wanted to say that
Here's our menu, sir.
AH!
Thank you.

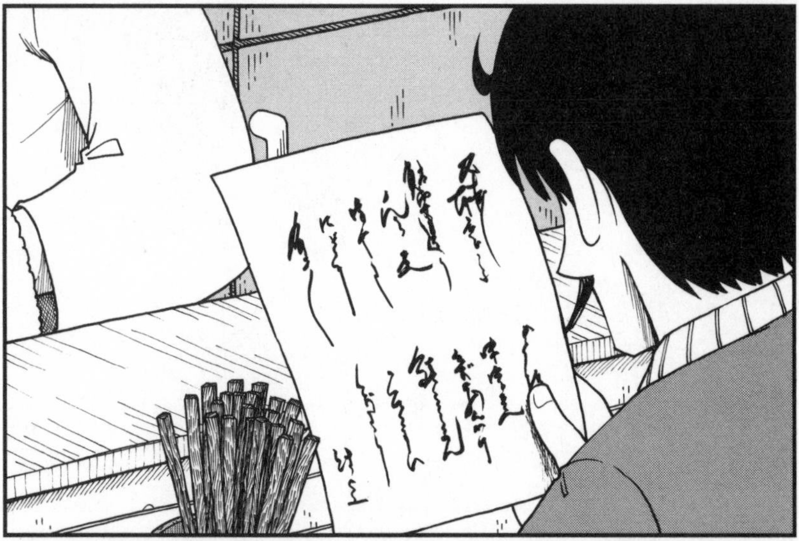

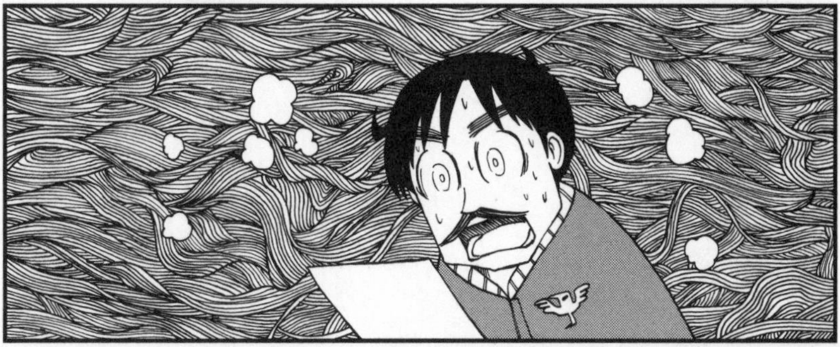

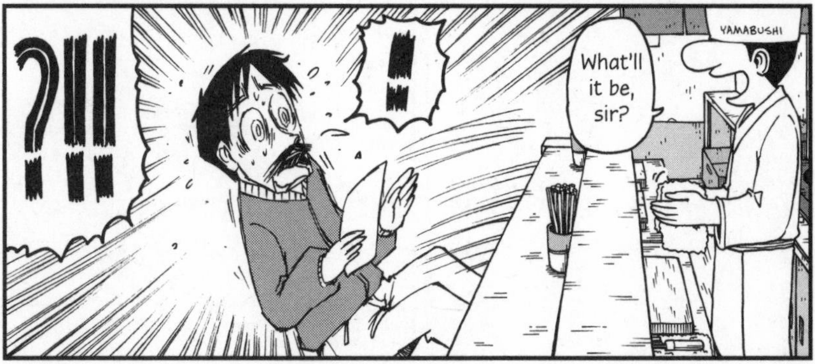
YAMABUSHI
What'll it be, sir?
!
?!!!

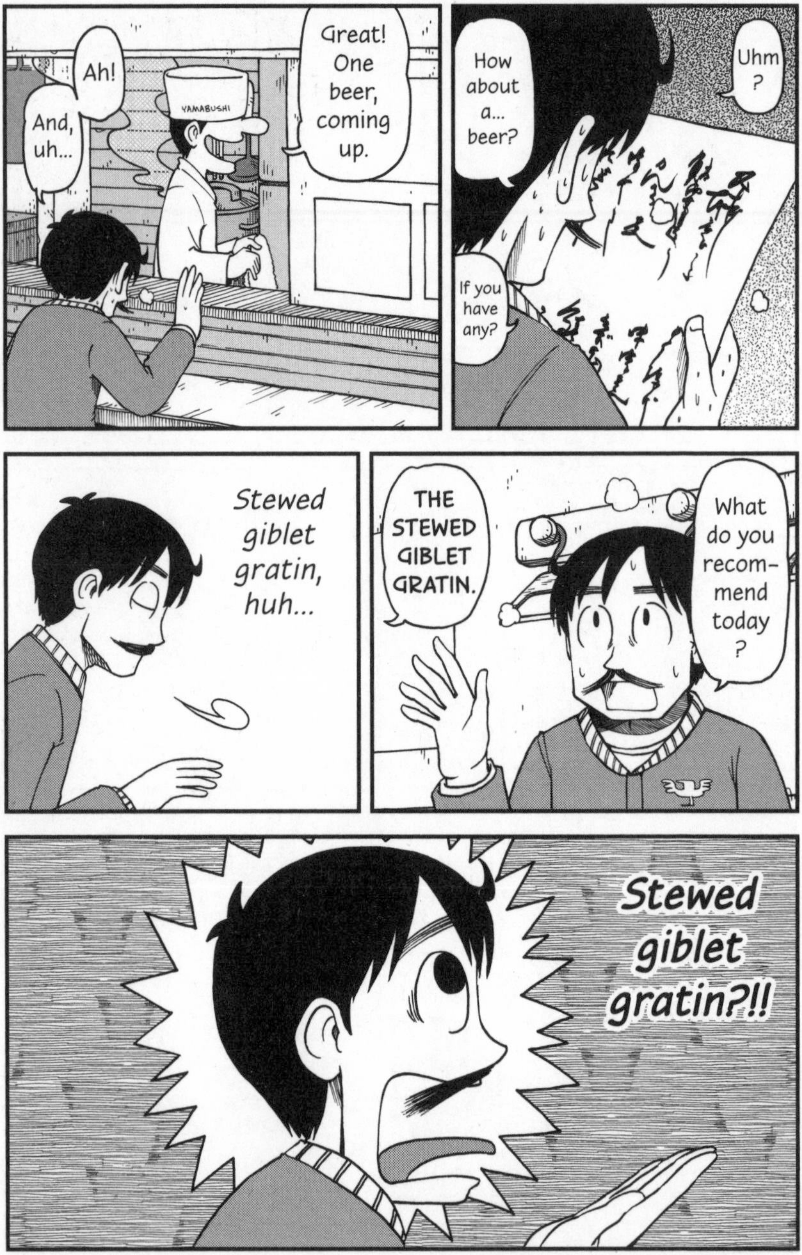
Uhm?
How about a... beer?
If you have any?
Great! One beer, coming up.
YAMABUSHI
Ah!
And, uh...
What do you recom-mend today?
THE STEWED GIBLET GRATIN.
Stewed giblet gratin, huh...
Stewed giblet gratin?!!

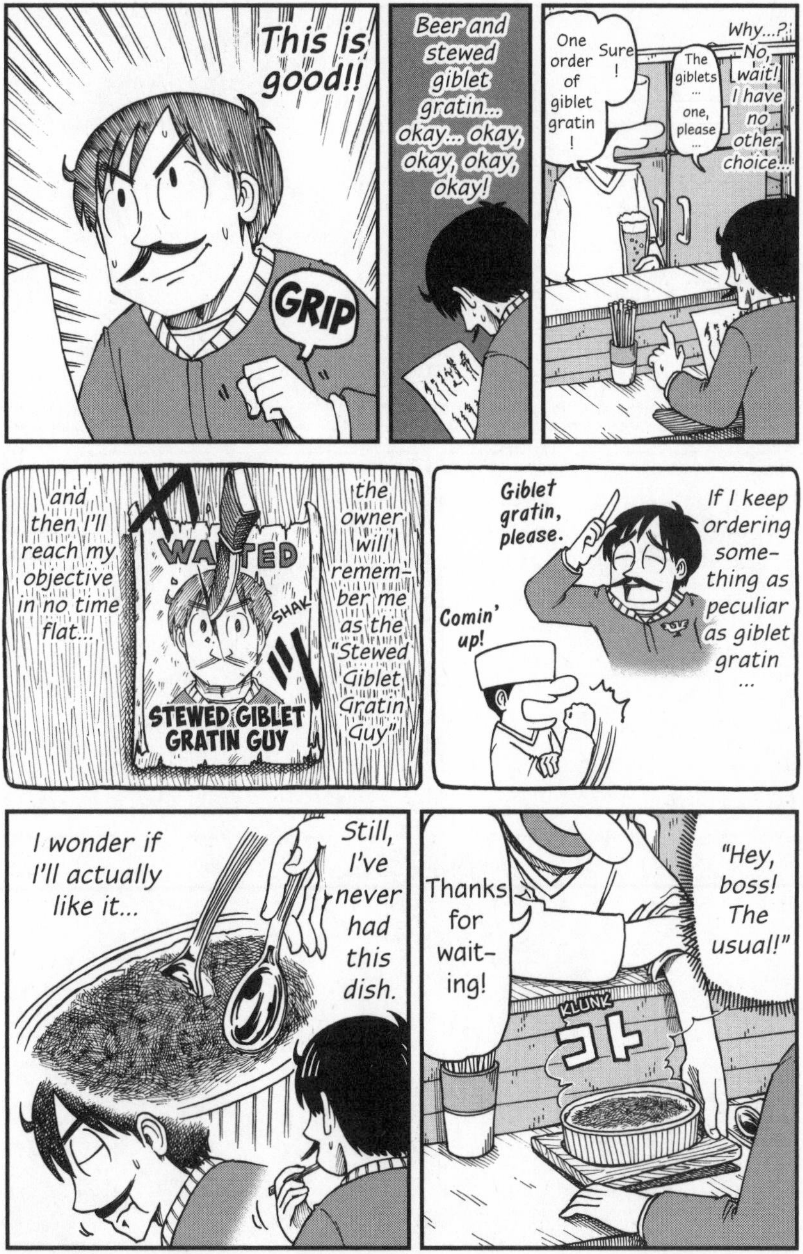

Why...? No, wait! I have no other choice...
The giblets... one, please...
Sure!
One order of giblet gratin!
Beer and stewed giblet gratin... okay... okay, okay, okay, okay!
This is good!!
GRIP
If I keep ordering something as peculiar as giblet gratin...
Giblet gratin, please.
Comin' up!
the owner will remember me as the "Stewed Giblet Gratin Guy"
WANTED
SHAK
STEWED GIBLET GRATIN GUY
and then I'll reach my objective in no time flat...
"Hey, boss! The usual!"
Thanks for waiting!
KLUNK
コト
Still, I've never had this dish.
I wonder if I'll actually like it...

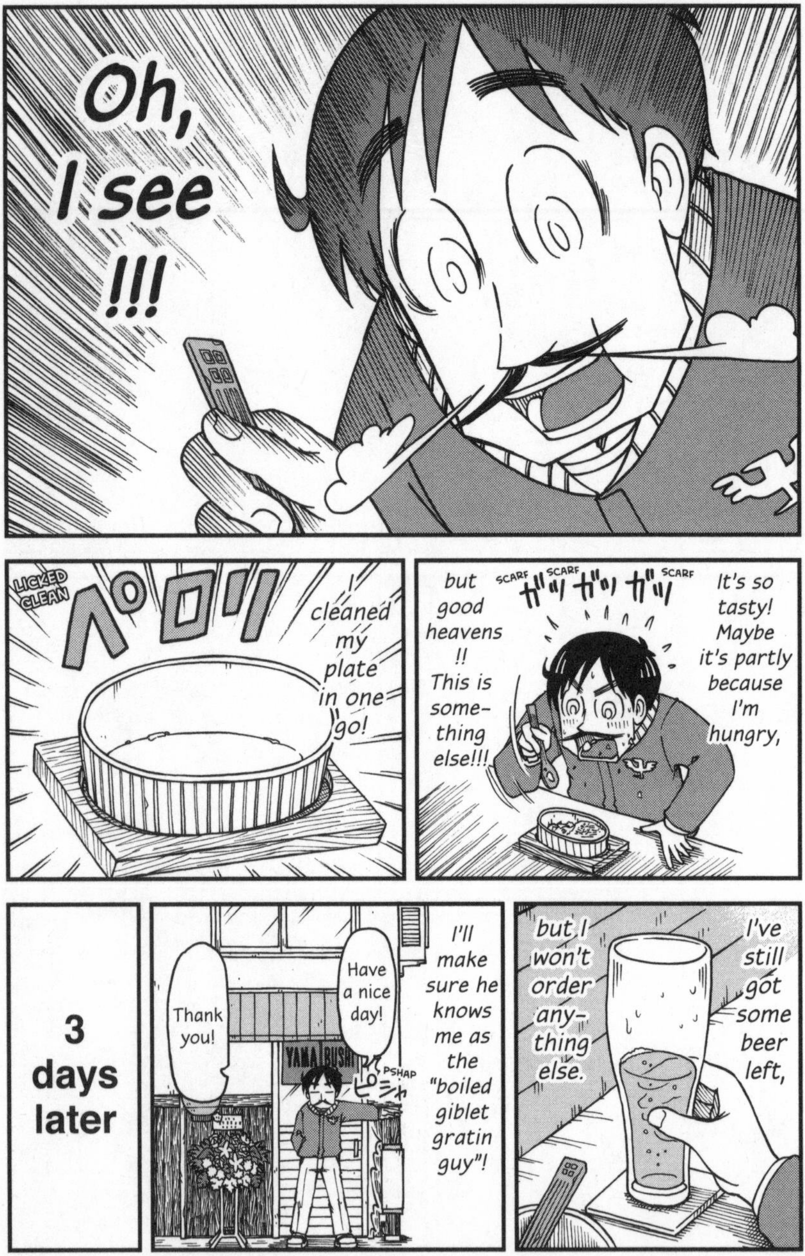

Oh, I see !!!
It's so tasty! Maybe it's partly because I'm hungry,
SCARF SCARF SCARF
but good heavens !! This is some-thing else!!!
LICKED CLEAN
I cleaned my plate in one go!
I've still got some beer left,
but I won't order any-thing else.
I'll make sure he knows me as the "boiled giblet gratin guy"!
Have a nice day!
Thank you!
YAMABUSHI
PSHAP
3 days later

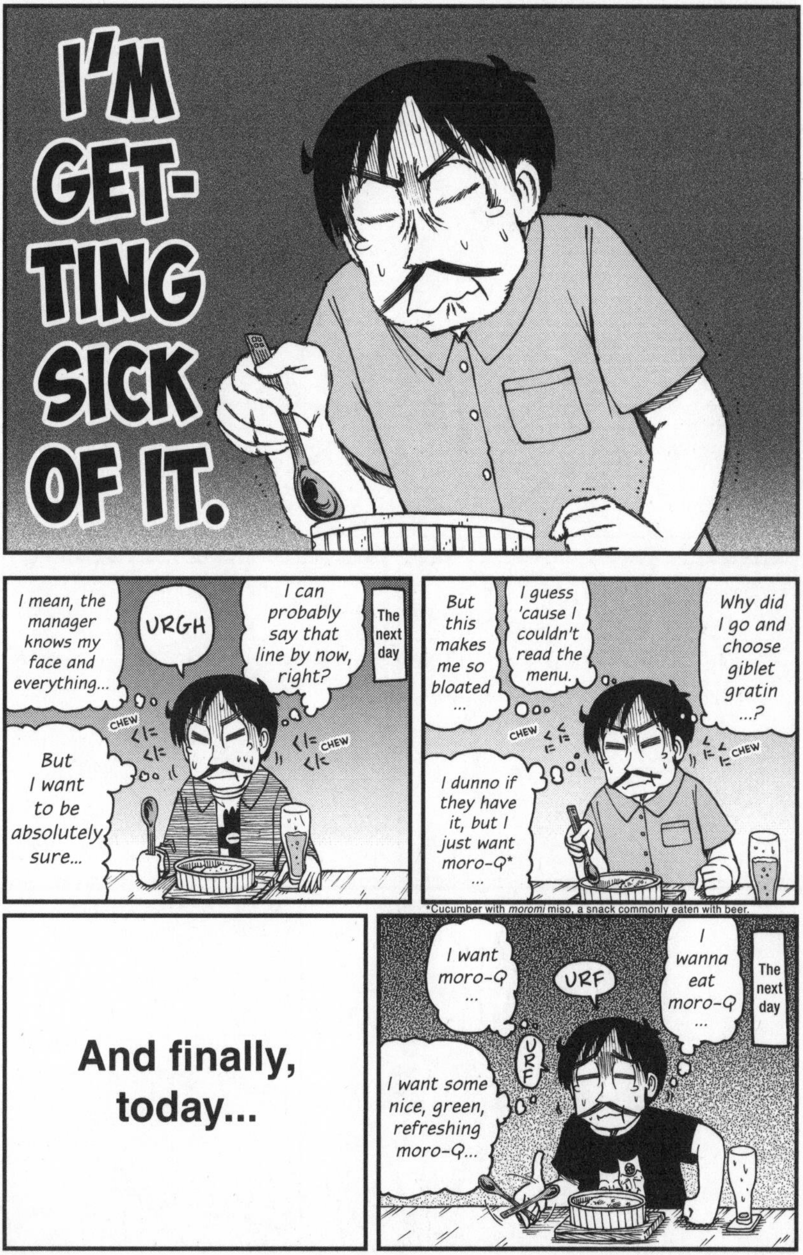
I'M GET-TING SICK OF IT.
Why did I go and choose giblet gratin ...?
I guess 'cause I couldn't read the menu.
But this makes me so bloated ...
CHEW
CHEW
I dunno if they have it, but I just want moro-Q* ...
The next day
I can probably say that line by now, right?
URGH
I mean, the manager knows my face and everything...
CHEW
CHEW
But I want to be absolutely sure...
The next day
I wanna eat moro-Q ...
URF
I want moro-Q ...
URF
I want some nice, green, refreshing moro-Q...
And finally, today...

*Cucumber with *moromi* miso, a snack commonly eaten with beer.

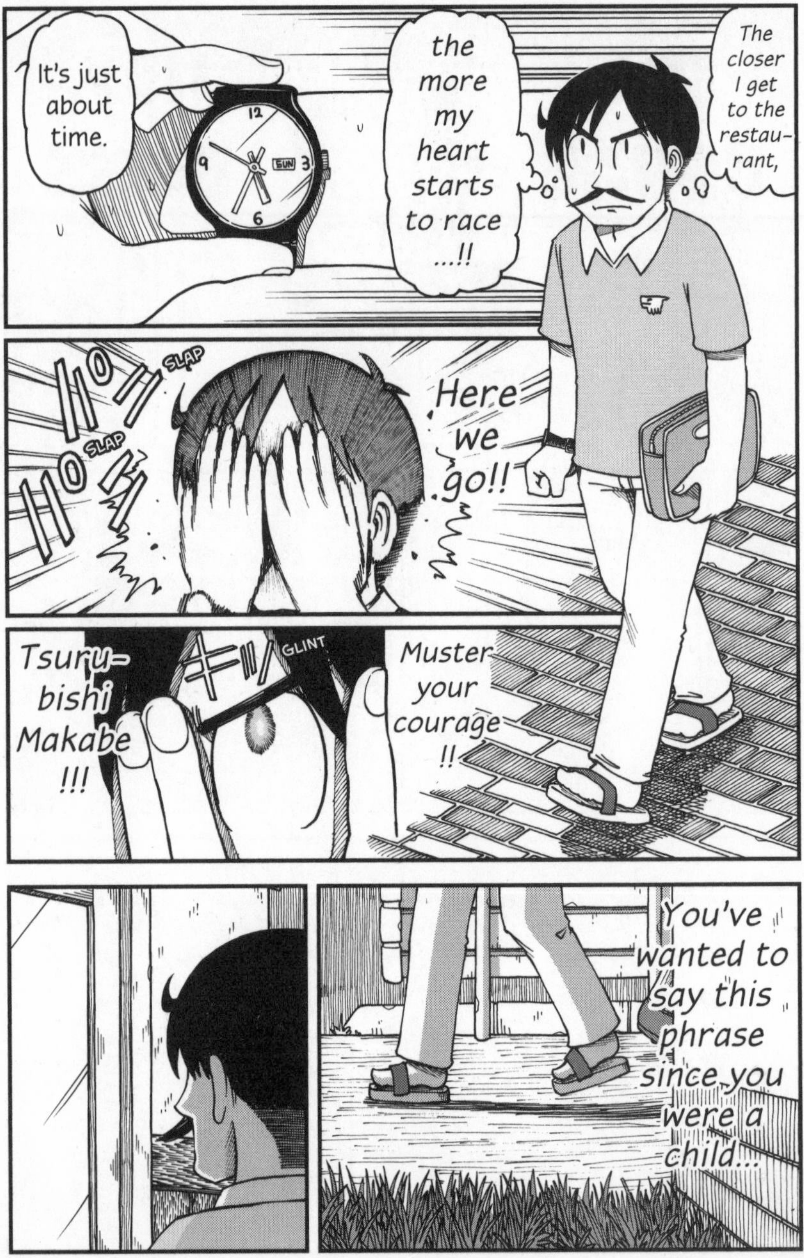
The closer I get to the restaurant,
the more my heart starts to race ...!!
It's just about time.
Here we go!!
SLAP
SLAP
Muster your courage !!
GLINT
Tsurubishi Makabe !!!
You've wanted to say this phrase since you were a child...

HEY, BOSS!
TENANT WANTED
Sentoboshi Office
1-800-221-2233
THE USUAL!!
Ha...
Ha ha...
ASAYO
EAR
Ha ha ha ha ha ha.
TENANT WANTED
Sentoboshi Office
1-800-221-2233

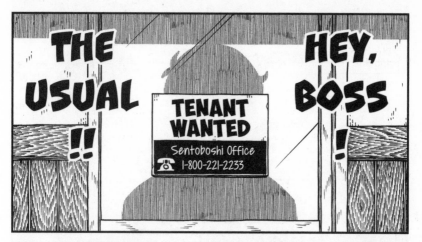

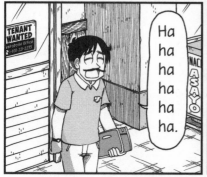

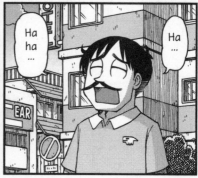

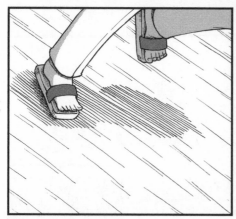

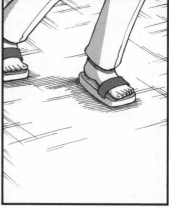

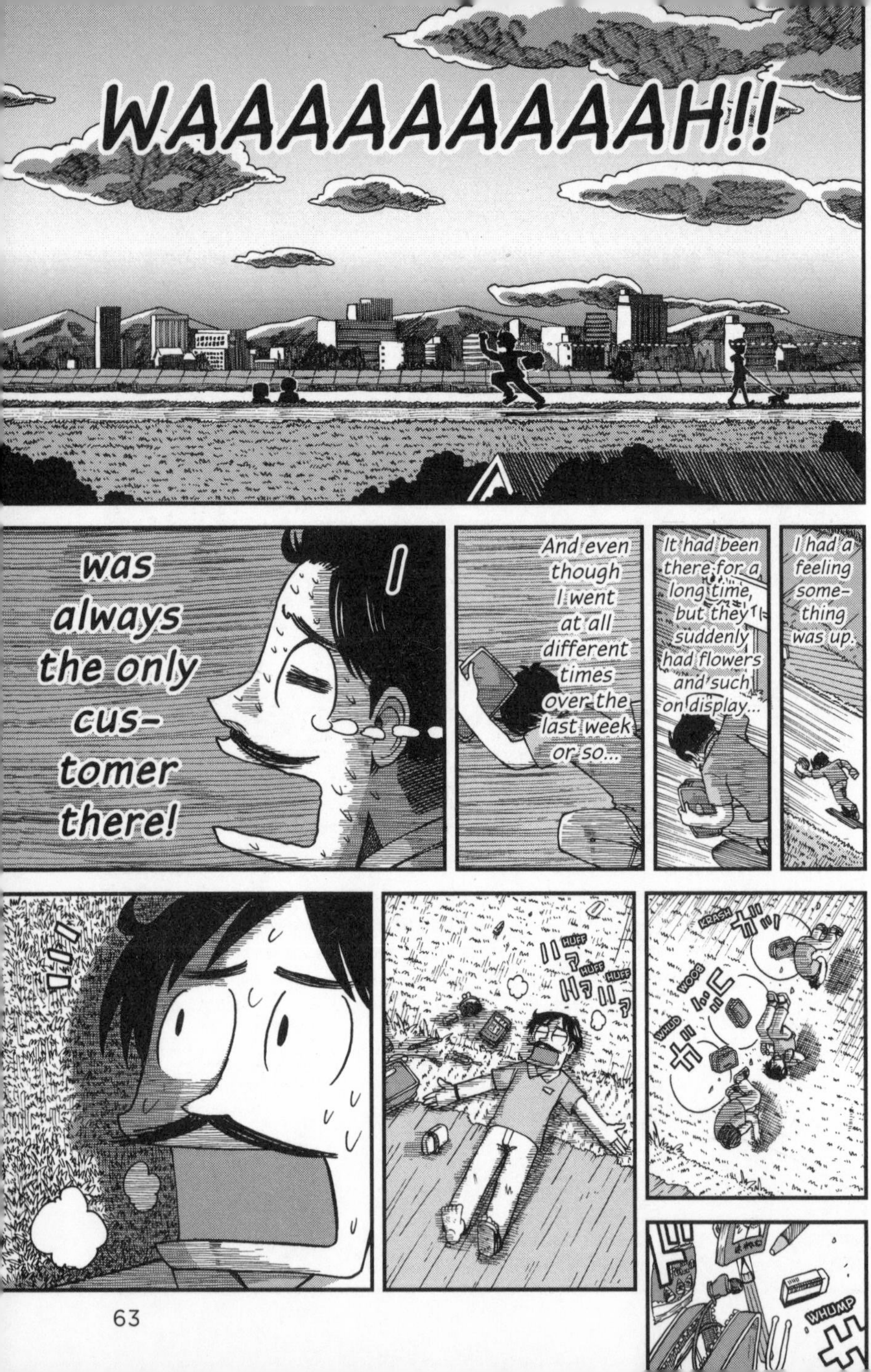

WAAAAAAAAAH!!
I had a feeling some-thing was up.
It had been there for a long time, but they suddenly had flowers and such on display...
And even though I went at all different times over the last week or so...
I was always the only cus-tomer there!
KRASH
BOOM
WHUD
WHUMP
HUFF
HUFF
HUFF

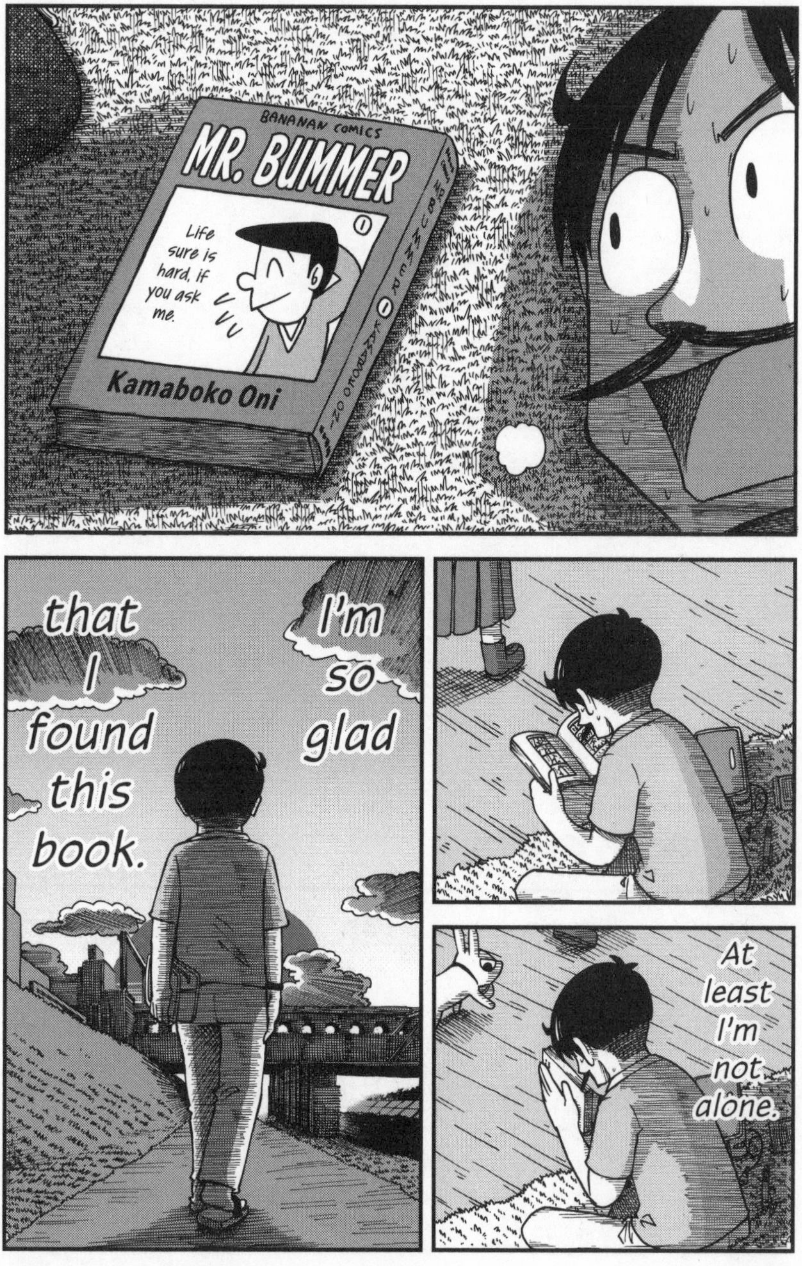
BANANAN COMICS
MR. BUMMER
Life sure is hard, if you ask me.
Kamaboko Oni
At least I'm not alone.
I'm so glad
that I found this book.

BANANAN COMICS
MR. BUMMER 1
KAMABOKO ONI
BANANAN COMICS
MR. BUMMER 2
KAMABOKO ONI
BANANAN COMICS
MR. BUMMER 3
KAMABOKO ONI
BANANAN COMICS
MR. BUMMER ~HARD TIMES~
KAMABOKO ONI
BANANAN COMICS
MR. BUMMER IN LOVE
KAMABOKO ONI
BANANAN COMICS
MR. BUMMER ~SUCCESS IN LIFE~
KAMABOKO ONI
BANANAN COMICS
MR. BUMMER ~DAYS OF YOUTH~
KAMABOKO ONI
BANANAN COMICS
MONSIEUR BUMMER
BANANAN COMICS
MR. BUMMER 4
KAMABOKO ONI

CITY

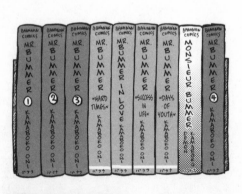

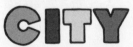

SUNDAY
8:40

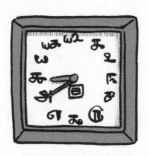

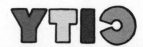

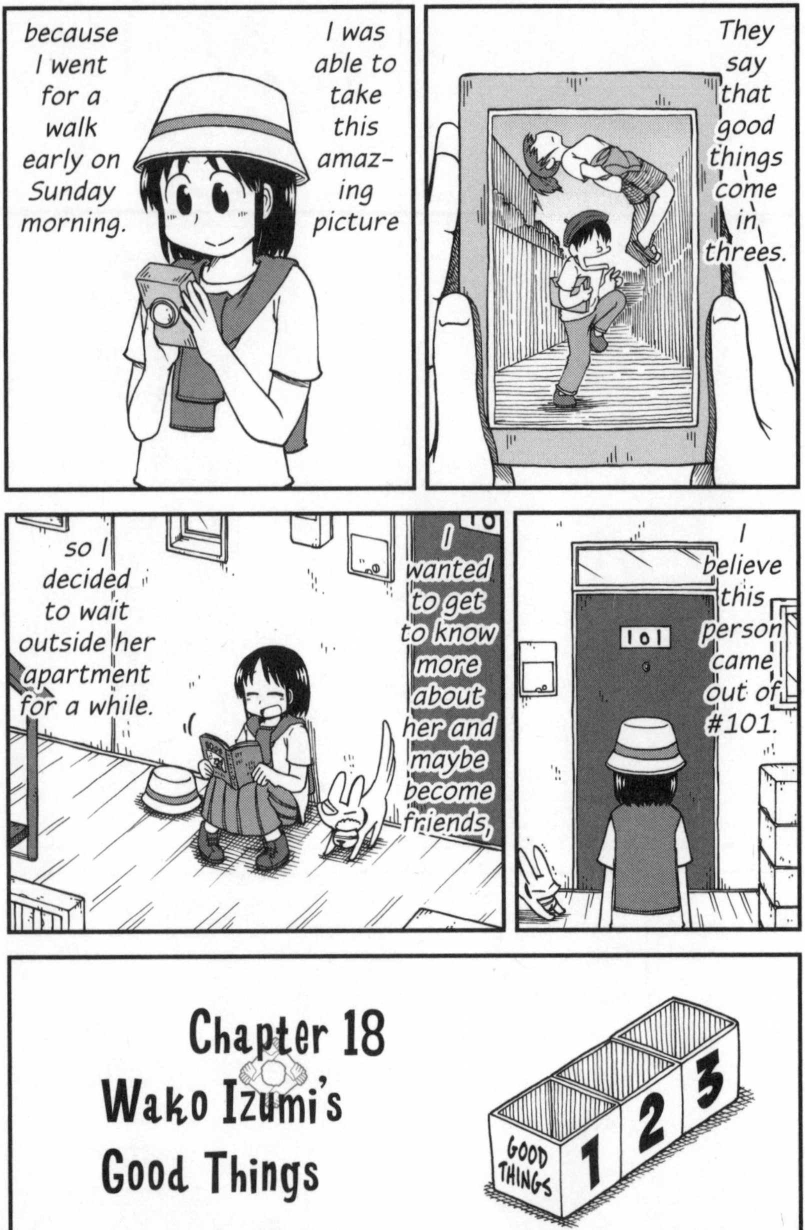
They say that good things come in threes.
I was able to take this amazing picture
because I went for a walk early on Sunday morning.
101
I believe this person came out of #101.
I wanted to get to know more about her and maybe become friends,
so I decided to wait outside her apartment for a while.
Chapter 18
Wako Izumi's Good Things
GOOD THINGS
1
2
3

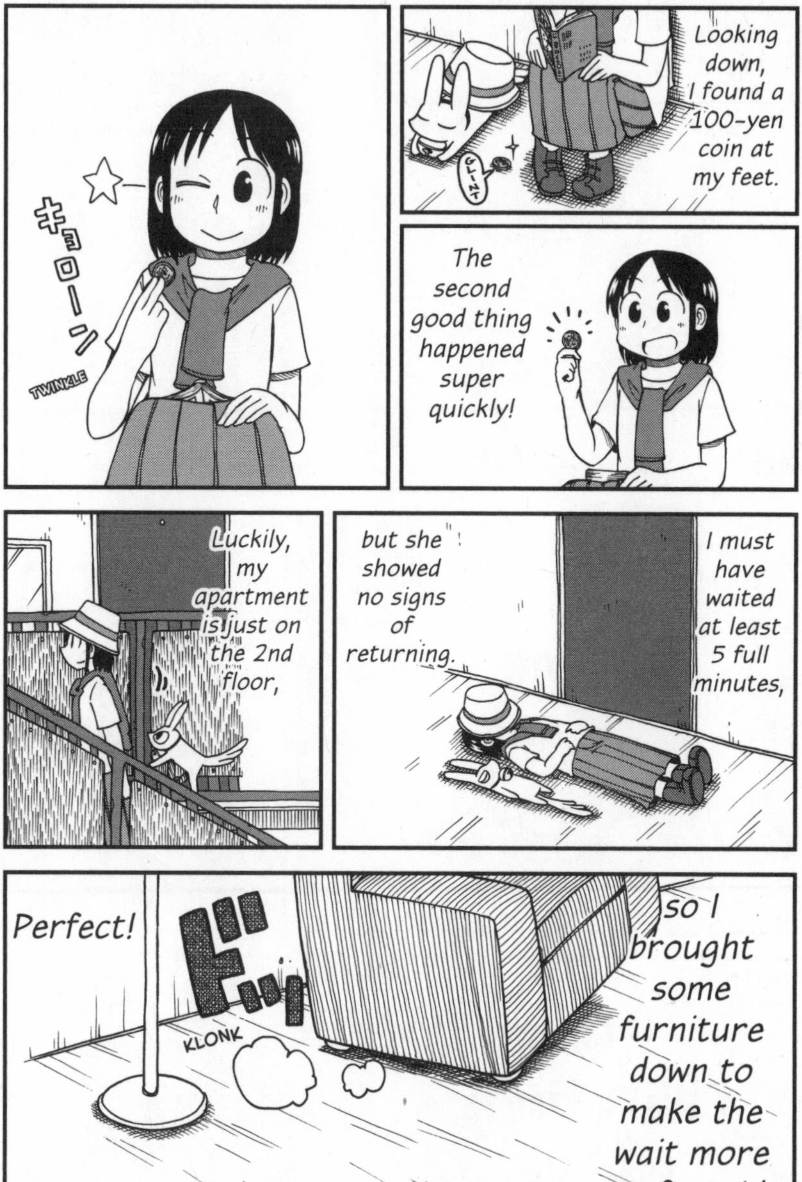

Looking down, I found a 100-yen coin at my feet.
GLINT
The second good thing happened super quickly!
TWINKLE
I must have waited at least 5 full minutes,
but she showed no signs of returning.
Luckily, my apartment is just on the 2nd floor,
so I brought some furniture down to make the wait more comfortable.
KLONK
Perfect!

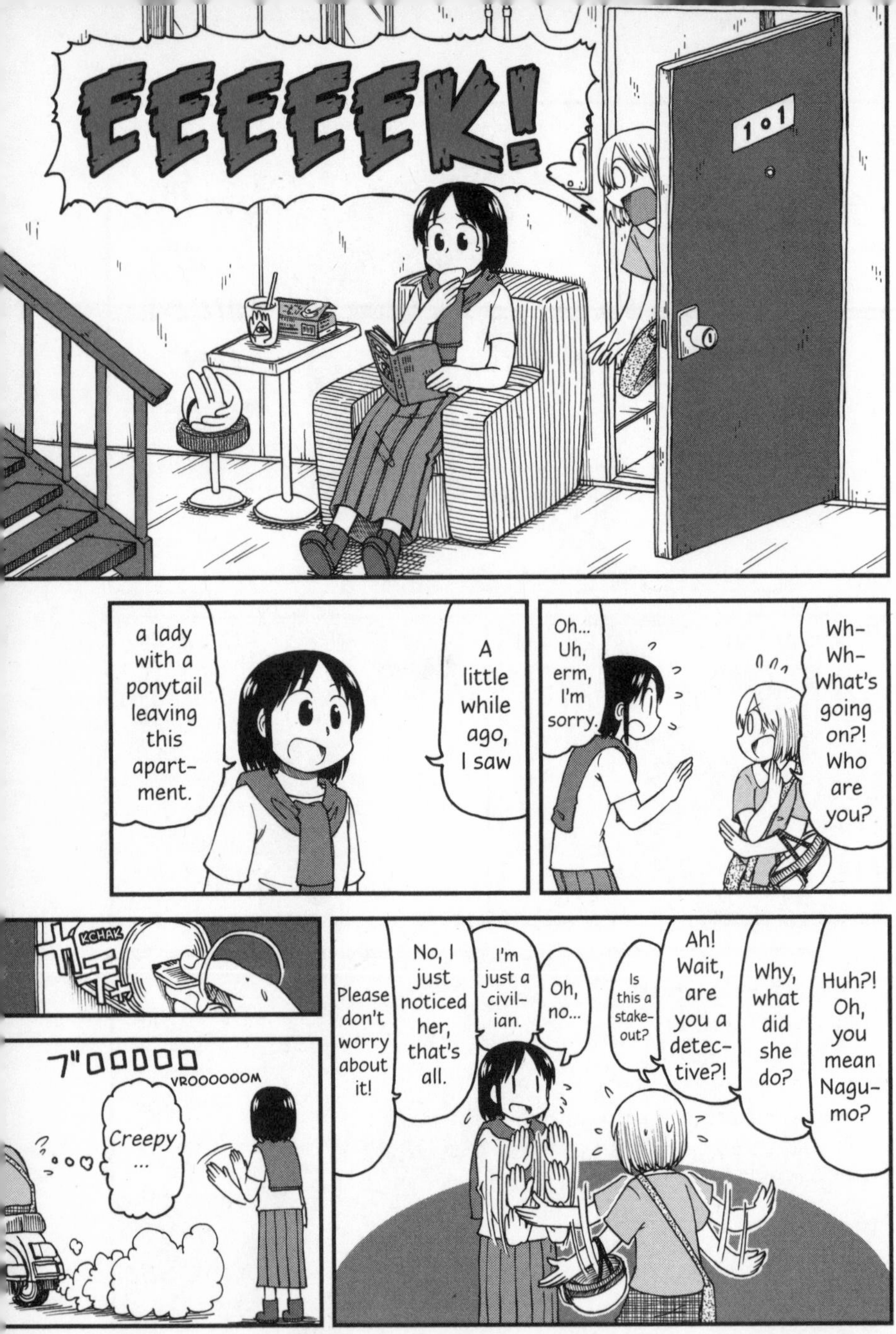
EEEEEK!
101
Wh- Wh- What's going on?! Who are you?
Oh... Uh, erm, I'm sorry.
A little while ago, I saw
a lady with a ponytail leaving this apartment.
Huh?! Oh, you mean Nagumo?
Why, what did she do?
Ah! Wait, are you a detective?!
Is this a stake-out?
Oh, no...
I'm just a civil-ian.
No, I just noticed her, that's all.
Please don't worry about it!
KCHAK
ブロロロロロ
VROOOOOOM
Creepy ...

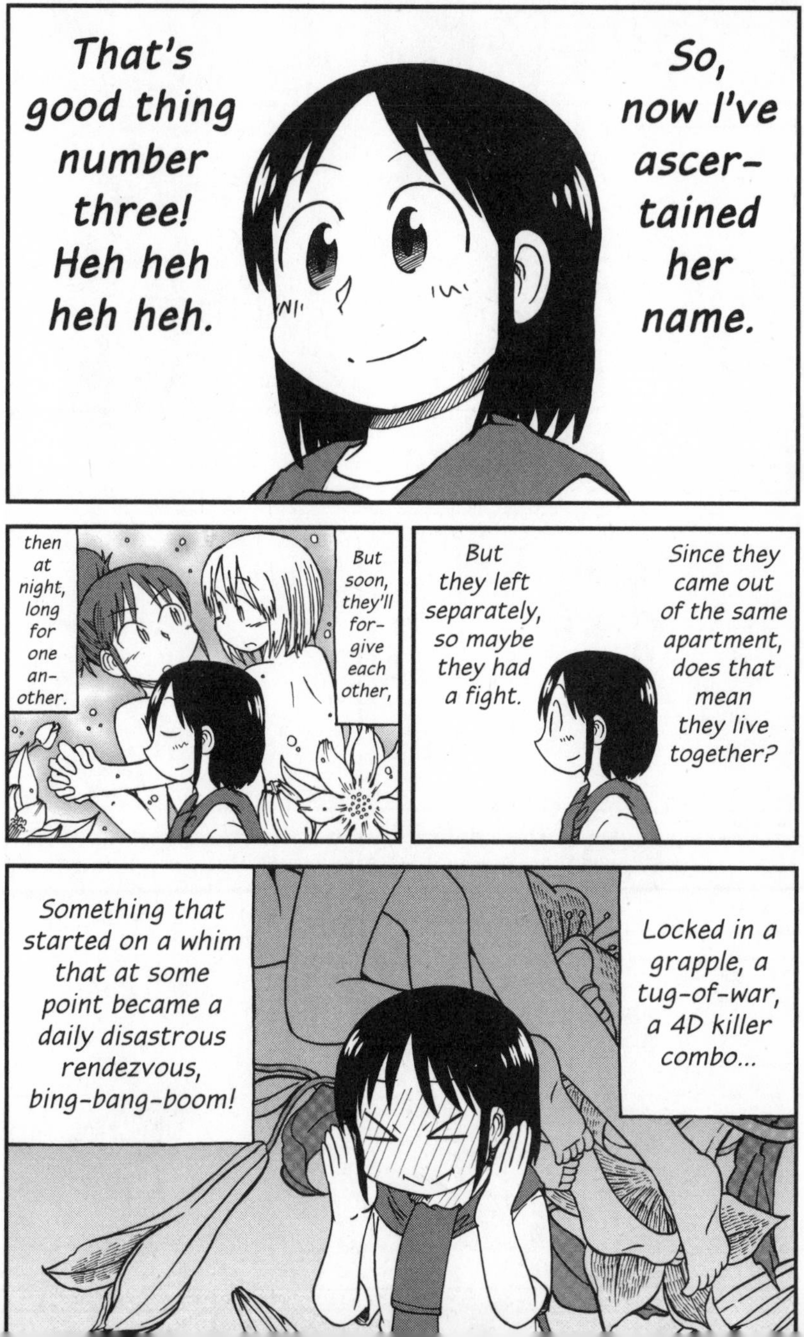
So, now I've ascer-tained her name.
That's good thing number three! Heh heh heh heh.
Since they came out of the same apartment, does that mean they live together?
But they left separately, so maybe they had a fight.
But soon, they'll for-give each other,
then at night, long for one an-other.
Locked in a grapple, a tug-of-war, a 4D killer combo...
Something that started on a whim that at some point became a daily disastrous rendezvous, bing-bang-boom!

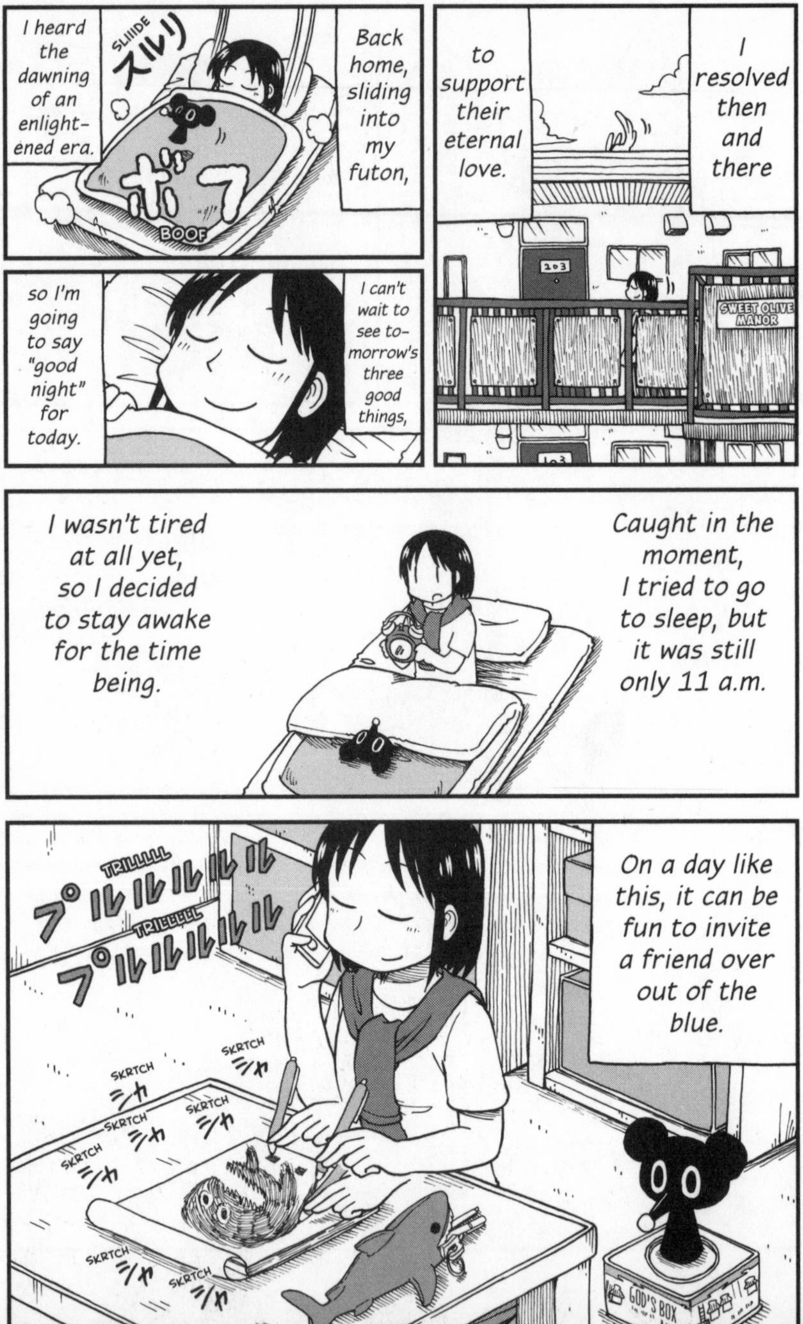
I resolved then and there
to support their eternal love.
203
SWEET OLIVE MANOR
Back home, sliding into my futon,
SLIIIDE
スルリ
ボフ
BOOF
I heard the dawning of an enlight-ened era.
I can't wait to see to-morrow's three good things,
so I'm going to say "good night" for today.
Caught in the moment, I tried to go to sleep, but it was still only 11 a.m.
I wasn't tired at all yet, so I decided to stay awake for the time being.
On a day like this, it can be fun to invite a friend over out of the blue.
TRILLLLL
プルルルルル
TRILLLLL
プルルルルル
SKRTCH
シャ
SKRTCH
シャ
SKRTCH
シャ
SKRTCH
シャ
SKRTCH
シャ
SKRTCH
シャ
SKRTCH
シャ
GOD'S BOX

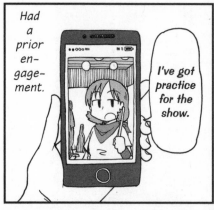

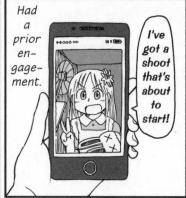

I've got a shoot that's about to start!
Had a prior en-gage-ment.
I've got practice for the show.
Had a prior en-gage-ment.
I called my younger sister, but she, too...
MNAH MNAH ...
MNAH MNAH MNAH ...
had a prior en-gage-ment.
This must all be because I'd received my three good things so early in the day.
I'm over capacity, with no room to accept another good thing.
Na gu mo
100
GOOD THINGS
1
2
3
So, since only one of these good things is returnable, I set off for the police box.

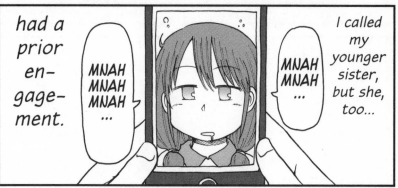

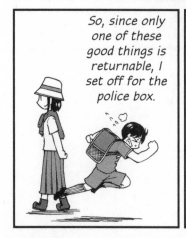

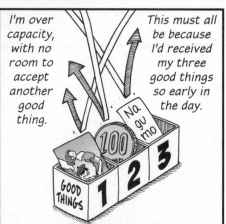

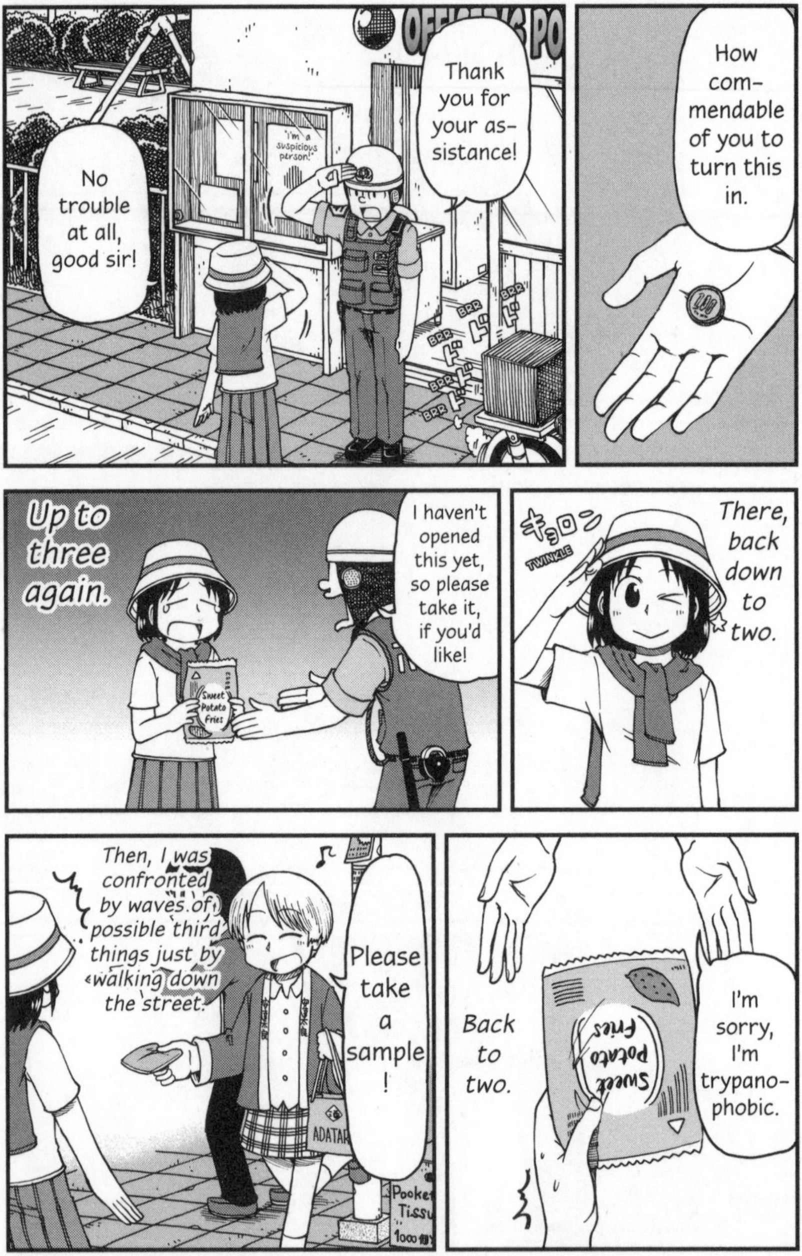
How commendable of you to turn this in.
OFFICER'S PO
Thank you for your assistance!
I'm a suspicious person!
No trouble at all, good sir!
BRR ド
BRR ド
BRR ド
BRR ド
BRR
キョロン
TWINKLE
There, back down to two.
I haven't opened this yet, so please take it, if you'd like!
Up to three again.
Sweet Potato Fries
I'm sorry, I'm trypanophobic.
Back to two.
Sweet Potato Fries
Please take a sample!
Then, I was confronted by waves of possible third things just by walking down the street.
ADATAR
Pocket Tissu

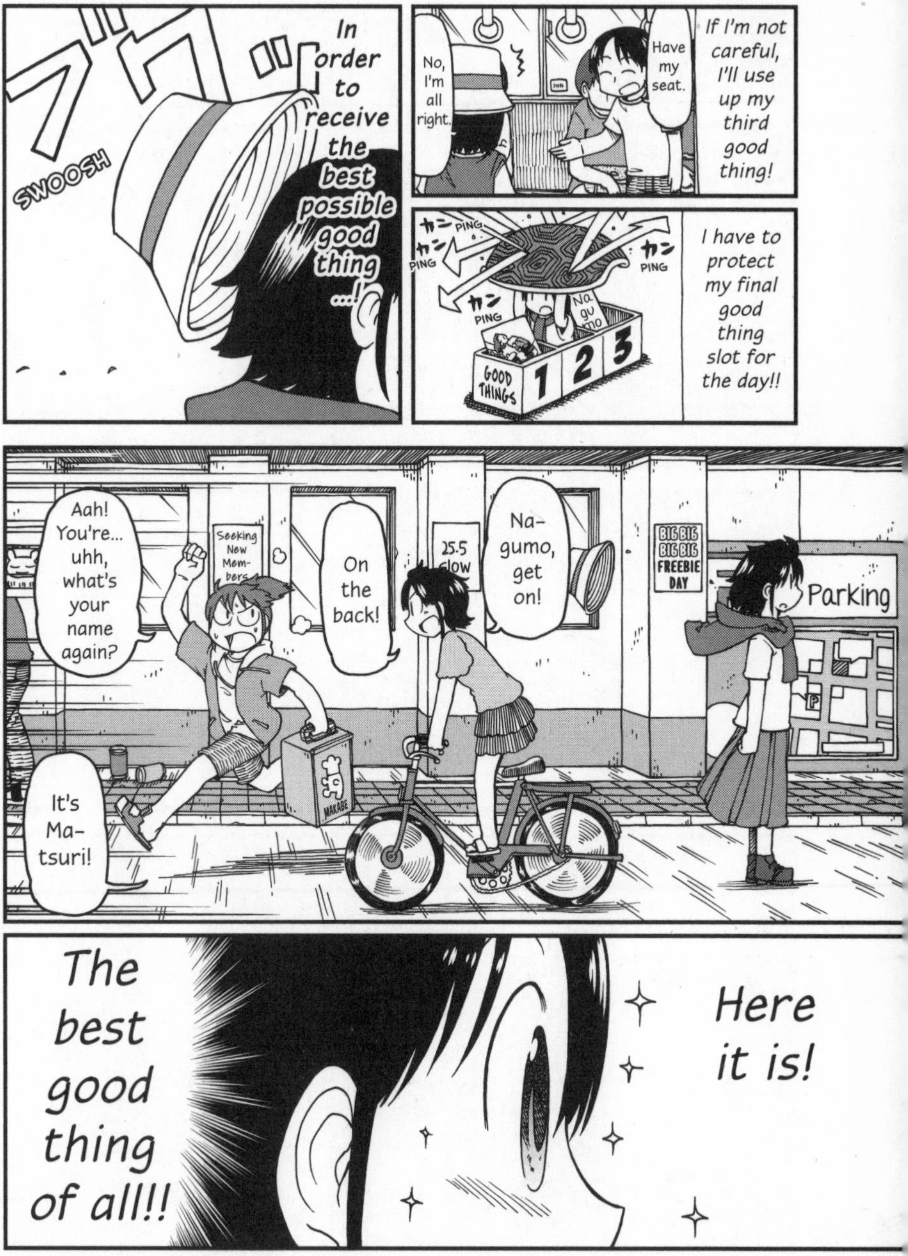
If I'm not careful, I'll use up my third good thing!
Have my seat.
No, I'm all right.
I have to protect my final good thing slot for the day!!
カン PING
カン PING
カン PING
カン PING
Nagumo
GOOD THINGS
1 2 3
In order to receive the best possible good thing...!
SWOOSH
Parking
BIG BIG BIG BIG FREEBIE DAY
Nagumo, get on!
On the back!
Seeking New Members
Aah! You're... uhh, what's your name again?
It's Matsuri!
MAKABE
Here it is!
The best good thing of all!!

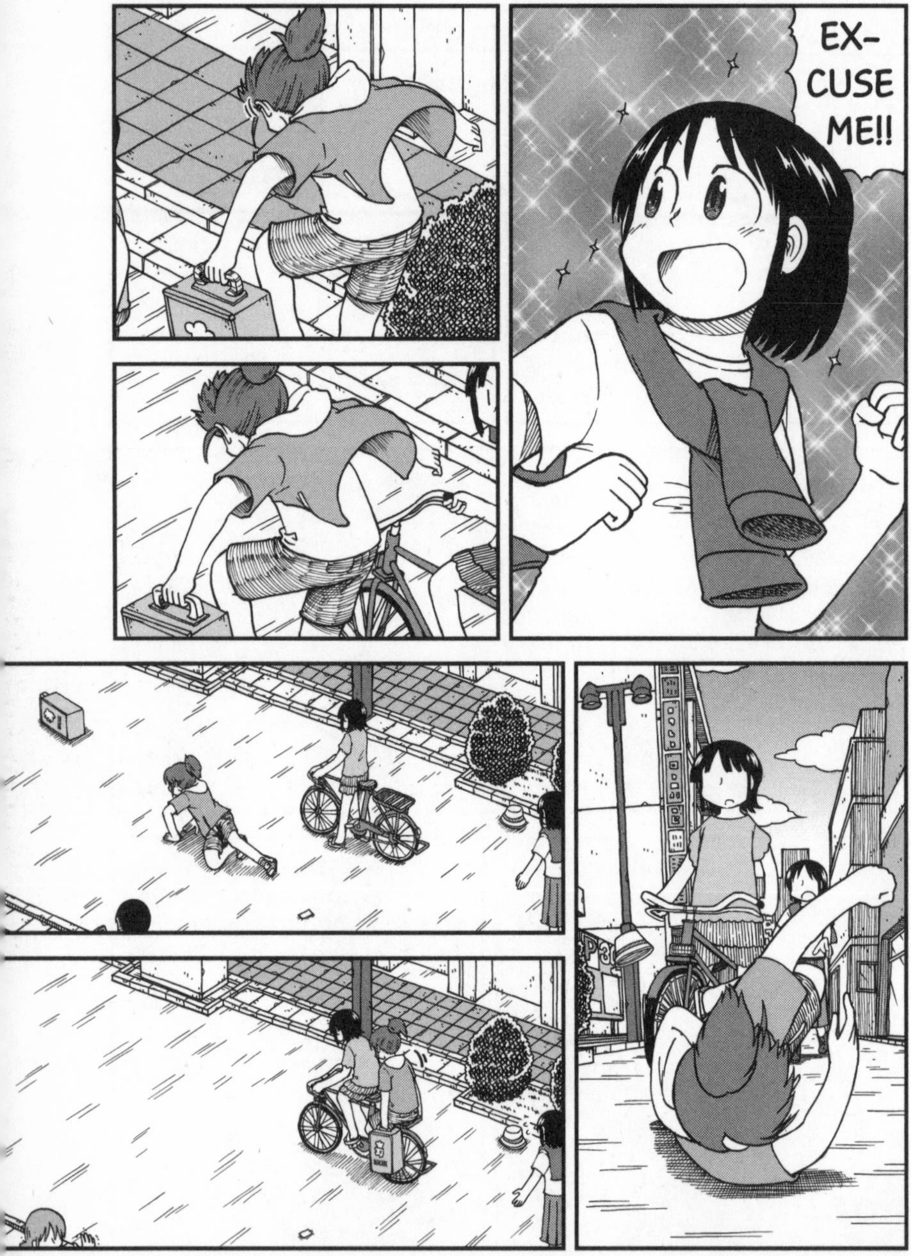
EX-
CUSE
ME!!

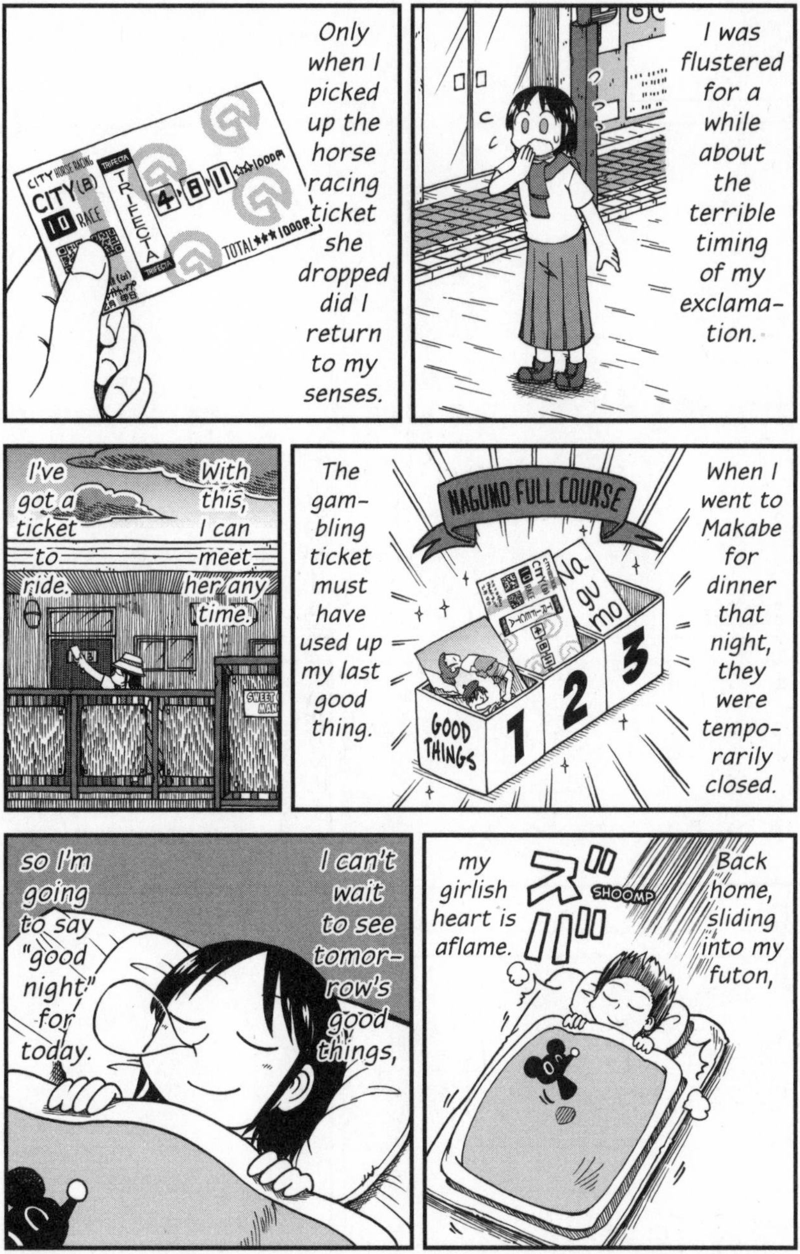
I was flustered for a while about the terrible timing of my exclamation.
Only when I picked up the horse racing ticket she dropped did I return to my senses.
CITY HORSE RACING
CITY (B)
10 RACE
TRIFECTA
4 8 11
TOTAL
When I went to Makabe for dinner that night, they were temporarily closed.
The gambling ticket must have used up my last good thing.
NAGUMO FULL COURSE
Na gu mo
GOOD THINGS
1 2 3
With this, I can meet her any time.
I've got a ticket to ride.
Back home, sliding into my futon,
my girlish heart is aflame.
SHOOMP
I can't wait to see tomorrow's good things,
so I'm going to say "good night" for today.

RACE START: SUNDAY 15:30 **SAWAYAKA CUP** 4+ OPEN LAWN 1600 CITY fun **PRIZE MONEY:** ① 23 MILLION ② 9 MILLION ③ 5 MILLION

#	Name	Sex/Age	Jockey	YAMA SHITA	YAMA NAKA	YAMA UE			Comment
1	JAM~JAM **JAMBALAYA** BALAYA	MALE 5	SAKA-UCHI					PAN-THER 2 S	Gets into a better rhythm with each chase
2	VEHICLE **TRAVELMIN** MOTION SICKNESS	MALE 5	ISHI-ZATO	○				SILVER CUP 7	Improves when struck
3	WHISKEY **ADULT FLAVOR** BON~BON	MALE 6	KITA-MURA		▲			HUN-GRY 1	Nimble movements
4	LICKEY **COOKIE CUTTER** SOAK	MALE 9	IKE-MURA					CY-PRESS 14	Steady at a low level
5	YAN~YAN **SUMMERLAND** NUN~NUN	MALE 8	AKI-NO		◎			ZU CUP 6	Compact and small; runs so-so
6	SUMMER ENERGY **VEGGIE OIL SET** GREETING	MALE 5	NIS-SHIN			▲		BUD-DHA CUP 9	Not too good, not too bad
7	RAKKYOU **HANARAKKYOU** FLOWER	MALE 4	AKI-KINE	◎	△	◎		BLACK PINE PRIZE 8	Looks sleepy
8	CHILD **SKELETON** LOVE	MALE 18	SALA-MAN-DER					QUEEN C 12	Steady and unchanging
9	BATHROOM BREAK **WHAT TO DO** C'EST BON, DON'T HAVE TO	MALE 6	AKI-MAE		○			SAKURA 98 CUP 3	Just middling
10	TIGRIS **MESOPOTAMIA** EUPHRATES	MALE 4	SUMER	△		○		PULPIT 6 S	Slightly plump, easygoing
11	ONE SLICE **SAINT PAUL** FORESEE	MALE 5	BAR-BA-ROSSA					AMANI PRIZE 11	Continually the worst
12	OLD LADY **GATE BALL** DAY OFF	MALE 6	PECK	▲		△		WO-DERSH-INS S 8	More passable every time

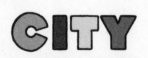

MONDAY
12:26

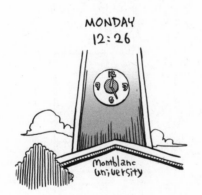

Montblanc
University

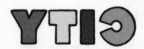

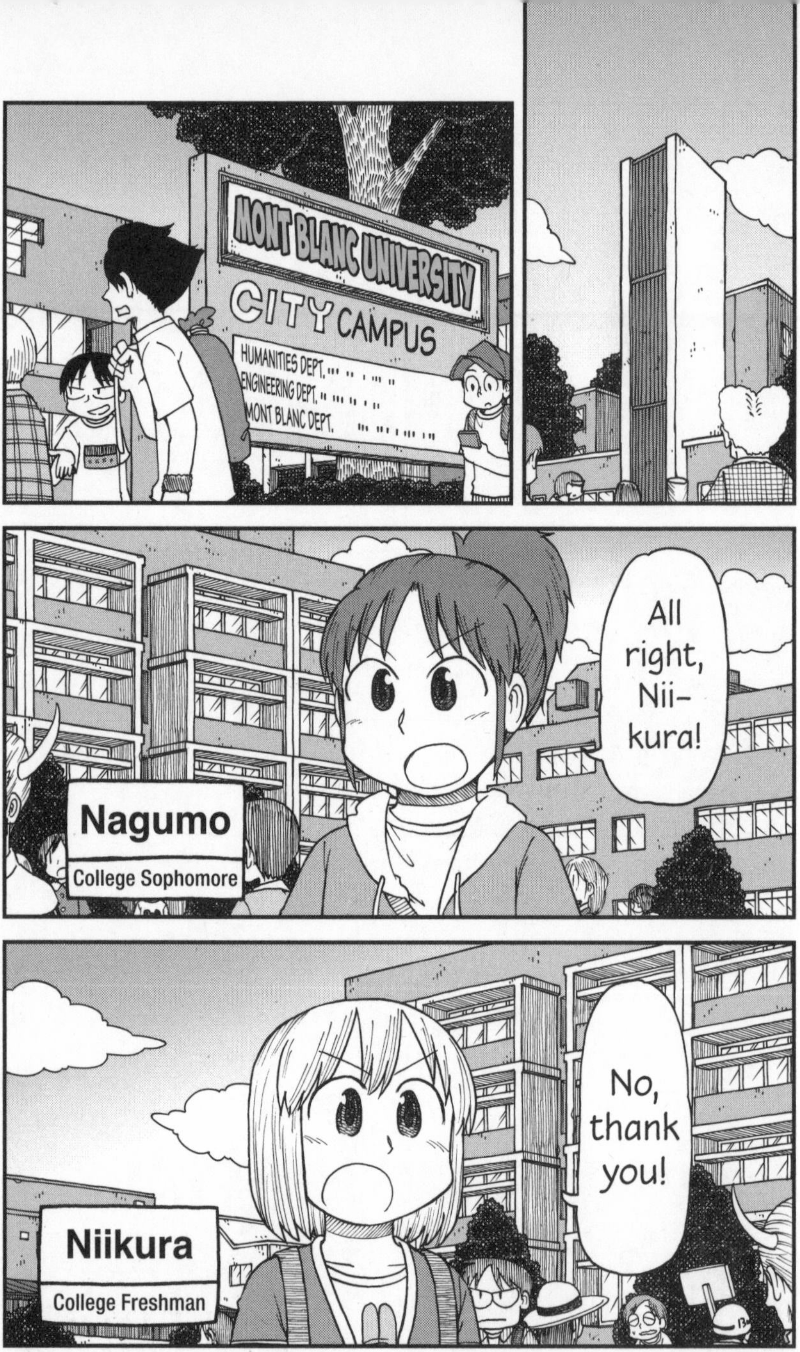
MONT BLANC UNIVERSITY
CITY CAMPUS
HUMANITIES DEPT.
ENGINEERING DEPT.
MONT BLANC DEPT.
All right, Nii-kura!
Nagumo
College Sophomore
No, thank you!
Niikura
College Freshman

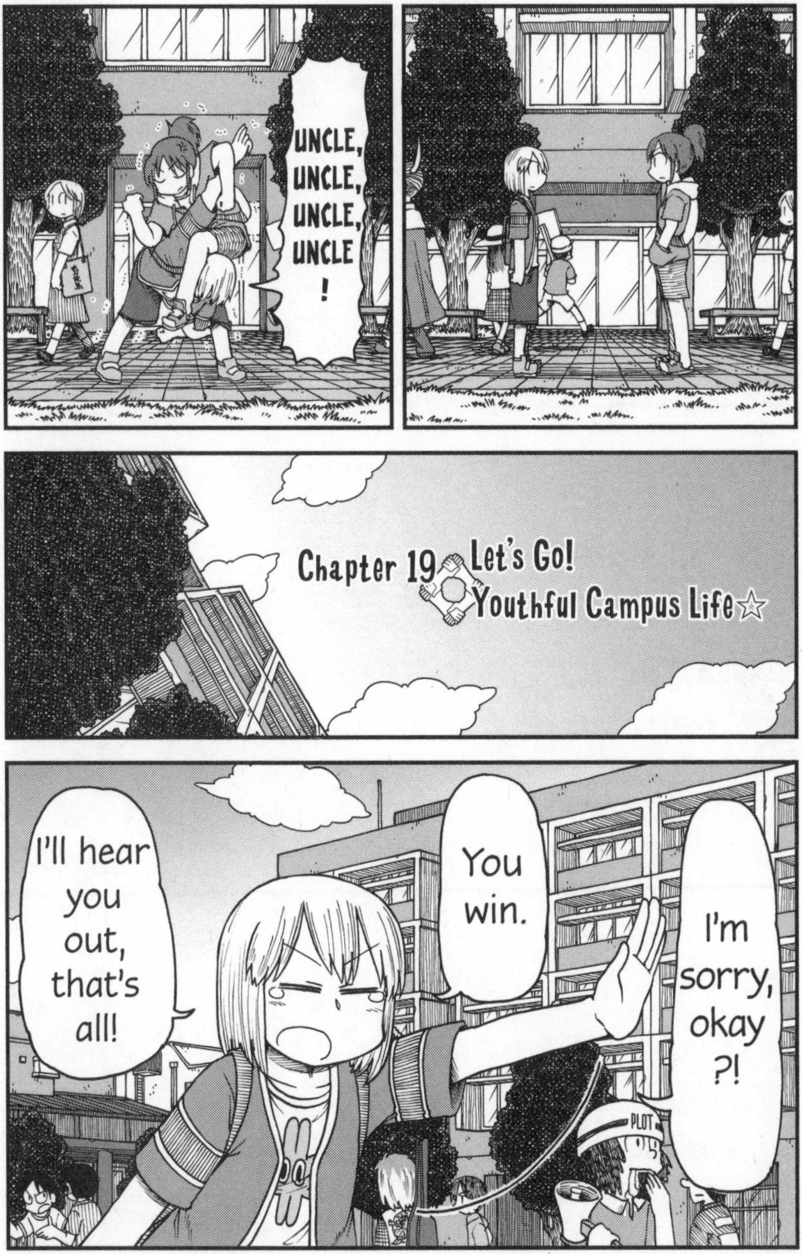
UNCLE, UNCLE, UNCLE, UNCLE!
Chapter 19 Let's Go! Youthful Campus Life☆
I'm sorry, okay?!
You win.
I'll hear you out, that's all!
PLOT

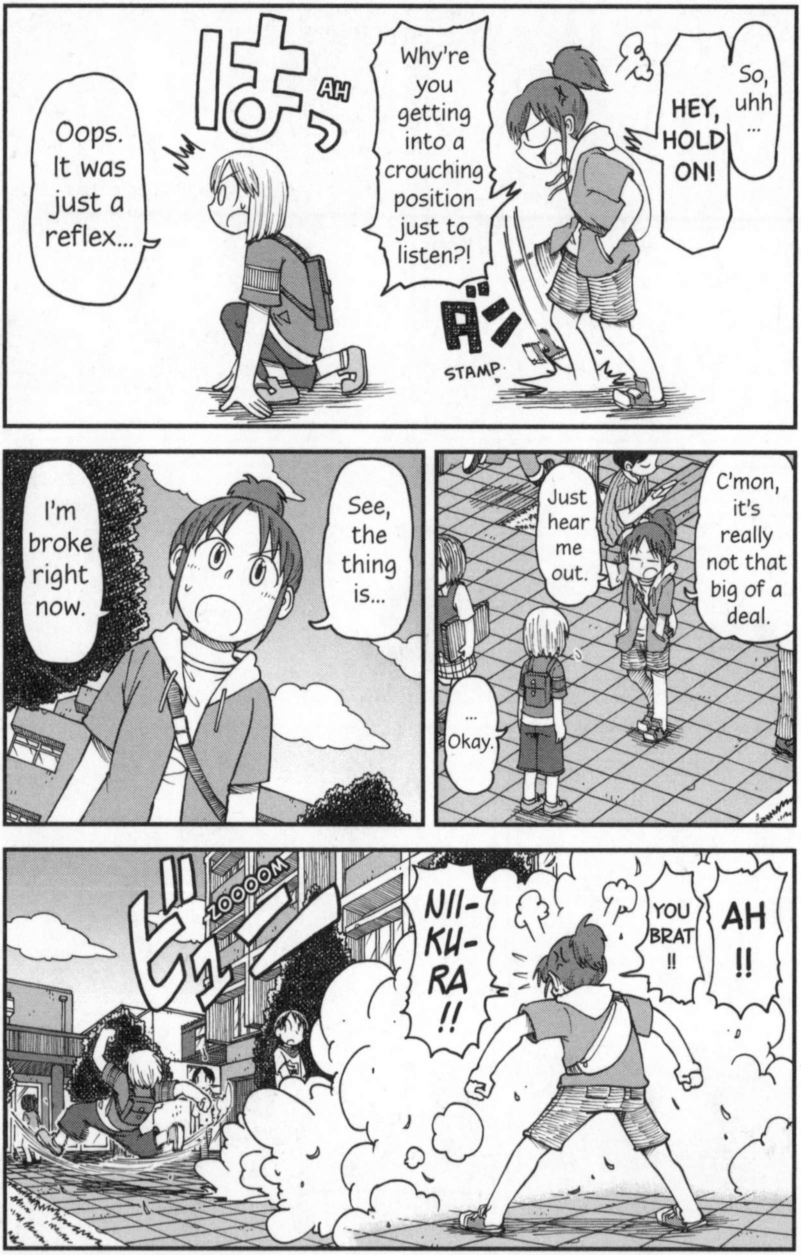
So, uhh ...
HEY, HOLD ON!
Why're you getting into a crouching position just to listen?!
AH
Oops. It was just a reflex...
STAMP
C'mon, it's really not that big of a deal.
Just hear me out.
... Okay.
See, the thing is...
I'm broke right now.
AH !!
YOU BRAT !!
NII-KU-RA !!
ZOOOOM

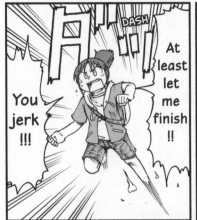

I knew it!!
I can never let my guard down with her.
Run away!
At least let me finish!!
DASH
You jerk!!!
WHA!
WHA!
WHA!
AAAAAAAH!
Wako Izumi
College Sophomore
Heeeey!
Over here!

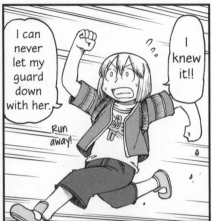

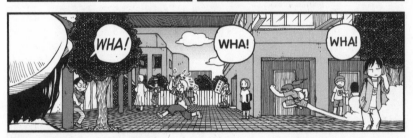

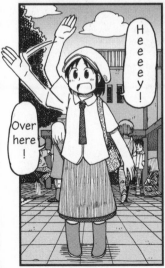

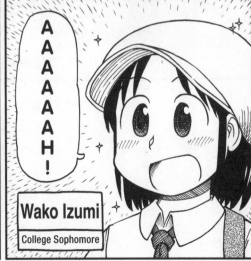

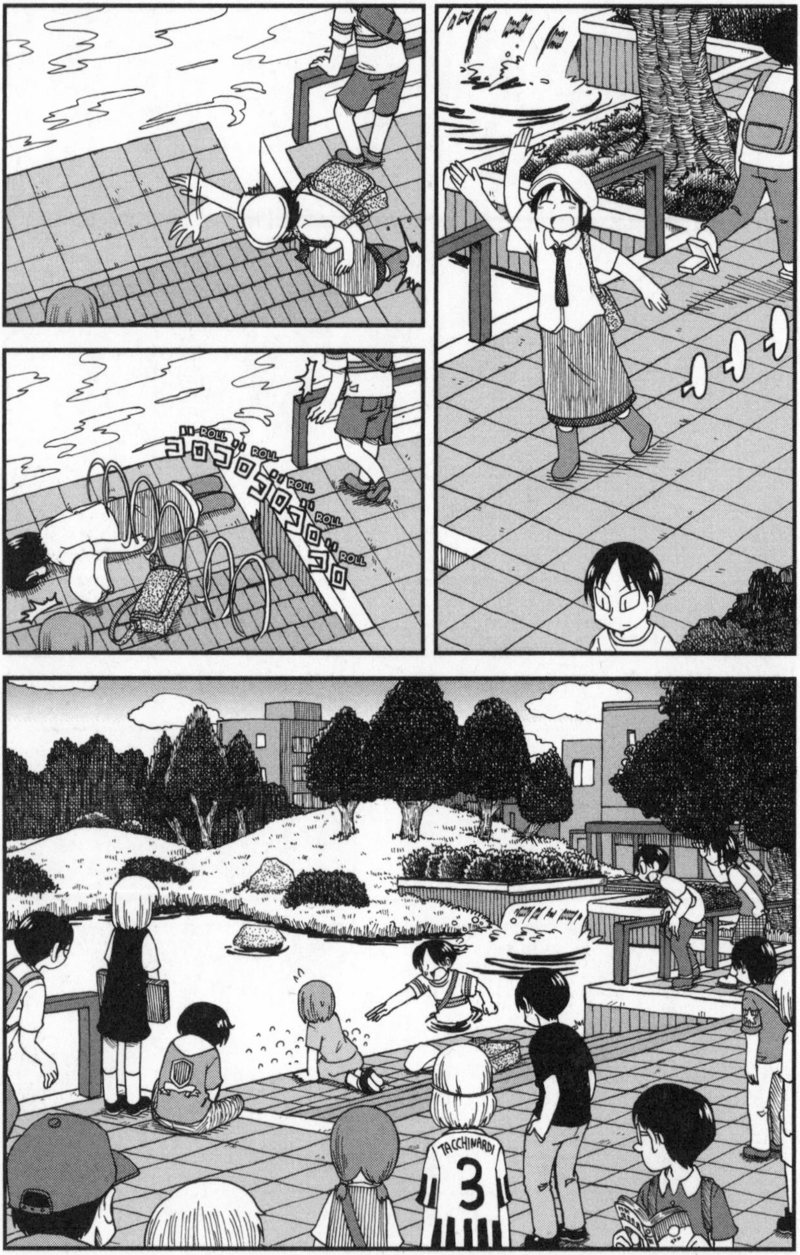
ゴロゴロゴロゴロゴロ
ROLL ROLL ROLL ROLL ROLL
TACCHINARDI
3

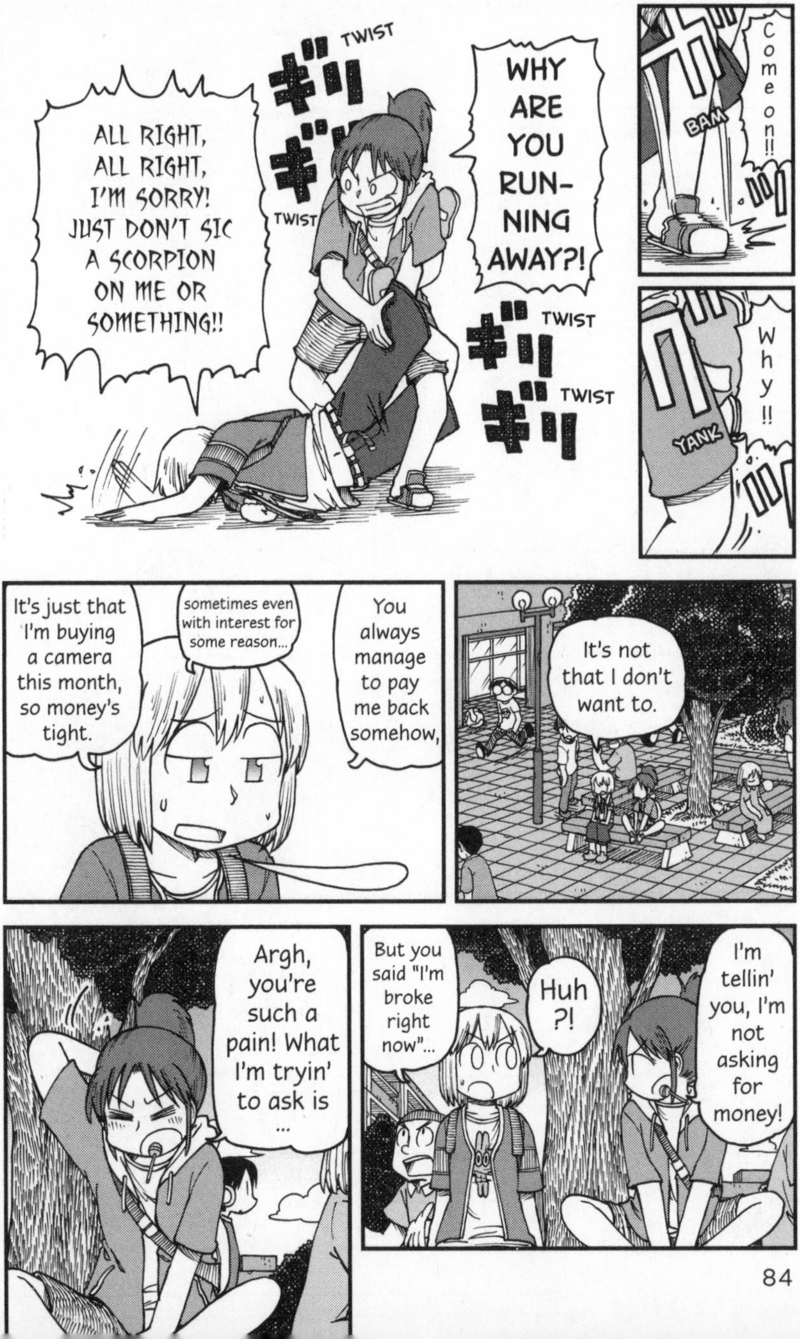
Come on!!
BAM
Why!!
YANK
WHY ARE YOU RUN-NING AWAY?!
TWIST
TWIST
ALL RIGHT, ALL RIGHT, I'M SORRY! JUST DON'T SIC A SCORPION ON ME OR SOMETHING!!
TWIST
TWIST
It's not that I don't want to.
You always manage to pay me back somehow,
sometimes even with interest for some reason...
It's just that I'm buying a camera this month, so money's tight.
I'm tellin' you, I'm not asking for money!
Huh ?!
But you said "I'm broke right now"...
Argh, you're such a pain! What I'm tryin' to ask is ...

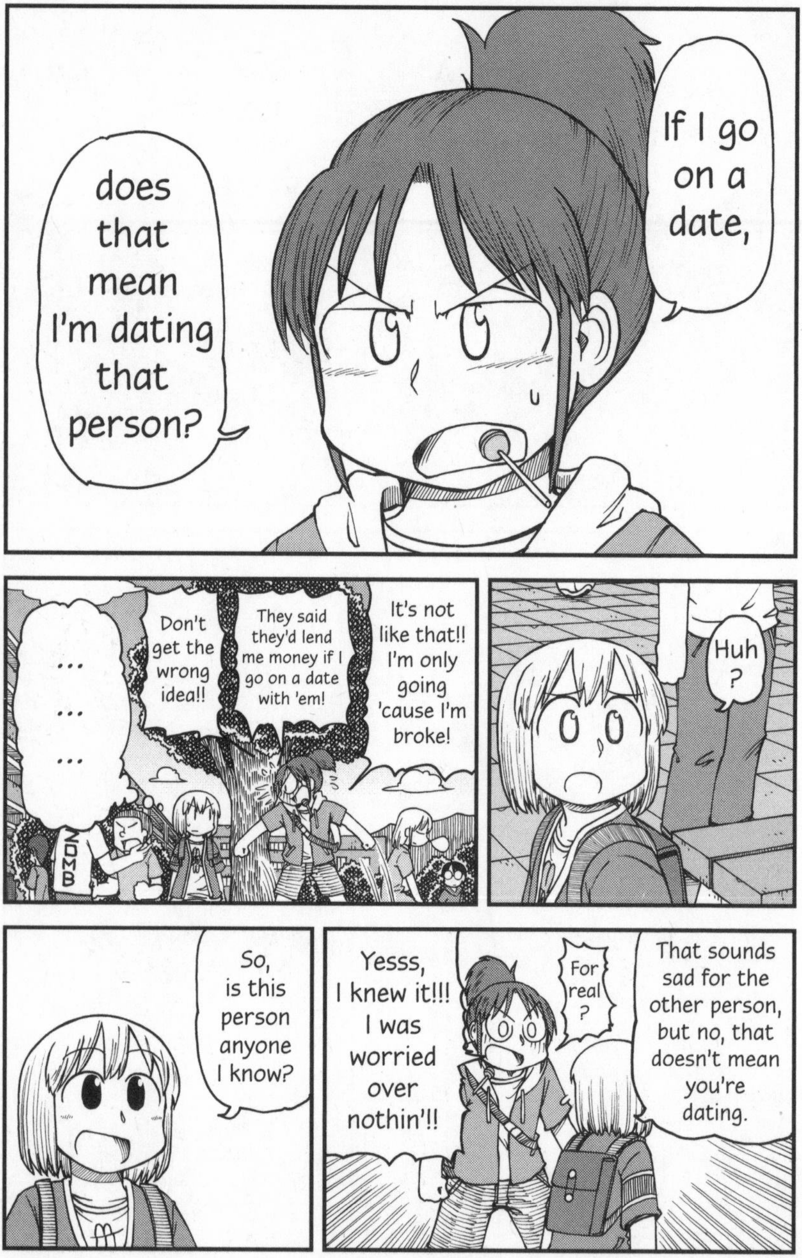
If I go on a date,
does that mean I'm dating that person?
Huh?
It's not like that!! I'm only going 'cause I'm broke!
They said they'd lend me money if I go on a date with 'em!
Don't get the wrong idea!!
... ...
ZOMB
That sounds sad for the other person, but no, that doesn't mean you're dating.
For real?
Yesss, I knew it!!! I was worried over nothin'!!
So, is this person anyone I know?

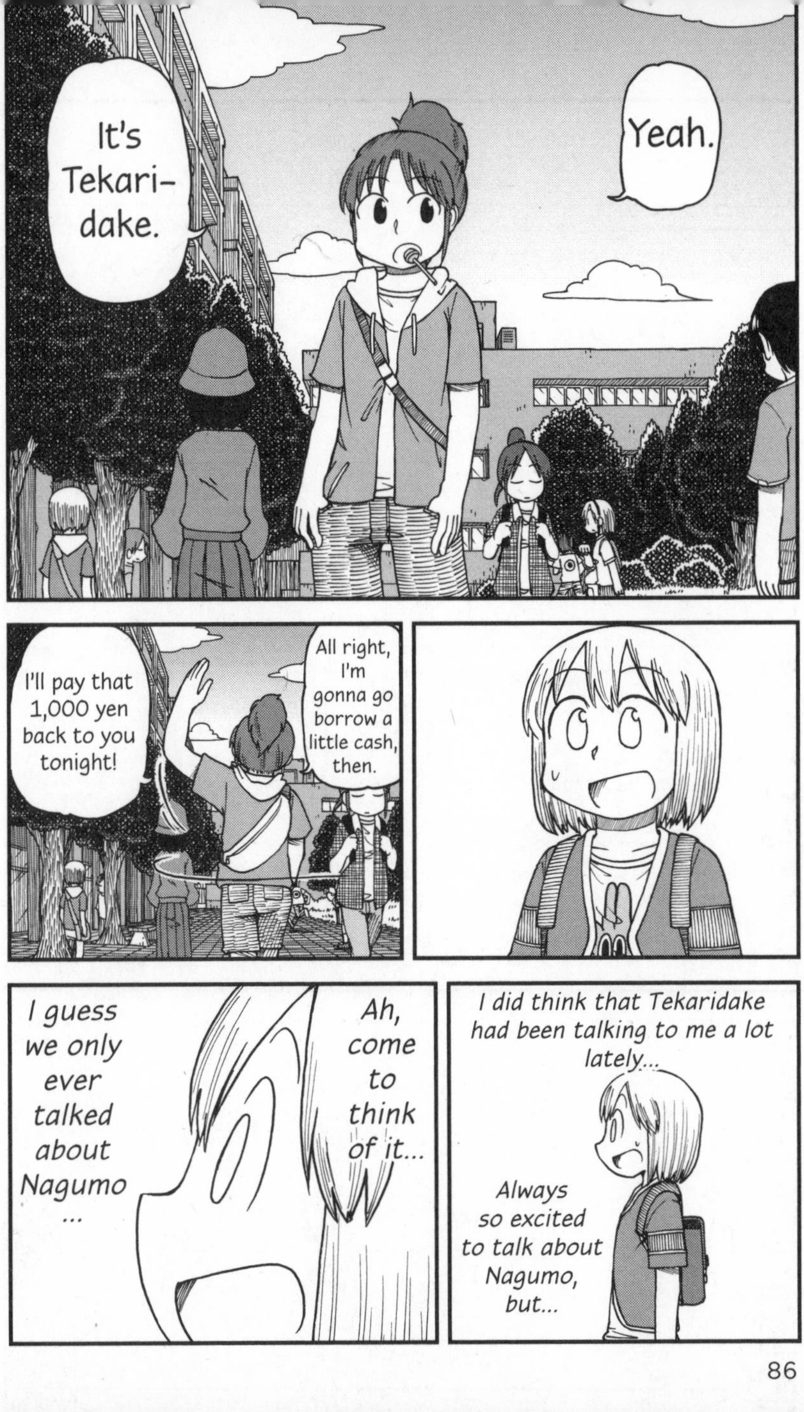
Yeah.
It's Tekari-dake.
All right, I'm gonna go borrow a little cash, then.
I'll pay that 1,000 yen back to you tonight!
I did think that Tekaridake had been talking to me a lot lately...
Always so excited to talk about Nagumo, but...
Ah, come to think of it...
I guess we only ever talked about Nagumo...

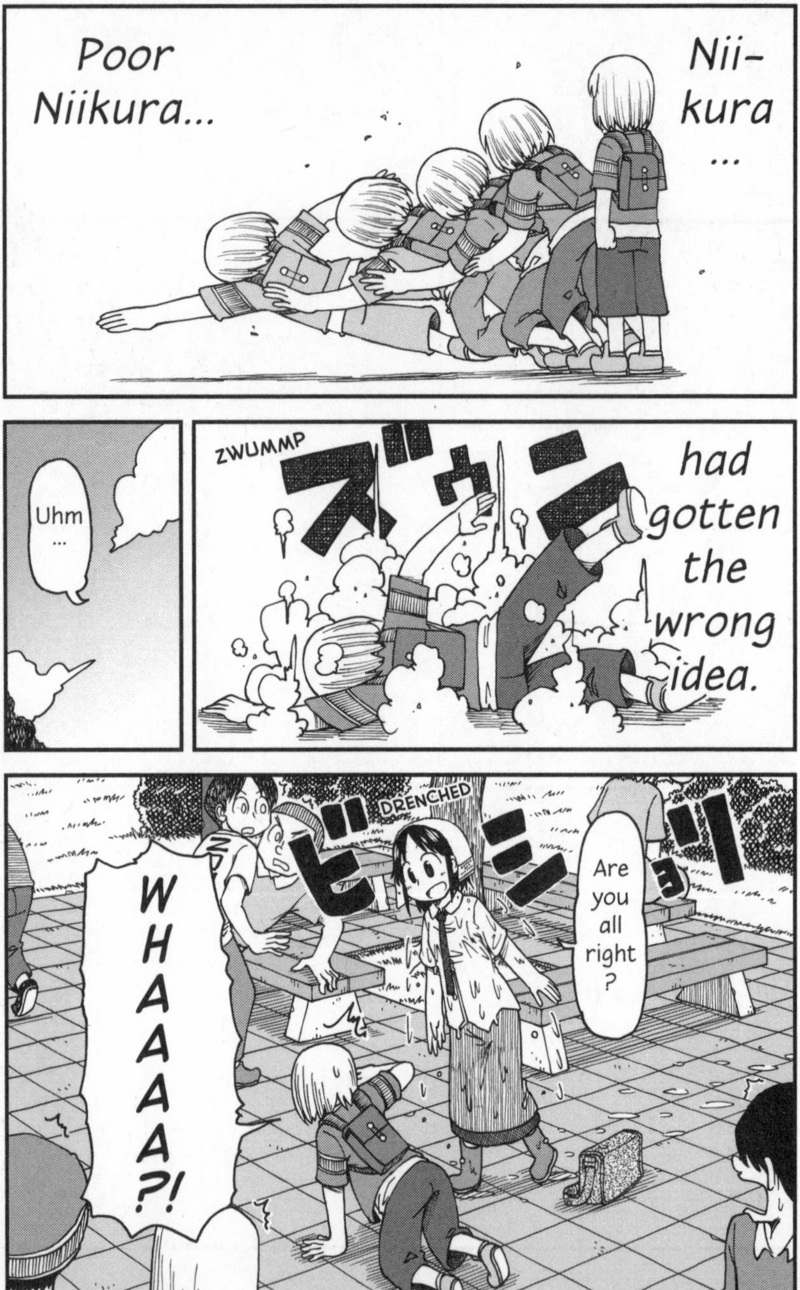
Nii-kura...
Poor Niikura...
ZWUMMP
had gotten the wrong idea.
Uhm...
DRENCHED
Are you all right?
WHAAAAA?!

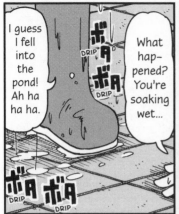

Ah! You were in front of my door yesterday !!
Yup.
I didn't know we went to the same school.
ZOMB
What hap-pened? You're soaking wet...
I guess I fell into the pond! Ah ha ha ha.
DRIP
DRIP
DRIP
DRIP
!
What about you? What's going on?
I se-cretly got my hopes up,
then se-cretly got jilted ...
...
...
...
SHPLAT
There, there.
NOOOOOOOOO!!!

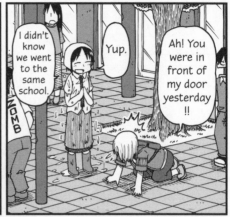

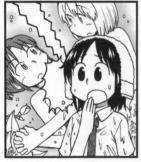

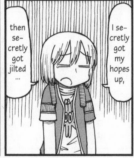

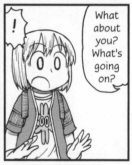

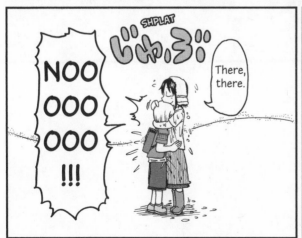

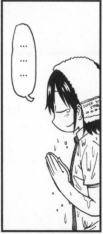

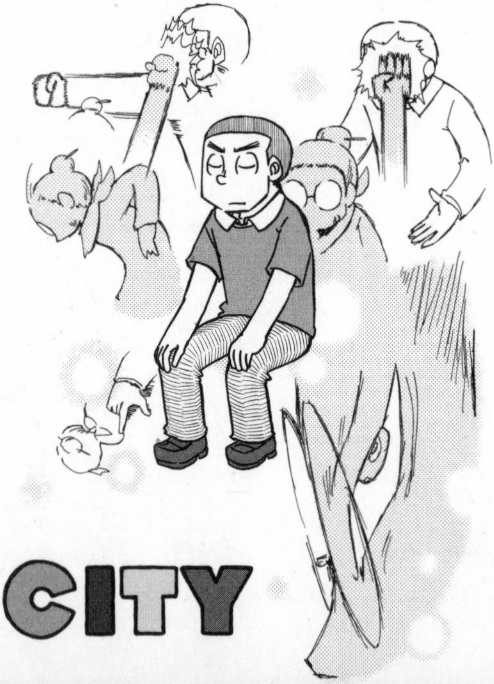
CITY

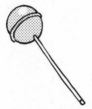

Golden Banana Milk Flavor
(very sweet)

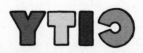

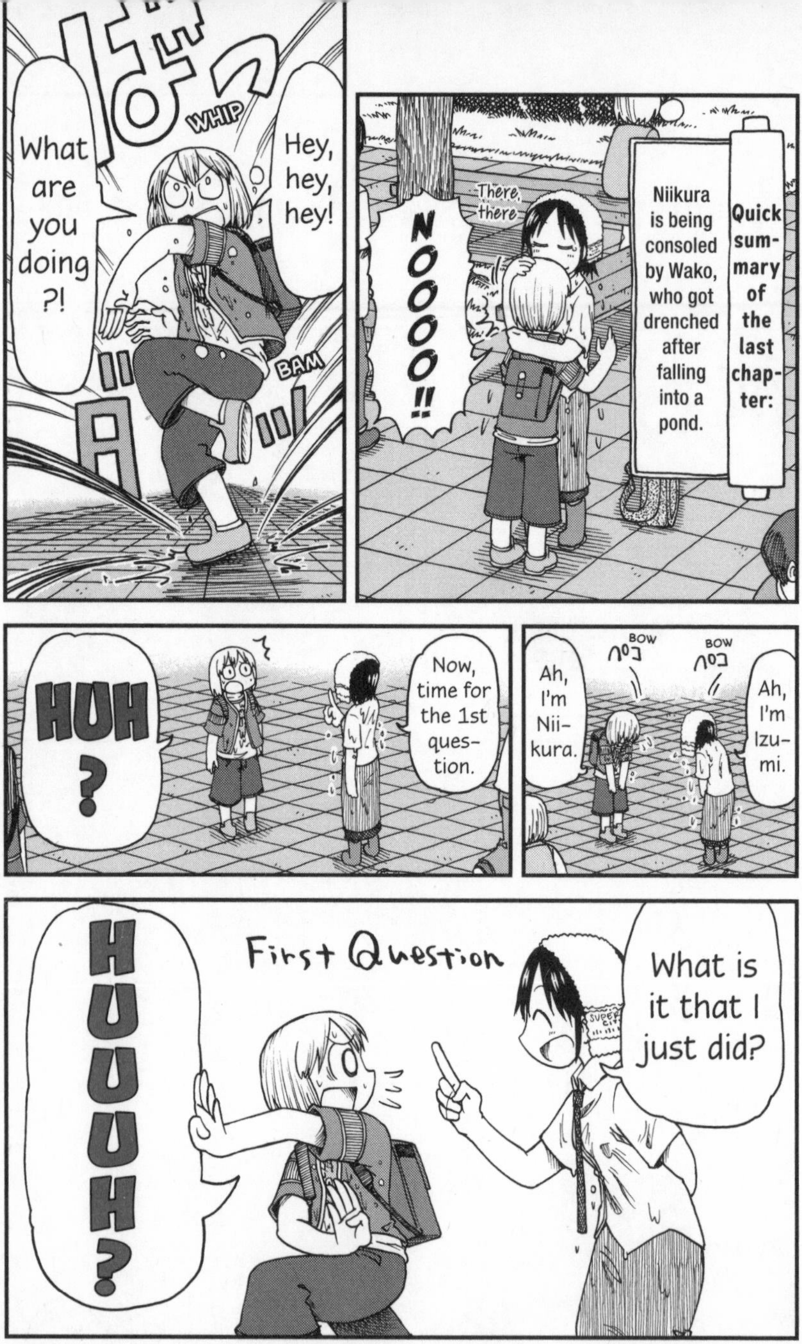
Quick summary of the last chapter:
Niikura is being consoled by Wako, who got drenched after falling into a pond.
There, there
NOOOOO!!
Hey, hey, hey!
WHIP
What are you doing?!
BAM
BOW
Ah, I'm Izumi.
BOW
Ah, I'm Niikura.
Now, time for the 1st question.
HUH?
What is it that I just did?
First Question
HUUUH?

Chapter 20 ◇ Wako Izumi's Questions

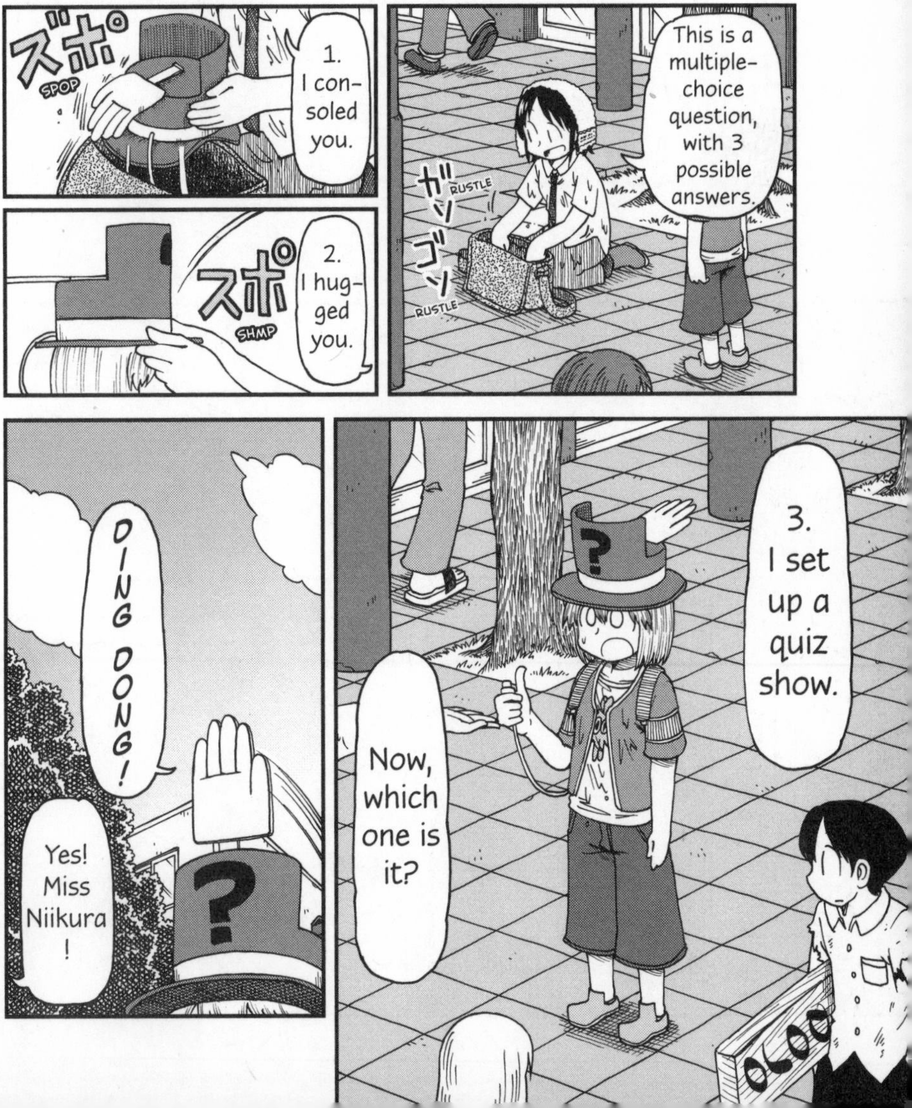
This is a multiple-choice question, with 3 possible answers.
RUSTLE
RUSTLE
ズポ
SPOP
1. I consoled you.
スポ
SHMP
2. I hugged you.
3. I set up a quiz show.
Now, which one is it?
DING DONG!
Yes! Miss Niikura!

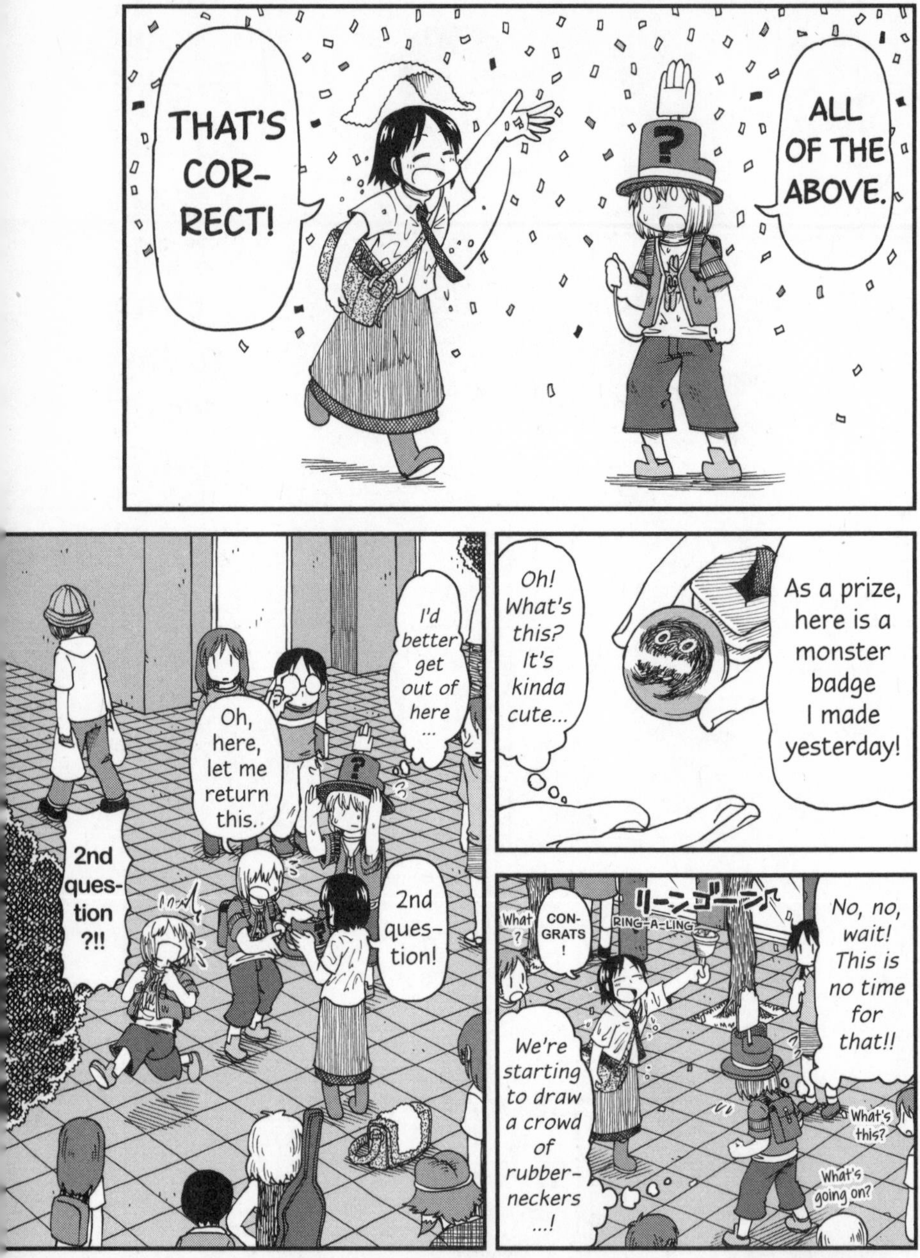
ALL OF THE ABOVE.
THAT'S COR-RECT!
As a prize, here is a monster badge I made yesterday!
Oh! What's this? It's kinda cute...
No, no, wait! This is no time for that!!
リーンゴーン♪
RING-A-LING
CON-GRATS!
What?
We're starting to draw a crowd of rubber-neckers...!
What's this?
What's going on?
I'd better get out of here...
Oh, here, let me return this.
2nd ques-tion!
2nd ques-tion?!!

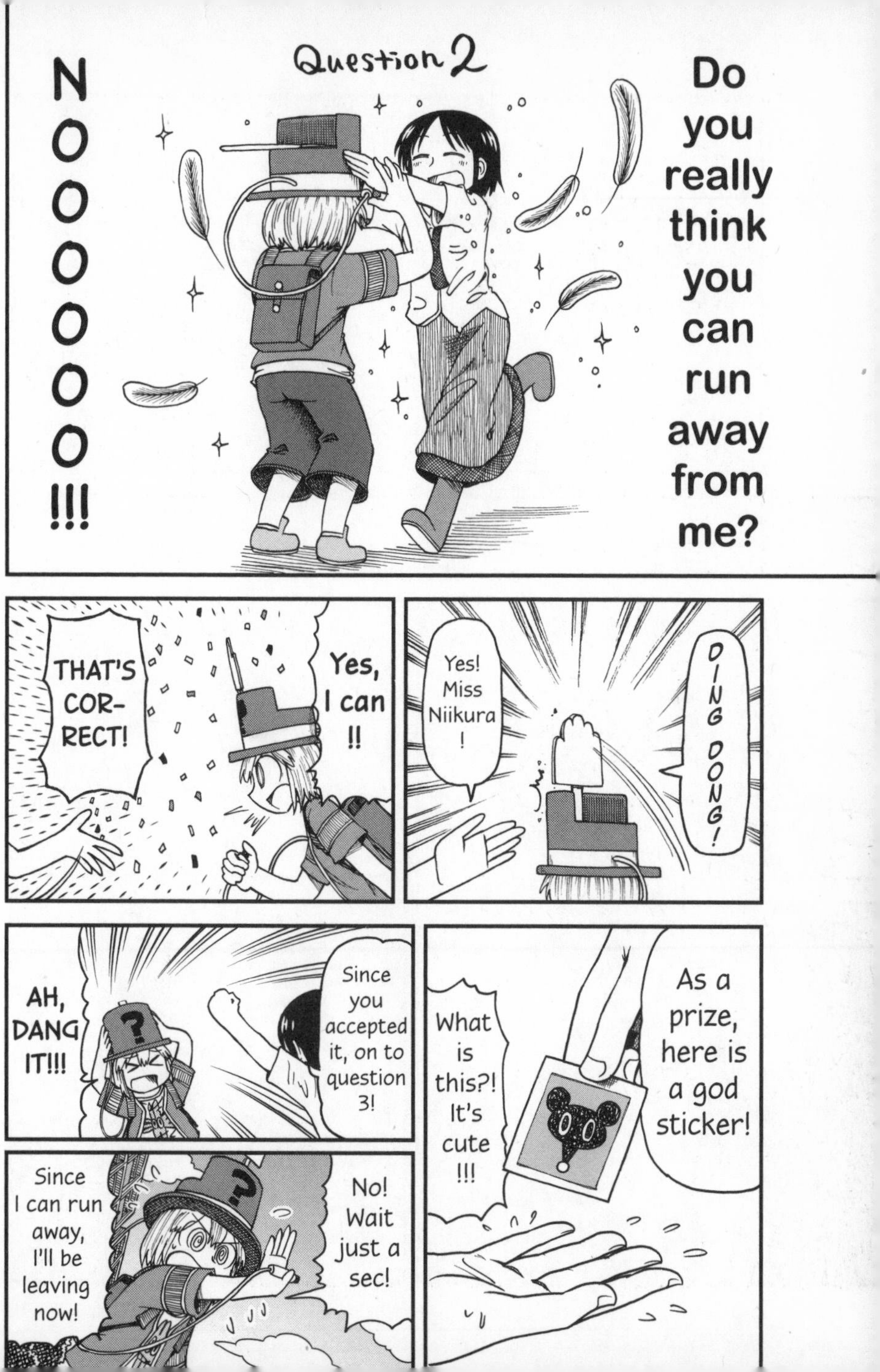
Question 2
Do you really think you can run away from me?
NOOOOOO!!!
DING DONG!
Yes! Miss Niikura!
Yes, I can!!
THAT'S COR-RECT!
As a prize, here is a god sticker!
What is this?! It's cute!!!
Since you accepted it, on to question 3!
AH, DANG IT!!!
No! Wait just a sec!
Since I can run away, I'll be leaving now!

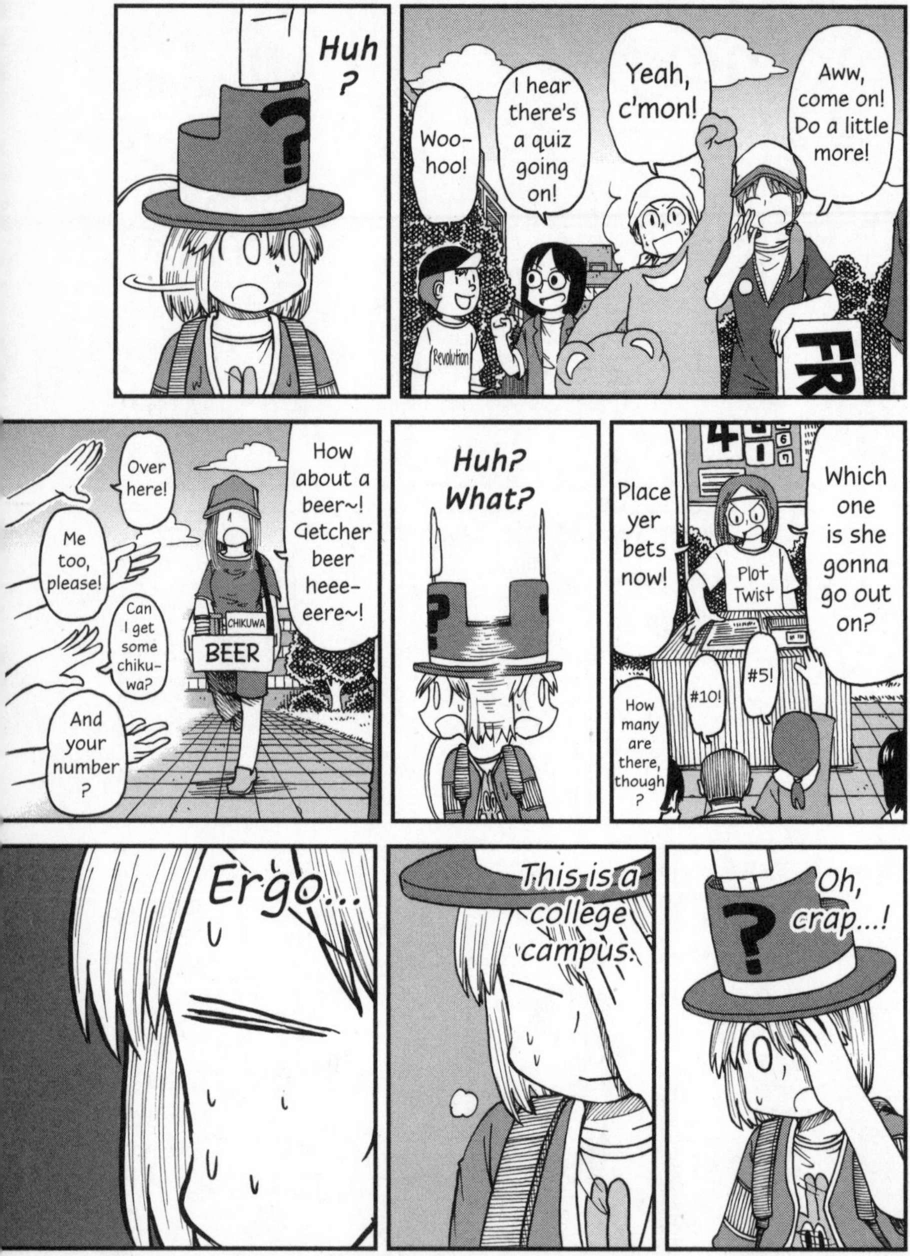

Aww, come on! Do a little more!
Yeah, c'mon!
I hear there's a quiz going on!
Woo-hoo!
Revolution
Huh?
Which one is she gonna go out on?
Place yer bets now!
Plot Twist
#5!
#10!
How many are there, though?
Huh? What?
How about a beer~! Getcher beer heeee-eere~!
Over here!
Me too, please!
Can I get some chiku-wa?
And your number?
CHIKUWA
BEER
Oh, crap...!
This is a college campus.
Ergo...

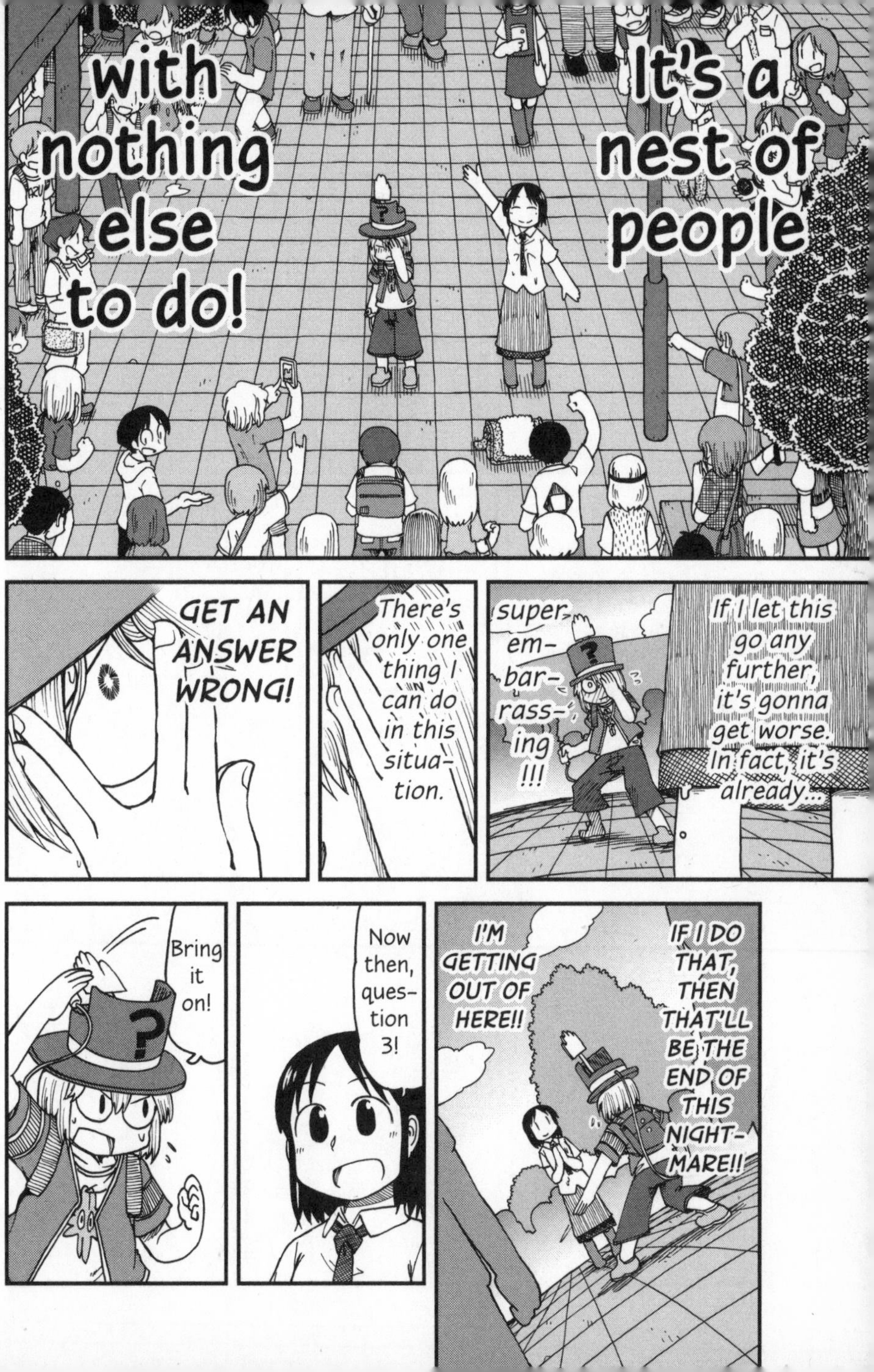
It's a nest of people
with nothing else to do!
If I let this go any further, it's gonna get worse. In fact, it's already...
super-embarrassing!!!
There's only one thing I can do in this situation.
GET AN ANSWER WRONG!
IF I DO THAT, THEN THAT'LL BE THE END OF THIS NIGHTMARE!!
I'M GETTING OUT OF HERE!!
Now then, question 3!
Bring it on!

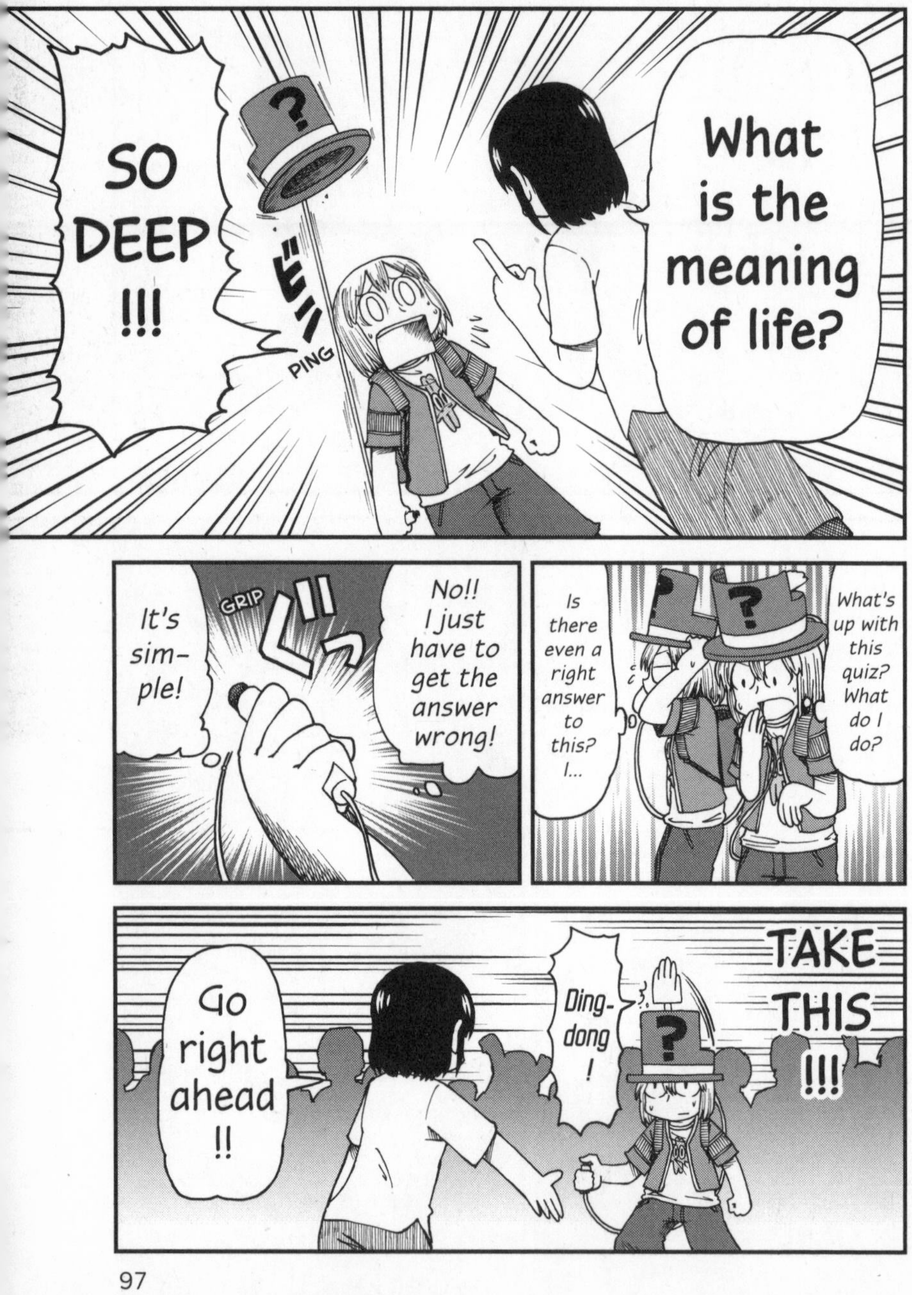
What is the meaning of life?
SO DEEP !!!
PING
What's up with this quiz? What do I do?
Is there even a right answer to this? I...
No!! I just have to get the answer wrong!
GRIP
It's sim-ple!
TAKE THIS !!!
Ding-dong!
Go right ahead !!

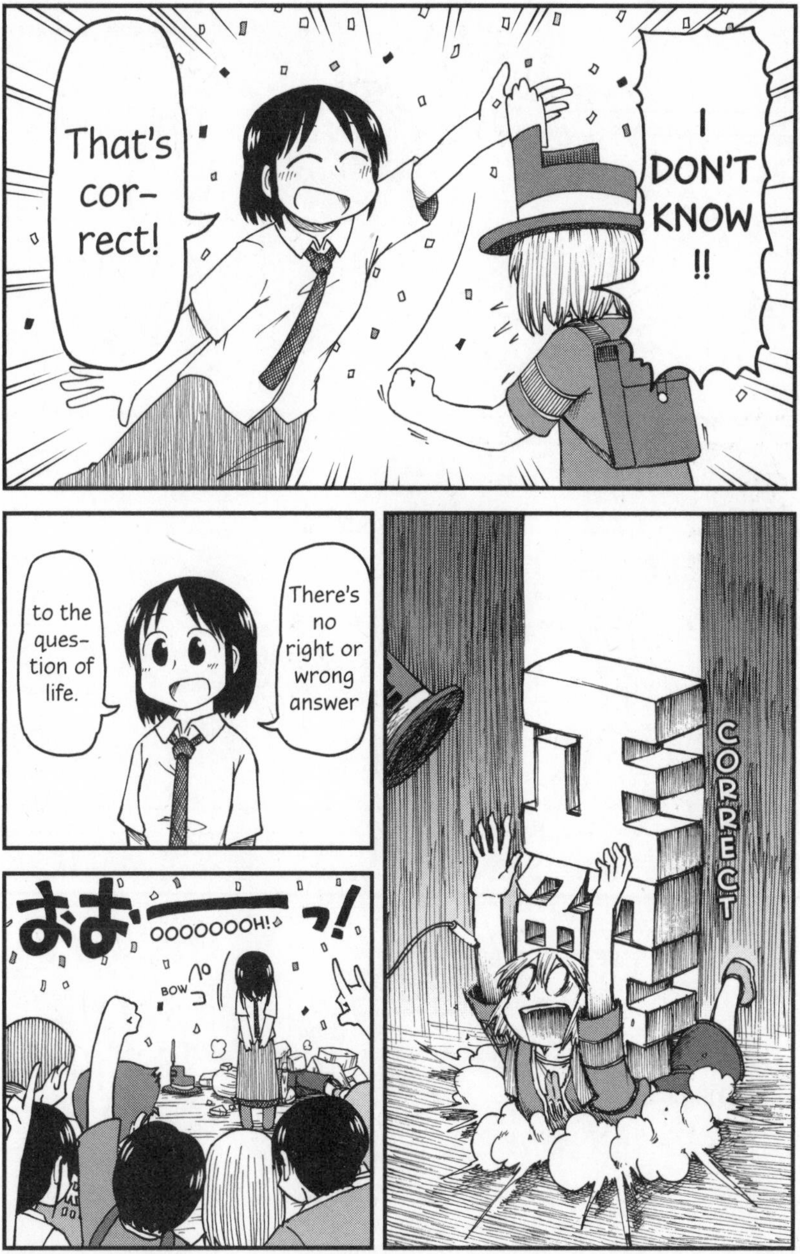
I DON'T KNOW !!
That's cor-rect!
CORRECT
There's no right or wrong answer
to the ques-tion of life.
おお——っ!
OOOOOOOH!
ペコ
BOW

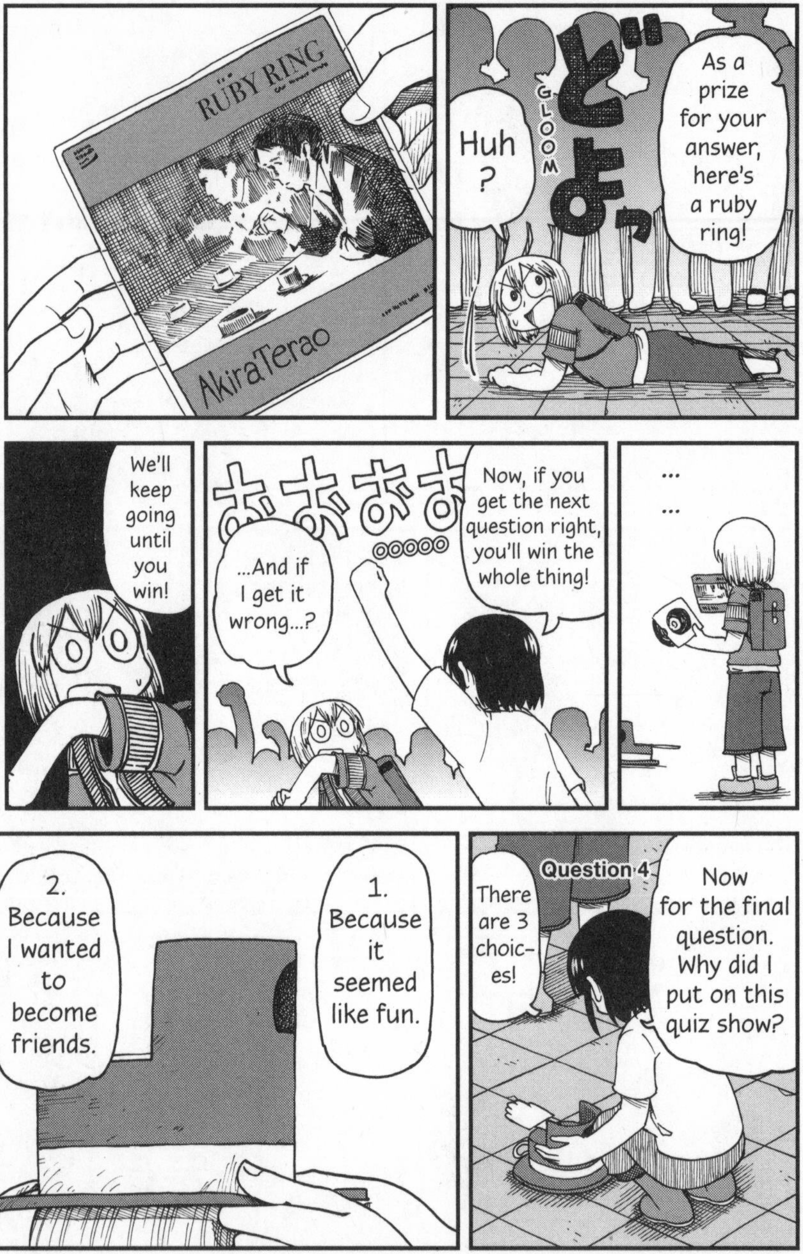

As a prize for your answer, here's a ruby ring!
どよっ
GLOOM
Huh ?
RUBY RING
AkiraTerao
...
...
Now, if you get the next question right, you'll win the whole thing!
おおおお
ooooo
...And if I get it wrong...?
We'll keep going until you win!
Question 4
Now for the final question. Why did I put on this quiz show?
There are 3 choic-es!
1. Because it seemed like fun.
2. Because I wanted to become friends.

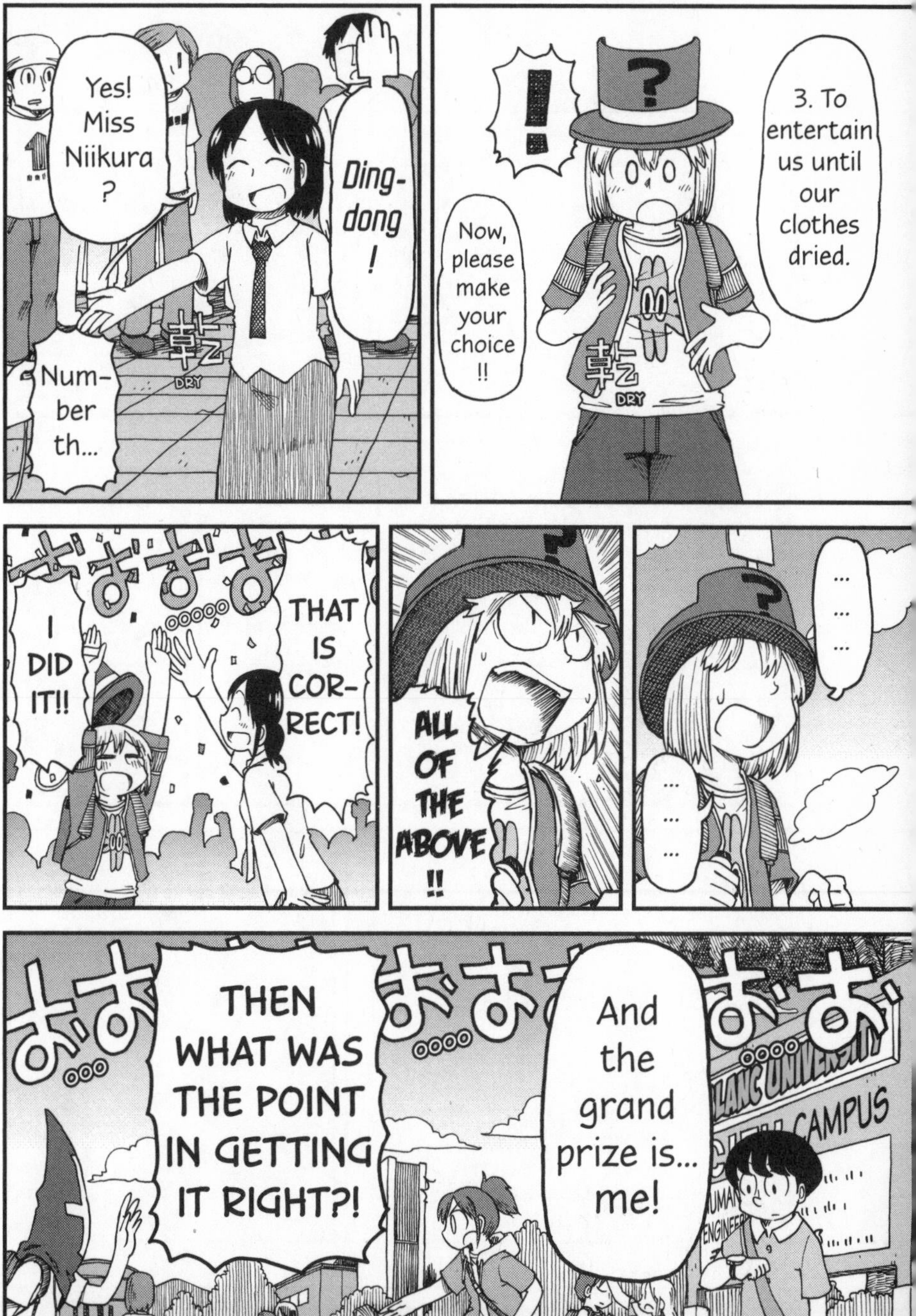
!
3. To entertain us until our clothes dried.
乾
DRY
Now, please make your choice !!
Ding-dong !
Yes! Miss Niikura ?
乾
DRY
Number th...
... ...
... ...
ALL OF THE ABOVE !!
おおおお
THAT IS CORRECT!
ooooo
I DID IT!!
And the grand prize is... me!
THEN WHAT WAS THE POINT IN GETTING IT RIGHT?!
CAMPUS

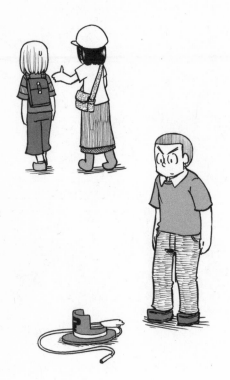

CITY

MONDAY
13:24

CITY South
High School

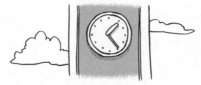

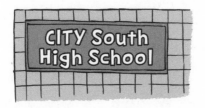

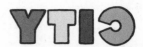

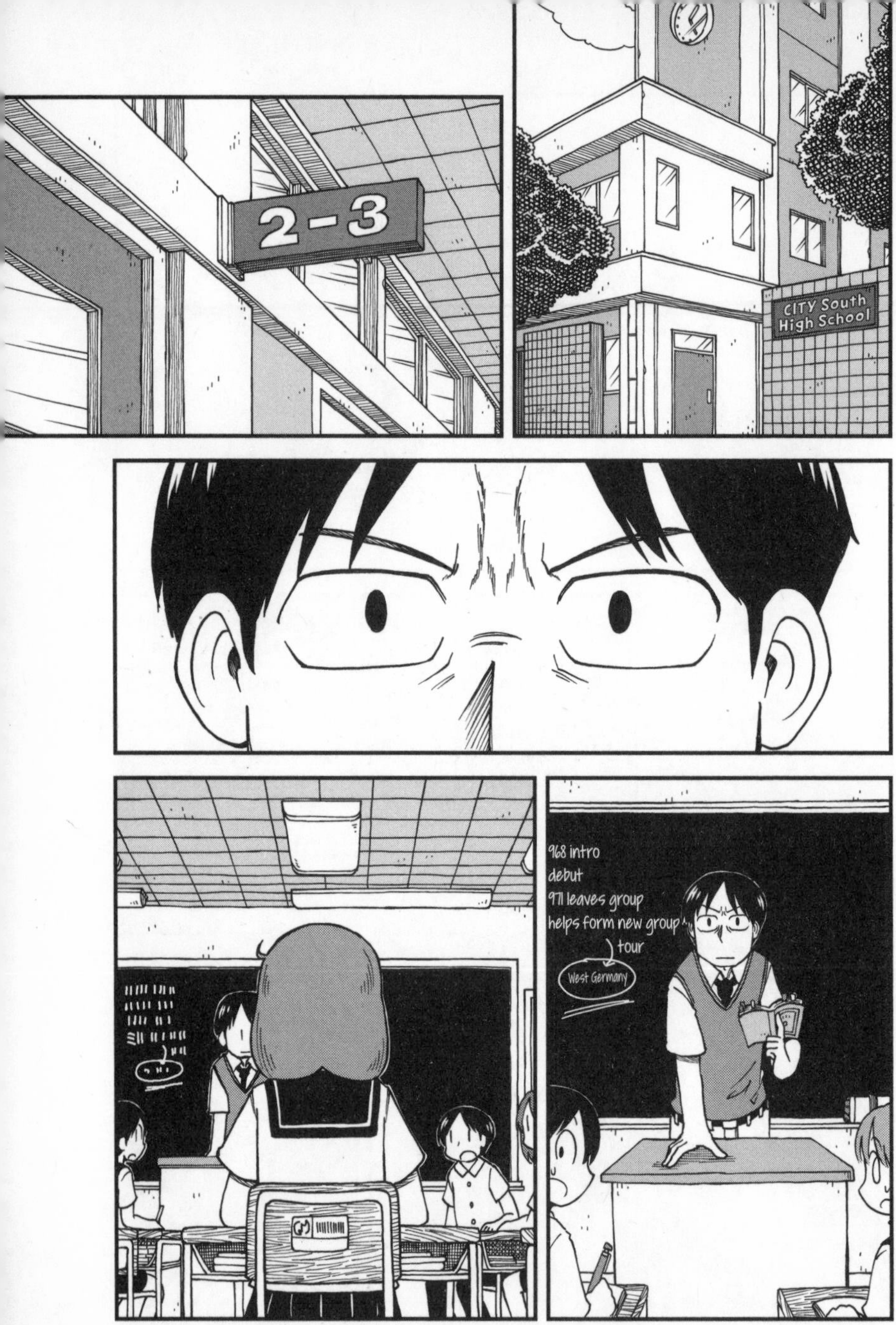
CITY South
High School
2-3
968 intro
debut
971 leaves group
helps form new group
tour
West Germany

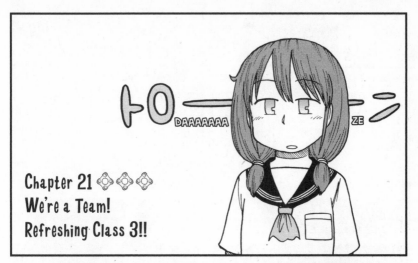

DAAAAAAA
ZE
Chapter 21
We're a Team!
Refreshing Class 3!!
Who was Osamu Kido's trainer
who taught him the art of wrestling ?
One more time ...
He's giving her a second chance ...
Come on, notice ...!
MUTTER
MUTTER
SNAP
Showa* Era History
Riko Izumi.
·but
l leaves group
lps form new grou
tour
West Germa

*1926-1989

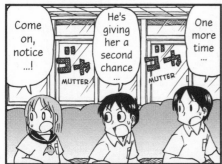

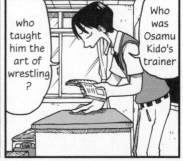

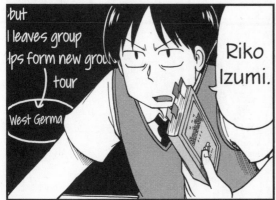

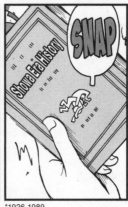

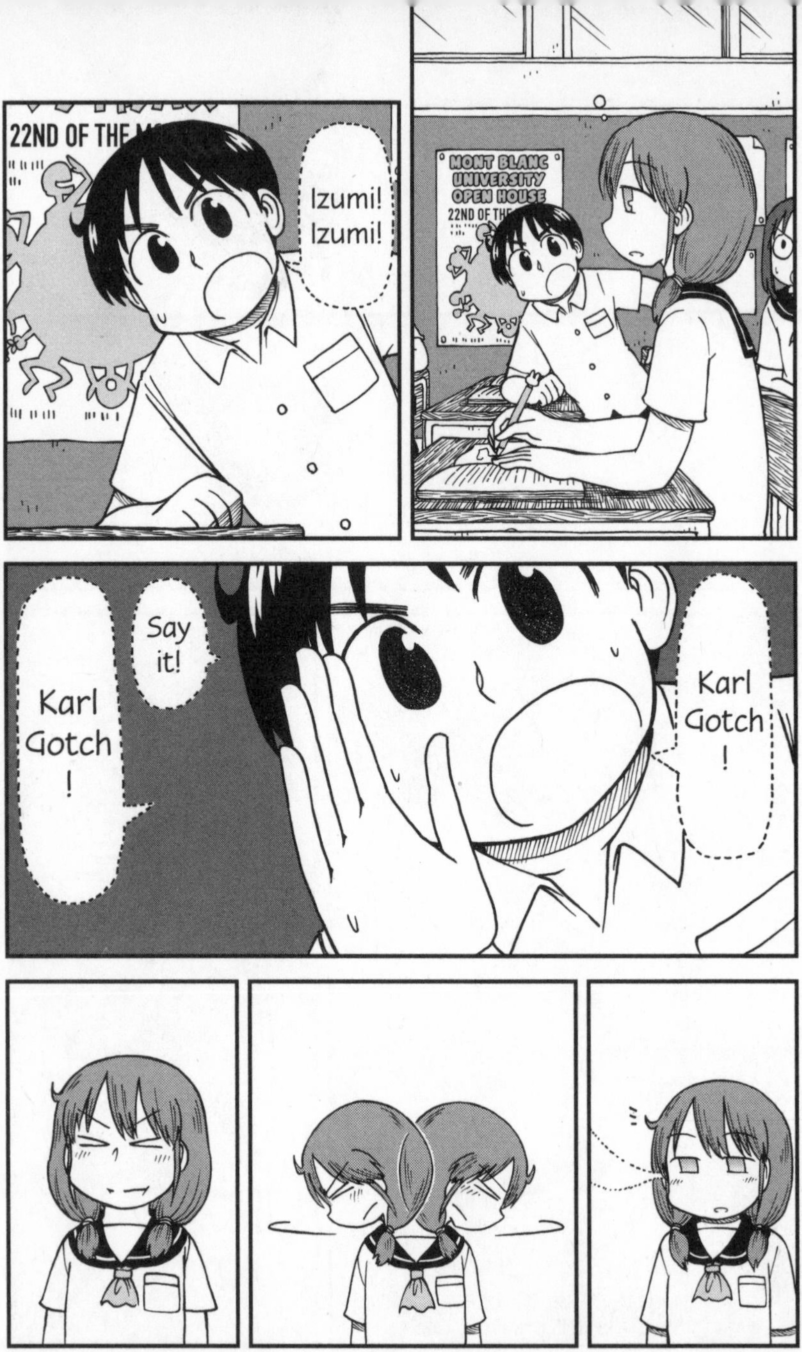
MONT BLANC UNIVERSITY OPEN HOUSE
22ND OF THE
22ND OF THE
Izumi! Izumi!
Karl Gotch !
Say it!
Karl Gotch !

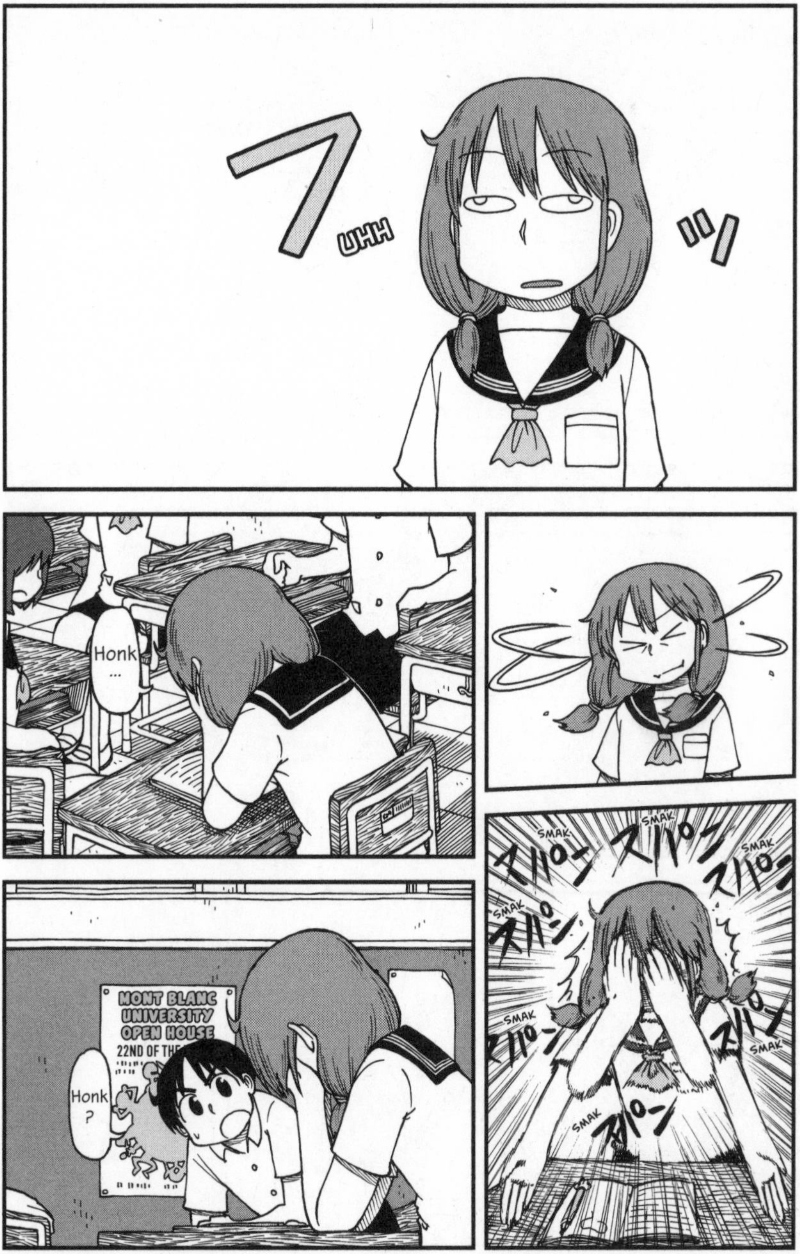
UHH
Honk
...
SMAK
SMAK
SMAK
SMAK
SMAK
SMAK
SMAK
MONT BLANC
UNIVERSITY
OPEN HOUSE
22ND OF THE
Honk
?

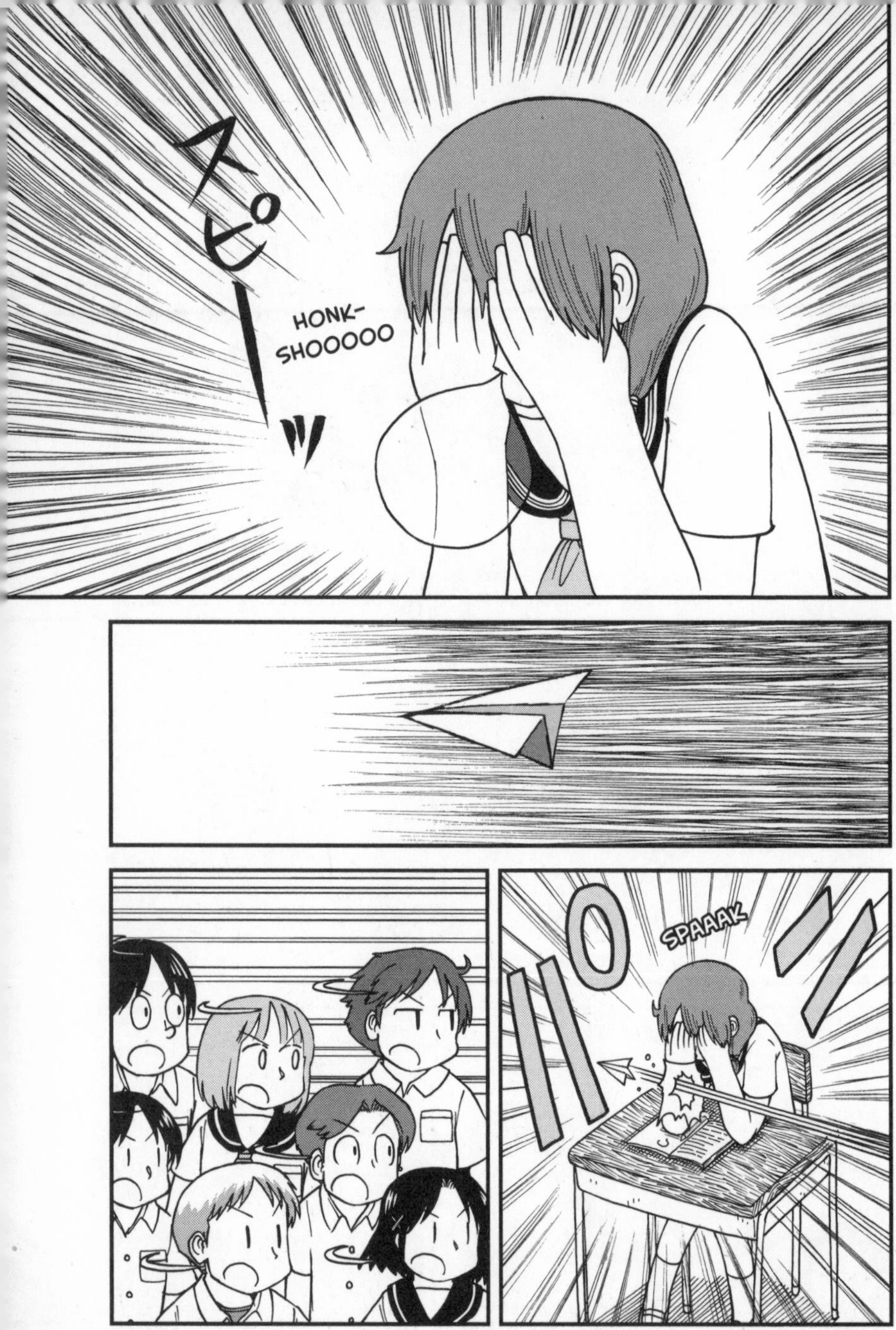
スピーッ
HONK-SHOOOOO
SPAAAK

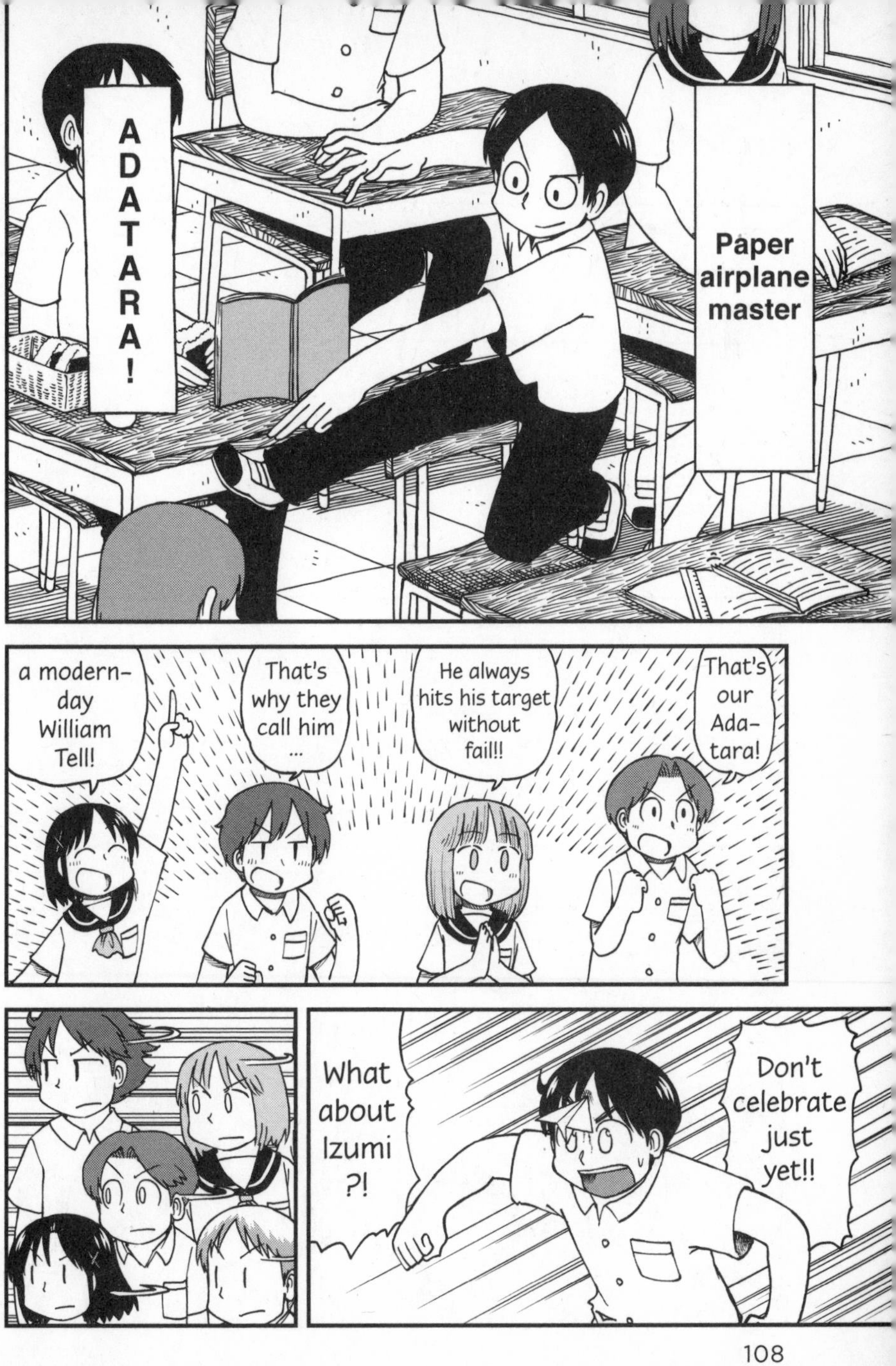
Paper airplane master
ADATARA!
That's our Ada-tara!
He always hits his target without fail!!
That's why they call him ...
a modern-day William Tell!
Don't celebrate just yet!!
What about Izumi ?!

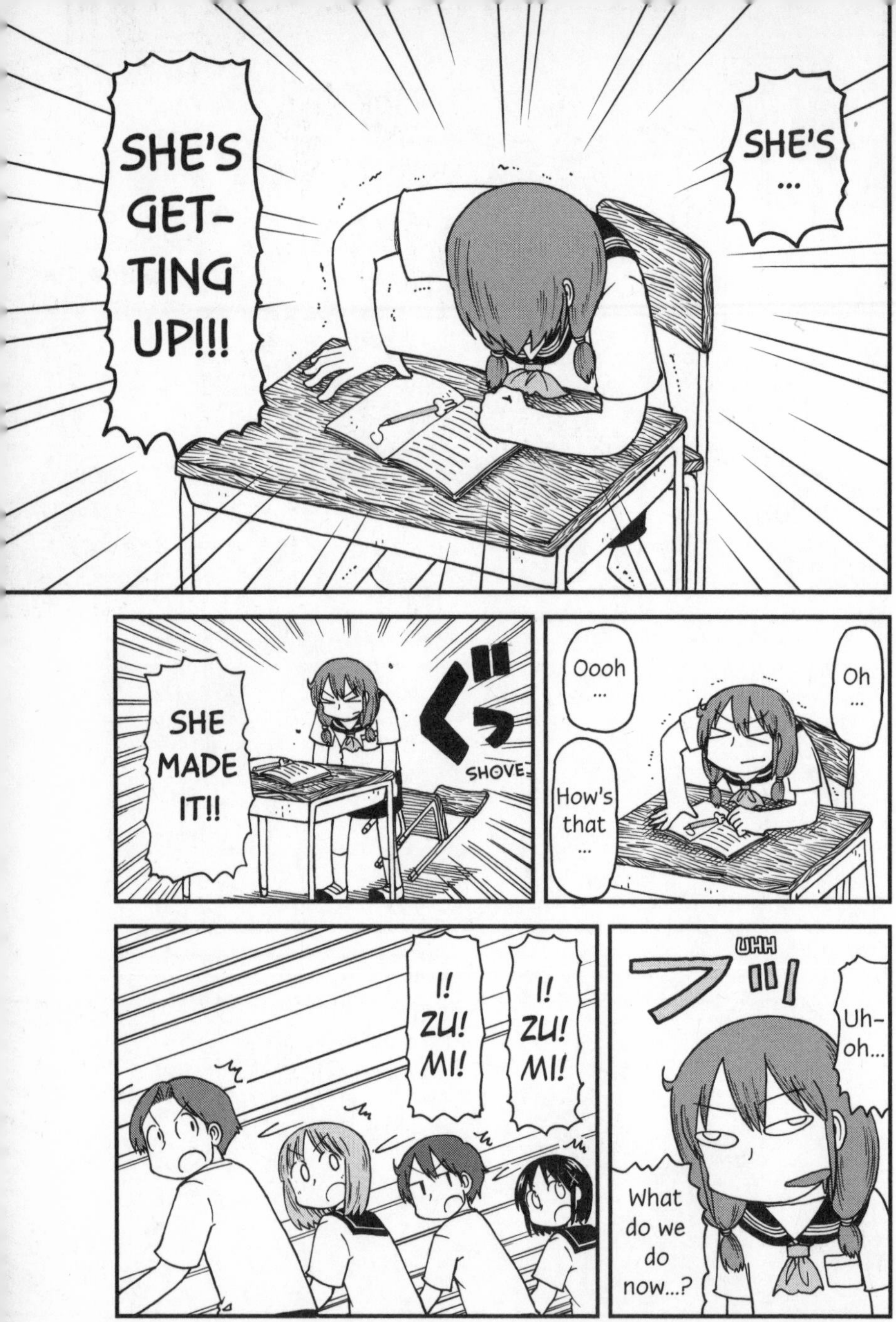
SHE'S ...
SHE'S GET-TING UP!!!
Oh ...
Oooh ...
How's that ...
ぐっ
SHOVE
SHE MADE IT!!
ブッ
UHH
Uh-oh...
What do we do now...?
I! ZU! MI!
I! ZU! MI!

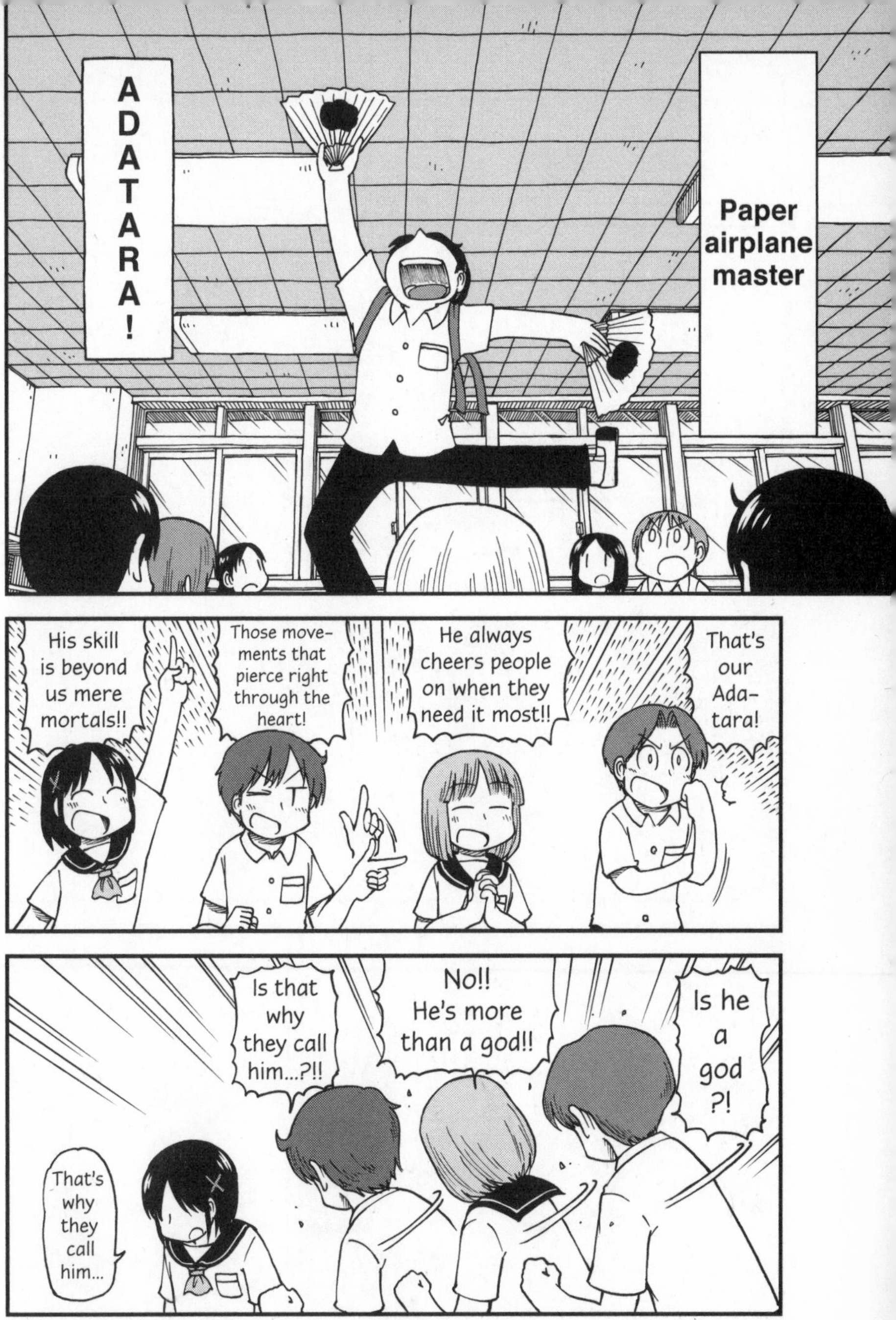
Paper airplane master
ADATARA!
That's our Adatara!
He always cheers people on when they need it most!!
Those movements that pierce right through the heart!
His skill is beyond us mere mortals!!
Is he a god?!
No!! He's more than a god!!
Is that why they call him...?!!
That's why they call him...

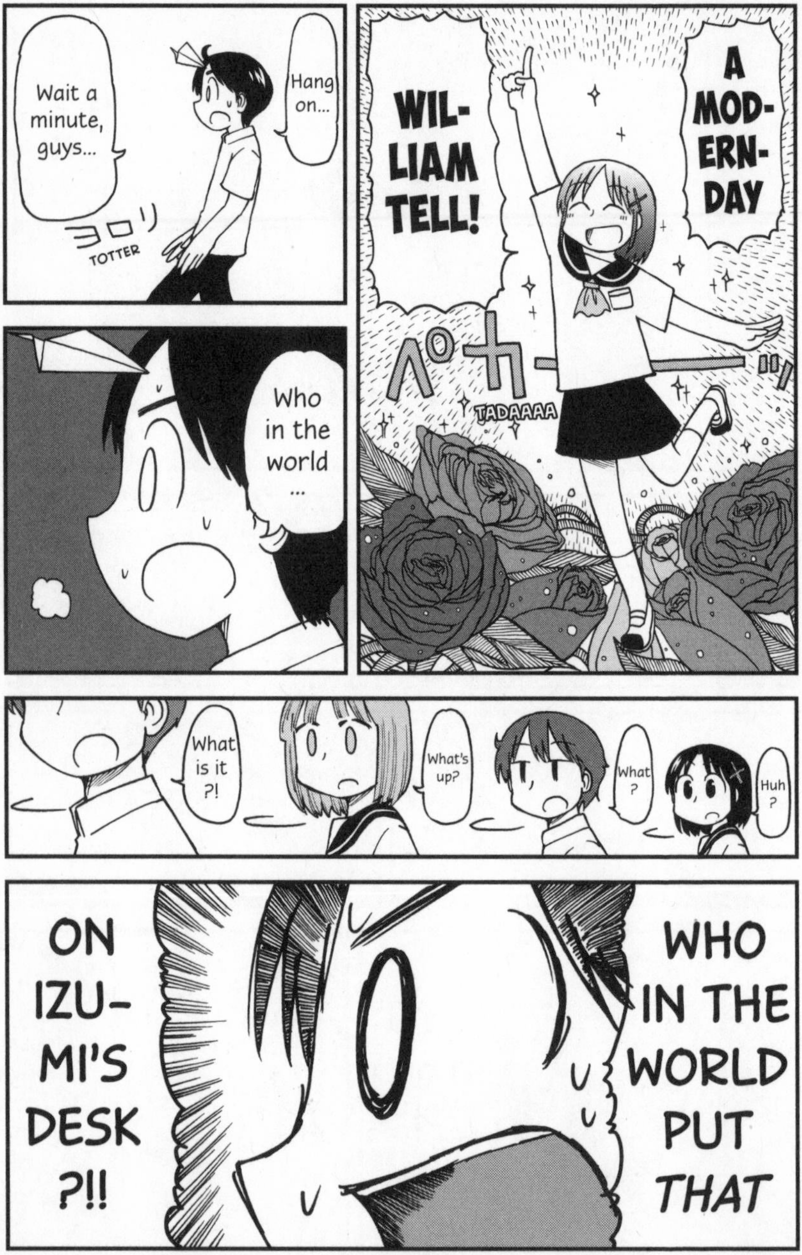
A MODERN-DAY
WILLIAM TELL!
ヘカー
TADAAAA
Hang on...
Wait a minute, guys...
ヨロリ
TOTTER
Who in the world ...
Huh ?
What ?
What's up?
What is it ?!
WHO IN THE WORLD PUT THAT
ON IZUMI'S DESK ?!!

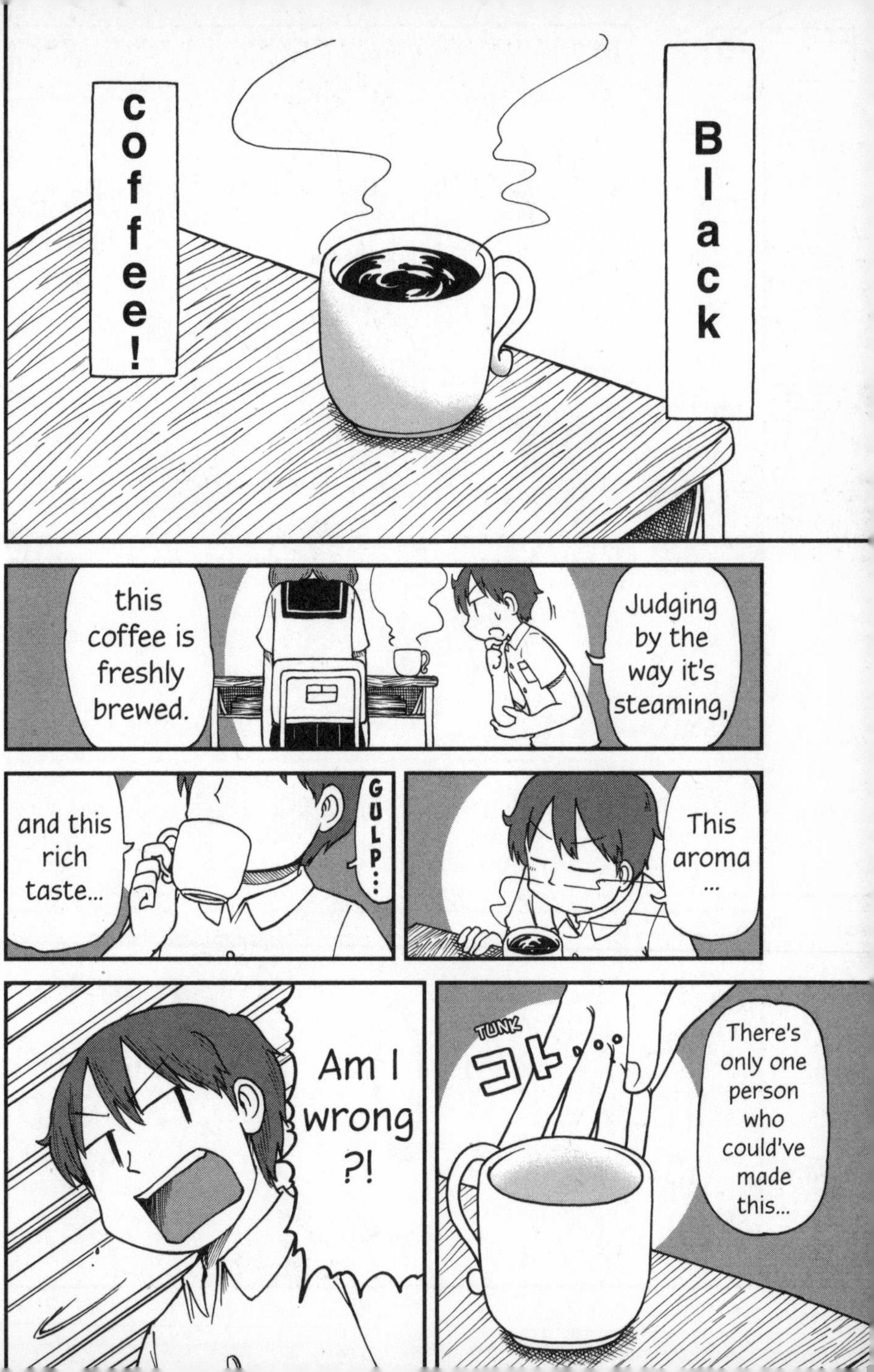
Black
coffee!
Judging by the way it's steaming,
this coffee is freshly brewed.
This aroma ...
GULP...
and this rich taste...
TUNK
There's only one person who could've made this...
Am I wrong?!

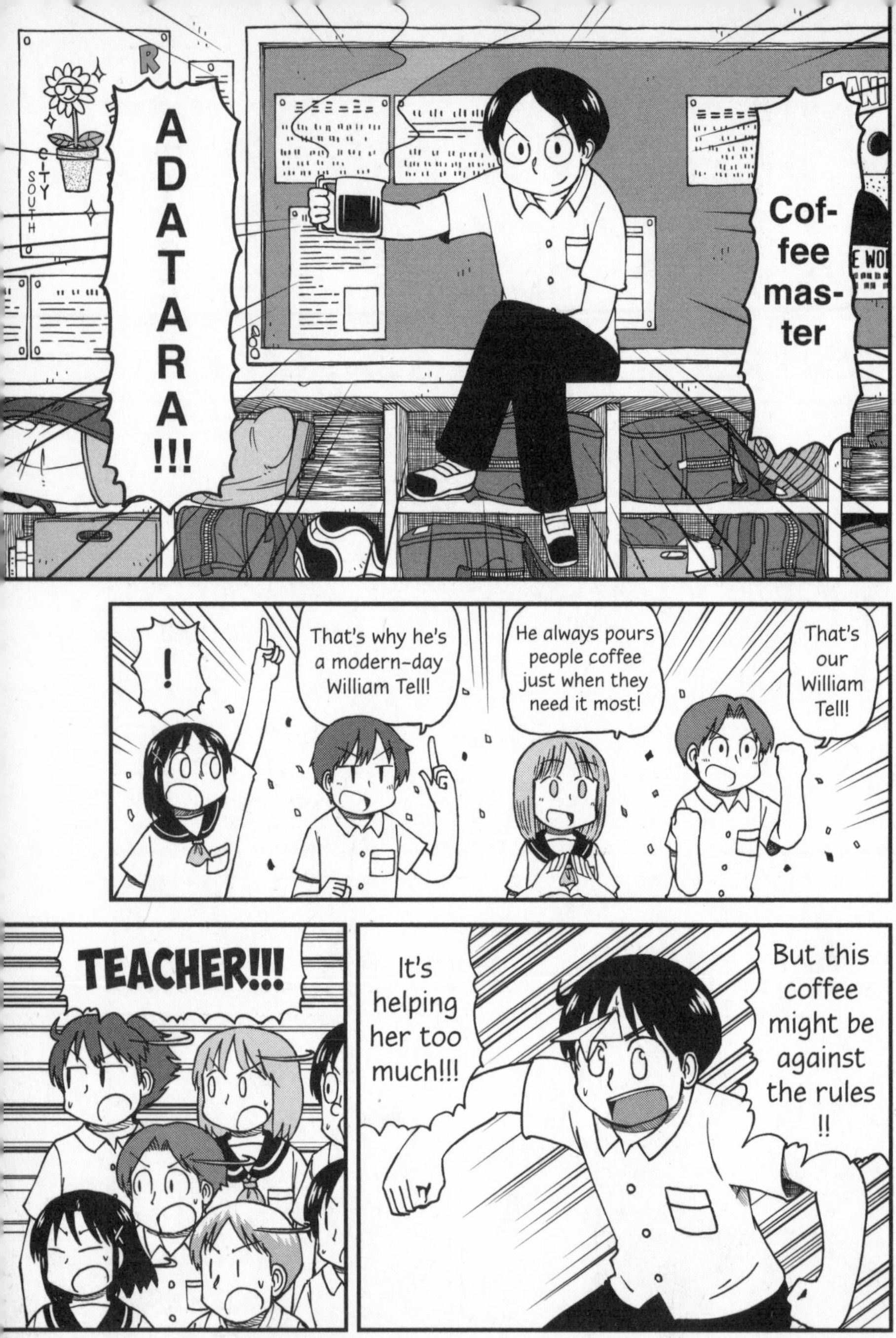
Cof-fee mas-ter
ADATARA!!!
That's our William Tell!
He always pours people coffee just when they need it most!
That's why he's a modern-day William Tell!
!
But this coffee might be against the rules !!
It's helping her too much!!!
TEACHER!!!

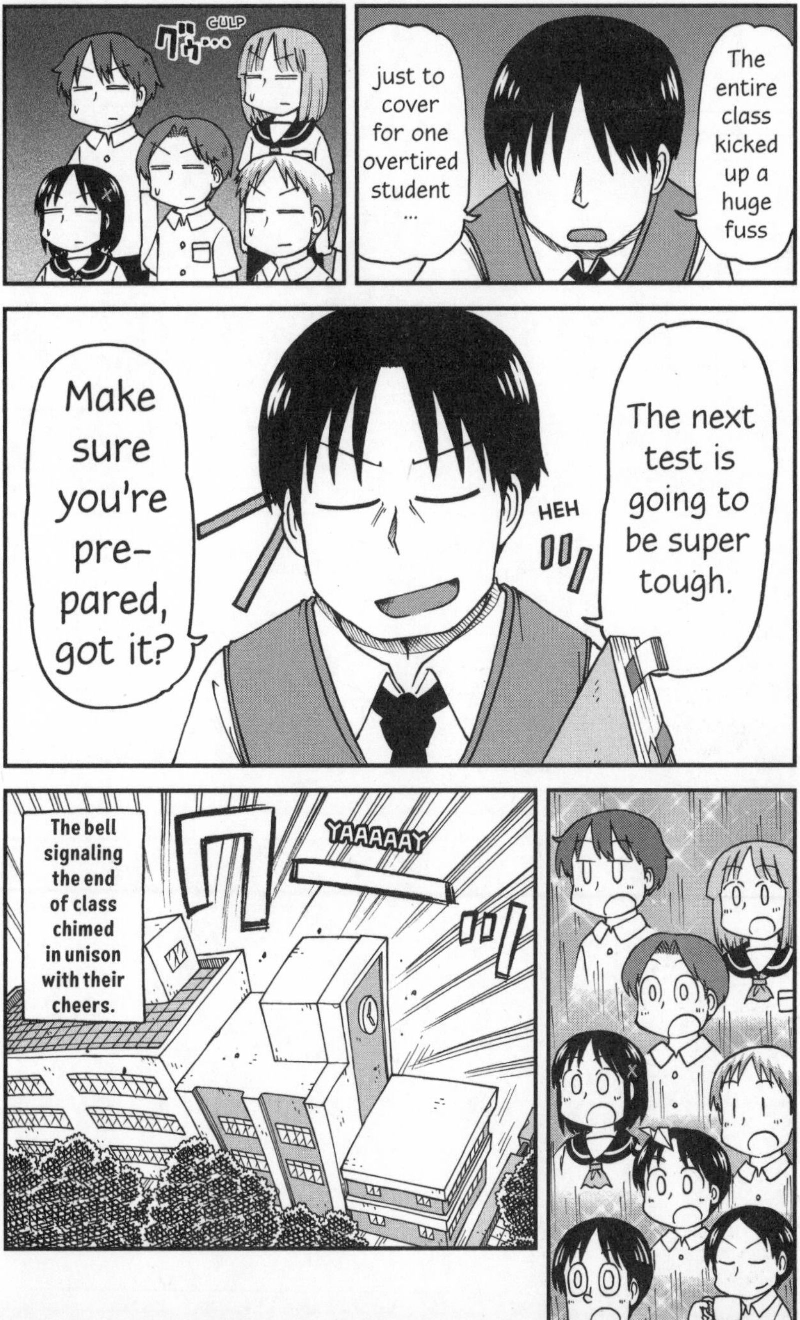
The entire class kicked up a huge fuss
just to cover for one overtired student ...
GULP
グゥ…
The next test is going to be super tough.
HEH
Make sure you're pre-pared, got it?
YAAAAAY
The bell signaling the end of class chimed in unison with their cheers.

Sch.
CITY South Middle School
tile
Sch.
tofu
CITY South High School
CITY South HS Day Care

CITY

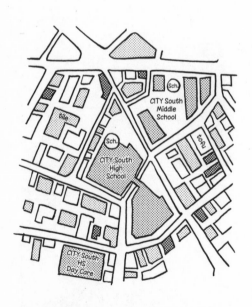

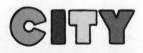

MONDAY
16:00

CITY
South
Middle
School

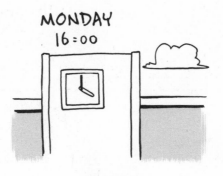

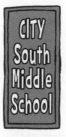

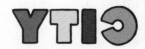

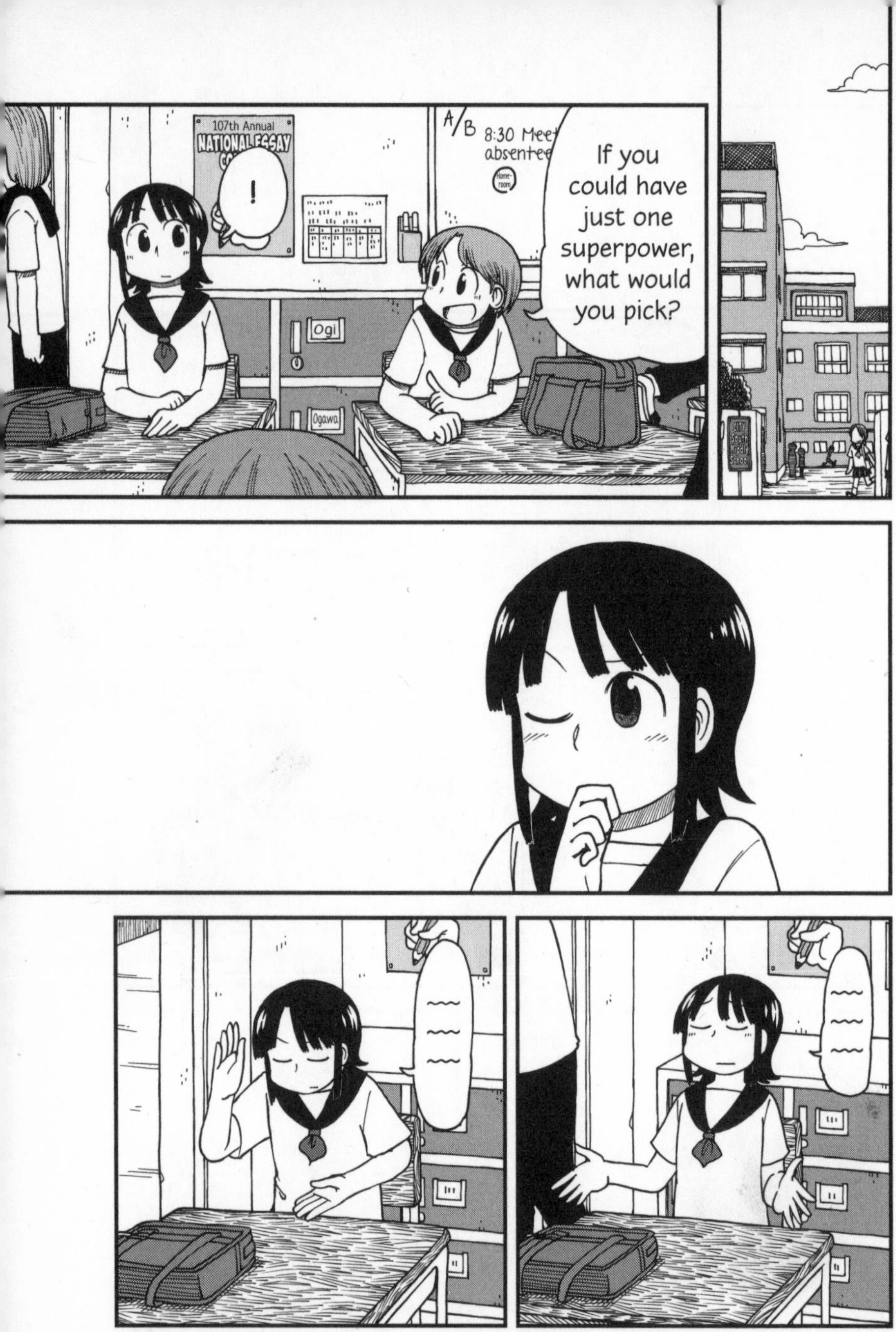
107th Annual
NATIONAL ESSAY CO
A/B
8:30 Meet
absentee
Home-room
Ogi
Ogawa
If you could have just one superpower, what would you pick?
!
~~~ ~~~ ~~~
~~~ ~~~ ~~~

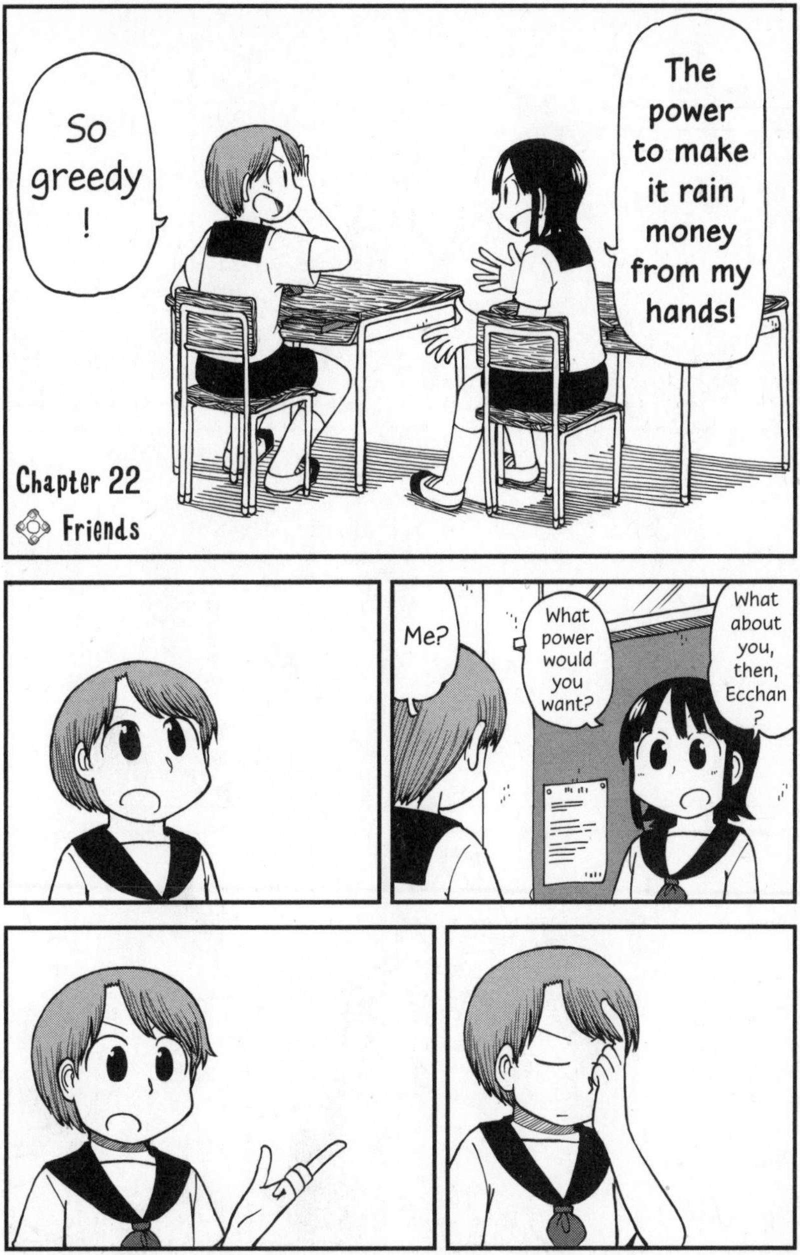
The power to make it rain money from my hands!
So greedy!
Chapter 22
Friends
What about you, then, Ecchan?
What power would you want?
Me?

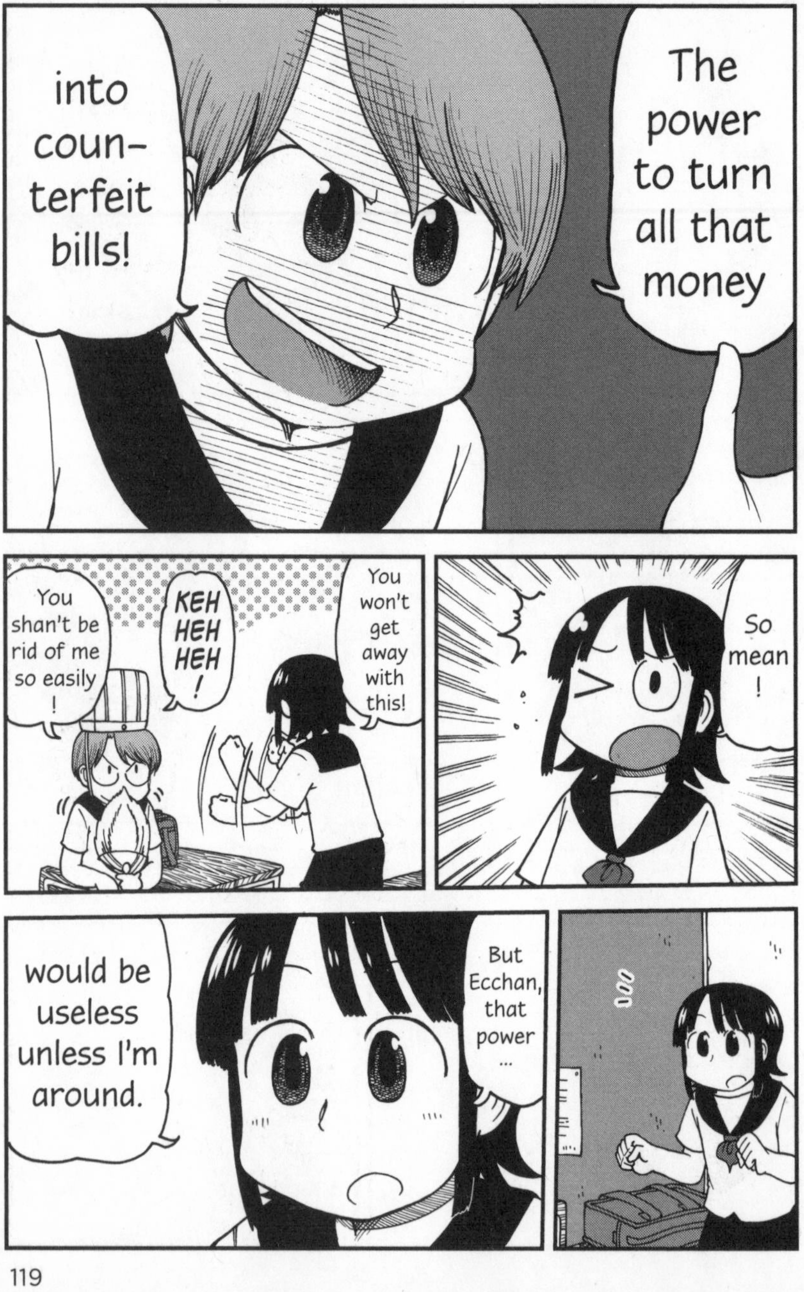
The power to turn all that money
into coun-terfeit bills!
So mean!
You won't get away with this!
KEH HEH HEH!
You shan't be rid of me so easily!
But Ecchan, that power...
would be useless unless I'm around.

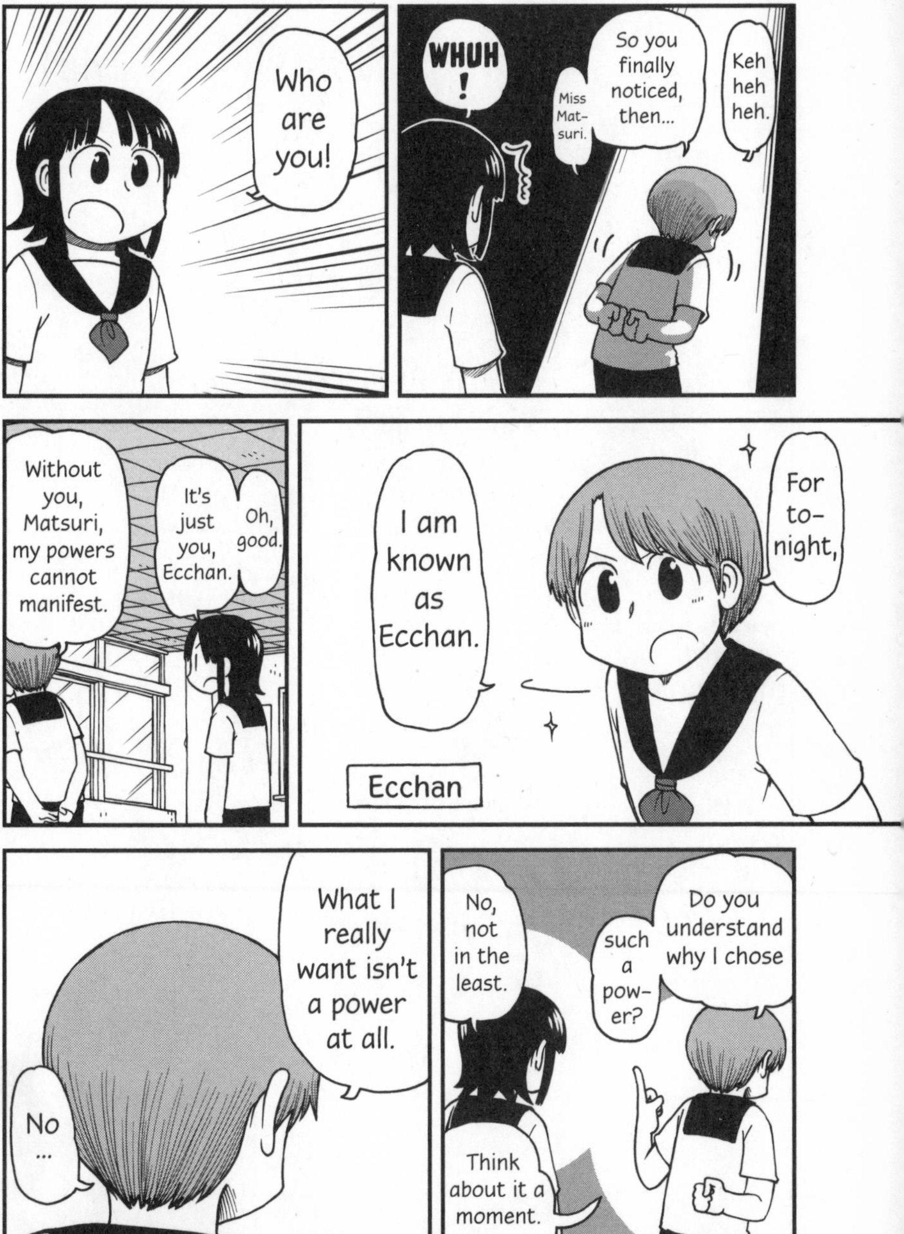
Keh heh heh.
So you finally noticed, then...
Miss Mat-suri.
WHUH !
Who are you!
For to-night,
I am known as Ecchan.
Ecchan
Oh, good.
It's just you, Ecchan.
Without you, Matsuri, my powers cannot manifest.
Do you understand why I chose
such a pow-er?
No, not in the least.
Think about it a moment.
What I really want isn't a power at all.
No ...

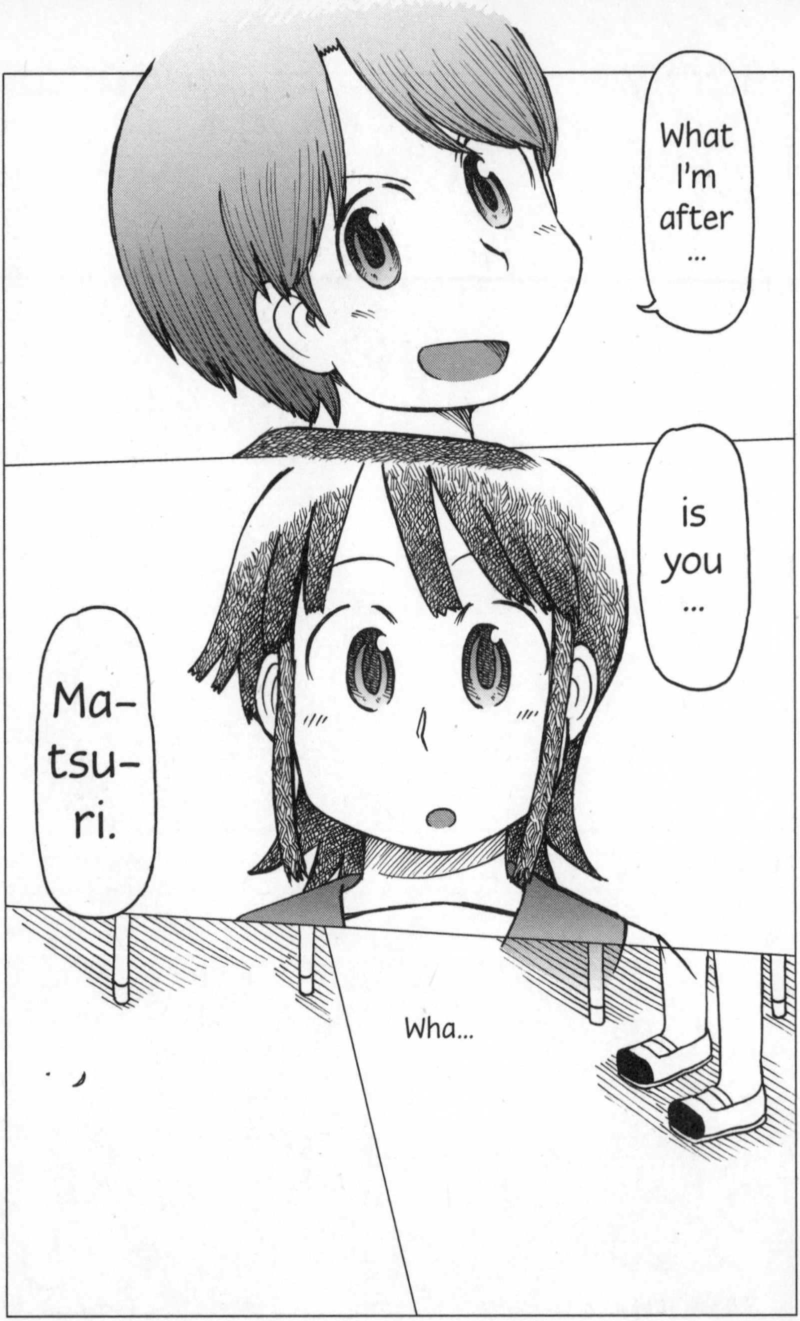
What I'm after ...
is you ...
Ma-tsu-ri.
Wha...

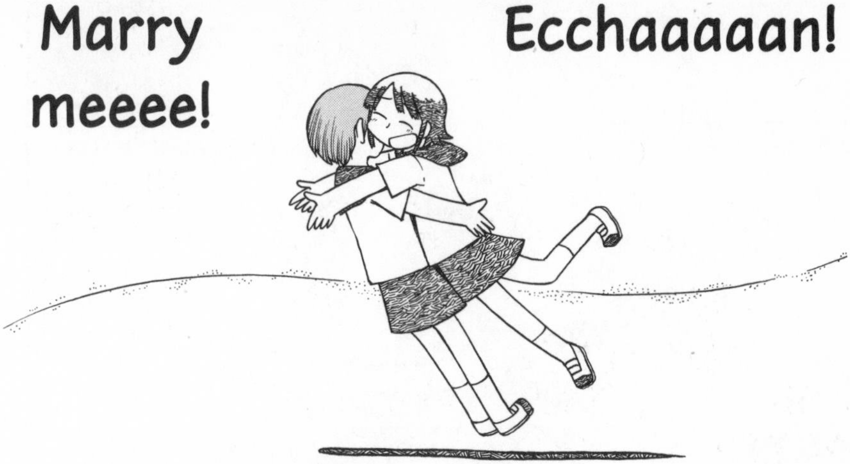
Ecchaaaaan!
Marry meeee!

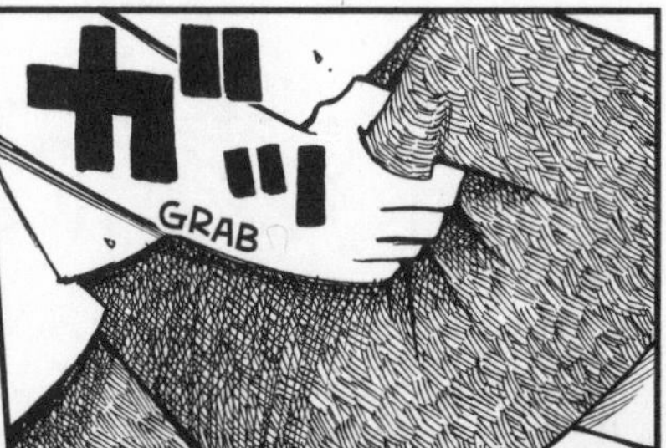
ガッ
GRAB

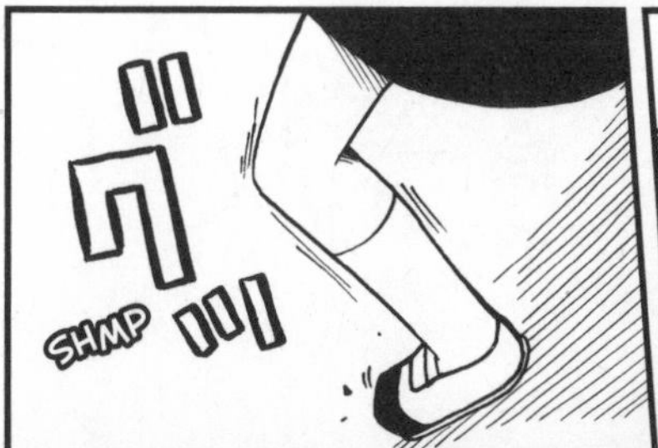
グッ
SHMP

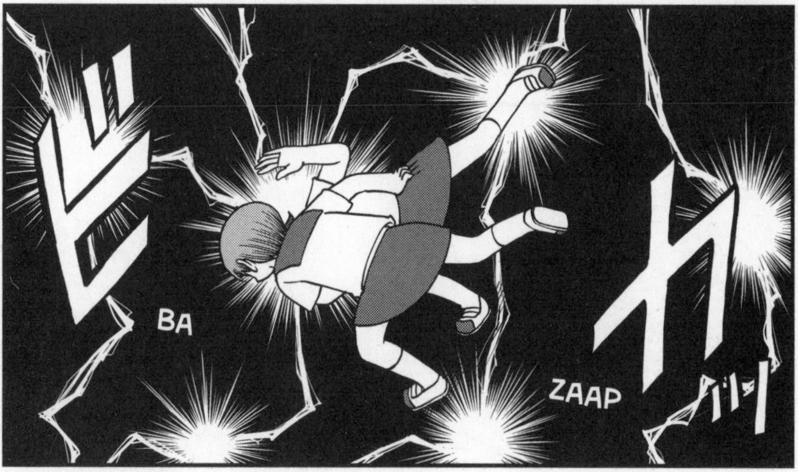
BA
ZAAP

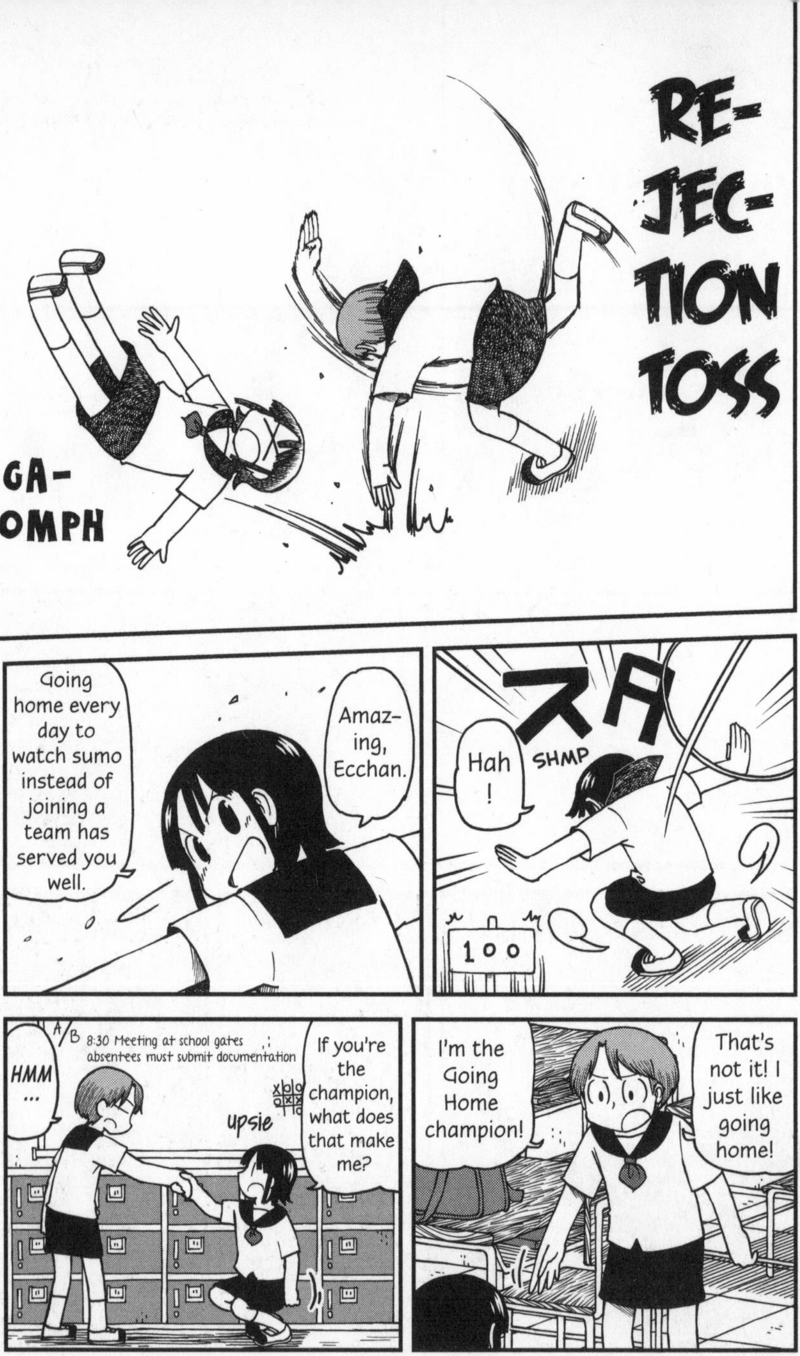
RE-JEC-TION TOSS
GA-OOMPH
スタ
Hah!
SHMP
100
Amazing, Ecchan.
Going home every day to watch sumo instead of joining a team has served you well.
That's not it! I just like going home!
I'm the Going Home champion!
If you're the champion, what does that make me?
upsie
8:30 Meeting at school gates
absentees must submit documentation
HMM...
A/B

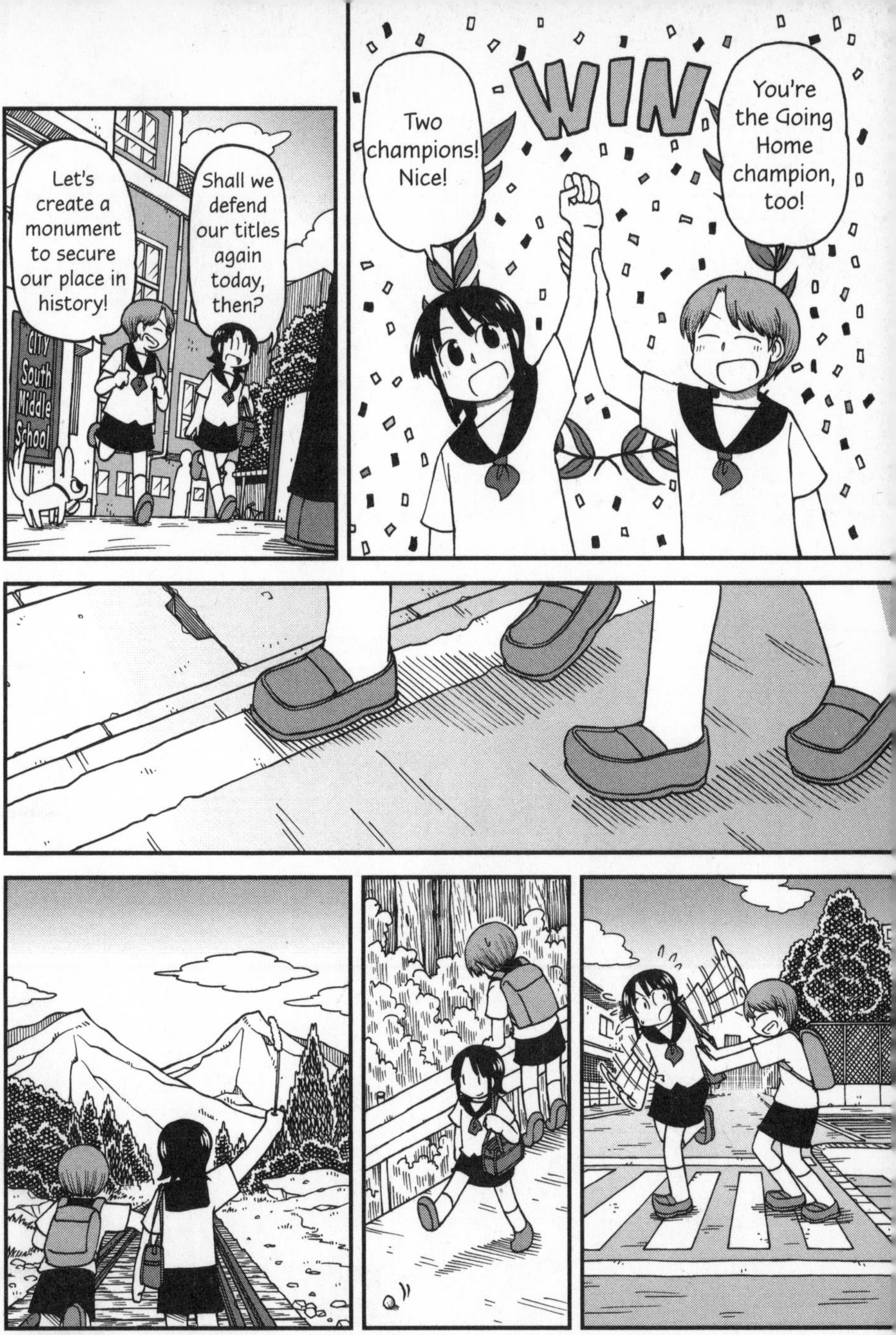
You're the Going Home champion, too!
WIN
Two champions! Nice!
Shall we defend our titles again today, then?
Let's create a monument to secure our place in history!
City South Middle School

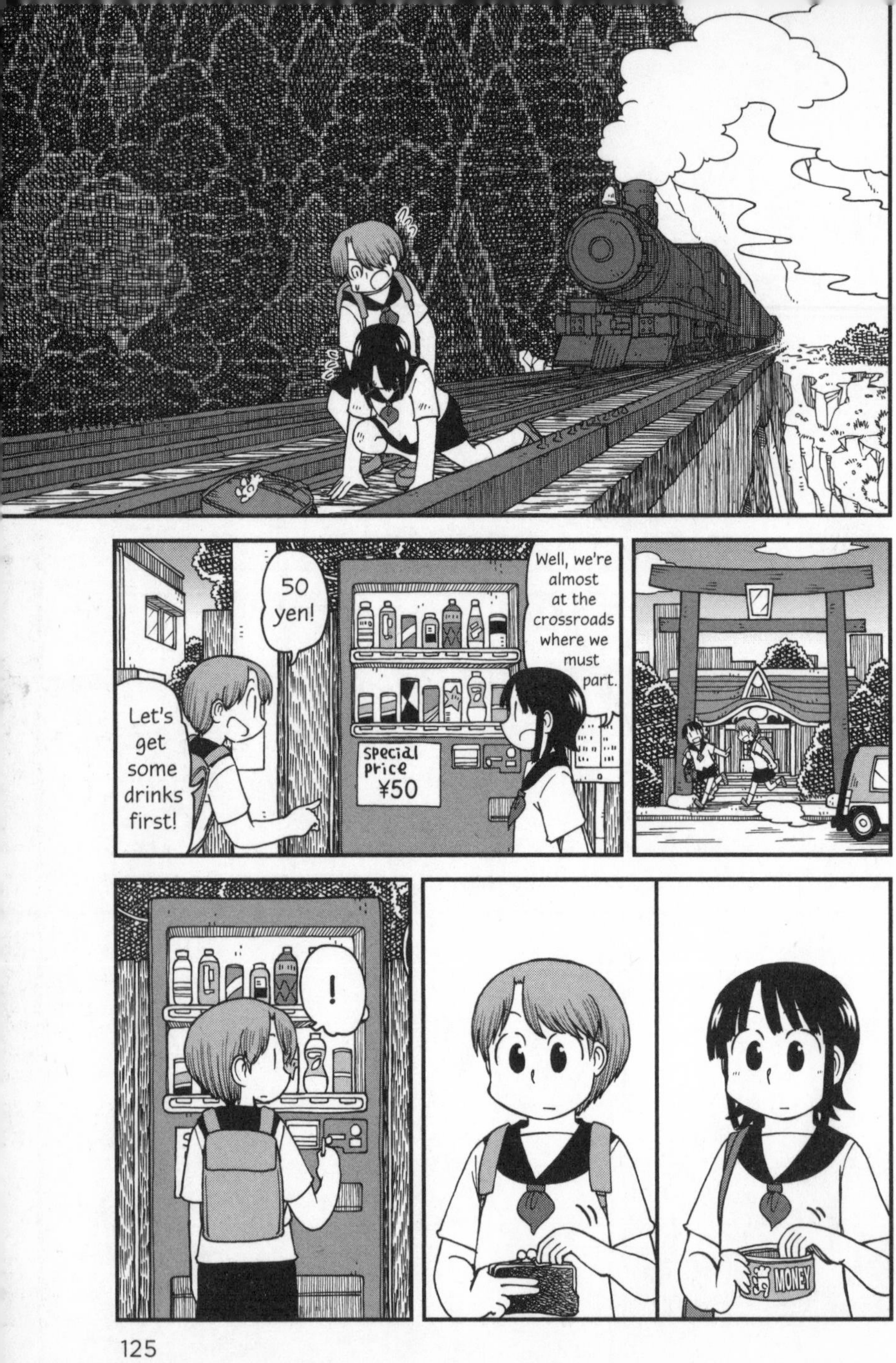
Well, we're almost at the crossroads where we must part.
50 yen!
Let's get some drinks first!
Special price ¥50
!
MONEY

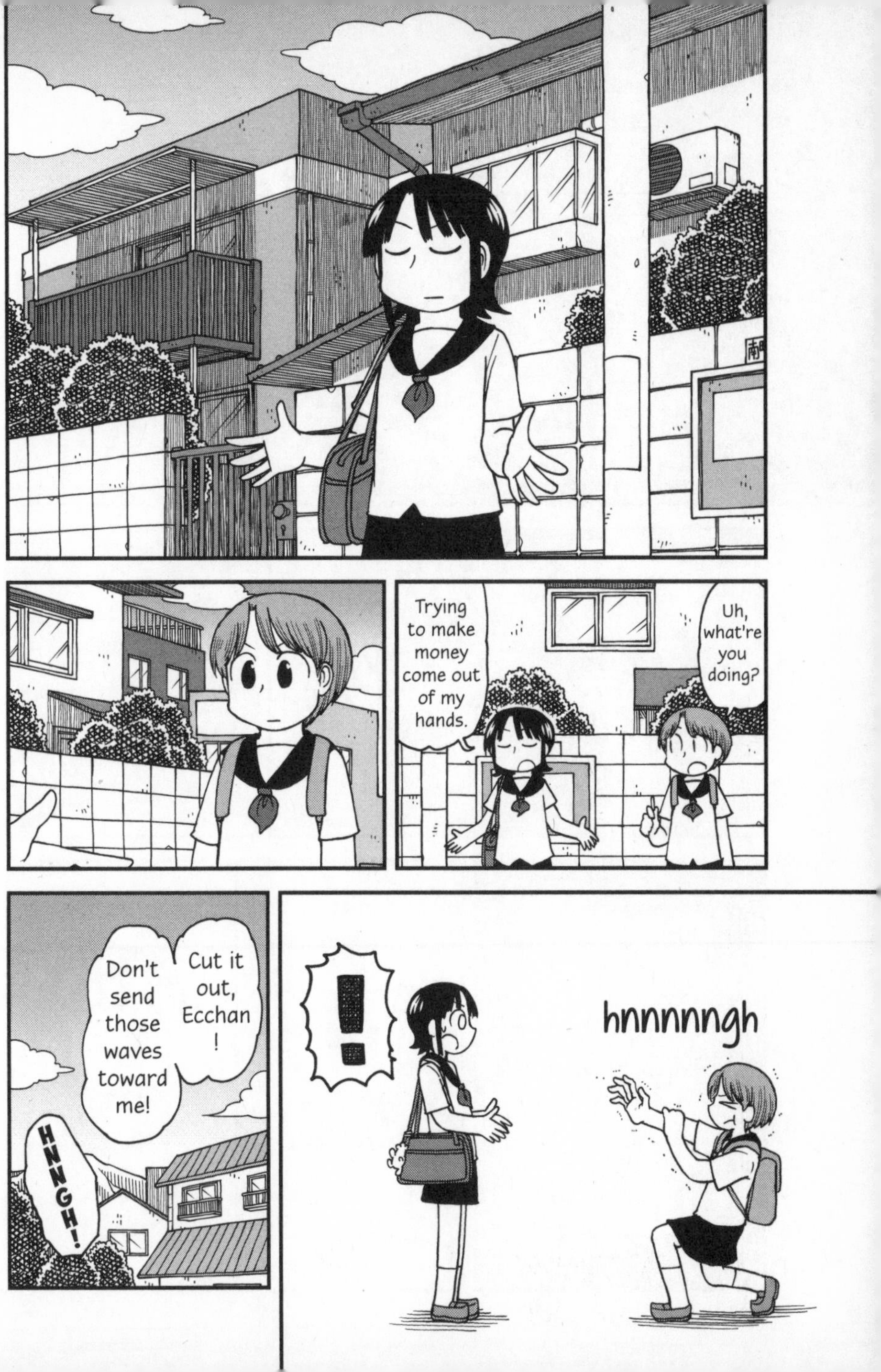
Uh, what're you doing?
Trying to make money come out of my hands.
!!
hnnnnngh
Cut it out, Ecchan!
Don't send those waves toward me!
HNNGH!

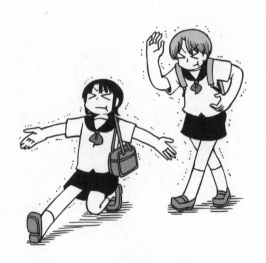

CITY

CITY

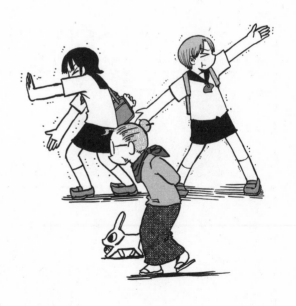

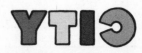

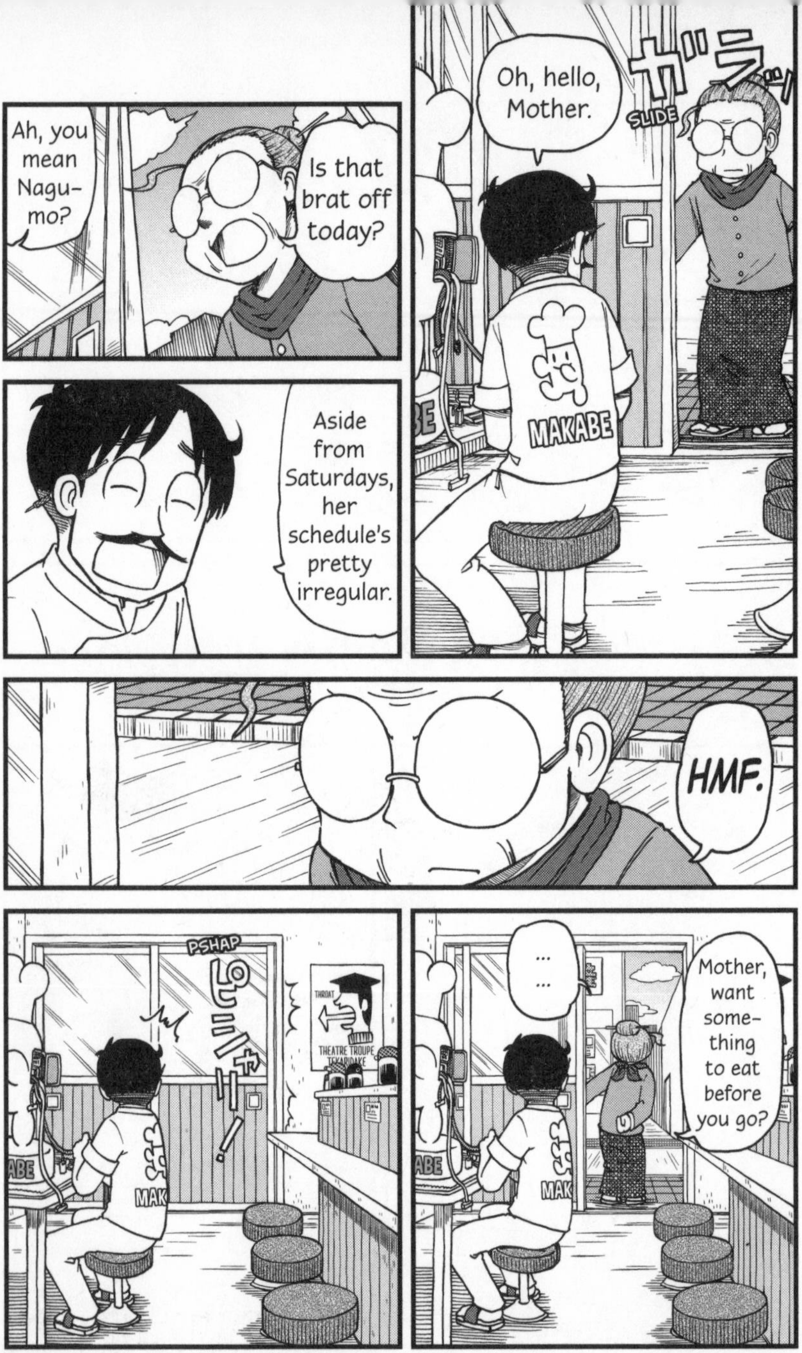
SLIDE
Oh, hello, Mother.
MAKABE
Is that brat off today?
Ah, you mean Nagu-mo?
Aside from Saturdays, her schedule's pretty irregular.
HMF.
Mother, want some-thing to eat before you go?
... ...
PSHAP
THROAT
THEATRE TROUPE

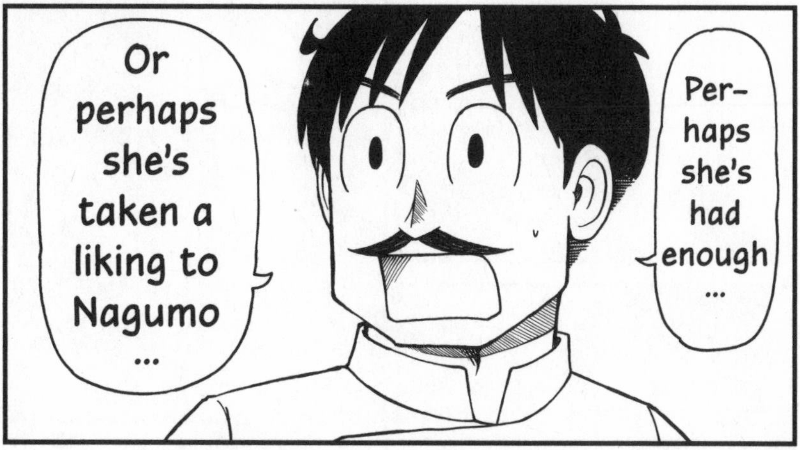
Per-haps she's had enough...
Or perhaps she's taken a liking to Nagumo...

Chapter 23 ◇ Back Alley Revenge

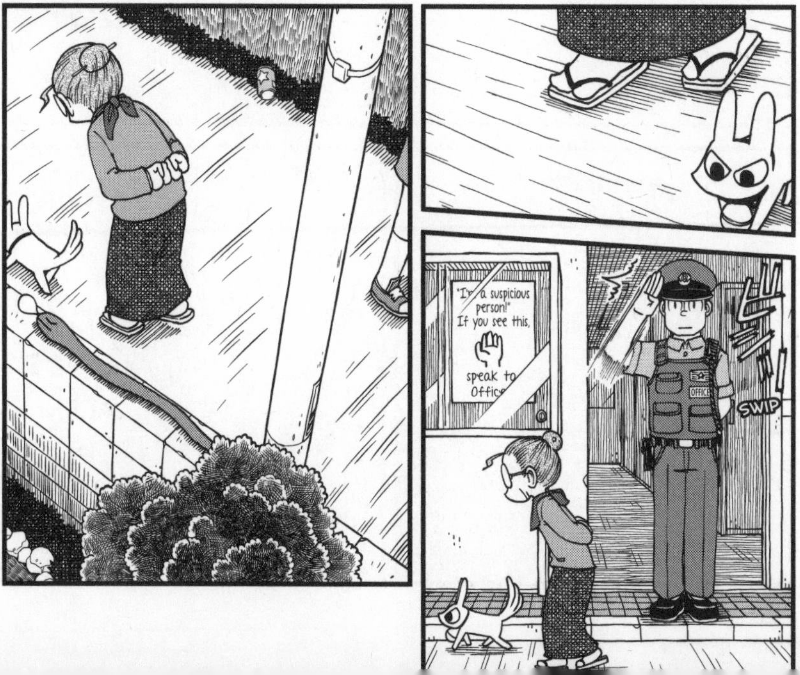
"I'm a suspicious person!" If you see this, speak to Offic
SWIP

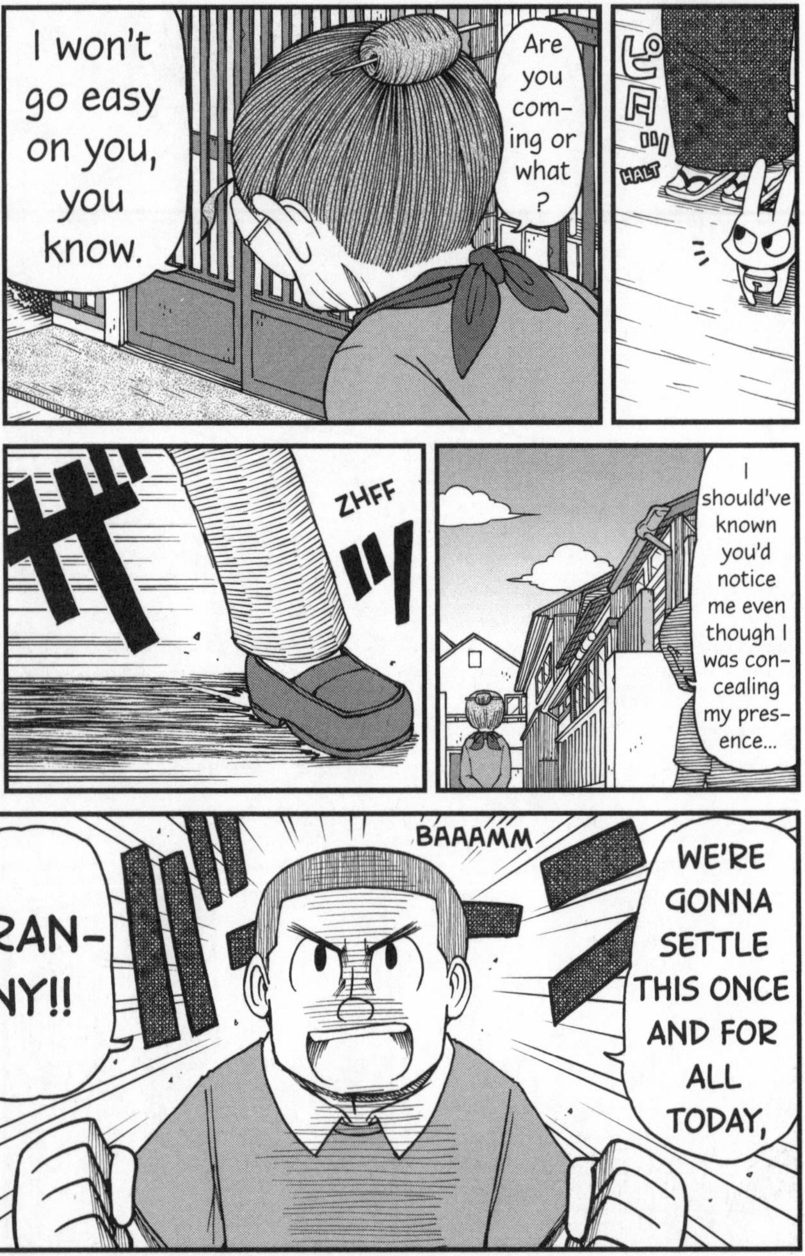
HALT
Are you com-ing or what?
I won't go easy on you, you know.
I should've known you'd notice me even though I was con-cealing my pres-ence...
ZHFF
BAAAMM
WE'RE GONNA SETTLE THIS ONCE AND FOR ALL TODAY,
GRAN-NY!!

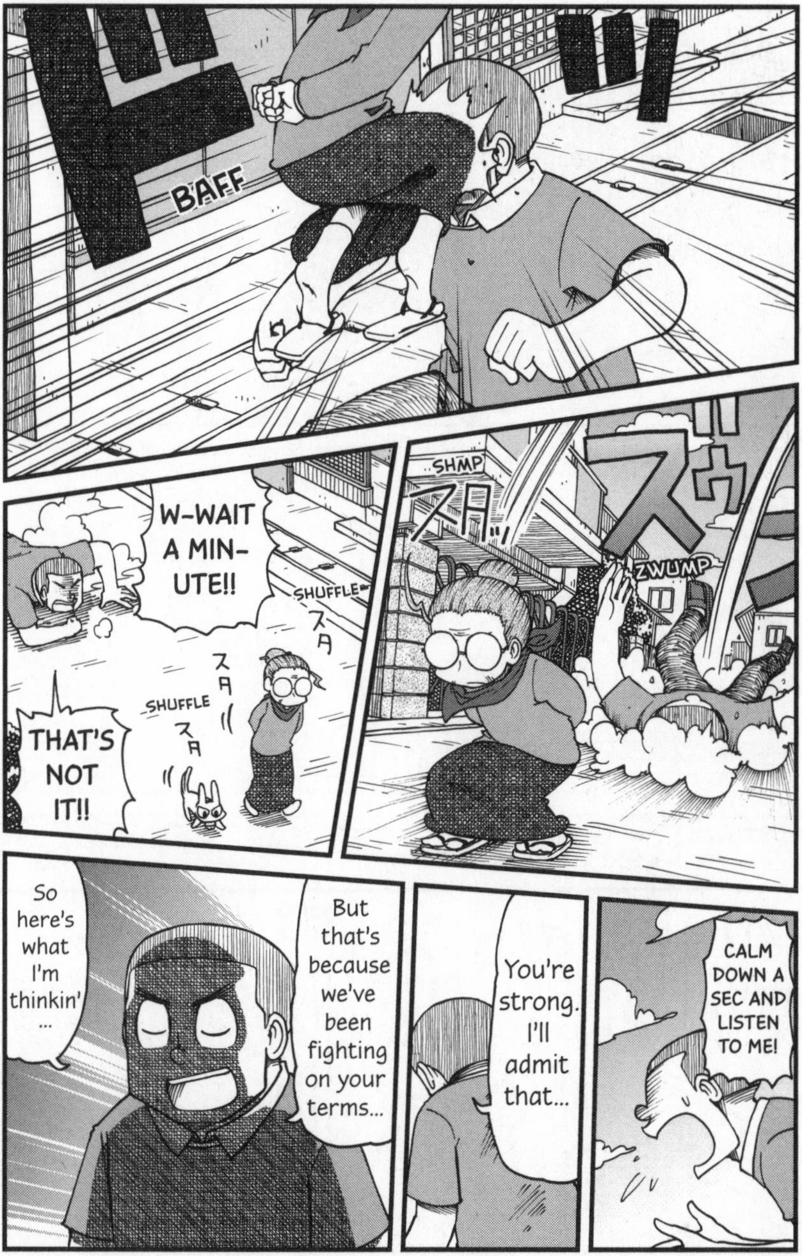
BAFF
SHMP
ZWUMP
W-WAIT A MIN-UTE!!
SHUFFLE
SHUFFLE
THAT'S NOT IT!!
CALM DOWN A SEC AND LISTEN TO ME!
You're strong. I'll admit that...
But that's because we've been fighting on your terms...
So here's what I'm thinkin'...

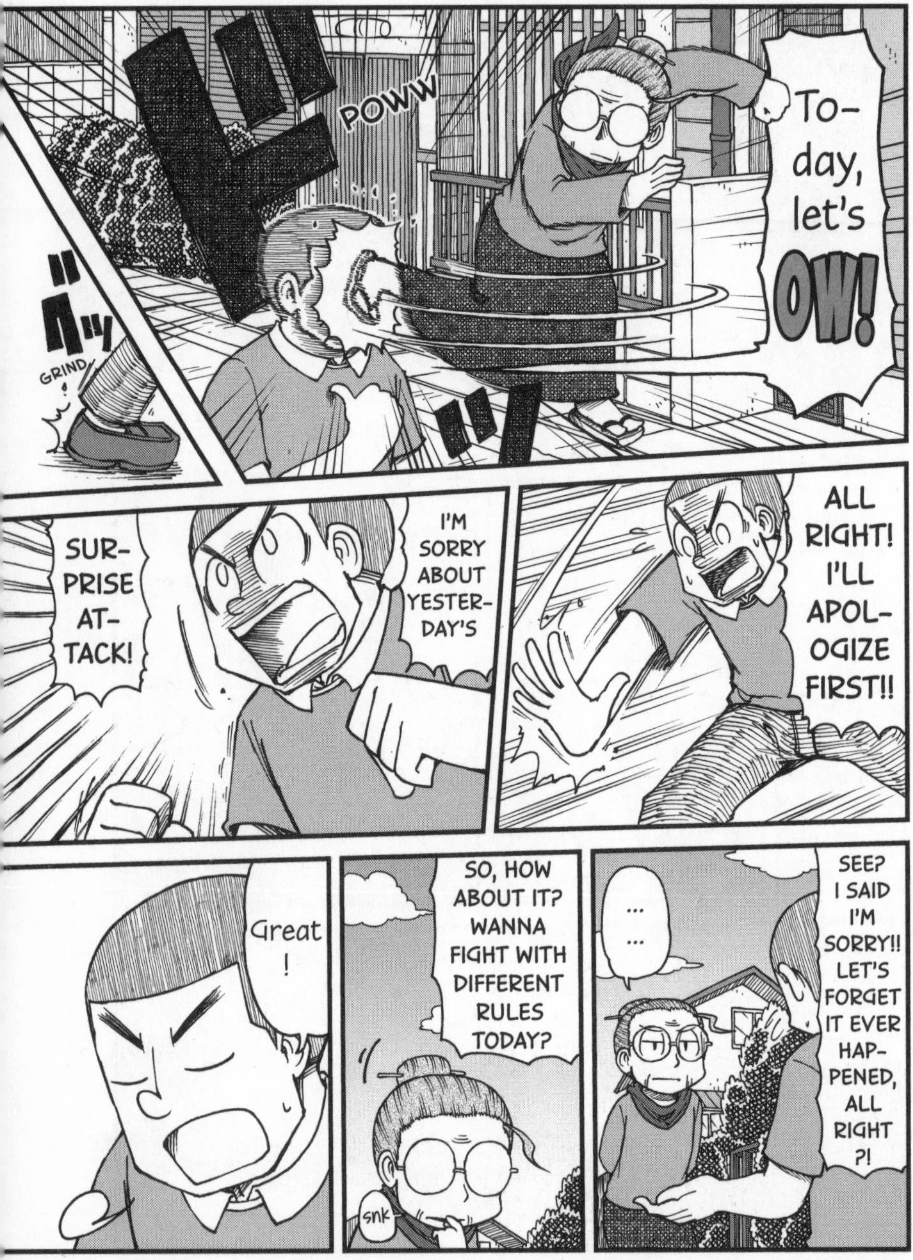
Today, let's OW!
POWW
GRIND
ALL RIGHT! I'LL APOLOGIZE FIRST!!
I'M SORRY ABOUT YESTERDAY'S
SURPRISE ATTACK!
SEE? I SAID I'M SORRY!! LET'S FORGET IT EVER HAPPENED, ALL RIGHT?!
... ...
SO, HOW ABOUT IT? WANNA FIGHT WITH DIFFERENT RULES TODAY?
snk
Great!

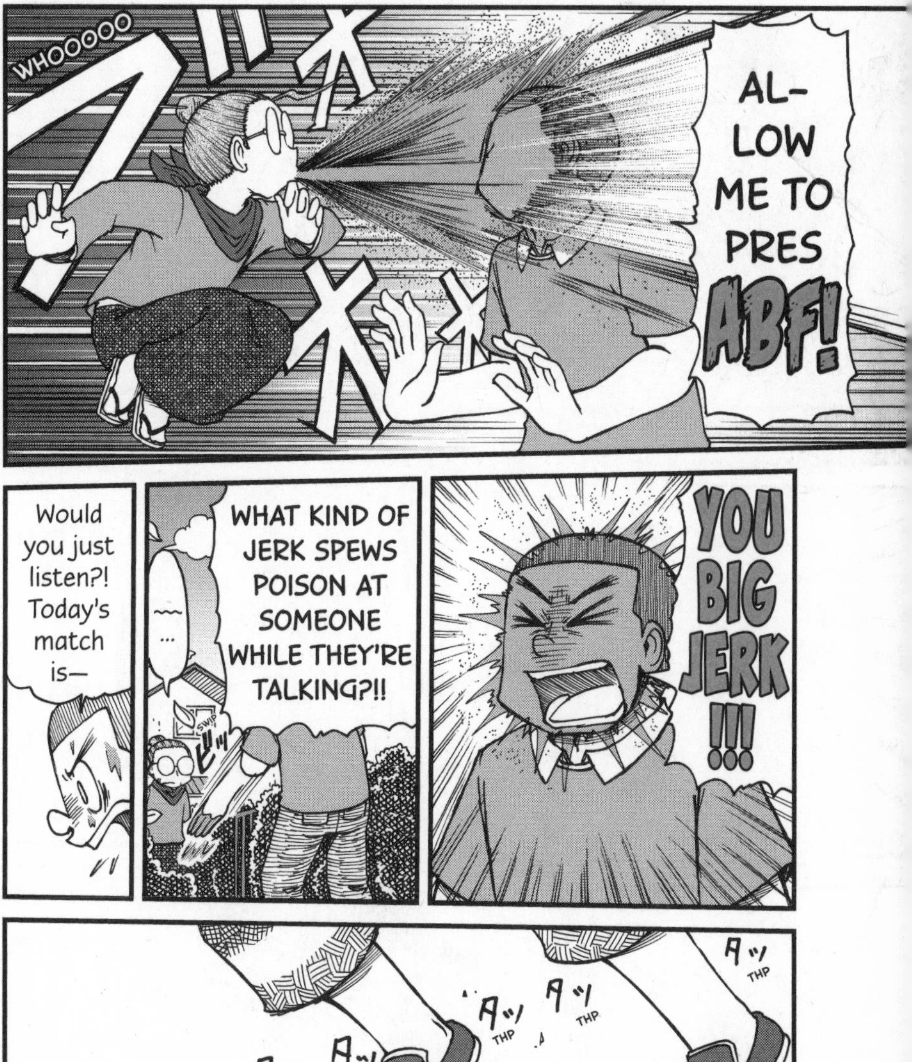
AL-LOW ME TO PRES ABF!
WHOOOOO
YOU BIG JERK!!!
WHAT KIND OF JERK SPEWS POISON AT SOMEONE WHILE THEY'RE TALKING?!!
~~ ...
SWIP
Would you just listen?! Today's match is—
THP
THP
THP
THP
THP
THP
THP
THP

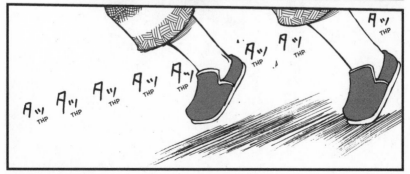

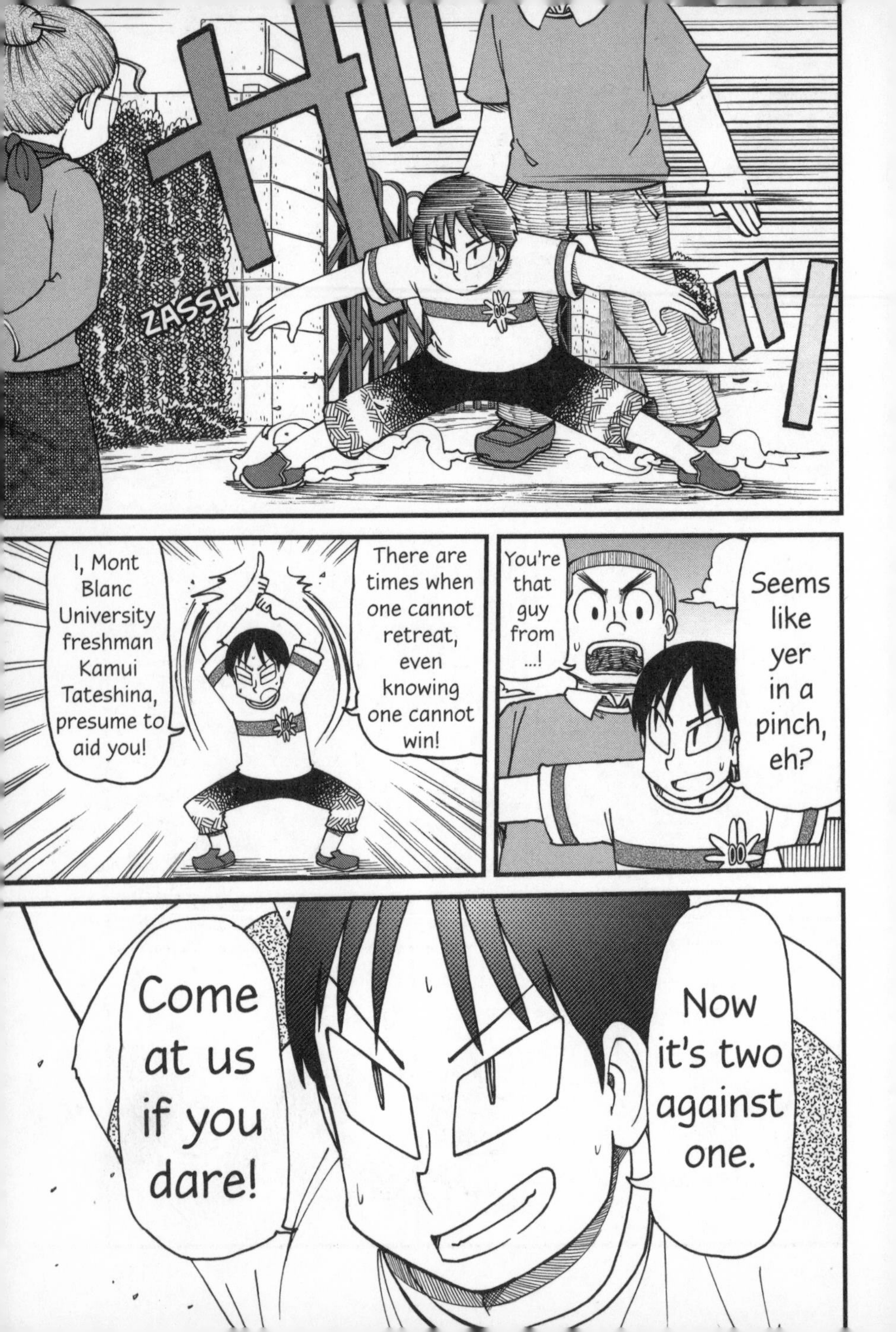
ZASSH
Seems like yer in a pinch, eh?
You're that guy from ...!
There are times when one cannot retreat, even knowing one cannot win!
I, Mont Blanc University freshman Kamui Tateshina, presume to aid you!
Now it's two against one.
Come at us if you dare!

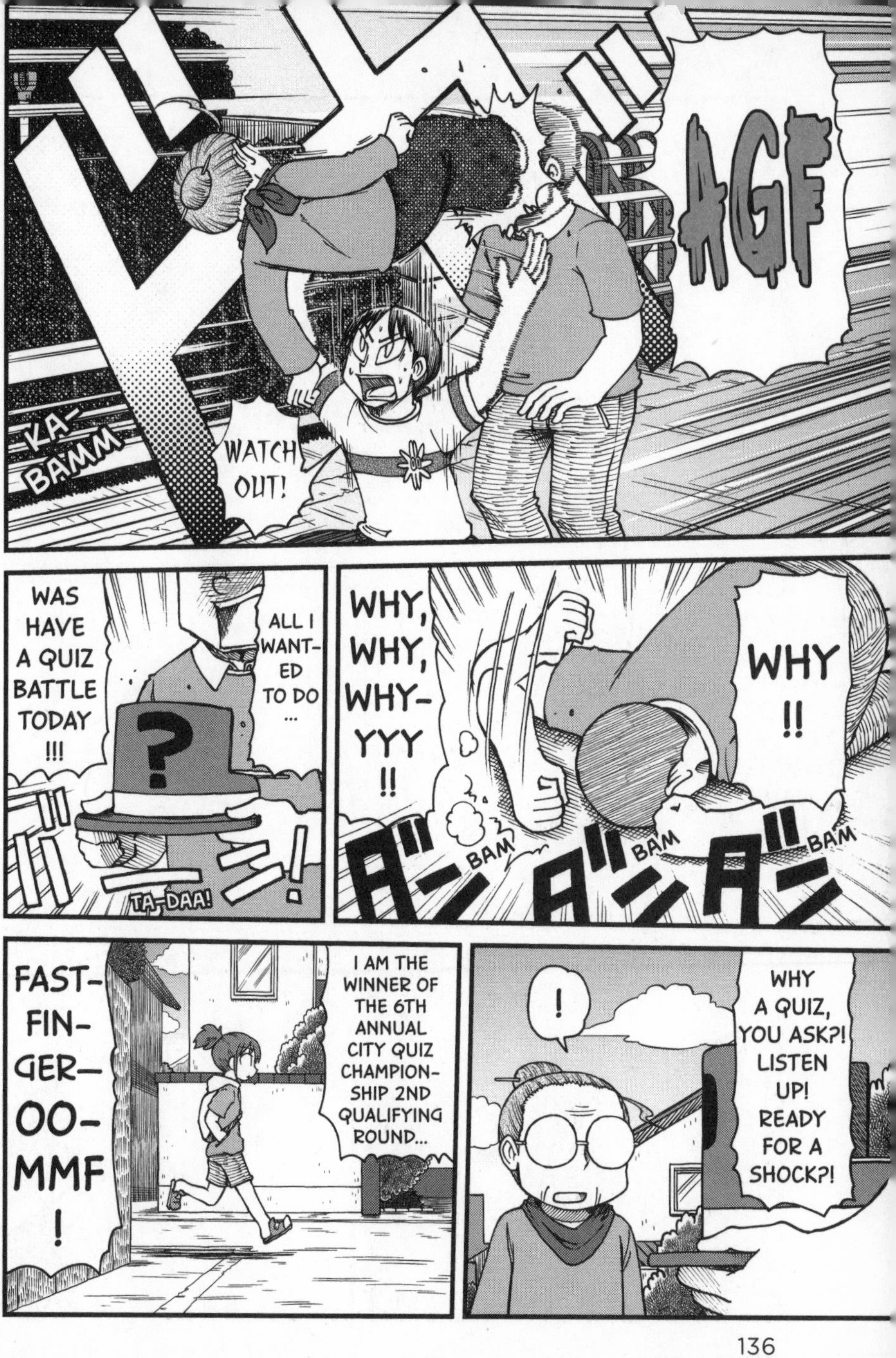
AGF
WATCH OUT!
KA-BAMM
WHY !!
WHY, WHY, WHY-YYY !!
BAM
BAM
BAM
ALL I WANT-ED TO DO ...
WAS HAVE A QUIZ BATTLE TODAY !!!
TA-DAA!
WHY A QUIZ, YOU ASK?! LISTEN UP! READY FOR A SHOCK?!
!
I AM THE WINNER OF THE 6TH ANNUAL CITY QUIZ CHAMPION-SHIP 2ND QUALIFYING ROUND...
FAST-FIN-GER—OO-MMF !

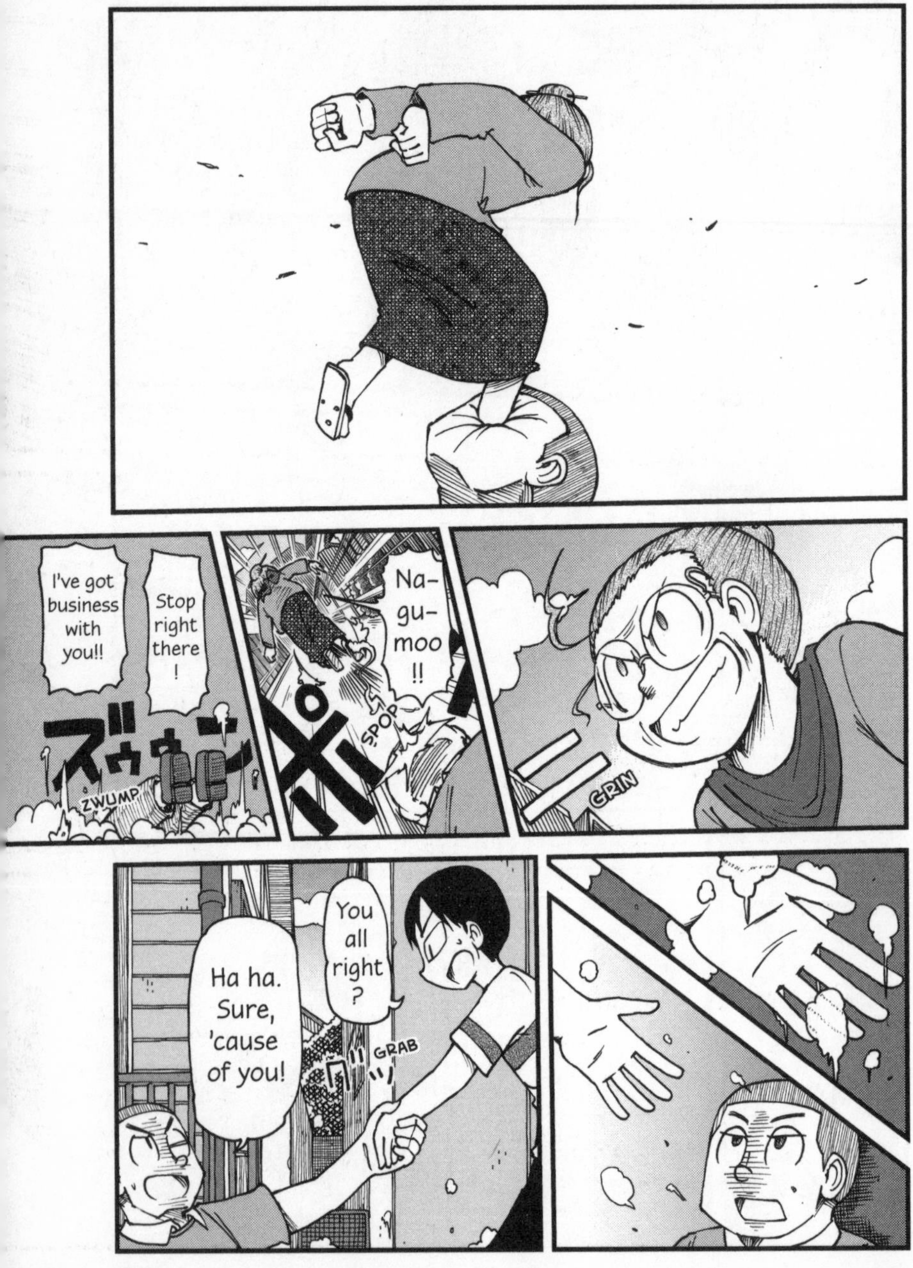
GRIN
Na-gu-moo!!
SPOP
Stop right there!
I've got business with you!!
ZWUMP
You all right?
Ha ha. Sure, 'cause of you!
GRAB

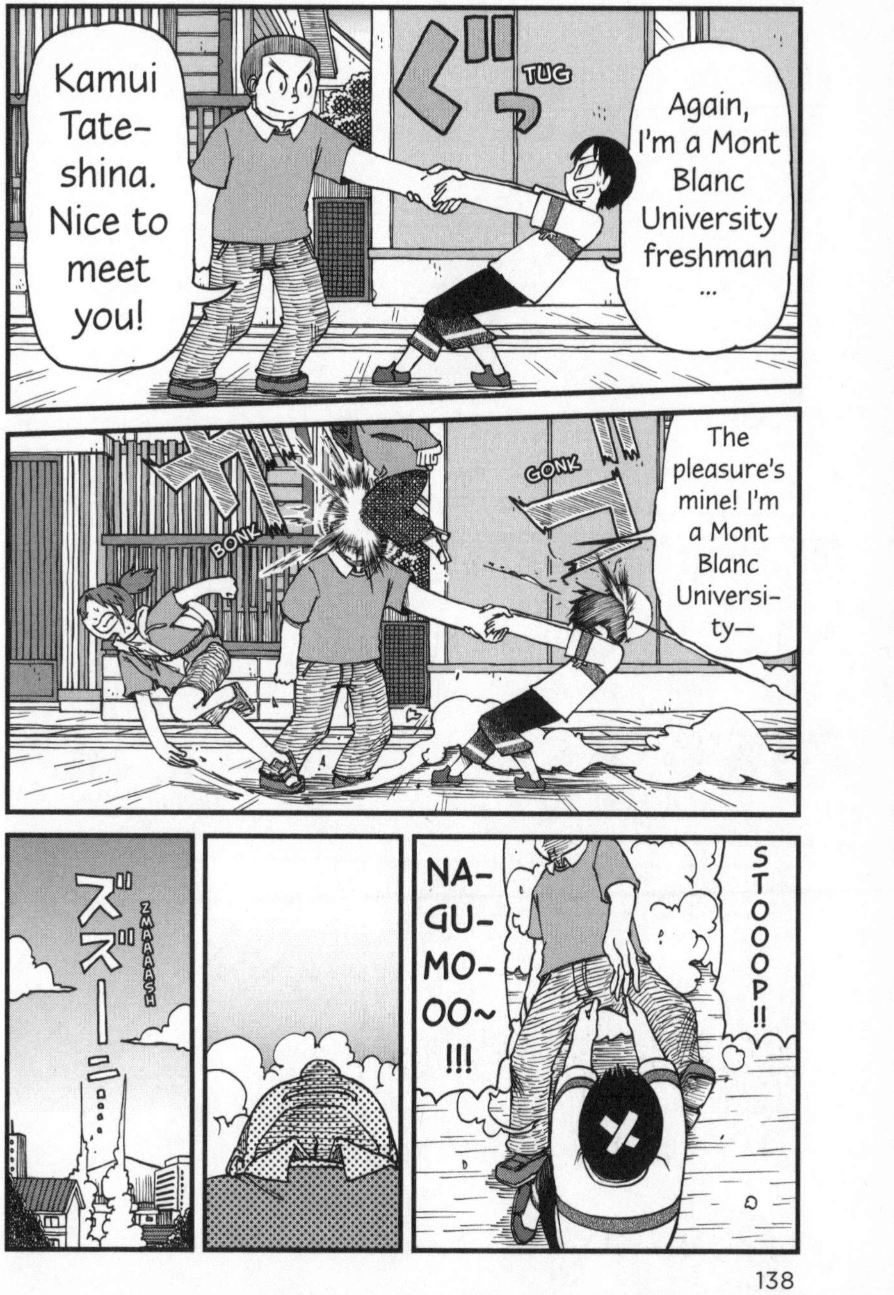
Again, I'm a Mont Blanc University freshman ...
TUG
Kamui Tate-shina. Nice to meet you!
The pleasure's mine! I'm a Mont Blanc Universi-ty—
GONK
BONK
STOOOP!!
NA-GU-MO-OO~ !!!
ZMAAAASH

CITY

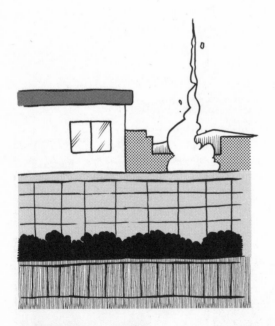

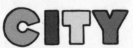

CITY

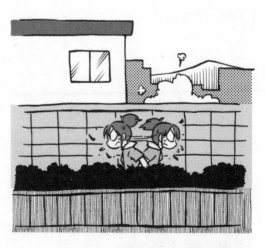

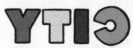

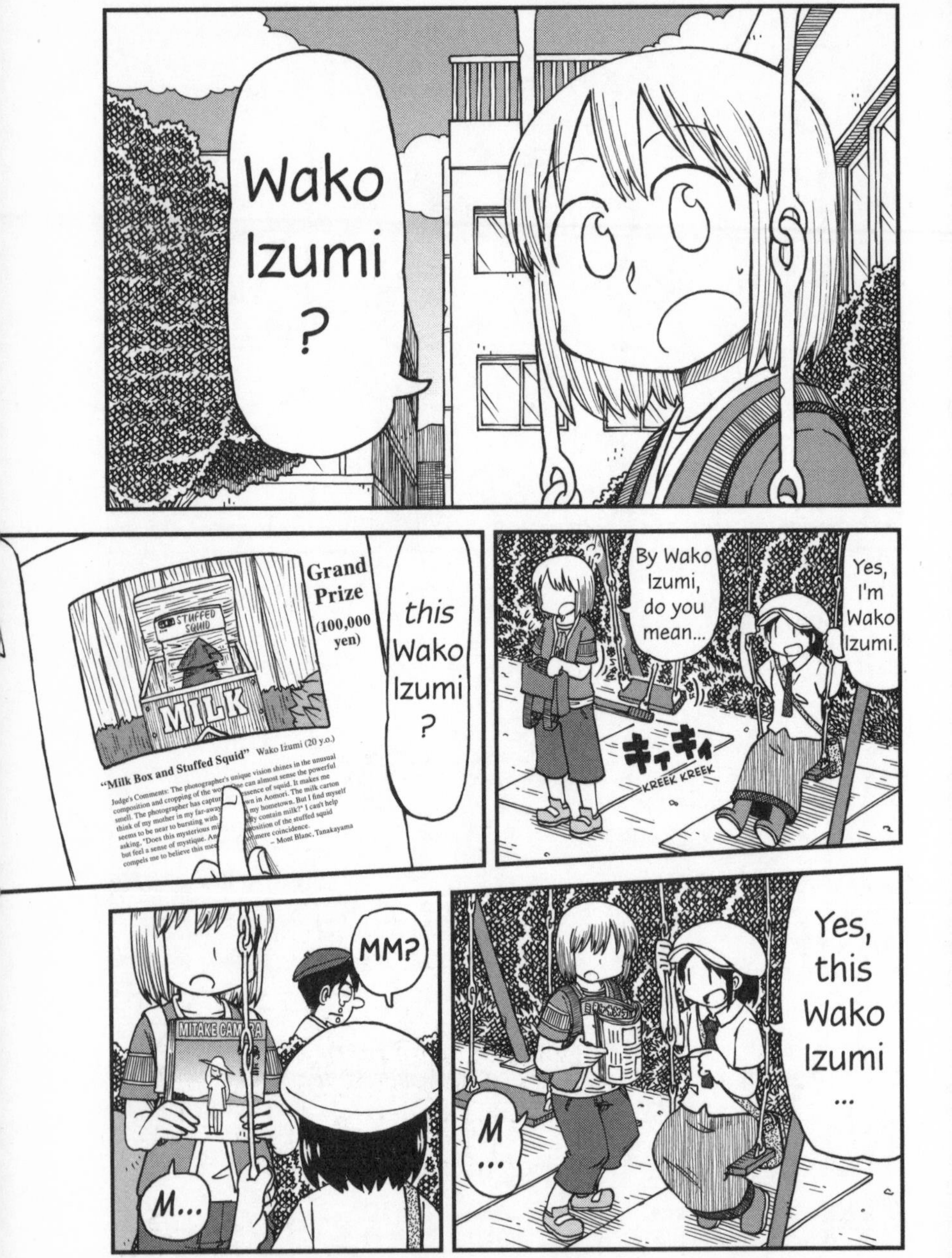
Wako Izumi ?
Yes, I'm Wako Izumi.
By Wako Izumi, do you mean...
キィキィ
KREEK KREEK
this Wako Izumi ?
Grand Prize (100,000 yen)
STUFFED SQUID
MILK
"Milk Box and Stuffed Squid" Wako Izumi (20 y.o.)
Yes, this Wako Izumi ...
M ...
MM?
MITAKE CAMERA
M...

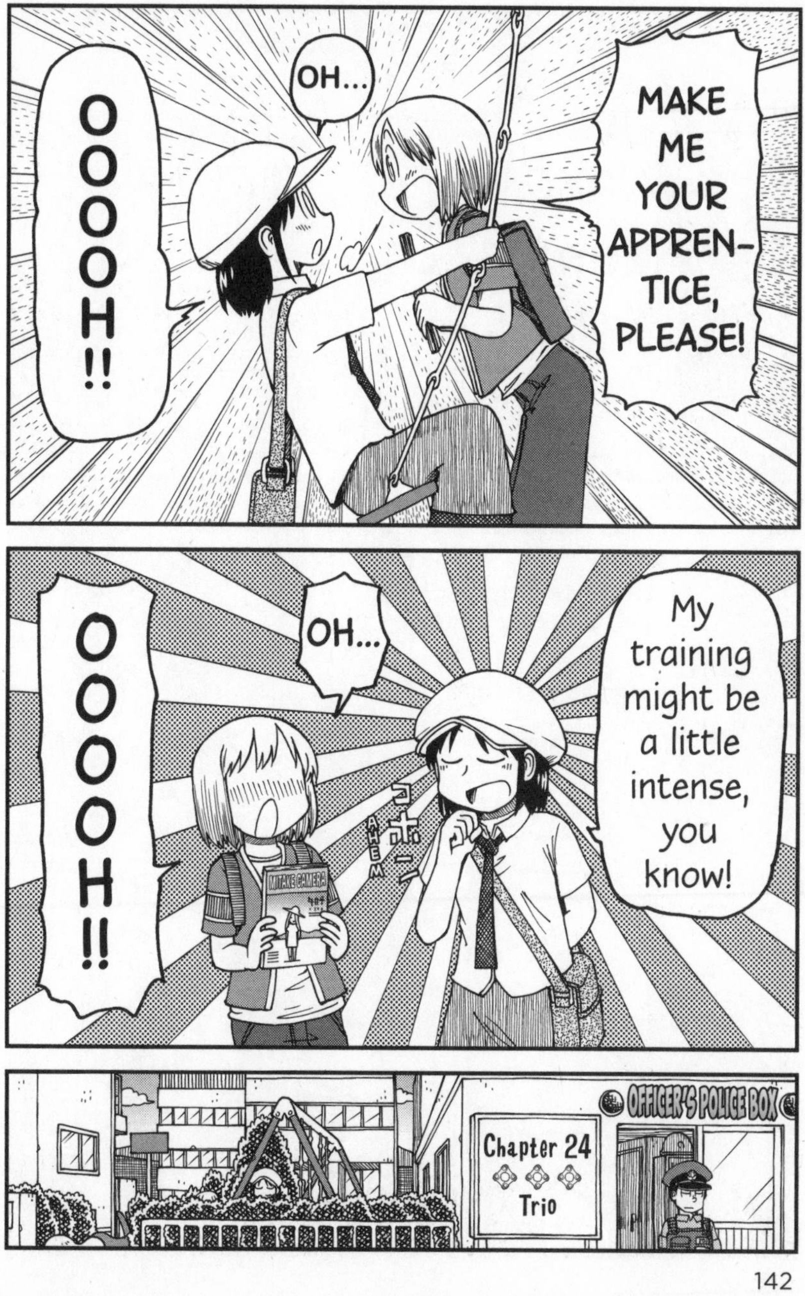
MAKE ME YOUR APPREN-TICE, PLEASE!
OH...
OOOOH!!
My training might be a little intense, you know!
AHEM
MITAKE CAMERA
OH...
OOOOOH!!
OFFICER'S POLICE BOX
Chapter 24
Trio

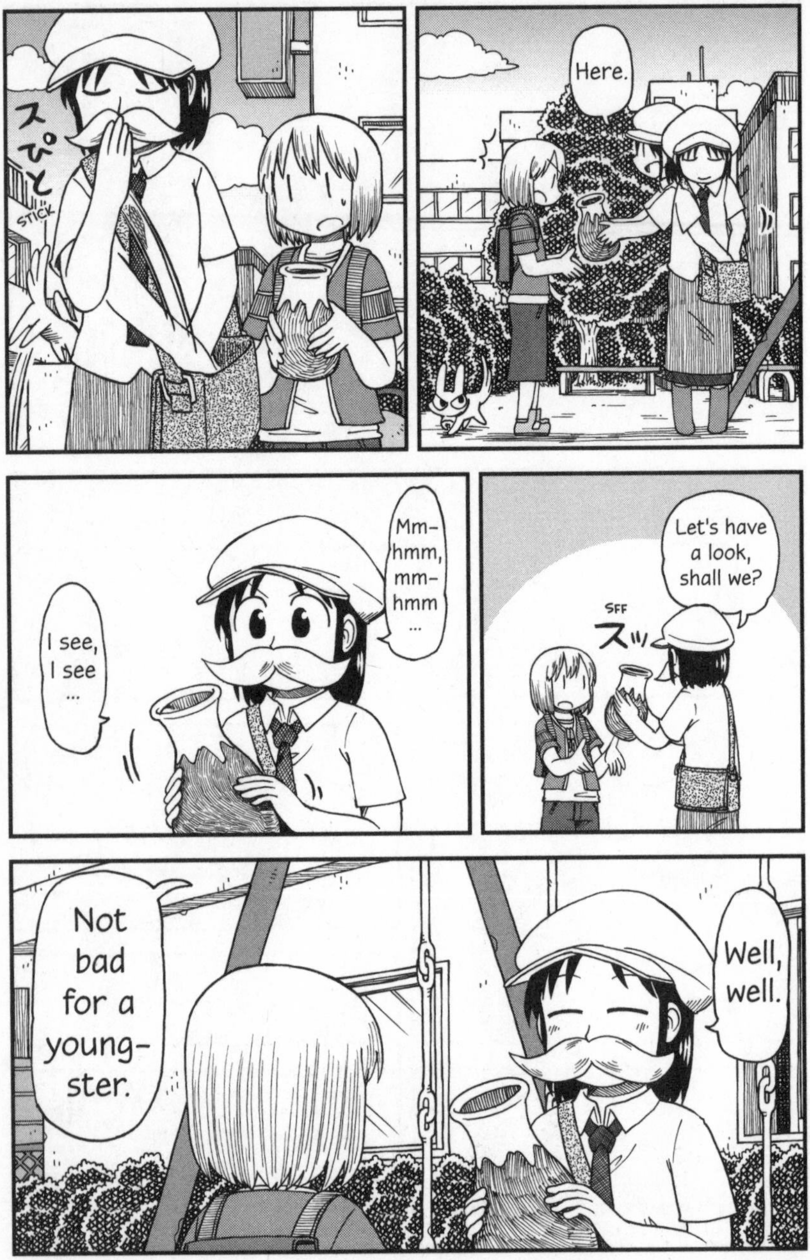
Here.
スぴと
STICK
Let's have a look, shall we?
SFF
スッ
Mm-hmm, mm-hmm ...
I see, I see ...
Well, well.
Not bad for a young-ster.

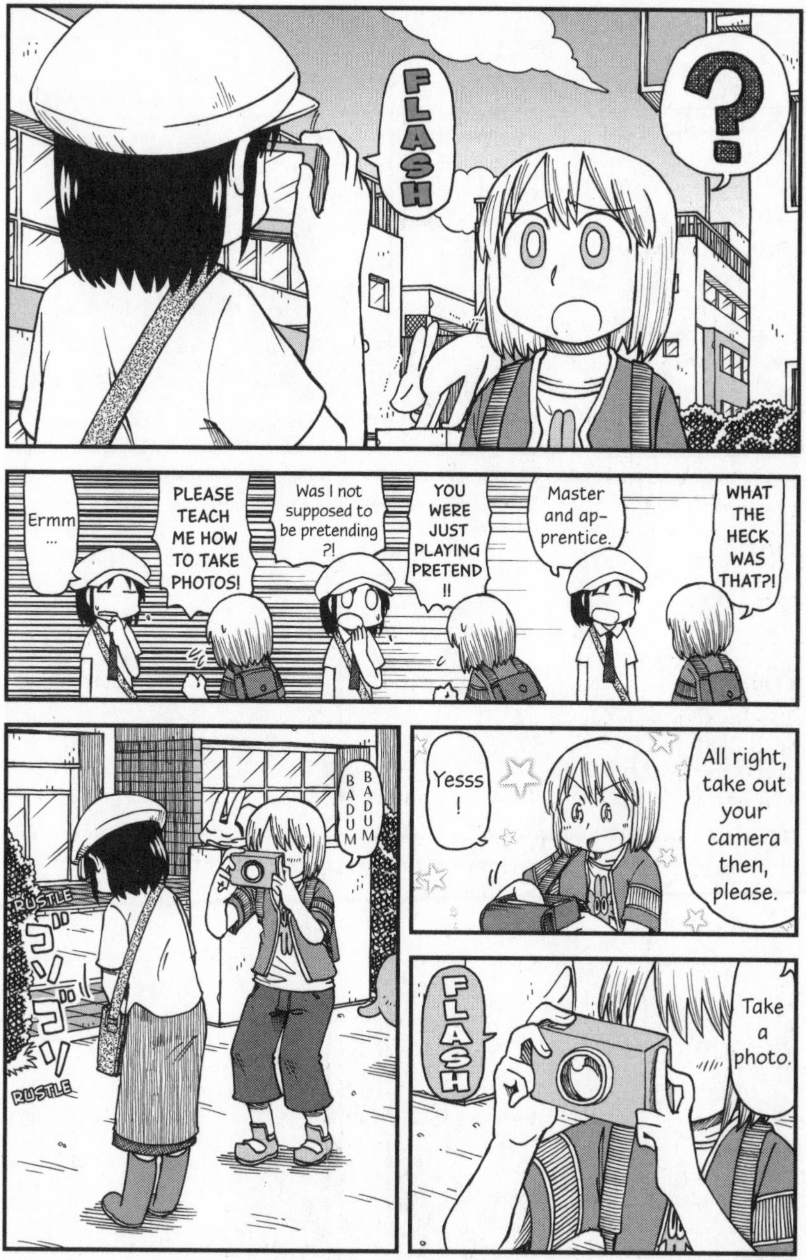
?
FLASH
WHAT THE HECK WAS THAT?!
Master and ap-prentice.
YOU WERE JUST PLAYING PRETEND !!
Was I not supposed to be pretending ?!
PLEASE TEACH ME HOW TO TAKE PHOTOS!
Ermm ...
All right, take out your camera then, please.
Yesss !
Take a photo.
FLASH
BADUM BADUM
RUSTLE
RUSTLE

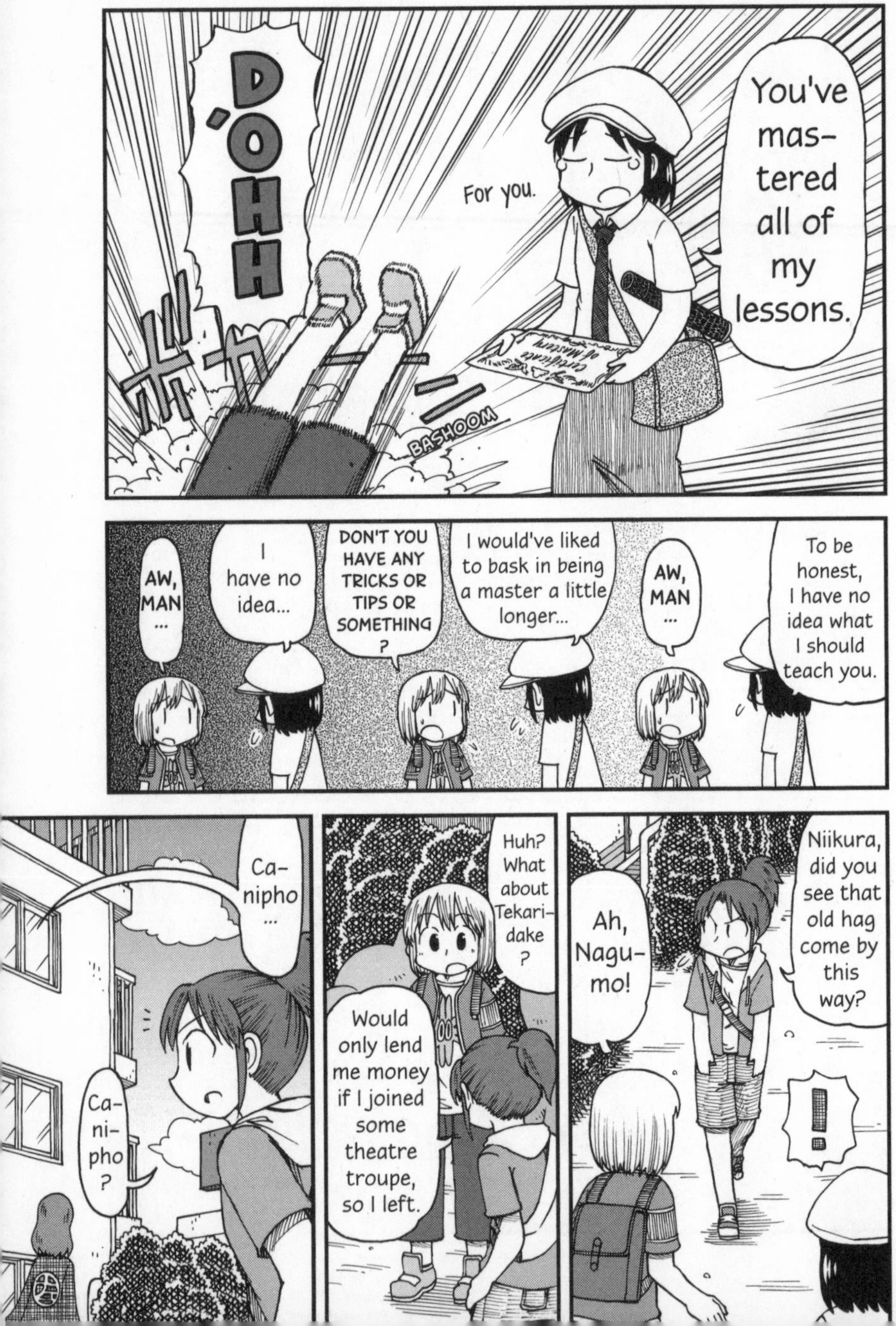

You've mastered all of my lessons.
For you.
Certificate of Mastery
D'OHH
BASHOOM
To be honest, I have no idea what I should teach you.
AW, MAN ...
I would've liked to bask in being a master a little longer...
DON'T YOU HAVE ANY TRICKS OR TIPS OR SOMETHING ?
I have no idea...
AW, MAN ...
Niikura, did you see that old hag come by this way?
!
Ah, Nagumo!
Huh? What about Tekaridake ?
Would only lend me money if I joined some theatre troupe, so I left.
Canipho ...
Canipho ?

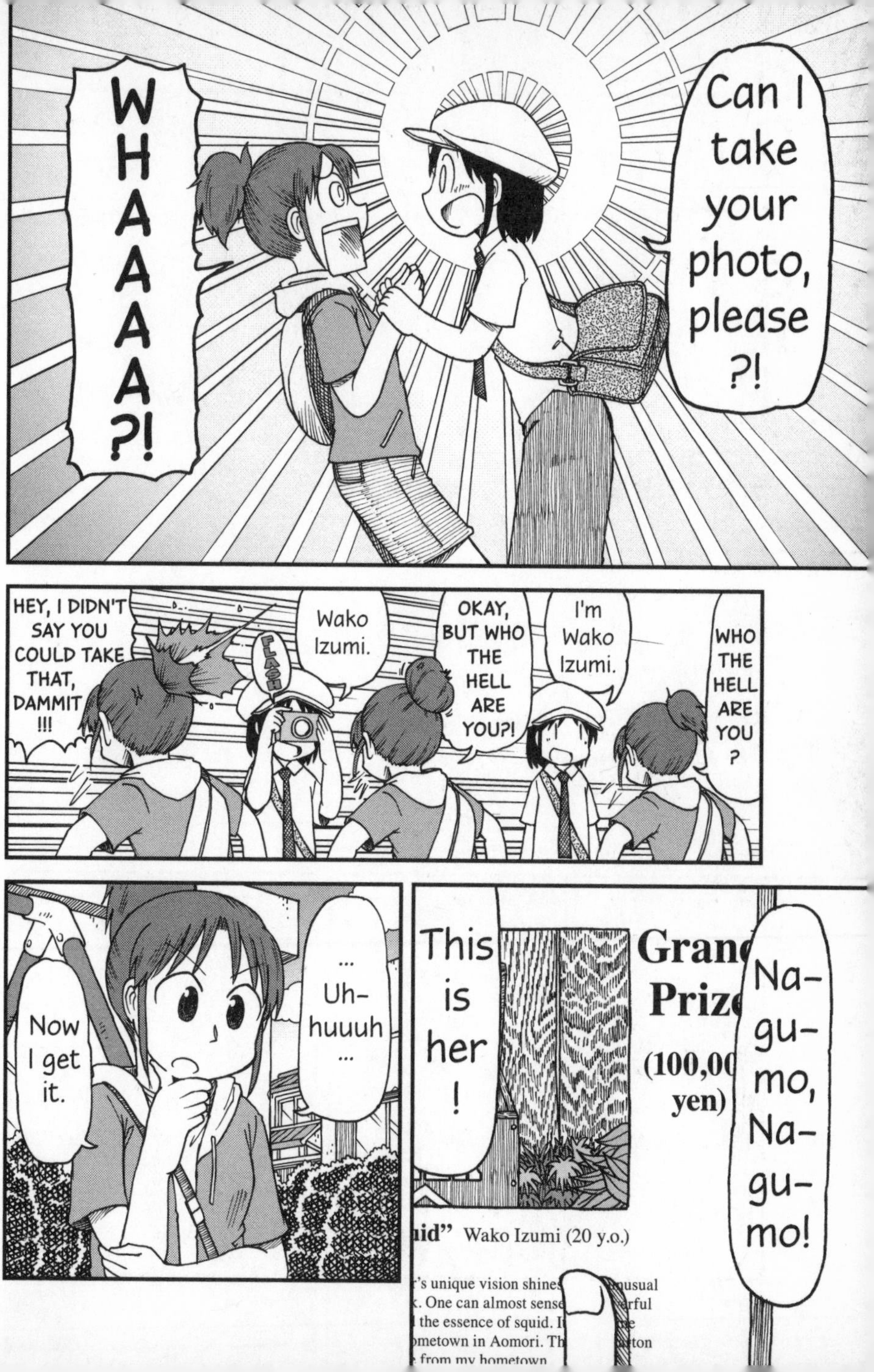
Can I take your photo, please?!
WHAAAA?!
WHO THE HELL ARE YOU?
I'm Wako Izumi.
OKAY, BUT WHO THE HELL ARE YOU?!
Wako Izumi.
FLASH
HEY, I DIDN'T SAY YOU COULD TAKE THAT, DAMMIT!!!
Na-gu-mo, Na-gu-mo!
This is her!
Gran
Prize
(100,00
yen)
uid" Wako Izumi (20 y.o.)
r's unique vision shines nusual
k. One can almost sense erful
l the essence of squid. I e
ometown in Aomori. Th ton
e from my hometown
... Uh-huuuh ...
Now I get it.

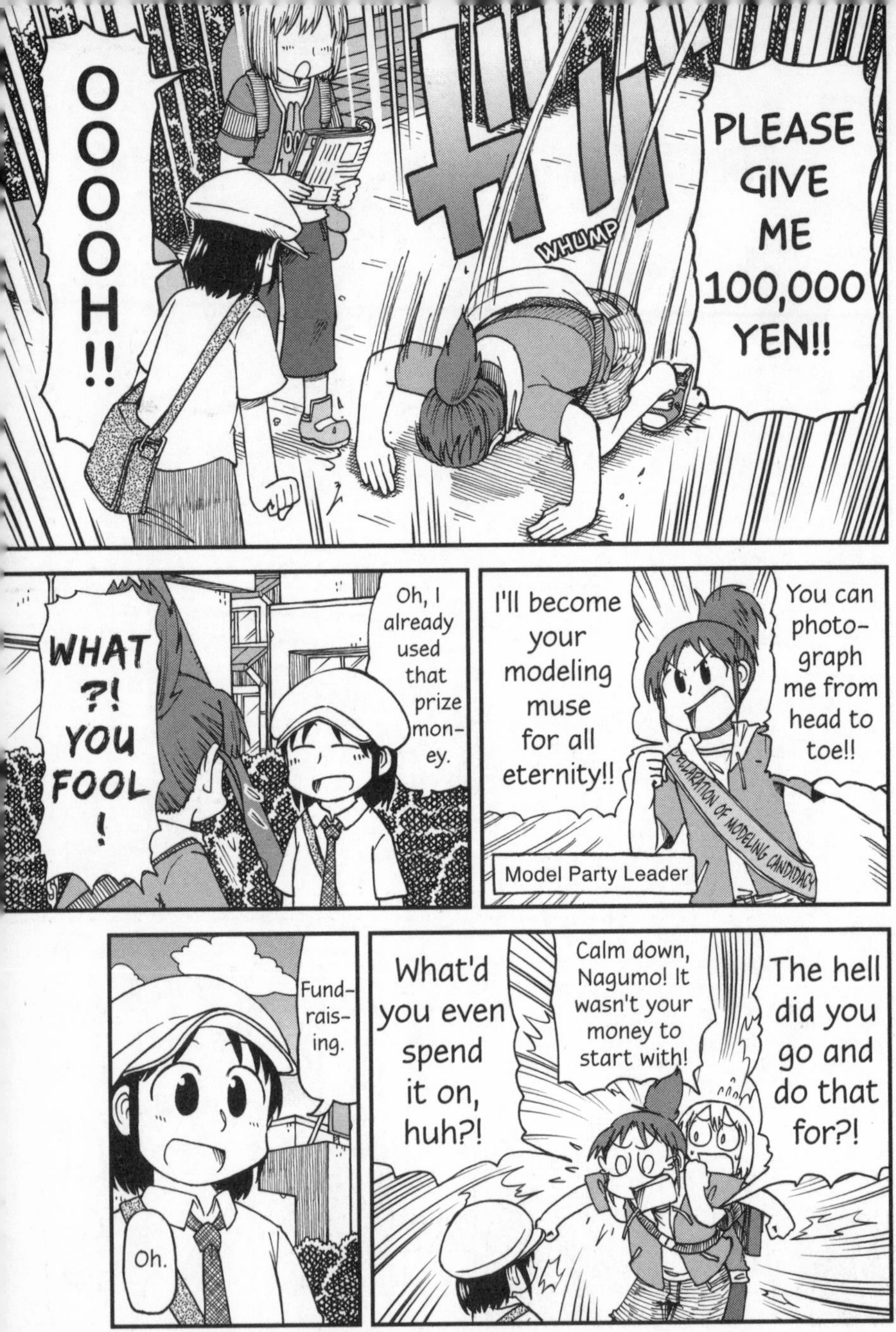
PLEASE GIVE ME 100,000 YEN!!
WHUMP
OOOOH!!
You can photo-graph me from head to toe!!
I'll become your modeling muse for all eternity!!
DECLARATION OF MODELING CANDIDACY
Model Party Leader
Oh, I already used that prize mon-ey.
WHAT?! YOU FOOL!
The hell did you go and do that for?!
Calm down, Nagumo! It wasn't your money to start with!
What'd you even spend it on, huh?!
Fund-rais-ing.
Oh.

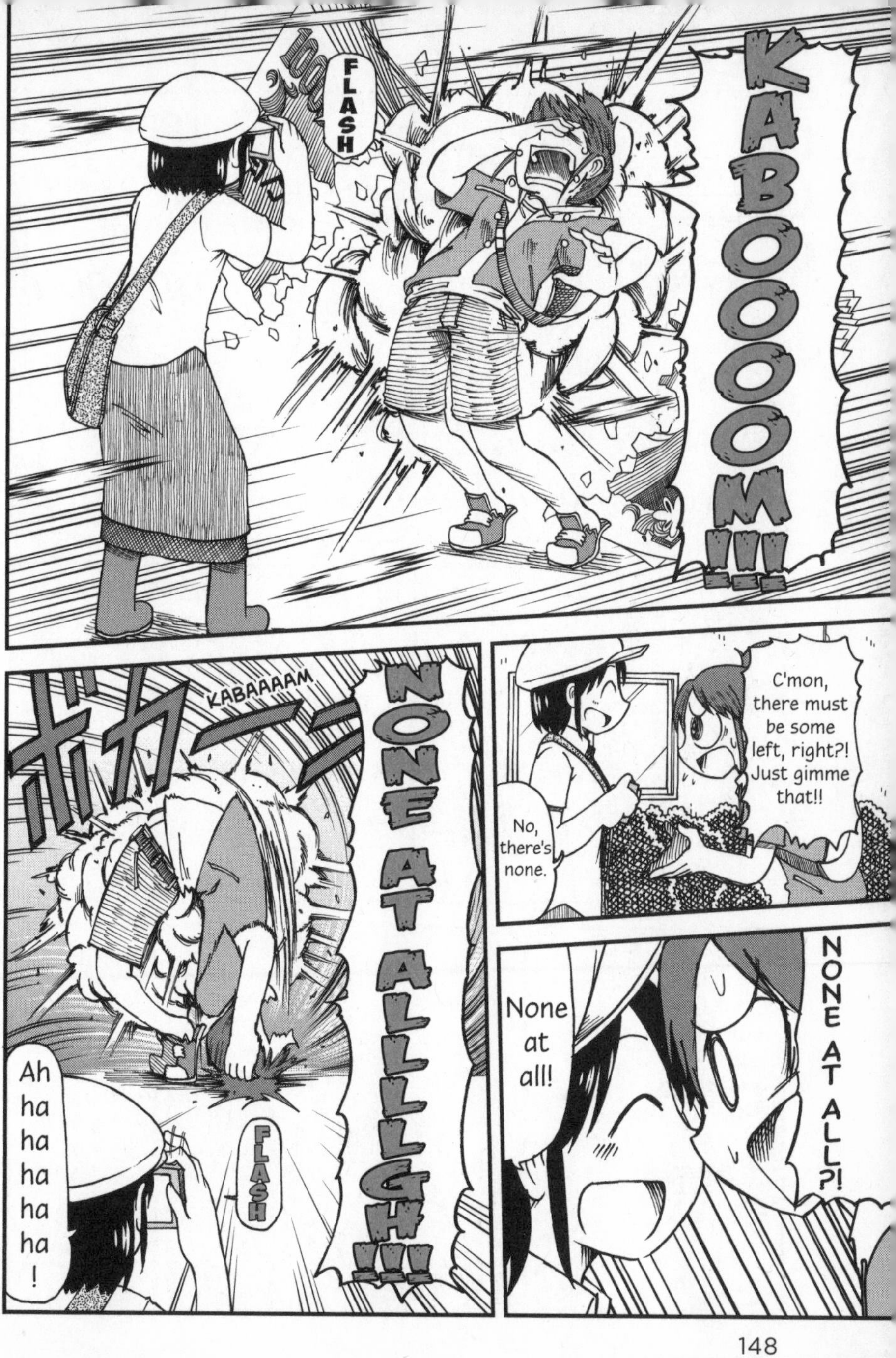
KABOOOOOM!!!
FLASH
C'mon, there must be some left, right?! Just gimme that!!
No, there's none.
NONE AT ALL?!
None at all!
KABAAAAM
NONE AT ALLLLGH!!!
FLASH
Ah ha ha ha ha ha!

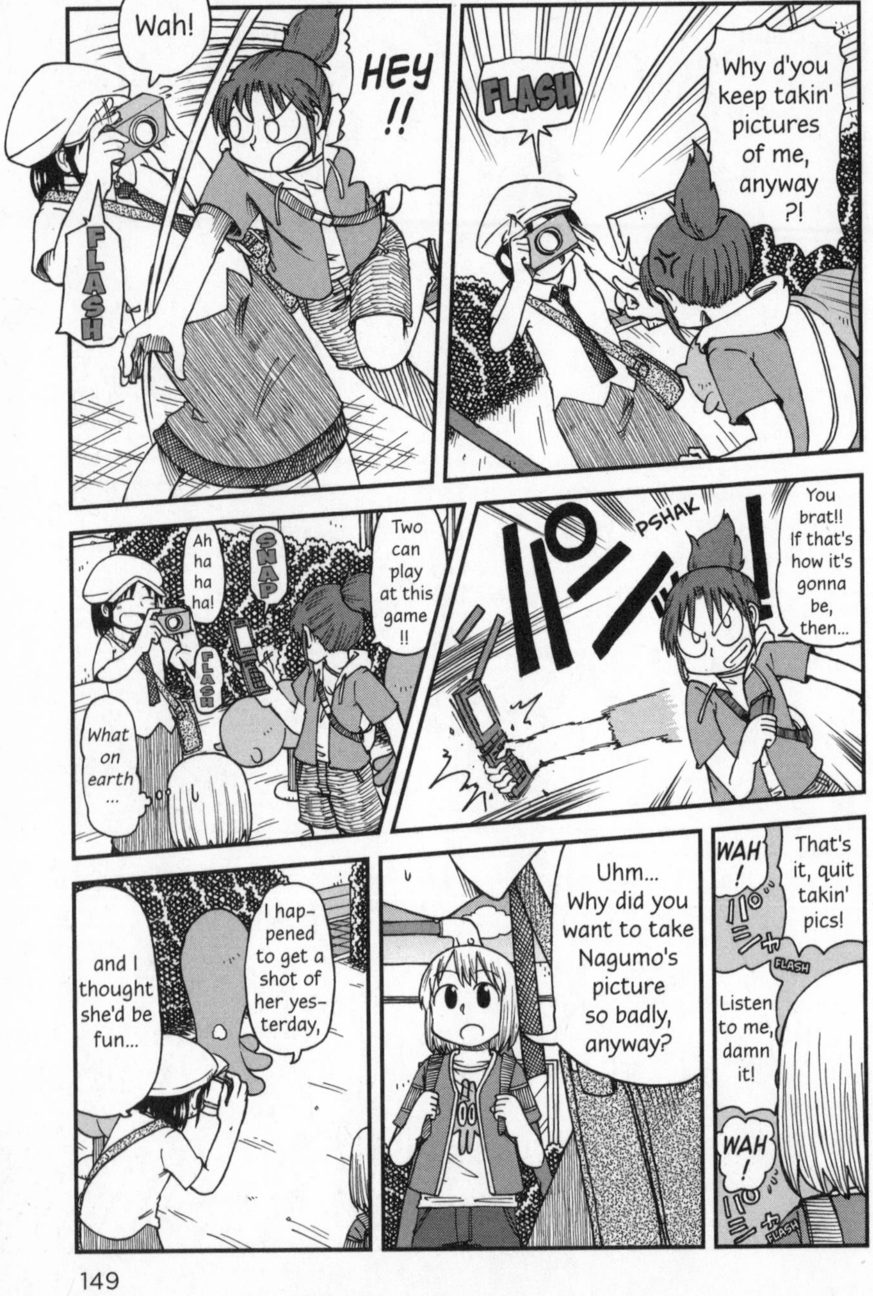
FLASH
Why d'you keep takin' pictures of me, anyway ?!
HEY !!
Wah!
FLASH
You brat!! If that's how it's gonna be, then...
PSHAK
Two can play at this game !!
SNAP
Ah ha ha ha!
FLASH
What on earth ...
That's it, quit takin' pics!
WAH !
FLASH
Listen to me, damn it!
WAH !
FLASH
Uhm... Why did you want to take Nagumo's picture so badly, anyway?
I hap-pened to get a shot of her yes-terday,
and I thought she'd be fun...

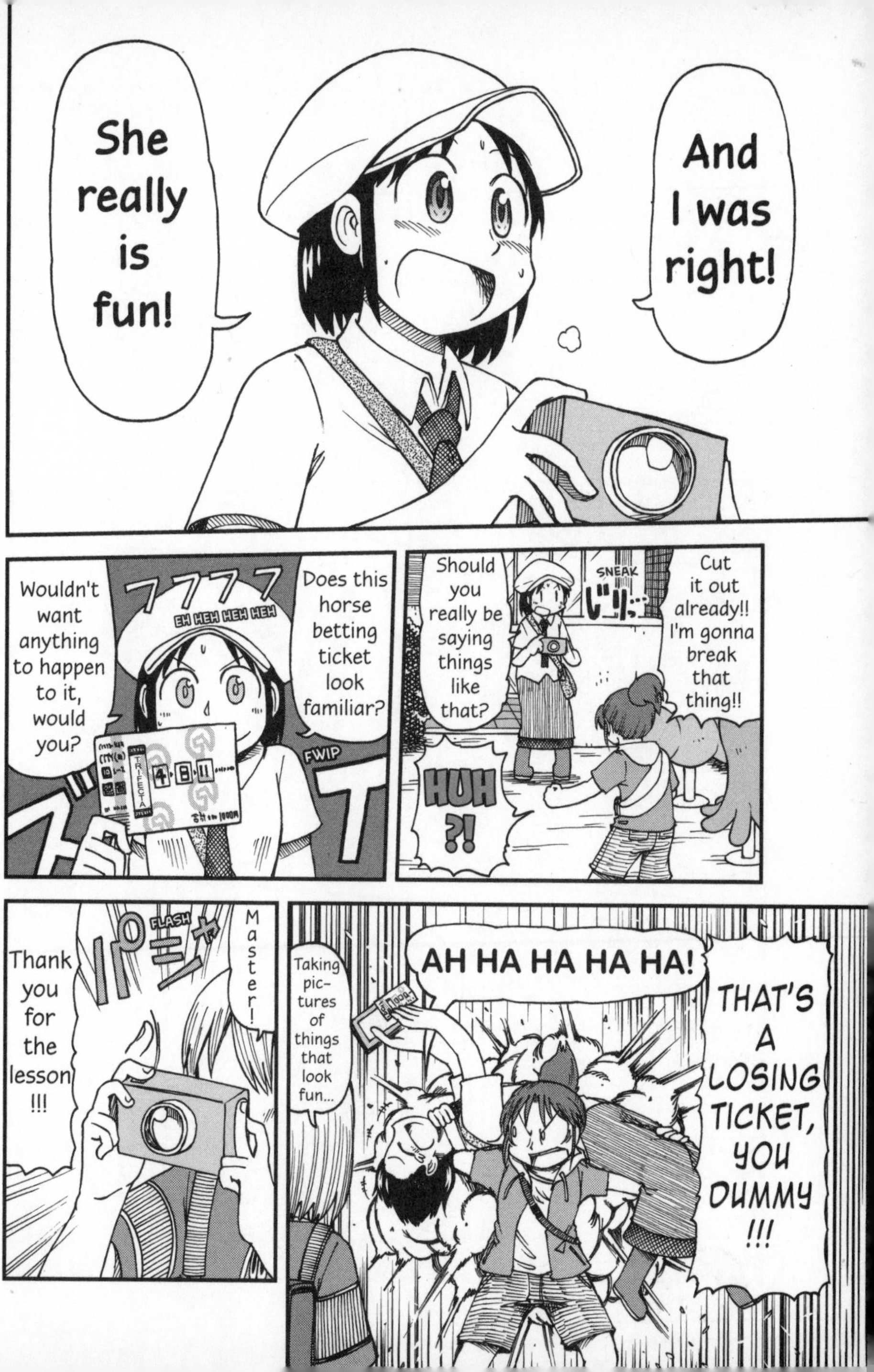
And I was right!
She really is fun!
Cut it out already!! I'm gonna break that thing!!
SNEAK
Should you really be saying things like that?
HUH ?!
Does this horse betting ticket look familiar?
EH HEH HEH HEH
Wouldn't want anything to happen to it, would you?
TRIFECTA
FWIP
AH HA HA HA HA!
THAT'S A LOSING TICKET, YOU DUMMY!!!
Taking pic-tures of things that look fun...
Master!
FLASH
Thank you for the lesson!!!

Rectangular Digi-cam

Product name: Rectangular Digital
Still camera

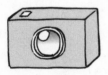

A simple design with as few
protruding parts as possible.
Medium performance for a
medium price, easy to use for
both amateurs and pros alike.
Stubbornly refuses to change
designs.

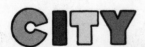

CITY

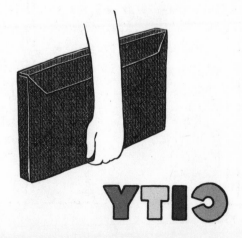

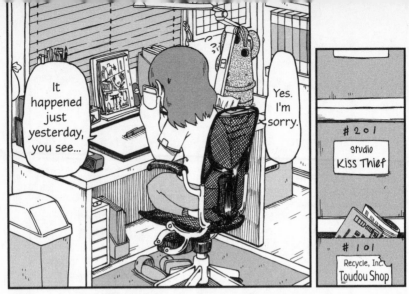

It happened just yesterday, you see...

Yes. I'm sorry.

#201 studio Kiss Thief

#101 Recycle, Inc. Toudou Shop

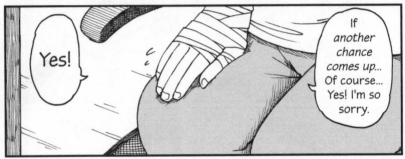

Yes!

If another chance comes up... Of course... Yes! I'm so sorry.

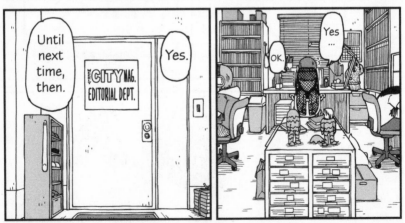

Until next time, then.

CITY MAG. EDITORIAL DEPT.

Yes.

OK.

Yes ...

Mr. Bummer #FINALE "A Flower Blooms in Bummer's Heart" by Kamaboko Oni

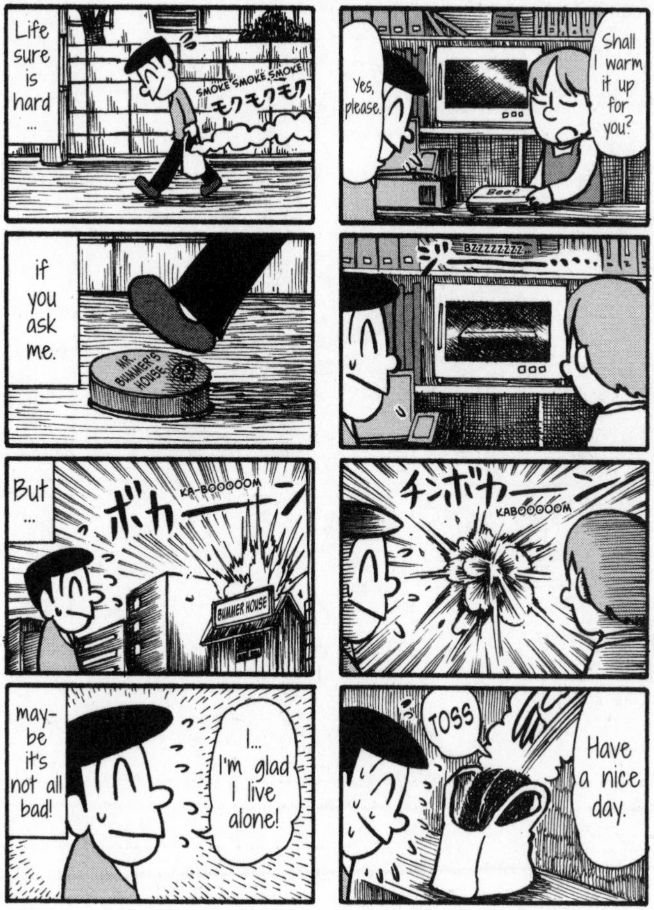
Shall I warm it up for you?
Yes, please.
Beef
Life sure is hard ...
SMOKE SMOKE SMOKE
モクモクモク
BZZZZZZZZ
if you ask me.
MR. BUMMER'S HOUSE
チンボカーン
KABOOOOOM
But ...
ボカーン
KA-BOOOOOM
BUMMER HOUSE
Have a nice day.
TOSS
I... I'm glad I live alone!
may-be it's not all bad!

Chapter 25 The Manga Way

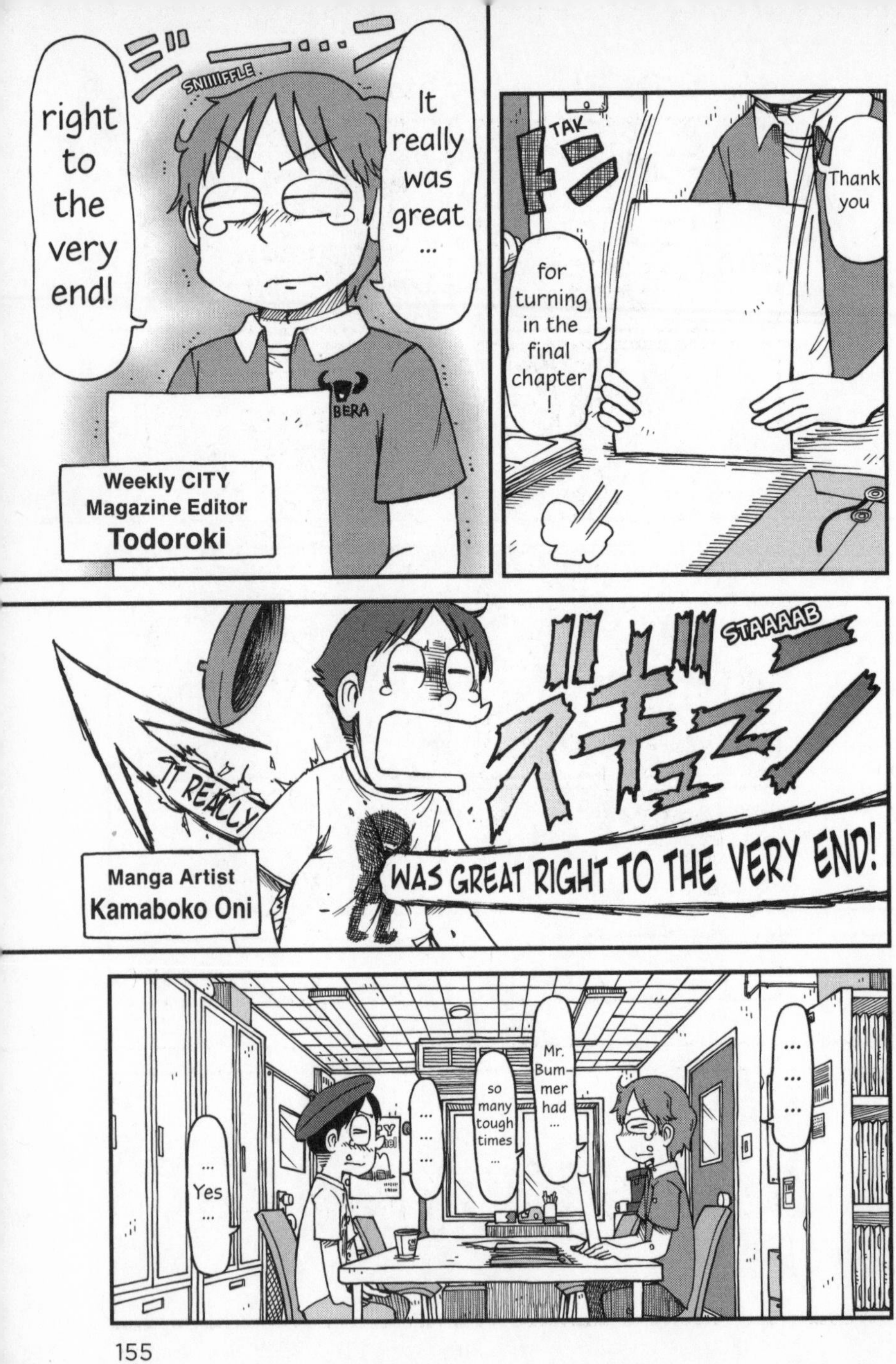
TAK
Thank you
for turning in the final chapter!
SNIIIFFLE
It really was great...
right to the very end!
Weekly CITY Magazine Editor Todoroki
STAAAAB
IT REALLY
WAS GREAT RIGHT TO THE VERY END!
Manga Artist Kamaboko Oni
... ...
Mr. Bummer had ...
so many tough times ...
... ...
... Yes ...

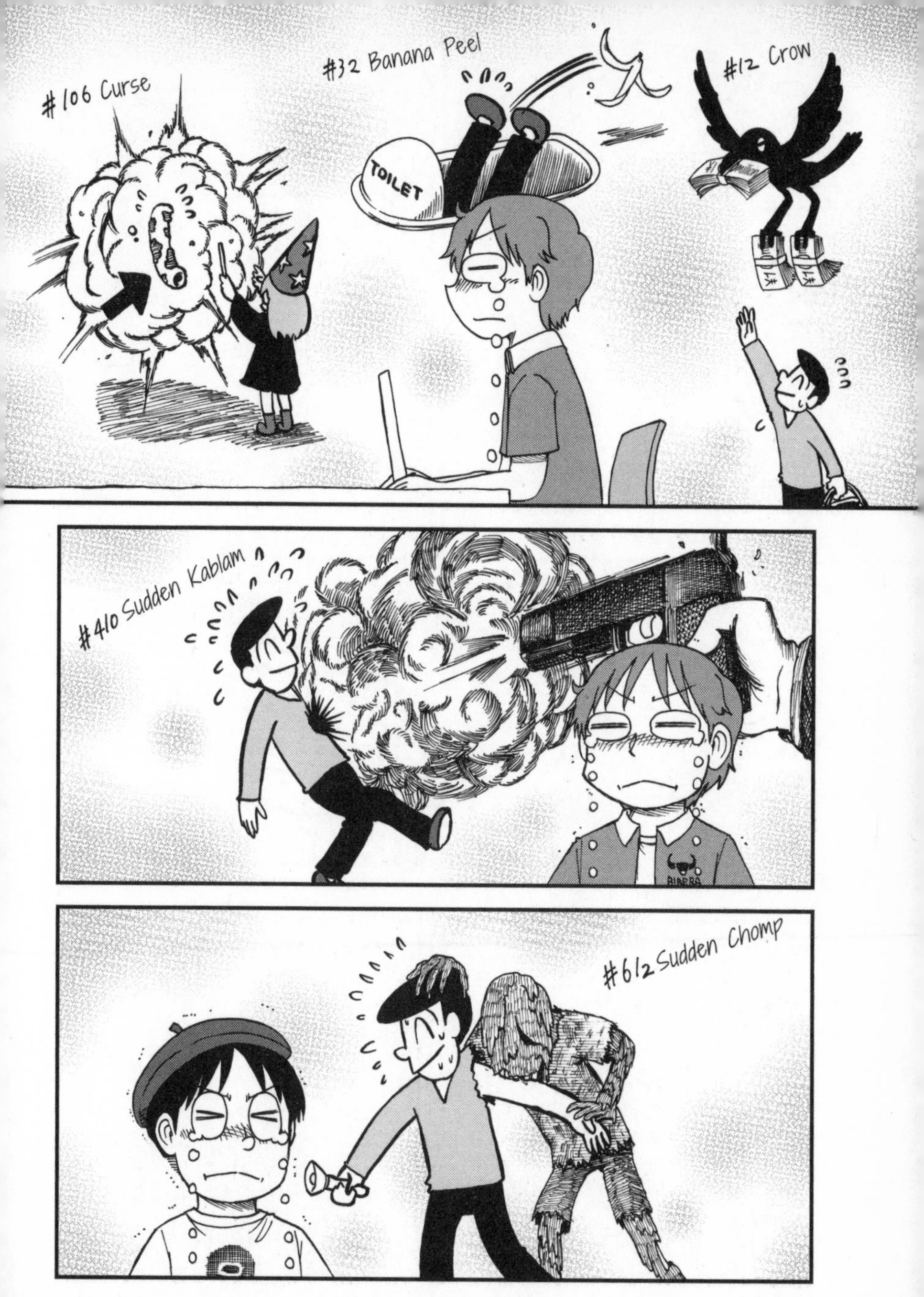
#12 Crow
#32 Banana Peel
TOILET
#106 Curse
#410 Sudden Kablam
#612 Sudden Chomp

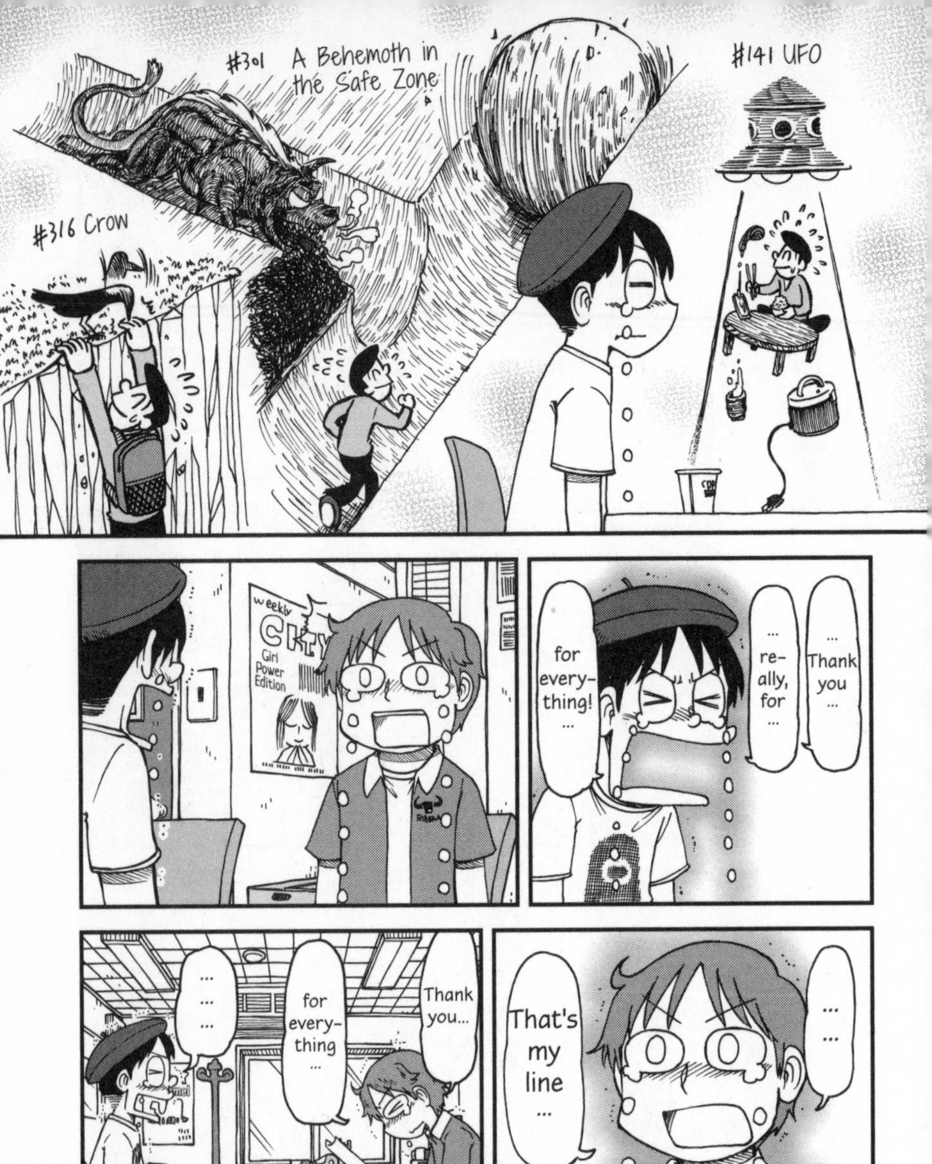
#141 UFO
#301 A Behemoth in the Safe Zone
#316 Crow
... Thank you ...
... re-ally, for ...
for every-thing! ...
weekly
Girl Power Edition
... ...
That's my line ...
Thank you...
for every-thing ...
... ...

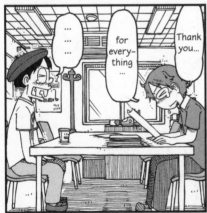

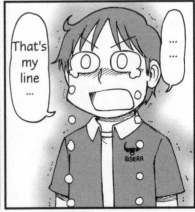

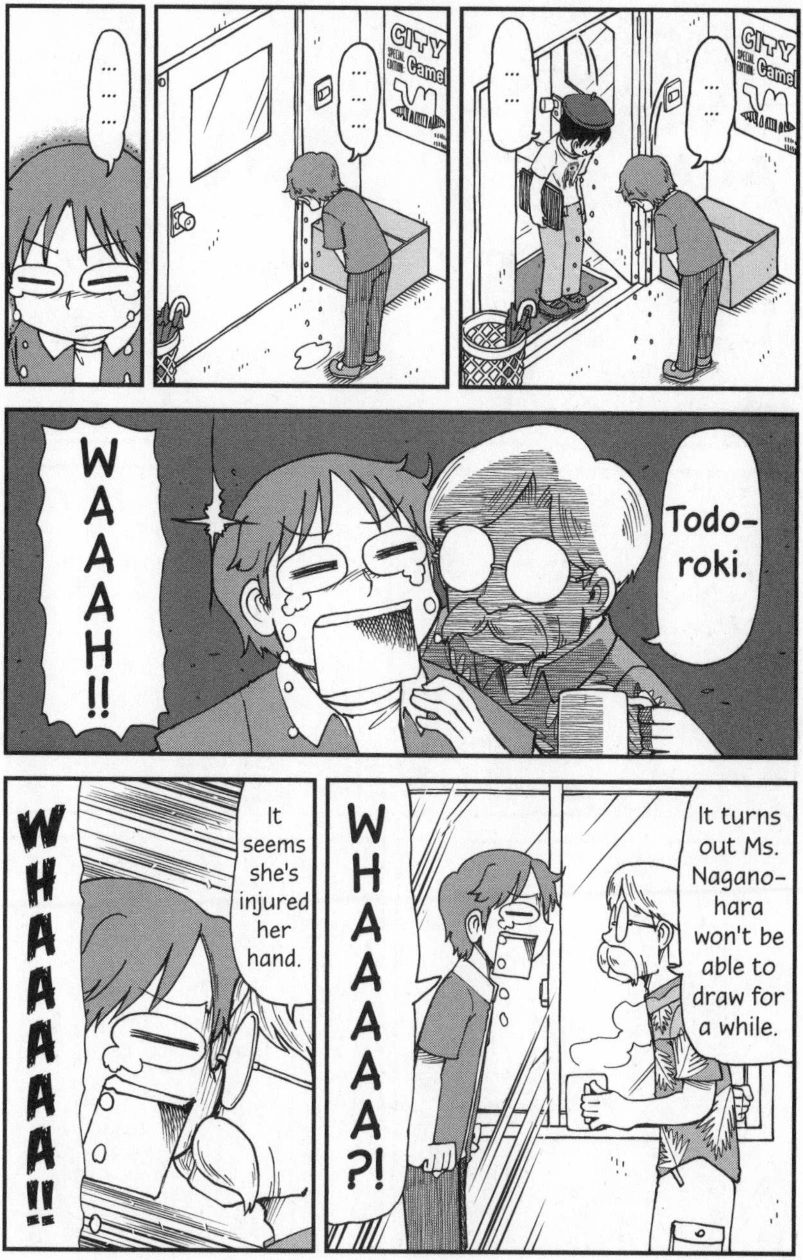
... ...
... ...
... ...
Todo-roki.
WAAAAH!!
It turns out Ms. Naganohara won't be able to draw for a while.
WHAAAAAA?!
It seems she's injured her hand.
WHAAAAAA!!

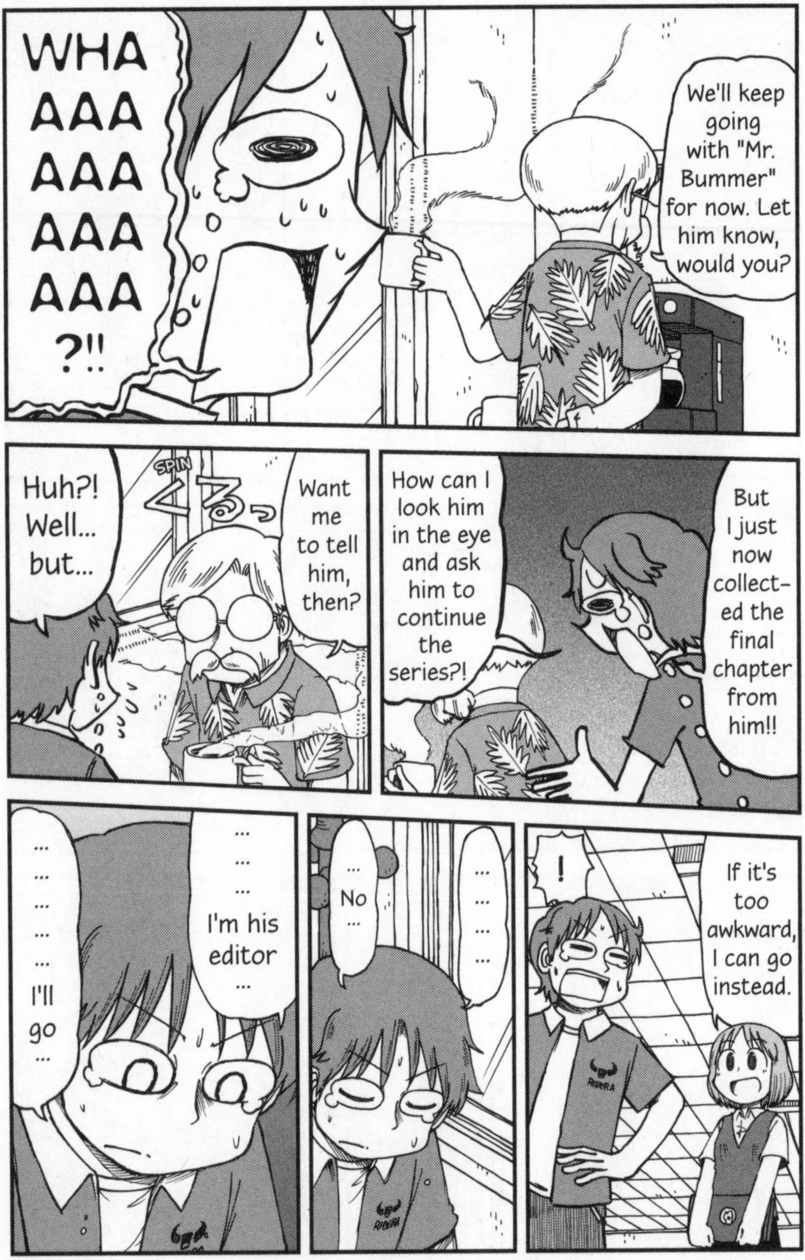
We'll keep going with "Mr. Bummer" for now. Let him know, would you?
WHAAAAAAAAAAAAAA?!!
But I just now collect-ed the final chapter from him!!
How can I look him in the eye and ask him to continue the series?!
Want me to tell him, then?
SPIN
くるっ
Huh?! Well... but...
!
If it's too awkward, I can go instead.
... ...
... No ...
... ... I'm his editor ...
... ... I'll go ...

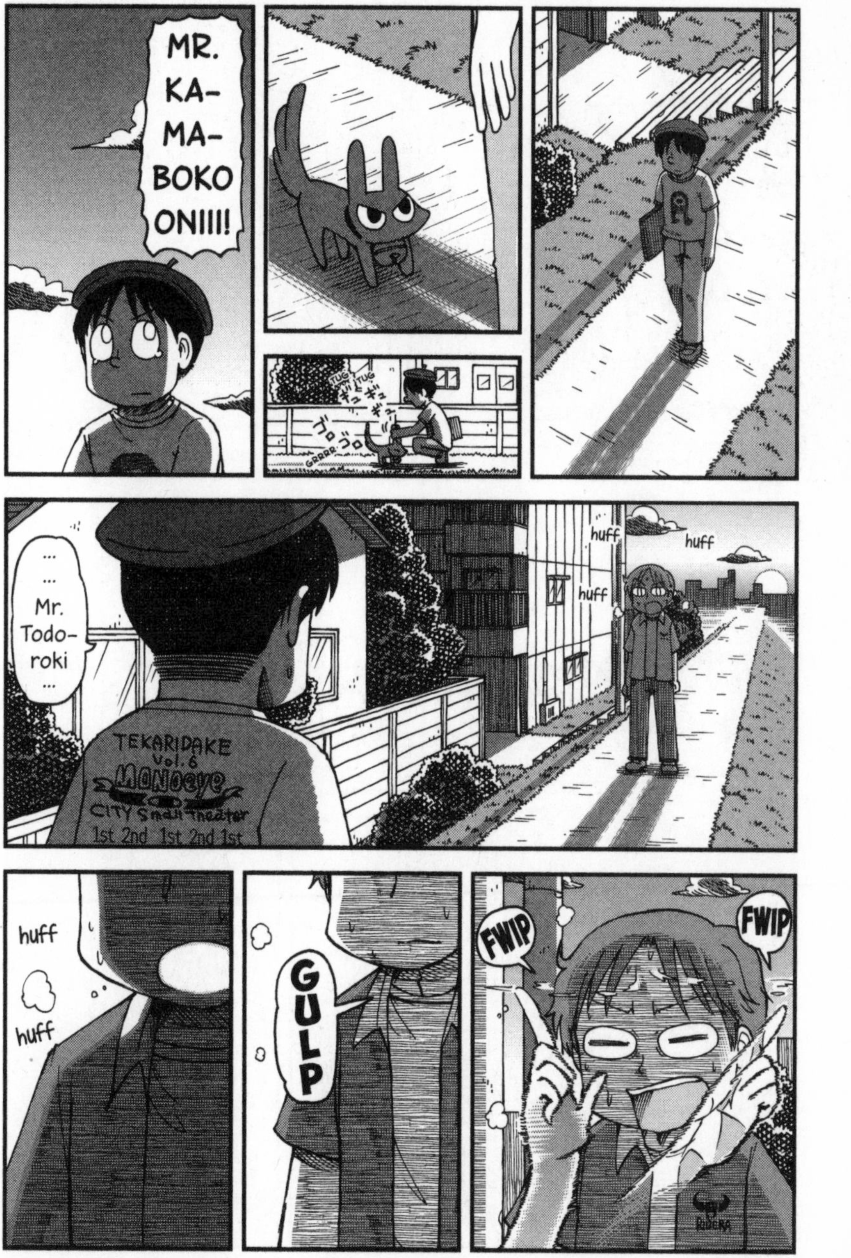
TUG TUG
ギュ ギュ
ゴロ ゴロ
GRRRR
MR. KA-MA-BOKO ON!!!!!
huff
huff
huff
... ... Mr. Todo-roki ...
TEKARIDAKE Vol.6
CITY Small Theater
1st 2nd 1st 2nd 1st
FWIP
FWIP
GULP
huff
huff

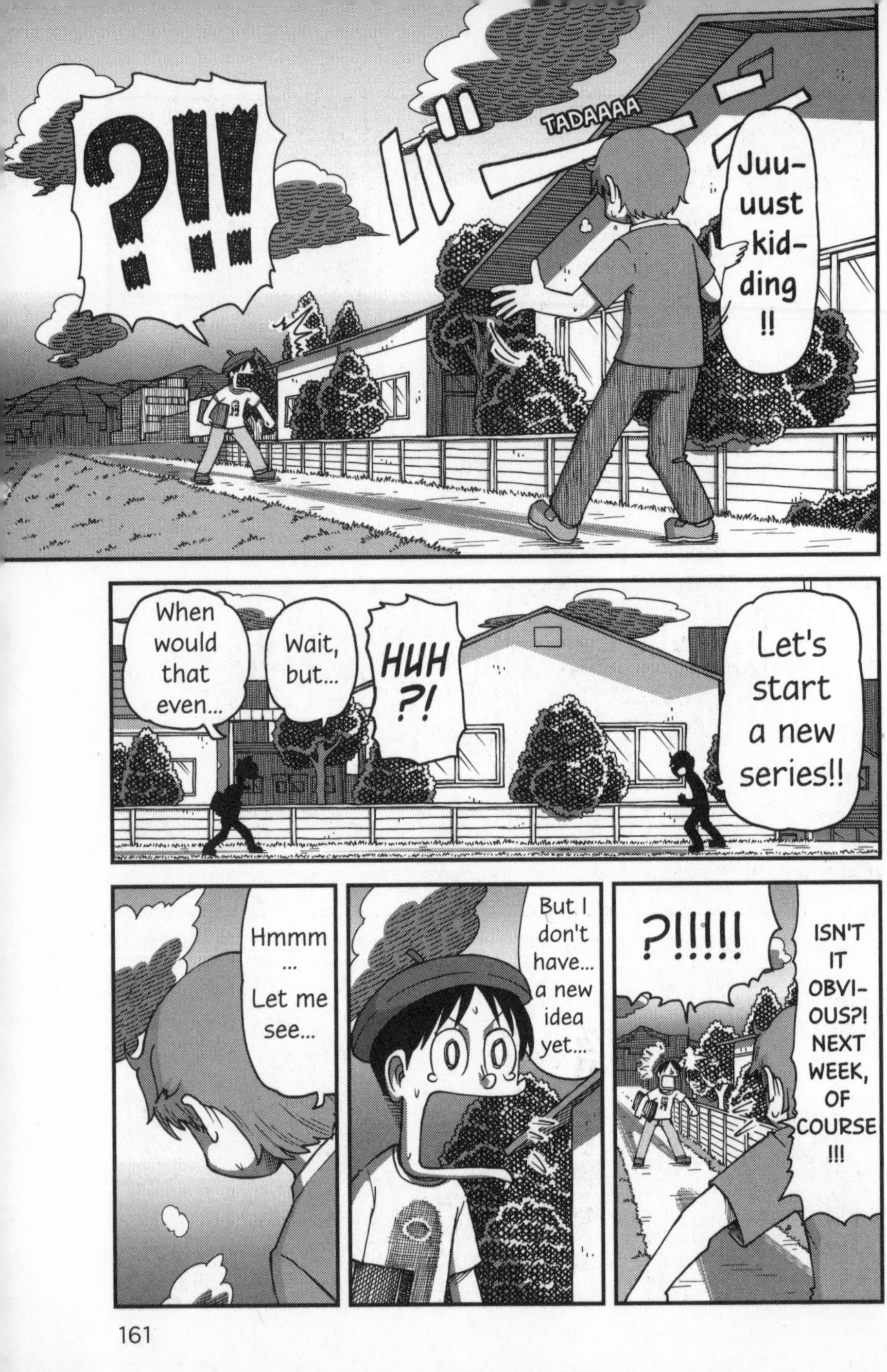
Juuu-uust kid-ding!!
TADAAAA
?!!
Let's start a new series!!
HUH?!
Wait, but...
When would that even...
ISN'T IT OBVIOUS?! NEXT WEEK, OF COURSE!!!
?!!!!!
But I don't have... a new idea yet...
Hmmm... Let me see...

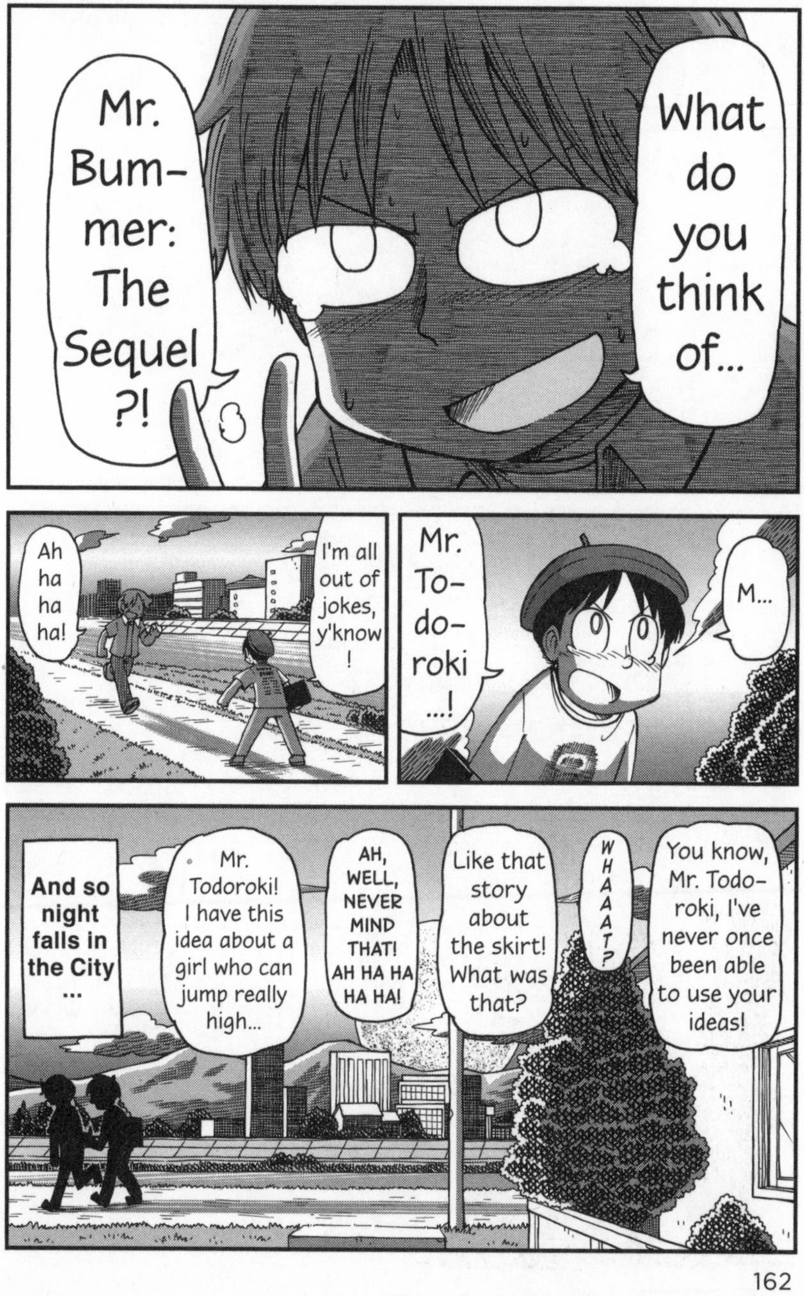
What do you think of...
Mr. Bummer: The Sequel?!
M...
Mr. Todoroki...!
I'm all out of jokes, y'know!
Ah ha ha ha!
You know, Mr. Todoroki, I've never once been able to use your ideas!
WHAAAT?
Like that story about the skirt! What was that?
AH, WELL, NEVER MIND THAT! AH HA HA HA HA!
Mr. Todoroki! I have this idea about a girl who can jump really high...
And so night falls in the City...

CONTENTS

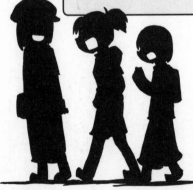

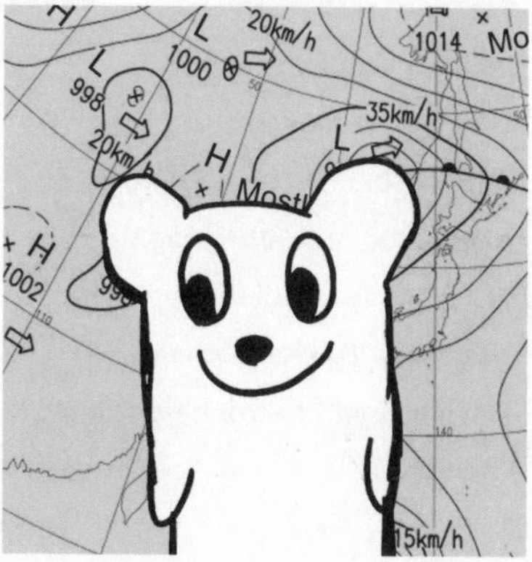
H
L
20km/h
1000
L
998
20km/h
1014
35km/h
L
H
H
1002
15km/h

Recent Author Photo

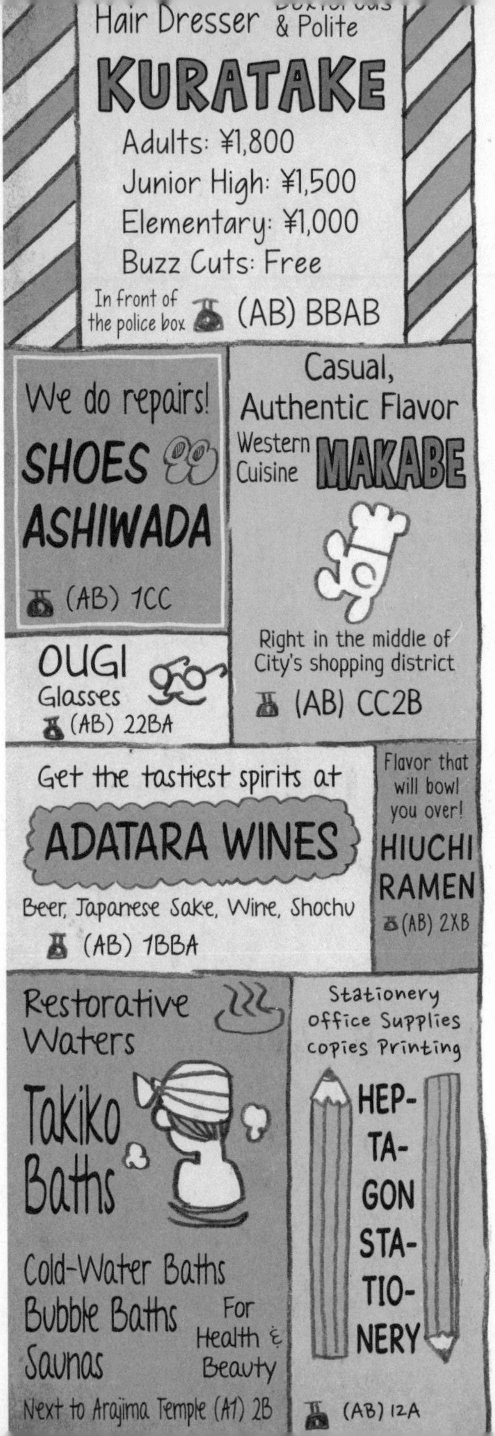
Hair Dresser
& Polite
KURATAKE
Adults: ¥1,800
Junior High: ¥1,500
Elementary: ¥1,000
Buzz Cuts: Free
In front of the police box
(AB) BBAB
Casual, Authentic Flavor
Western Cuisine
MAKABE
Right in the middle of City's shopping district
(AB) CC2B
We do repairs!
SHOES ASHIWADA
(AB) 1CC
OUGI
Glasses
(AB) 22BA
Flavor that will bowl you over!
HIUCHI RAMEN
(AB) 2XB
Get the tastiest spirits at
ADATARA WINES
Beer, Japanese Sake, Wine, Shochu
(AB) 1BBA
Stationery
Office Supplies
Copies Printing
HEP-TA-GON STA-TIO-NERY
(AB) 12A
Restorative Waters
Takiko Baths
Cold-Water Baths
Bubble Baths
Saunas
For Health & Beauty
Next to Arajima Temple (A1) 2B

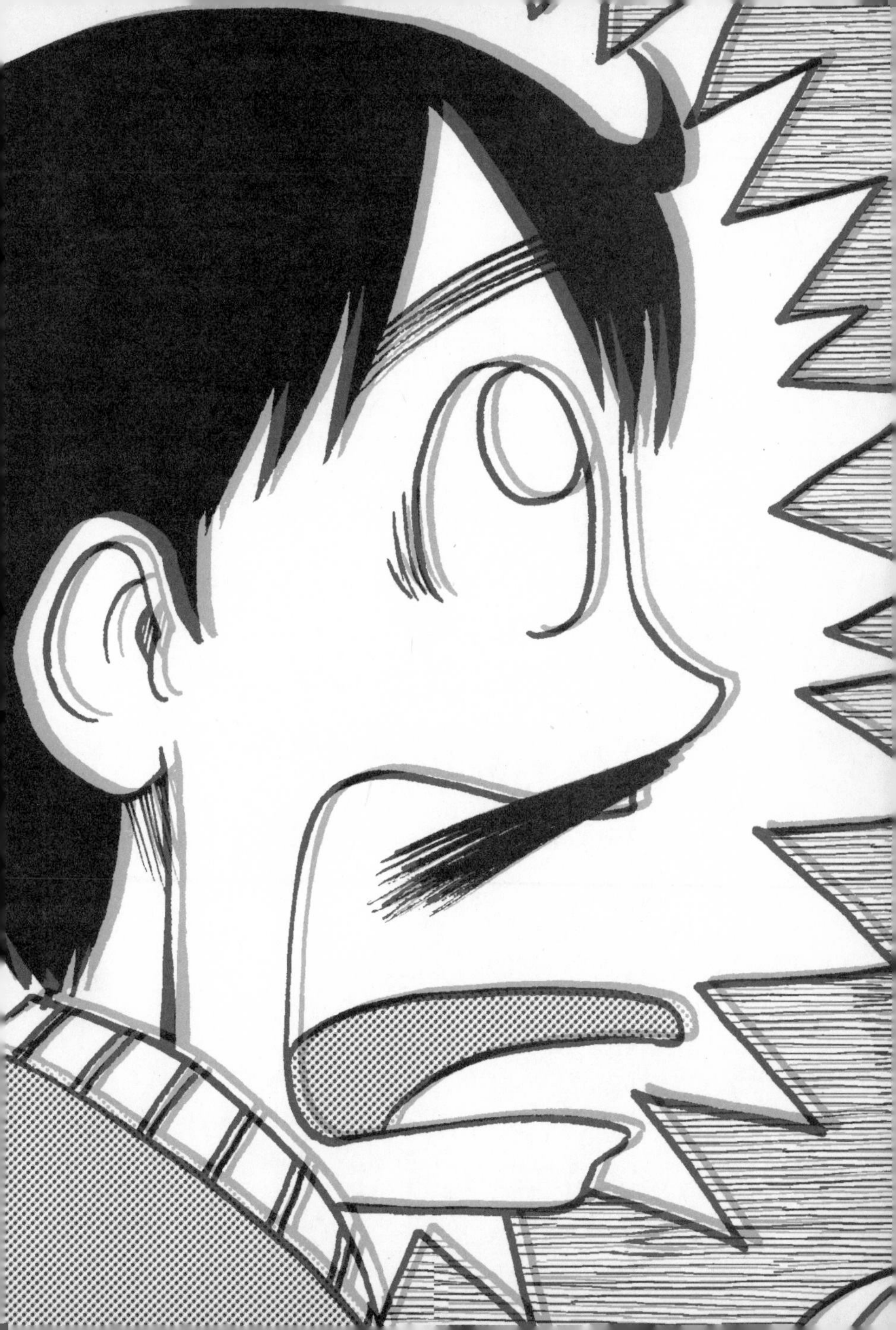

CITY

2

MAKABE

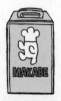

define "ordinary"

in this just-surreal-enough take on the "school genre" of manga, a group of friends (which includes a robot built by a child professor) grapples with all sorts of unexpected situations in their daily lives as high schoolers.

the gags, jokes, puns and random haiku keep this series off-kilter even as the characters grow and change. check out this new take on a storied genre and meet the new ordinary.

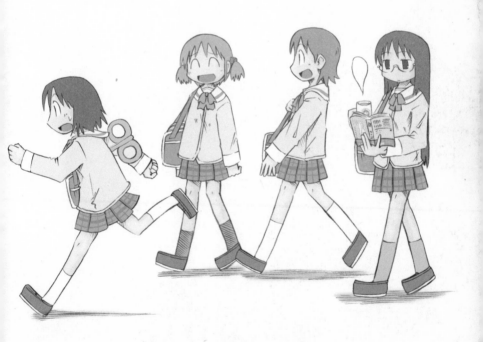

all volumes
available now!

nichijou

my ordinary life

keiichi arawi

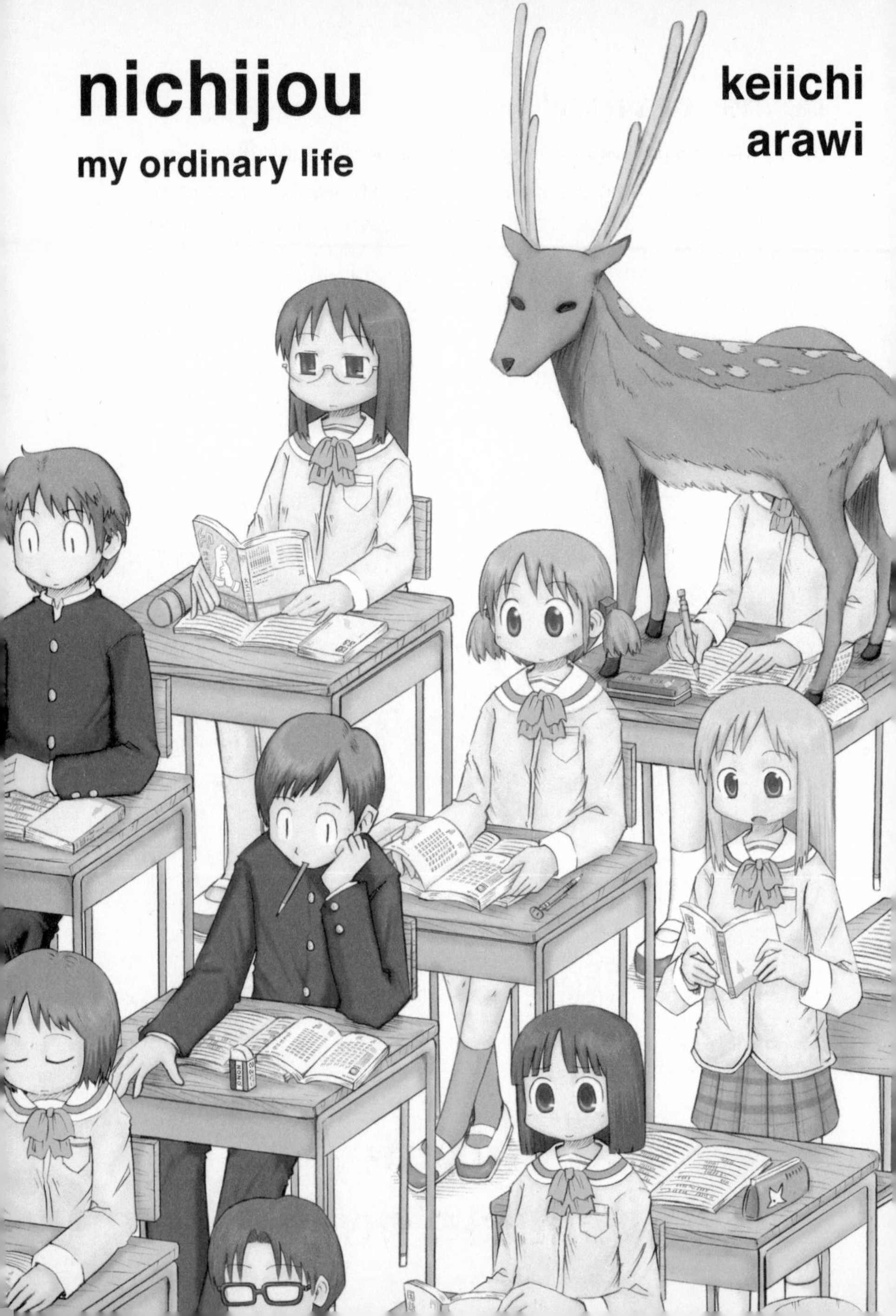

The follow up to the hit manga series *nichijou*,
Helvetica Standard is a full-color anthology of
Keiichi Arawi's comic art and design work.
Funny and heartwarming, **Helvetica Standard**
is a humorous look at modern day Japanese
design in comic form.

Helvetica Standard is a deep dive into the artistic
and creative world of Keiichi Arawi. Part comic, part
diary, part art and design book, **Helvetica Standard**
is a deconstruction of the world of *nichijou*.

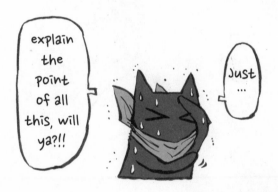

Both Parts Available Now!

Keiichi Arawi

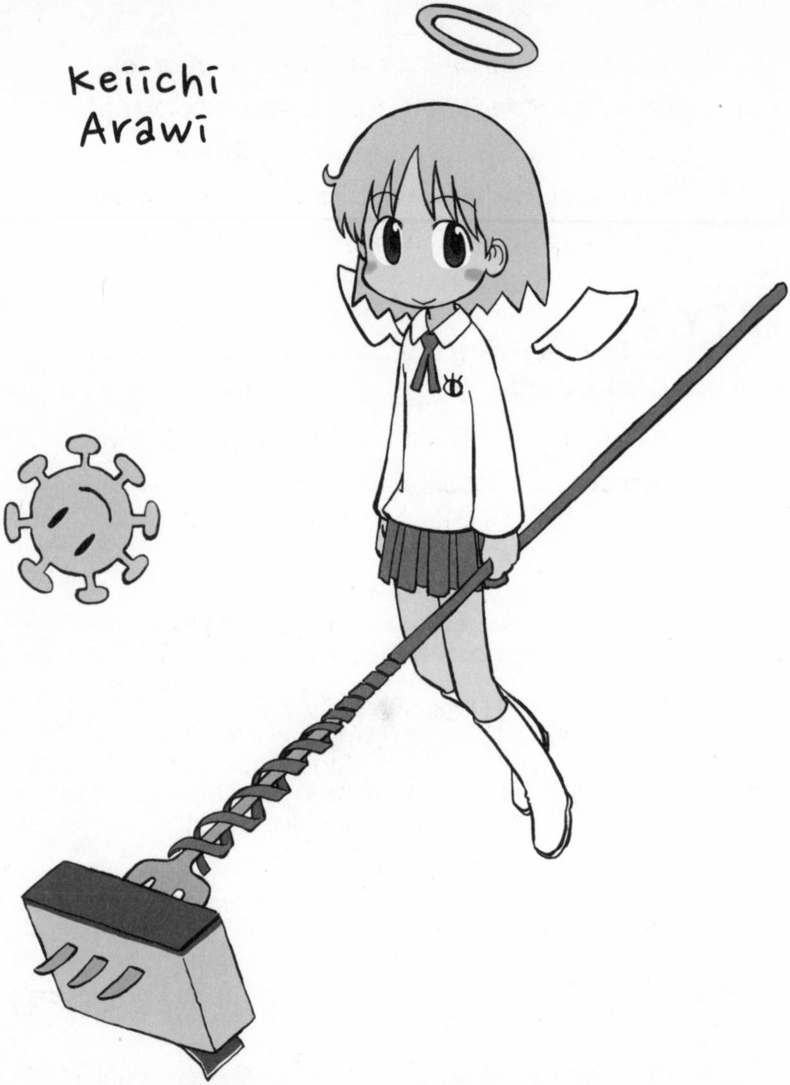

Helvetica Standard

CITY 2

A Vertical Comics Edition

Translation: Jenny McKeon
Production: Grace Lu
            Hiroko Mizuno

© Keiichi ARAWI 2017
First published in Japan in 2017 by Kodansha, Ltd., Tokyo
Publication rights for this English edition arranged through Kodansha, Ltd., Tokyo
English language version produced by Vertical, Inc.

Translation provided by Vertical Comics, 2018
Published by Vertical Comics, an imprint of Vertical, Inc., New York

Originally published in Japanese as *CITY 2* by Kodansha, Ltd.
CITY first serialized in *Morning,* Kodansha, Ltd., 2016-

ISBN: 978-1-945054-79-2

Manufactured in Canada

First Edition

Vertical, Inc.
451 Park Avenue South
7th Floor
New York, NY 10016
www.vertical-comics.com

Vertical books are distributed through Penguin-Random House Publisher Services.